GUARDIAN

BECCA SULLIVAN

GUARDIAN by Becca Sullivan

beccasullivanbooks.com

First published by Feather & Flame Publishing Ltd. 2025

Copyright © 2025 by Becca Sullivan

First edition

DEDICATION

Writing this book has been a journey more than fifteen years in the making, and I couldn't have done it without the incredible support and love of those around me.

First, to my husband — thank you for your unwavering support and constant belief in me, even

when this dream felt far away.

To my daughter, my very first reader — your honest feedback means the world to me.

Thank you for being brave enough to tell me everything.

To my family and friends — you are my foundation. And to my cousins, thank you for the magical

adventures that sparked my imagination from the very beginning.

A special thank you to my editor, Fran — your sharp eye, thoughtful insights, and genuine care helped shape this story into something I'm truly proud of. Your guidance has been a gift.

To my readers—thank you for embracing my words and for allowing me to share this story with you.

Your enthusiasm and support make this all worthwhile.

Finally, I am deeply grateful to the muses, the late-night inspirations, and the countless cups of coffee that fueled this book.

With all my gratitude,

Becca

"It was pride that changed angels into devils; it is humility that makes men as angels." – Saint Augustine

Chapter One

I stood before the familiar staircase, clutching my luggage with trembling hands. Swallowing back tears, I repeated to myself that this was what I needed, what was best for me. Time with Nan and my cousins always brought me solace. I gently touched the star-shaped scar on my right palm and circled it with my thumb. It always calmed me to do so. I had had it for as long as I could remember, but I had no idea how I had gotten it.

I looked up at the house I had grown up in. It looked smaller now than I remembered, with its single staircase curving up to the front door. The black shutters were now sun-bleached to a deeper gray. The trees in front of the house were taller. Their branches almost touched each other as they climbed toward the sky. Their leaves were green and shiny like emeralds touched with dew. Red and white roses stood tall in the flowerbed and were in full bloom from the summer's heat. Their sweet perfume lingered in the air. I took a deep breath and remembered my cousins and me tumbling down the grassy hill in front of the house when we were kids, and I couldn't help but smile.

As she made her way up the stairs and into the house, I lingered outside for a moment longer, taking in my surroundings. The homes in this neighborhood curved downward towards the local high school at the end of the block, but Nan's house stood proudly atop the hill.

The thunderous roar of an engine echoed through the air, startling me from my reverie. I turned to see a sleek muscle car pulling up behind me, its engine still growling like a beast ready to pounce. A somewhat familiar voice called out to me, cutting through the rumble. "Damn, girl, is it possible to get any taller?"

My cousin Steve leaned out the car window, and my heart lifted when I saw him. He shoved open the door and grabbed me into a giant bear hug. "Good to see you, cousin," he said against the shell of my ear. His hugs were stronger than the last time I saw him. "We all missed you." His voice was gruff as he loosened his hug, not letting me go completely. Steve was taller than me now, so tall that I had to tilt my chin to look him in the eye. He was still lean, but his muscles strained his t-shirt. He was very attractive, and he seemed like he knew it with his cocky grin. His dirty blonde hair brushed his shoulders as he swept a hand through it, pushing it off his face.

"Steve... you're so...um HUGE!" I said.

He chuckled. "Like I told you before, one day I'd be bigger than you, Amazon girl."

I glanced behind him as a boy got out of the car. He was handsome; dark hair pulled back away from his face in a band, olive skin that hinted at Italian or Greek origins, and a white tank top revealing a large black cross tattooed on his right arm. Before he stopped where we stood, I managed to steal a glimpse of his eyes— they were dark emerald green with flecks of gold like fallen leaves on a perfect fall day. His stare made me look away quickly, and I kept my eyes fixed on the ground.

Steve turned, the sun glinting off his blonde hair as he welcomed the boy beside him. "Justin, this is my cousin Rhi," he introduced, gesturing towards me with a warm smile. "Rhi, this is Justin."

Justin's piercing green eyes ran over me slowly, causing a strange warmth to spread over my skin. His lashes were long and dark, framing his intense gaze. My body suddenly felt too hot, and I nervously tucked a strand of hair behind my ear.

My palms felt clammy. I was a disheveled mess. "Um, nice to meet you," I managed to say shyly.

"I don't recall hearing about a cousin Rhi..."

"Yeah, dude, I told you about her, remember?" Justin shrugged, not seeming to care either way.

"My dad got home and told me he just dropped you off at Nan's." Steve squeezed me into him again. "It's good to have you back."

"Thanks," I smiled meekly. My uncle, who was my mom's only sibling, my aunt, and my cousins lived only two blocks away. It was sweet of him to come over right away, although I wish I had time to change and wash up a bit.

It had been seven long years since my mother and I left here to move across the country. The year when fear and panic gripped the world as the new millennium approached. The infamous Y2K scare had everyone on edge, expecting chaos and disaster to ensue. But it only revealed how easily fear could spread like wildfire. However, while the rest of the world seemed to carry on without much change, my world began unraveling. Soon after, my mother met my now stepfather, and everything changed. Her demeanor shifted her once vibrant personality, dimming into something unrecognizable. It was like someone had flipped a switch, and she was no longer the same person I had known for my entire life. He was controlling not only to her but also to me. I felt like Cinderella, only I had an evil stepfather and no happy animals to tell my troubles to.

I had no idea what my mother had told any of them about why she wanted me to move out of that suffocating house. It got more unbearable as time passed, and I would run away to friends' houses and sleep on their couches when I couldn't take it anymore. I guess she believed sending me back here was better than that. I wasn't surprised to find myself back. Since my seventeenth birthday, my mother insisted that I stay with my grandmother. She said things like 'it's nice and safe there.'

"What's up guys?!" a melodious voice interrupted my reverie.

I looked over my shoulder to see a young girl on the neighbor's front porch. She had short, curly black hair and smooth, ebony skin. She was bent over a book and wearing a black T-shirt and jean shorts. Her hair was pulled into a tight bun, and the sides of her head were shaved. She caught my eye, smiling broadly before walking down her steps towards us. A faint memory of a neighbor with clunky glasses and a love for bugs came to mind. Could it be the same girl?

I leaned in towards Steve and Justin, "Who is she?"

"That's Mia. She's lived there for as long as I can remember. I think she's a senior this year, too. She's a bit, well, eccentric." Steve said.

I nodded, still staring at her as she got closer. There was something about her that I couldn't quite put my finger on. "Do you know her well?"

He gave me an inquisitive look. "Not really. We've talked a few times at parties, but that's about it." He shrugged. "Why do you ask?"

I shook my head, feeling silly. "No reason."

"Let me introduce you," Justin said, calling out to Mia.

"Hey, Mia! How's it going?" Justin asked as she made it to us. Mia had the large, thick, heavy book in her hands. It looked very old. "Hey Justin, I'm good. I'm just reading."

"You remember Rhiannon, don't you?" Steve motioned to me.

Mia's eyes flicked over to me, and she nodded. "Yeah, I remember Rhiannon. We used to play together when we were little."

I smiled at her, "Yeah, I remember you too. You used to collect bugs, right?"

Her face lit up in surprise. "Yeah, I did. How did you remember that?"

"I used to watch you from my bedroom window." I shrugged, feeling embarrassed.

Mia giggled. "That's cute. I still collect bugs, actually. It's one of my things."

Steve looked at me, amused. "I told you she was eccentric."

Mia rolled her eyes at him. "Hey, I prefer the term 'quirky.' It's more charming."

I laughed, feeling a sense of warmth towards her. "I like 'quirky'. It suits you."

I glanced at the book in her hands. It was definitely old and well-worn, and the cover had some unique symbols on it. "What are you reading there?" I asked, nodding towards it.

She held it up for me to see. "It's a book of witchcraft. My great-grandmother gave it to me before she passed away."

My eyes widened in surprise. "Wow, that's unique. Do you practice?" I asked, intrigued.

Mia smirked. "I'm still learning, but I find it interesting. A long time ago, there was a coven up by the reservation. There's lots of lore about them in this town."

"Don't freak her out, Mia," Justin said. "She just returned; we don't want her to run off too soon."

I glanced his way, seeing a mischievous look in his eyes.

Mia leaned in, her eyes sparkling with excitement. "Justin, don't interrupt me." She laughed up at him. "The stories say that there used to be a group of witches that lived in the forest up on the reservation. They were powerful and wise, and people would come to them for help with various problems. But then, one day, something happened. Nobody knew exactly what, but the witches disappeared, and the forest was cursed. People say that if you go in there, you'll never come out or that you'll come out a different person."

I shuddered. "That's creepy."

Mia lifted her sunglasses and looked me in the eyes. "We even had our own witch trials here."

Justin shot her an exasperated look. "Seriously, Mia."

Mia turned to face him. "It's not just a story, Justin. There is evidence about them here as well." She gestured to the book cradled in her arms.

We talked for a few more minutes until Justin nudged Steve in the arm, "We should probably go. We need to pick up those parts."

"Yeah, we do," Steve smiled warmly at me. "I'll text you later and maybe we can hang out soon."

"Sure," I said, plastering on a smile. "I'd like that."

I turned to Mia, "It was nice seeing you again, Mia."

"Hey, if you want, you can come with me to check out the Witch's Well in a couple of weeks. It's supposed to be a full moon."

I paused, considering. I had no idea if Nan would let me go out with Mia, let alone to some supposedly haunted location. "Maybe I will. Thanks for inviting me."

Mia headed back up her stairs to her front porch, waving at us. I turned to go when Justin called after me, "I'll see you later." I looked over my shoulder at the dark and handsome boy. He was watching me with a wicked grin on his face. I looked away swiftly but still felt his eyes on my back as I climbed the stairs slowly, feeling like I was walking through wet concrete.

Nan was bustling around in the kitchen, which seemed frozen in time. The room was still a cheerful yellow hue and felt inviting and cozy. She was making tea on the same stove she'd had for years. "Do you want some?" she asked without looking up.

"Is there any soda in the house?"

"Yes, it's in the fridge," she replied, gazing towards me. She looked exhausted. Looking at me once more, sadness settled into her brown eyes. "You need new clothes," she said.

"You don't have to do that, Nan," I mumbled, staring at the ground.

"But I want to," she assured me with a smile. "We have to go shopping anyway for your cousin's baby shower."

My oldest cousin, Taylor, was pregnant with her first child, and I was excited to attend her baby shower. She was five years older than me and seemed to have a fairy tale life.

Nan's voice cut through my thoughts. "I'm going to run to the grocery store, Rhiannon," she said, smoothing my cheek. "Is there anything special you would like me to pick up?"

After some consideration, I asked her to pick up cookie-dough ice cream. "Do you mind if I get the pint-sized version, Nan?" Ice cream always made things better.

She patted me on the cheek again, her hands soft. "Of course," she said as she grabbed her keys and shuffled out the door.

I dragged my luggage up to my childhood bedroom, and as I walked in, it seemed like time had stood still. My mom was pregnant with me at nineteen. She had been going to nursing school at the time and moved back home to my grandparents' house so she could continue going to school and have some help with me. I didn't know my father. I didn't even have a photo of him; my mother never talked about him.

I sighed as I flicked on the dim light and looked around at the cobwebs and dust covering every surface. My comforter was still there, faded with alternating light blue and white squares. When I was a kid, yearning to be a princess, I had a small white nightstand with a lamp shaped like a tiara. Seeing it made me smile. In one corner stood a daybed loaded with teddy bears of all shapes and sizes. I couldn't believe I'd left them behind. It seemed as if they were silently accusing me of the loneliness this room held. Loneliness was something I often encountered in this space – being an only child raised by a single mother. Thankfully, when my cousins came over, life filled this room.

I stopped to look at the small shelf holding my collected childhood trinkets. On top of it stood a cross, reminding me of my Grandma's strong Catholic faith and the images that hung in nearly every room of Mary and Jesus. The phrase inscribed on the cross read: *"How great the dignity of the soul, since each one has from his birth an angel commissioned to guard it."* – St. Jerome.

A chill ran down my spine as I paused for a moment. The room felt cold despite being July and having no air conditioning. I grabbed my luggage and crossed the hall to my mother's old bedroom. Shutting off the lights, I sealed those childhood memories behind me.

My mother's old room was just as I remembered it. It was bigger than mine, with a large four-poster bed that occupied most of the space. The room was decorated in shades of green, with a large window overlooking the backyard. I walked over to the window and looked at the old oak tree that still had my tire swing hanging from its limbs. It moved slightly in the wind. It was peaceful, unlike the chaos that had been my life for the past few months.

I turned around and walked over to a small bookshelf. On top of it was a framed picture of my mother and me. I picked it up and stared at it. My mother was smiling, her hazel eyes sparkling with joy. She had her arm wrapped around my shoulders, pulling me tightly to her. I was smiling, too, my brown eyes shining with happiness. I remembered the day so vividly. How things had changed.

I hurried downstairs, grabbed some sheets from the linen closet, and returned to my mother's old room. The sunlight shone through the windows, creating dancing shadows on the walls. As I watched, I thought I saw a large bird's wings in the shadows, but when I looked at the window, I saw only the swaying limbs of the trees outside.

In no time, I finished making the bed. My grandfather had crafted it himself. He loved working with wood. It was made of dark oak wood and adorned with carved roses on the bedposts. My mother wanted to take it when we moved, but hesitated. It was too big to disassemble without possibly ruining it. Lucky me, now it was all mine.

I stood back to admire the freshly made bed, wanting to curl up in a ball and let the tears spill that I had been holding in. I sighed and swiped at my eyes to remove the mist growing there. I traced the delicate rose carvings on the bedposts. This room held so many memories, both joyful and painful. It was a bittersweet inheritance.

I flopped back onto the bed, my body sinking into the soft mattress. Spreading my arms out on either side of me, I stared at the ceiling.

I was sent back here in hopes of finding a fresh start. Away from my mother and her new husband, away from the constant belittling that had become a daily occurrence. Despite the distance, his words still echoed in my mind, taunting me.

"You're no good, lazy, a burden. You're nothing." His words echoed in my head.

But being here, in this room, I felt I could finally breathe. Nan's house was where I could leave behind the weight of anger and expectations and forge my own path.

As I stared at the ceiling, I told myself this move was good and made sense. I was strong enough to start over again and create a life for myself that was free from my stepfather's toxic influence. For the first time in a long while, I felt a glimmer of hope in my heart. I told myself that tomorrow would be better and eventually drifted into an uneasy slumber.

Chapter Two

I woke up to the sunlight streaming in through the thin white curtains of the window. I squinted, trying to keep the light out of my eyes. I could tell it was hot and humid outside because it was sweltering in the house. The weather here in New Jersey was so different from that in Colorado. The heat and humidity didn't seem to bother Nan, but I couldn't say the same.

The sweat ran down my back as I rolled out of bed and dug into my luggage. I grabbed a white tank top and cut-off shorts and headed out the door.

I spotted my childhood bedroom door slightly ajar. I swore I had closed it the night before. I pulled it shut again and found myself eyeing the light wood paneling next to it. My heart swelled at seeing my artwork. A giraffe, elephant, and lake among some palm trees—which I had drawn with a permanent marker after returning from an outing to the zoo. My mother wasn't pleased, but my grandfather laughed at me after seeing it. It never got sanded or redone, so it stood as another lasting reminder of my childhood.

Taking a few steps down the faded carpet, I called for Nan and descended into the living room. No response. Opening the front door, I realized her car was gone. She must have gone to The Pier, our family's restaurant. Nan swore her cousin had a sixth sense that helped make the restaurant so popular, but whatever the reason, it was well known in the entire state.

I noticed Nan's knitting bag on the couch with yarn spilling over onto the cushion. I assumed it would be something for Taylor's baby. It was pink, so she must be having a girl. She will undoubtedly look like her mother–blonde hair, blue eyes, and petite.

My stomach growled loudly. I hadn't eaten since yesterday morning. As I made my way to the kitchen, I caught sight of coffee cake sitting on the counter. I reached for a piece and washed it down with orange juice before leaning against the wall. This place made me happy and sad. A part of me wanted to stay here forever, but simultaneously, I felt like an outsider with no real home. Tears welled up in my eyes once again, but I slapped my cheeks with my hands to get rid of them before heading down the hall to the bathroom to wash up. "No more crying," I said out loud to myself.

When I exited the bathroom, Nan was back sitting at the dining room table. Even though I had blow-dried my hair, it still felt damp from the humidity. "Nan, how can you stand this weather?" I said as I pulled my hair away from my neck.

"I've lived here my whole life, and I'm used to it; you will get used to it, too," she replied as her eyes swept over me. "Your cousin's baby shower isn't until later. We can head to the mall and go by your uncle's to see if Kacey wants to go to the mall with us," Nan suggested.

"I'll grab my shoes!" Anxiety curled in my stomach. I hadn't seen Kacey in a few years and worried if we would still have the same connection.

Nan's car was an old police car Uncle Nick had gotten a good deal on. It was only two blocks to my uncle's house, and childhood memories flooded back when we parked in front of the white house with navy blue shutters.

A big dog appeared from the corner of the yard at the fence and barked once. "Hush, Bubba," Nan said, and he settled down.

"Bubba?" I asked in surprise. He greeted me with a bark.

"Don't blame me," Nan said with a laugh. "I didn't name him."

Bubba looked like a Labrador-Shepherd mix with gigantic feet and one ear standing straight up, the other flopping over his eye. I instantly adored him.

"Get down," Nan ordered when she opened the gate. He jumped on me and kissed me all over my face, and I fell even more in love with him.

"Bubba! Get off her!" Steve's voice came from the yard.

Bubba obeyed immediately, wagging his tail.

"Hello, Steve," Nan said.

"Hey, Nan," he wiped dirty hands onto his jeans. "I was just working on my car."

I glanced past him, hoping to see the dark-haired boy from yesterday. The garage was separate from the house and housed some of my uncle's toys. He loved refurbishing old cars and making them into showpieces. I didn't see anyone in the garage, though.

"Come inside, Kacey's waiting for you," Steve said.

"Really?"

"Of course, silly girl. She hasn't stopped talking about it since she heard you were coming back." Just then, the door flew open, and a blur of strawberry blonde hair raced towards me, almost knocking all the air out of my lungs as she embraced me in a hug.

"Told ya." Steve snickered.

"Oh my gosh! You finally made it! What took you so long?!" Kacey exclaimed in my ear.

"Well, I only got in last night, Kacey."

"Well, then you should have come over last night!" She scolded with a playful tone. She pulled herself away from me, and I noticed she was taller now, too—not nearly as tall as me, but I no longer towered over her. Her eyes looked wet with tears, and I felt a lump begin to form in my throat.

"I told Dad to bring you here first, but he said you were tired. Were you tired, or did you not want to see us?" Her eyes stared up at me like an owl.

"Huh?, no, no Kacey...I was indeed exhausted, jet-lagged. Uncle Nick didn't lie to you."

Nan spoke up. "Kacey, we need to go to the mall and pick out some dress clothes for Rhi. Do you want to come along?"

"Oh yes!" Kacey shouted enthusiastically. "I'll get my purse!"

"How about you, Steve?" Nan asked.

"No, thanks," he replied. "Girls' shopping trips aren't for me. I'll catch up with you later, Rhi." He gave me a playful wink before entering the house as Kacey flew back outside with a goofy grin on her face.

The drive to the shopping mall was swift, and I welcomed the air-conditioned car; Kacey chatted nonstop about anything and everything that crossed her mind, from school, boys, clothes, Taylor's baby, and music. When we arrived, Nan handed me a couple of hundred dollars. Guilt rose inside me again; I didn't want to be a burden.

"I'm heading to the bookstore," Nan said. "Be back here by noon so we can leave."

"No problem, Nan. We'll be back on time. Now let's go, Rhi- I know where the best sales are!" She grabbed my hand and tugged me with her.

Kacey was always charming, waving to people she knew. Her hair hung down to the middle of her back, sleek and straight despite the humid weather, unlike my untamed waves, which looked like a squirrel had taken up residence in them. Although Kacey was getting closer to my height, she was still considered petite – with a thin waist, slender hips, and skinny legs. She belonged in a garden surrounded by other fairies.

"With the money Nan gave you, you could get a lot of outfits here!" Kacey said excitedly.

"I don't want to spend it all; I want some money to give back to Nan," I said.

She looked disappointed, her lips tightening into a sad pout. "They *want* you to have some nice things. She paused, biting her bottom lip. "Oh, not that you look bad now! I'm really messing this up," Kacey apologized quickly as a blush crawled across her cheeks.

"No, Kacey, it's not that," I began slowly. "I don't want them to think that I'm being too...needy. Before I came here, I was managing just fine." In truth, my mother had pushed me onto them, and now they felt obligated to take care of me financially. My pride was getting in the way of their charity.

"Please, Rhi, we all want to do this for you. We all love you. You can pay Nan back if you want, but don't forget to get something. She'll be hurt if you don't." She spoke pleadingly like she could read my mind.

"Ok...only clearance items...nothing too extravagant..." I said with a sigh. Kacey let out a delightful squeal and clapped her hands together in joy.

"Yay! What size? let me guess...eight?" I nodded in agreement, feeling amazed by her intuition. She skipped away, calling over her shoulder. "Stay put; I'll be right back with some clothes for you to try on."

While Kacey fluttered through the racks, I watched the passing people go by. It was so different from the tiny town I was from. There was a greater emphasis on fashion, something I knew little about. Jeans and a t-shirt girl. That was me.

I slumped forward, resting my elbows on my knees while I pressed my face into my hands. Even though I hadn't started school yet, I already knew I was doomed. Thoughts of convincing Nan to let me get my GED ran through my head, but deep down, I knew it was a long shot. I was in advanced classes; there was no way she would permit it.

Instead of letting myself wallow in self-pity, I gazed out the window at a music store across the hall with Black Eyed Peas and Nickelback posters in the window.

In the window's reflection, I saw my little fairy cousin bouncing towards me with clothes piled in her arms. At once, my lips curved into a smile — she seemed to have that effect on everyone around her.

"Here! Are you ready?" I couldn't believe she could hold so much in her tiny arms.

"Kacey, I only have two hundred dollars," I pointed out.

"It should be fine since we're shopping clearance," She grinned confidently. "I'm guessing it will only add up to around a hundred seventy-five dollars." She smiled wickedly at me.

"Are you serious?"

"If there is one thing I'm good at, Cuz... It's shopping! Now go try them on!" She plopped the pile of clothing in my arms and shoved me towards the dressing room.

"No need," I assured her. "I'm sure they will fit."

Her bottom lip jutted out slightly in disappointment. "But I wanted to see how they looked on you."

I rolled my eyes playfully. "Alright, alright, when we get back to the house, I'll put them on and give you a mini fashion show! Does that make you happy?"

Her face lit up with delight. "Yay! But what if you don't like them?"

Chuckling, I waved my hand around in an exaggerated motion at my current attire. "Do you see this? I'm not picky, Kacey."

I paid for my things, and she was right: One hundred seventy-six dollars and forty-five cents. She was good. Now, I owed her a fashion show.

Chapter Three

Nan had brought us back to my uncle's house, complete with two bags of new clothes. We eventually whittled it down to two outfits for the baby shower, and I suggested the pink one.

"I should go with the pink. Taylor is having a girl, right?" I said.

Kacey furrowed her brow. "No, Taylor is having a boy. Why did you think she was expecting a girl?"

"I assumed because Nan was knitting something pink. I should have known better than to assume. Anyway, blue it is!"

"Why don't you try the pink instead? It suits you better," Steve said, leaning against the doorway.

I turned around quickly. "How long have you been standing there?" I asked, attempting to feign indignation. "Not long. Don't worry, I didn't see anything. You were holding up clothes." He waved his hand dismissively and pushed himself off the door frame.

"You look better in pink. I remember little details." He tapped his finger to his head, smiling sweetly. "Photographic memory."

"Steve, get out of here. She needs to get dressed!" Kacey scolded him as she tried to push him out of the room.

"It's fine; I'll just change in the bathroom," I replied before putting the outfit back into the bag.

I got up and headed down the hall. The bathroom was small, but the shower doors were mirrored, and a large mirror edged in gold was hung above the sink. I could see myself from every angle. I knew Kacey was generous when she said I looked great, stunning, and spectacular in all the outfits.

I would be the judge of that.

I pulled on the flower-printed shirt, stepped into the skirt, and zipped it up along the side. The pink Steve had suggested was flattering, and I must admit he was right. I took a second to check myself from all sides and concluded that Kacey hadn't been lying: my butt didn't look huge. I looked pretty. However, I thought most guys liked small, petite girls like Kacey rather than tall, curvy, dark-haired girls like me.

I glanced up into the mirror. Dark circles framed my eyes. "Perfect," I thought sarcastically. Sighing, I opened the door, hearing Kacey's voice as I walked back down the hall.

"See? Pink! What did I say?" Steve grinned. I offered a half-hearted smile before glancing at Kacey. "Kace, can you help me with some makeup?"

Instantly, she jumped up from her bed. "Oh my gosh, yes! Come here, come here." She yanked a suitcase from underneath her bed and opened it to display rows upon rows of makeup products. I'd never seen so much in one case.

I explained that I only wanted something natural, nothing too glamorous.

She seemed slightly disappointed, "The natural look then." It took forever, but I thought I looked pretty when she was finished. Checking out the result in a hand mirror, I smiled.

Steve popped his head in the door. "We should get going now."

Kacey looked at him inquisitively. "You're taking us?"

He nodded his head. "Mom wanted to check everything was ready for the shower, so I offered to drive you guys there." He bowed. "At your service, ladies."

"Are you staying at the shower, too?" I asked.

He answered with a nonchalant shrug of his shoulders.

"I'll stay and help in the kitchen."

Kacey grabbed my hand warmly and pulled me towards the door.

"So, I met Justin yesterday. He's Taylor's fiancé's brother, right?" I asked.

"Yep, and they're night and day." She suddenly shot me a dazzling smile. "Just so you know, I had the hugest crush on Justin Rizzo for the longest time, and, okay, I kind of still do. But then he opens his mouth, and it's like all my feelings fly right out the window. That's why I always wonder, why are all the girls around here crazy about him?"

It could be because he looked like he walked off the pages of some dark romance novel. I thought to myself.

We stepped outside into the blazing heat. I needed one of those little hand-held fans that sprayed water living here. In front of the house was a gorgeous orange car with Steve behind the wheel. I ran down the porch steps, and he revved the engine, making it roar.

"I replaced the exhaust with a dual muffler." He grinned.

"Sounds good, right?!"

"It's amazing," I was intrigued and thrilled.

"This..." He said with reverence, running his hands along the wheel. "Is my baby. She's a 1972 Gran Torino. Her name's Hottie." He revved the engine again. "Now hurry up before my mother has my head for getting there late." He gave the seat beside him a light pat. "Kacey, hop in the back so Rhi can see how it feels from the front seat."

I eagerly hopped into the passenger side, and Kacey climbed into the back. The inside still needed some sprucing; the front seats were frayed and faded, but the stereo was brand new. Steve shoved it into gear and spun the tires as we took off.

"Steve! Dad will kill you!" Kacey yelped as she was flung against the backseat.

"How's he going to know, Kacey?" Steve replied with a smile. "Besides, he does it too."

"You're such a show-off," I said, shaking my head. He grinned back at me wickedly.

"Can I drive it?" I asked excitedly.

"You don't even have a license," he took the corner sharply, giving the car more gas. "And her name is Hottie, not *It*."

"Actually, I do. We get our driver's licenses at sixteen in Colorado." I said proudly. "It's up to Nan if I can drive here though."

"More like my dad; he's the cop," Steve said. He then turned down a familiar street to The American Legion Hall. Typically, everyone brought something, and it was like a big potluck dinner. But when we had more people than just family, we got food catered from The Pier instead.

I turned back to Steve. He still hadn't answered my question. I'm sure it meant no. I wasn't going to let it go, though. I wanted to drive the car. I mean, Hottie, but I wanted to tease him even more.

"So, can I drive back then?" I asked imploringly.

"No, nobody drives my car, Rhi."

"But I thought I was your favorite cousin?" I pouted, just like Kacey did when she wanted something.

"Nice try, but still no."

"I'm not your favorite cousin?"

He chuckled, "Yes, you're my favorite cousin; NO, you aren't driving my car." Steve pulled into a parking spot and reached over, ruffling my hair.

"Hey, it isn't anything personal. I just worked every summer for the past four years and never spent a penny. All that money went to my dad, who put it away and bought this car from the police auctions. I've put everything I have into Hottie, that's all."

He exited the car and held the door open for Kacey. Nan was waiting for us on the porch.

Steve side-hugged me. "What's with the frown?"

"Nothing." I paused before we reached nan, "You and I should hang out later, maybe...if you want."

He grinned, "Sure. But you're not driving my car."

I walked up the stairs to meet Nan. She gave me a warm smile and gently touched my face as if I were a child. "You look great," she said as she patted my cheek. "Come on in and eat. They've got mashed potatoes, your favorite."

"Oh, those yummy Pier mashed potatoes with garlic?!" I could already feel my mouth watering at the thought of them.

"That's right, and Taylor has been dying to see you."

My grin widened as I replied, "Really?"

"Yes, Rhi. She missed you terribly."

Nan ushered me inside, and the smell of The Pier's mashed potatoes hit me as soon as I entered the room. "Hmm", I thought to myself. "Mashed potatoes or Taylor?" Well, Taylor, of course, but maybe we could walk through the kitchen to get to her, and I could stick a spoon in the mashed potatoes to hold me over.

Too late, I saw her, and she saw me, and the thought of the mashed potatoes vanished. Taylor smiled, excused herself from the person she was talking to, and rushed towards me with teary eyes. She hadn't changed a bit: petite stature with hair down to her waist - not strawberry blonde like Kacey's, but almost pale white when hit by the sunlight streaming through the windows. Her skin was porcelain white, and her powder blue eyes searched mine when she reached me. She wrapped her slim arms around my neck and drew me close. I followed suit, albeit timidly—this gesture of intimacy in front of people made me feel uncomfortable. She pulled away, her eyes brimming with tears.

"You look nice." She whispered.

"So do you," I replied.

She giggled at that. "I'm huge!"

"That's just the baby, silly." Her legs and arms were still slender, but her belly was full of life, and she rubbed the roundness affectionately. Another set of hands joined hers in a gentle caress on her baby bump. I lifted my gaze to meet those of the man standing behind her; he kissed her daintily on the cheek, and she blushed shyly.

"Scott, this is Rhiannon, my cousin. I told you about her." She said. "Rhi, this is Scott, my boyfriend."

"Fiancé." He corrected.

I looked down at their entwined hands but didn't see a ring. Taylor and Scott are like real-life Barbie and Ken.

Scott was easily a foot taller than Taylor and had a stunning light olive complexion. His short blonde hair was combed to perfection. He was rubbing Taylor's belly with a gentle touch. He wore a short-sleeved, white button-up shirt, revealing an intricate tattoo on his right arm that said "Taylor" underneath it.

Upon noticing my gaze, Scott inquired with a smile, "You like tattoos?"

"Some of them can be nice," I answered.

Scott rolled up his sleeve and revealed an angel tattoo. The details were exquisite.

"She is my angel," he said. Then I remembered that this was Justin's brother, and they shared the same brilliant green eyes.

"It's stunning," I said, pulling my eyes away from his. "And a little spooky."

He seemed taken aback by my comment and pulled his sleeve back over the tattoo.

"Spooky?" he replied incredulously, staring at Taylor and patting her baby bump gently again. "You don't believe in angels?" he asked.

"Well, yes, I suppose," I said hesitantly. However, I trusted in them as much as I believed in fairies, vampires, and Prince Charming.

"You suppose?" A voice I didn't recognize whispered near my ear.

I spun around and saw Justin standing there. All black clothes adorned his body, and he crooked one midnight black brow at me. "What did you mean by that?" I snapped.

He frowned slightly before quickly masking it with a dazzling smile full of pearl-white teeth. No wonder all the girls swooned over him. "Mean by what?"

"You whispered in my ear," I said, rolling my eyes at him.

He looked perplexed, "I didn't."

I must be losing my mind. I know I heard someone and even felt their breath in my ear.

"Taylor!" a tall, redheaded woman with too much makeup and a curvy figure beckoned her. "Come sit, honey. It's time for some games." She patted an empty chair in the middle of a circle of other women.

"Games?" both Justin and Scott said in unison.

"I didn't know there were games at these things?" Scott actually looked alarmed. "I can do presents and food, but I don't think I can sit with thirty women playing baby games. I'll be in the kitchen if you need me."

"Of course, sweetie." Taylor brushed her lips against his cheek, "Just try to stay away from the food until we're finished."

"Who, me?" Scott batted his emerald eyes at her. He kissed her gently on the forehead before he went towards the kitchen.

Justin was staring at me with breathtaking eyes. "Justin! let's go!" Scott called from the kitchen doorway.

"Right, yeah...um, I'll be in the kitchen too if you want me." He winked at me before looking away, and I scowled in response. Somewhere deep inside me, a strange feeling stirred. Was this god-like boy flirting with me? I couldn't help but stare at him as he walked back towards the kitchen.

"Rhi, will you come and sit with me?" Taylor asked, walking over to the chair of honor. I felt awkward as all eyes were on her, which meant they would wander towards me.

"Maybe I should sit with Nan?" I suggested.

"No, she is sitting with my mom. Besides, I need somebody to make me laugh during these games. Ooh! The baby is kicking!" She beamed with happiness. She grabbed my hand and placed it over her belly. "He's so feisty!" She grinned. "I already adore him so much. Being pregnant has been a magical experience."

I felt the tapping and swelling beneath her skin. "Is it uncomfortable?" I asked.

"Well, it is a bit now that I'm getting close to the end of my pregnancy. But generally speaking, it isn't too bad."

We took our seats, and Taylor shifted her weight onto her right hip, trying to find a more comfortable position. Kacey flounced over to us and took the chair on Taylor's other side.

When the red-haired woman I didn't know stood, the noise in the room faded. She raised a ball of blue yarn and said, "I want all of you to cut off a piece and guess how big around Taylor's stomach is!"

Taylor moaned. "I'm sure Cousin Julie will make it extra long to embarrass me."

"Well, mine will be extra small," I whispered to her.

She giggled and shifted on her seat again. "See, that's why I wanted you to sit next to me."

The game then began. The scissors and yarn were passed around as everyone tried to estimate Taylor's size. It reminded me of when we were kids playing together. Now, she was having a child of her own. Time really flew by too fast. The yarn came to me, so I unrolled it and speculatively pretended to study Taylor's shape before cutting off my piece much shorter than the others and passing it along.

When everybody had a piece of yarn, Taylor was asked to stand up, and we each took turns encircling her waist with our pieces. Mine was too small, but I knew it made her feel good. Julie was able to wrap the string almost twice around Taylor. In the end, the redheaded woman who had proposed the game got the best measurement.

"We have one more game, ladies, before we eat and get to presents." This time, it was my aunt Daphne speaking. She hadn't seemed to age at all.

"Ugh, I'm starving. Could you get me something Rhi that'll hold me over until dinner?" Taylor inquired.

"Sure thing. What would you like?" I asked.

"Anything."

I leaped up, relieved I'd have an excuse to escape the next activity. As soon as I heard my aunt talk about diaper fillings, I knew I lucked out. So, I politely made my way through the crowd toward the kitchen; the aroma of garlic mashed potatoes filled the air. It was heavenly. I pushed open the door and inhaled deeply. Yes, I had died and gone to heaven. My out-of-body experience was rudely interrupted by the sound of chuckling coming from the corner.

Steve stared at me with an amused smirk playing across his lips. "That good, huh?"

"What? They don't know how to cook in Colorado?" Justin snickered.

"Of course, they know how to cook." I blushed, trying to hide that I was craving the garlic mashed potatoes.

Justin hopped off the counter and grabbed a spoon. He opened one of the trays, scooped up a large helping of potatoes, and then turned to me. His green eyes taunted me as he lifted the spoon to my lips.

Damn him with his green eyes and mashed potatoes. "Go on, I could hear your stomach rumble from across the room. No one will know." His thumb tickled my chin as he offered me the spoon.

I suddenly felt embarrassed, swallowing quickly and grabbing the spoon from his hand. "Stop that! I need to get Taylor something to eat." I said firmly.

At the suggestion that Taylor was hungry, Scott leaped to his feet, and before I had time to object, he was at the door with a plate of food and drink in hand.

"Be careful out there," I hollered after him. "There's a diaper game going on."

He scrunched up his nose, flexed his arm muscles, and then disappeared through the door. I turned back to Steve and Justin. Steve was filling a plate and turned my way.

"I can't eat that much," I said, my voice wavering.

"Yes, you can," he replied as he handed me the plate of food. "I've seen you eat more."

"Are you trying to insult me?" I asked playfully. "Besides, I don't want to get caught eating; it will look rude."

"So, hand the plate to Justin; he's always rude." Steve joked.

Justin just smiled like the Cheshire Cat, shrugging his shoulders.

"Wow, full of compliments today, aren't we?" I said. Steve smiled and told me to eat. So I did, and they were the best potatoes I had ever tasted.

The remainder of the day went smoothly. Taylor and Scott opened gifts, and everyone rubbed Taylor's belly and shared their birthing stories. She listened attentively to each person, but I could tell she was beginning to tire. Before long, people began to take their leave, and Scott, Justin, and Steve loaded Taylor's car with gifts.

I went and sat with Taylor. "Rhi, you must come over and spend some time with us. I'm alone during the day while Scott is at work. I've been out on medical leave for a month."

"Why? Is something wrong? I asked, concerned.

"No, not really. I was having contractions early, and they had to stop them. No worries, though; I wasn't planning on heading back to work after the baby arrived anyway," she said before adjusting her position again. "So, will you be able to stop by?"

"Of course," I answered without hesitation; in truth, I couldn't wait to spend time with my older cousin.

At that moment, Nan walked up to see if I was ready to go home. Internally, I groaned since I still wanted to talk to Steve. She must have sensed my hesitation because she said, "Or if the kids will be home, you can go to your uncle's house."

"Let me go look for them and ask." As I stepped outside, I searched for Steve. He was the one I wanted to talk to about what the family was told about me. Dark clouds began to roll in, carrying a freshening scent of rain on the wind. Steve came around the corner as I made it to the foot of the stairs.

"Hey, you. Remember when I asked if we could talk later?"

He smiled, swinging an arm over my shoulders. "Yep, little cousin."

"So, what are you doing tonight? Would it be alright if we hung out and caught up?" I tried to keep it casual.

"How about checking out the view from the reservation? Most kids our age gather there if you want to meet some new people."

The idea of meeting strangers didn't appeal to me much; I preferred staying in the shadows. "Nah, I'd rather spend time with you, if that's alright?" I asked.

"Did you say the res? I want to go!" Kacey skipped down the stairs. "You can meet everyone there." Kacey rummaged in her bag until she fished out her cell phone. Steve blocked her attempts to make the call, grabbing her phone out of her hands.

"Kacey, Rhi doesn't want to meet a bunch of people yet. She just wanted to catch up with us first." Kacey looked disappointed as she took back her phone.

"Well, what if Kacey comes with us and hangs out with her friends while we do something else? We can come back and get her later?" I suggested, hoping to make Kacey happy again.

"Yes! Please, Steve? That way, I could still see Jake, and you two could go do whatever it is you want to do before coming back for me." Her eyes lit up as she spoke with excitement.

Steve hesitated, "Fine. But don't change plans, Kacey. You go with me and come home with me. When I say it's time to leave, I don't want to hear any complaining." Kacey did a small victory dance before heading back up the stairs again.

Nan was sitting with Taylor. They were about the same size. Nan always seemed bigger to me when I was a child. Now, she seemed like a tiny doll I needed to be careful with, or she would break.

"So, Steve and Kacey are going out. They said I could go with them if it's alright with you." I asked her.

"Of course you can, dear," Nan said, patting my back. "I'll see you later."

Steve stuck his head in the doorway. "Let's go, Rhi." "Guess that means I have to get up," Taylor groaned.

I reached down and gave her my hand to help her. As I pulled her upright, I saw Justin out of the corner of my eye, busy folding chairs and stacking them in the corner. His biceps bulged against the fabric of his black shirt as he worked. He paused to brush his dark hair out of his eyes and caught me watching him. I averted my gaze quickly, yet not before Taylor noticed.

"He is handsome, I will give you that." She sighed before continuing, "He's also egotistical, intolerable, and a remarkable womanizer." Taylor had a slight scowl on her face as she spoke. "But he is my baby's uncle, and he still has time to grow up."

As we looked in his direction, he observed us with his intense green eyes and a lopsided smirk. He strolled towards us as Steve popped his head through the entrance again. "Rhi, come on - we're waiting for you!" He called out.

"I know, I know. I was just saying goodbye to Taylor." Turning back to Taylor, I told her, "We'll get together soon."

"Where are you guys headed?" Justin asked me curiously.

"To the reservation."

He cocked an eyebrow at me. "Ah, planning to investigate Thirteen Witch's Road?"

Taylor cut in sharply, "She most certainly is not! Don't let Steve talk you into that Rhi - that road is genuinely haunted." She was serious in her warning.

Justin laughed. "That's just something our parents told us to keep us out of the woods."

"Rhi!" Steve shouted again from the doorway. "Move it!"

I hugged Taylor goodbye, saying, "Gotta go - see you later!"

Justin chuckled, "What, no hug for me?"

I shook my head and stepped towards the exit; "Nope!" I said over my shoulder, but my traitorous mind wondered what it would feel like to be hugged by him.

Chapter Four

High Mountain Reservation. It didn't make much sense since these hills weren't even close to the mountains back in Colorado, but that's what it was called. I came here as a kid with my family for picnics during the summer when many families would gather on the grass and relax. But now, as night approached, it was full of teens looking for freedom away from their parents' watchful eyes. As we reached the summit of one of the larger hills, I couldn't help but gasp at the view before me. It was as if I were on top of the world. The trees below were a sea of green. You could see right to New York City, where the lights got brighter as the sun began to set.

A few cars had already parked near the overlook. It was a steep drop off with a stone wall at the edge. It was especially beautiful here when it was completely dark, overlooking the city with its array of colorful lights that danced merrily beneath the stars.

We drove past some people as Kacey spoke on her phone. "We're almost there. Do you see the car? Wave! Oh, yes, I see you!" She waved to a tall guy with short black hair, wearing blue jeans and a white shirt. He was leaning against a Jeep.

"Steve, pull into that spot nearby," she pointed to an open parking space close to the Jeep. Steve eased up to the curb, and Kacey flew out of the car before he even came to a complete stop. She ran up to the good- looking guy and flung her arms around his neck. He hoisted her body into the air with little effort and embraced her warmly. "Rhi, this is Jake," she said as he placed her on the ground.

"Nice to meet you," I said shyly.

"Don't forget, I'm coming right back here to find you—not down the street or around the corner. Right here, understand?" Steve called after her as she and Jake moved to stand by a group of people.

I scrambled out of the backseat, hopping into the front of the car. Steve was smiling at me. It was like he was a different person than the pig-headed big brother he was with Kacey.

"I haven't been here since I was a kid when we used to come for picnics," I said, looking around the park. "Are there still lots of deer around?"

"Yup, but you won't see them in the dark. People come here at night for the view," he scowled at Kacey, who was giggling with Jake. "And other activities."

He swung his arm on the seat, letting it fall on my shoulders. "Let's go before it gets too crowded," Steve suggested, backing out of the parking space, "If talking is what you're into, this isn't the place for it. We'll have to drive down into the woods if you want some privacy. Everyone hangs out here to socialize and Kacey loves to talk...obviously," he laughed, "so hiding in my car won't work long; she'll inevitably come over to drag you out."

A knot formed in the pit of my stomach as I sank further into the seat. "Let's go to the deepest, darkest part of the woods," I sighed.

He laughed out loud and thrust the vehicle into gear.

As darkness descended, the roads snaked through the reservation, illuminated only by slivers of moonlight.

"That place Mia mentioned, Thirteen Witches Road. Justin mentioned it too before we left." I looked around but did not see any street signs. "Have you been before?" I asked.

"To Thirteen Witches Road? Yeah, I have," he replied. "The well is very eerie. It's on the side of a wooded hill called The Mount near some ancient stone altar called the Holy Holy. They say it's where the Jersey Devil is imprisoned. But it's all just stories people tell kids so they don't venture up there." He shrugged. "It's a bunch of nonsense if you ask me." Turning right, he glanced at me and said, "There are a few old houses and structures up there too. Once, I went to a party there; it wasn't a good scene."

I nodded, taking in his words. The thought of going to a place with such a dark history made me nervous, but I was also intrigued by the lore.

He glanced my way, "Why do you ask?"

"Mia invited me to go the next time the moon is full, remember?"

"I do. Maybe take one of us with you. Well, not Kacey because she's a chicken or Taylor because she's pregnant." He shrugged. "I guess that leaves me."

"Or Justin."

Steve slowed the car, narrowing his eyes at me.

"What? Mia invited him too."

"Yeah, I guess she did, but maybe just you and I should go with her."

I wasn't sure what Steve's problem was with Justin coming. I guessed it was the same thing as Taylor thought. He was a womanizer, and I shouldn't get involved with him.

"Okay," I sighed dramatically. "I do want to go. I think local legends and stories are interesting."

"Cool, just let me know when Mia plans on going."

Steve continued to glide down the snake-like road until we pulled off the main stretch onto an overgrown path too narrow for his vehicle.

"It goes back quite a bit, but I'm not scratching my car on these trees and bushes," he declared, cutting off the headlights and opening his window. The breeze that filtered in blew his hair away from his face. He had grown up since I had last seen him; gone were his skinny legs and goofy smile of my memories, replaced by this handsome young man I didn't know if I knew anymore.

"It feels like we're in a secret forest mixed with urban sounds," I said.

Steve nodded in agreement, "Yeah, that's the beauty of this place. You feel like you're far away from everything, but you're really not. It's the perfect place to escape to when you need some space from the rest of the world." We sat in silence for a few moments, taking in the stillness of the surrounding forest.

Occasionally, the leaves rustled in the wind, and an owl would hoot. He leaned back in his seat, his hand reaching for the radio. "You mind some music?"

I shook my head, and he turned on the radio, tuning it to a classic rock station. The sound of Led Zeppelin's 'Stairway to Heaven' filled the car, and Steve hummed along.

"My friends and I would drive in the mountains in Colorado and find places to hang out and make campfires." My eyes scanned the forest around us. "We'd have fun, but if you walked away just a bit, all you could hear was the wind through the trees. It was beautiful and peaceful, but also kinda scary."

"Do you miss it?" he asked me in a gentle voice.

"Yes. I miss my friends, but I'm glad to be here with all of you. You make me feel wanted." I said that last part almost too softly for him to hear.

"We do want you here," he replied, looking at me intensely with a serious expression on his face.

His stare made me feel exposed and embarrassed. I didn't know if I could let anyone else in on my secrets. I quickly changed the subject. "So, what do you like to do for fun?" I asked, trying to sound casual.

He hesitated momentarily as if he wasn't sure how to answer the question. "I like to explore," he finally said. "I like to see new places and try new things. Life is too short to stay in one place all the time."

I smiled, feeling a little more at ease. "I bet you would love Colorado then. I wish I could be more like that."

"You can be," he said, his voice softening. "You just have to be willing to take risks and step out of your comfort zone."

I nodded, feeling a strange mix of excitement and fear. I had always been someone who played it safe, who didn't take risks. But something about how he looked at me made me want to be brave. "Maybe I will," I said, surprising myself with the confidence in my voice, but it quickly faded. My past haunted me, and my future terrified me.

Ghostly images flooded my mind of the smoky form of my stepfather - the embodiment of cruelty and indifference. Every gruff word he uttered, every cold stare that he shot at me, was like a shiver sent down my spine. His disapproving glares were a constant reminder of what a disappointment he thought I was. I vividly recalled the late hours I used to spend alone in my room, knees pulled up to my chest, drowning out his thunderous voice reverberating through the walls with music. The absence of my real father reminded me of a gaping maw ready to swallow me whole any time I dared think about it too much. My mother never really talked about him. The few times she did, her voice would drop down into a whisper as though saying his name aloud would break some spell and bring forth unwanted demons from her past.

Now, here I was, facing an unfamiliar future. A new town meant a new school, which meant an onslaught of questioning glances from classmates just waiting to judge what they didn't know or understand.

Maybe I could reinvent myself—shed the skin of my past like trees shed their autumn leaves. I envisioned myself as someone carefree, someone who laughed too loud and loved too much, someone whose spirit danced freely and loved openly, a girl whose inner light shone so bright that it kept her personal demons at bay.

"If only I were that brave," I said to myself.

I decided to change the subject: "Do you have a girlfriend?" I asked.

That caught him off guard, and he looked bewildered. "Um, kind of. Not really. She is serious, but I don't know..." His voice trailed away.

"Oh, okay. You didn't mention her before, and I can't believe someone like you would be single," I ventured. "Aren't you worried she's with someone else?"

He chuckled at that. "I wish! It would make me feel less guilty if she weren't so obsessed with me." His gaze drifted to the darkness outside. "She's a great girl, but I'm not into the exclusivity thing. New places, new things, remember? She claims she doesn't mind me seeing other people, but I know that isn't true. She won't even look at another guy. It's suffocating." He let out a deep sigh.

"Do you want to break up with her?" I asked tentatively.

"Yes and no. I'd still see her if she weren't so serious about it, but when I mention it, she erupts in anger."

"You shouldn't stay with her because you feel guilty," I suggested.

"I know. It's just that I feel like I have to take care of people I care about. That includes her. I'd love to keep seeing her if she could stop being so possessive." He ran his fingers through his hair and then balled his hands into fists. "Sorry, I didn't mean to get upset."

"It's not your fault," I muttered, twirling the hem of my skirt around my fingers.

"You brought me here to talk about you, and now I'm complaining about my girl problems." He turned down the radio slightly. "So, spit it out already. What is it?"

The time had come for me to open up. I could learn what they knew, but some part of me wasn't sure if I wanted them to know yet. It was sometimes better to remain in the dark.

I took a deep breath, my chest pounding with anticipation. I didn't want to lose these few people who cared about me, but what would they think of how I ran away to escape my crazy home life? Then, a voice near my ear said, *It's okay to tell him.* The sensation passed quickly, leaving a chill in its wake, like stepping out into the snow.

"Hello?" Steve inquired, his face showing concern. "Were you daydreaming? You were staring off into space, and you just jumped a little bit. Are you all right?"

"I don't know." My voice sounded distant to me. I stared out the window into the woods around us. "It's okay to tell you," I mumbled.

"Of course, it's okay to tell me." He said a bit sharply.

I gazed into his deep blue eyes, illuminated by the dashboard lights. It was clear that he cared deeply. He wanted to know what was wrong and protect me. I put my hand in his and felt him squeeze it gently. Tears started rolling down my face, and I found myself in his embrace. I told myself I wouldn't cry, and yet here I was soaking Steve's shirt with my tears.

"If you just need to cry, that's okay," he whispered softly. "You don't have to tell me anything if you don't want to."

I wanted to cry, but I also didn't. I thought it was weak and that I should not show weakness because weakness leads to getting hurt. The voice in my head said to tell him, yet my sobs and tearful embraces expressed more than any words I could have uttered. I don't know how long we stayed like that; it felt like an eternity. He didn't grow weary of cradling me in his arms as he whispered reassuring words. When I tried to separate, he drew me closer, making me want to cry for an entirely different reason. Softly, he asked if I felt better. Through sniffles and tear-stained eyes, I nodded.

"Are you up to talking then?" he asked. There was a long pause before he softly said, "We know that you ran away."

I stiffened in his embrace, unable to find the courage to meet his eyes.

"Back home..." I began, my voice barely above a whisper. "It was... it was too much." My gaze dropped to my trembling hands.

All memories of home seemed tainted with pain and despair. Every corner of the house echoed with heartache; every room a mausoleum of abandoned dreams and shattered hopes. There were nights when the sound of boots stumbling drunkenly down the hall filled me with terror.

"Running away," I continued, "It wasn't a decision, more like an instinct... survival." I stared intently at the scenery outside the car window as if it held answers.

My past flowed from me like a burst dam – tales of torment and despair in a house that I could not call a home. I told him about my mother's quiet suffering, her tears soaking the pillow late at night when she thought I was asleep. About how our lives revolved around avoiding my stepfather's wrath just to keep peace in our tormented home.

Tears welled again, and I fought them back. "I wasn't really living on the street; most of the time, I stayed with friends."

"Look at me," he said softly but firmly. I hesitated, lifting my chin but still refusing to meet his gaze. "I will always believe you," he murmured. "Trust me, Rhi."

"Does Nan think badly of me?" I asked, feeling my lips quiver.

"I don't think so. Nan doesn't have anything but good thoughts about you."

The relief that washed over my body was immense, and I sighed, relief filling me.

"We can see the hurt behind your eyes, and when you're ready, any of us-me, Nan, Kacey, or Taylor-will be here to listen to you." He smiled reassuringly.

I felt better. The ropes around my heart had slackened, and I felt I could trust Steve to protect my heart.

I knew the mysterious voice in my head was right. I could tell him everything. My body was exhausted, and I stifled a yawn, but it still escaped audibly.

"Are you tired already?" Steve asked.

"I haven't cried like that in front of someone in years."

"Glad I could be here for you," he murmured, squeezing my hand in his. "But one thing before I take you back. Justin Rizzo."

My eyes flew open at the mention of Justin. "What about him?"

He scowled. "Justin has a reputation." His face got serious again. "You're the newest car on the lot to him; he likes to have them all first."

"You are suggesting I'm a car?"

"Yes."

"What kind of car am I?" I asked with a smile.

"I'm being serious, Rhi!"

"So am I!" I retorted.

"Alright, you are a Mustang."

That sounded all right to me. "What year?"

"Oh, come on, this isn't the point of our conversation."

"It is for me! I need to know."

He let out an exasperated sigh. "1968...Cherry red. Are you satisfied now?"

I smirked. "Okay, so Justin wants to try out the 1968 cherry red Mustang....a
nd...?

He shook his head and replied, "And he'll use it, abuse it, and it will end up in
the junkyard along with all the other cars he's ruined before. I mean, you will end
up being used." He huffed.

"I'm not his type," I said.

"Justin doesn't have a type. He likes girls. Period. He just likes to score. He likes
to be the first to have them. He isn't interested in relationships at all and...."

I cut him off. "Neither are you."

"What?!"

"You told me you didn't want a serious relationship, and your girlfriend did."

"It isn't the same, Rhi. I treat the girls I am with respectfully. Justin just uses
them. He doesn't care about anyone but himself."

"I thought he was your friend."

"Well, we hang out sometimes. We both love cars. I've known him for years.
Plus, he is practically family with Taylor and Scott together, but I don't want
him near you or Kacey. All I ever see from Justin are girls crying over him, and he
couldn't care less."

"And no girls cry over you?" I arched one of my eyebrows at him. It wasn't hard
to imagine someone falling for Steve; he was very handsome.

He pressed his forehead against the steering wheel. "Yes, they do! But I don't
do it on purpose! I don't do it because I want to see them cry! Justin does. Girls
are just toys to him. He doesn't even consider their feelings! And you, Rhi...
the newest girl in town. Stay away from him! He will break your heart with no
remorse whatsoever."

I knew he meant every word of what he said. Still, Justin was gorgeous. I
couldn't see him having the least bit of interest in me, even as a plaything.

"Why is he that way?" I asked carefully.

"That's his own story," Steve replied gruffly.

He cast a sideward glance at me before turning his attention back out the
window. He drummed his fingers on the steering wheel as if he were debating

something. He eventually broke the silence. "Justin and Scott have different fathers," he began.

"These days, it's not uncommon," I said, shrugging my shoulders.

"It is for Justin and Scott's family, though," he sighed heavily. "Most people know that they don't have the same dad, but few know the full truth: They were born exactly one year apart."

I nodded in understanding. "His mom had an affair when Scott was only a couple of months old then."

"And she kept it secret, obviously. It didn't last long, according to Taylor. His mother must've been terrified when she found out she was pregnant again. Eventually, Justin came along, and they kept quiet about it since he resembled his mom; however, as he grew older, he started resembling his biological father more and more."

I felt like Steve was withholding some details. I didn't know if it was because he thought he shouldn't be talking about this with me, respect for Justin's family's privacy, or he just wasn't sure himself.

"Justin somehow is his dad's- the man who raised him- favorite. Well, at least he was. Justin was the perfect child. Then he found out. He insisted on knowing who his real father was. His mother told him, and it was a shock to him. To go from who raised him to who his biological father is....well, he just changed. He doesn't understand how his mother could do this. He blames her. He hates his biological father, and yet he works for him and has become like him. It's all bizarre. His mother has been a church-goer her entire life, which only added to Justin's confusion and disillusionment as he believed she could do no wrong. Taylor believes that Justin thought that if his saintly mother couldn't be perfect, then how could he be? He always put her on this pedestal, and when he found out she was human and made a mistake."

"You're calling Justin a mistake?" Suddenly, I was protective of him; I understood that feeling all too well.

"No, Rhi," Steve shook his head. "I'm saying that Justin thought his mother was infallible, and when he found out she had made an inexcusable mistake in his mind, something inside him snapped. If there was no hope for her to make the right decision, then why should he have any faith in himself? That's Taylor's theory, at least."

He took my hand in his. "Do you understand now? He doesn't trust women. He really doesn't trust anyone. He's just a player."

I rubbed my fingers over his knuckles. Steve really didn't want to see me get hurt. But, knowing now what I knew of Justin Rizzo, I thought there was one person in this town who might understand me better than anyone else. We both had parent issues. I couldn't promise Steve I would stay away. Looking up into his eyes, I saw the worry there. "I understand," I said confidently. "I won't let him hurt me."

I felt satiny fingertips squeeze my shoulders. I turned around to face the source of the touch, but no one was there. The air around me grew colder, and a shiver cascaded down my spine. I felt my heart race as I looked around for any signs of a presence. The car's interior was empty except for me and Steve, who looked at me curiously.

I tried to shake off the feeling of unease, thinking it was just my overactive imagination playing tricks on me, but I felt the hairs on the back of my neck stand up. I couldn't tell what it was, but the feeling of unease only grew stronger as I stared out into the darkness. The only sounds were the hum of the radio and the occasional rustle of leaves as the breeze passed through them. I swore there was someone or something in the car with us.

"Maybe I should get you home," Steve said.

I nodded, and we backed out of the darkness of the woods and onto the main road. Looking into the rearview mirror, I swore I saw the shape of a human standing where we were just parked.

Chapter Five

Nan was finishing breakfast when I came down the stairs the following morning. I had come home and fallen into my bed. Surprisingly, I had slept pretty well and felt unusually refreshed and upbeat. The last few days' events had taken their toll on me, but this morning, I felt lighter and even a bit happy. Nan picked up on my mood immediately.

"It's drizzling rain out today," Nan said as she sipped her tea.

I enjoyed the rain outside. "Maybe it will cool things down," I said as my eyes hungrily searched for more delicious coffee cake.

"Do you have any plans for the day?" Nan asked tentatively.

I shrugged. "No, not really. Taylor said she wanted me to visit, but maybe not today. And Kacey and Steve might want a break from me, too."

"I don't think that is true." She smiled, her eyes glinting with love and understanding. "Call Taylor. She moved into a bigger apartment for more space when the baby comes. I'm sure they aren't done unpacking or even decorating the baby's room. They could probably use the help."

I stared at Nan. Her hair was cut short and neat with beautiful curls. Nan was in her late seventies and still beautiful. She was short and petite, and her skin was beginning to wrinkle with age. She wore a pink dress that was so faded from washing it many times that the pink was almost white. I remembered that dress from when I was a little girl. I had always called her Nana back then, but now she is just Nan.

"What about you?" I hadn't been back for long and felt I always left Nan alone. She'd lived by herself since my grandfather passed away five years ago, yet she still stayed in this same large house they once shared together. "I don't mind staying with you," I said.

"I'm planning on going to church and doing some grocery shopping. After that, there's an old movie I wanted to watch this afternoon on TV. Nothing exciting, sweetheart – go and have fun." She said, taking another sip of her tea.

After getting off the phone with Taylor and making plans for Scott to pick me up in an hour, I hurried through the shower and hastily ransacked the new clothes Kacey had picked at the mall. I rifled through a few items and found what I needed: a pair of jean shorts and a plain red T-shirt with a pretty scooped neck.

I thought I packed some lip gloss in my suitcase. I searched the suitcase one last time, which was still open near my bed.

Through the clothes within, I found nothing. There was one zipped compartment I hadn't looked in yet. I opened it and swished my hand back and forth inside. I bumped up against something, but it certainly wasn't lip gloss. Reaching in, I pulled out an envelope with my name written on it in my mother's handwriting. Anxiety began to grip me, so I placed it in the drawer in the nightstand beside the bed and decided not to confront those feelings today. I had woken up in a good mood. I wanted to have a good day. I would deal with those demons later.

Staring at the messy suitcase and the disarray of shopping bags made me realize I needed a dresser. I had a small one in the other room. I would have to ask for help moving it, though. I didn't want to scratch the wood floor in the bedrooms. I would ask Scott when he picked me up.

"I'm off now, Rhi!" Nan's call came from downstairs. I rushed down the stairs to say goodbye.

"I'm going to have a key made for you tomorrow. In the meantime, the extra one is under the white rock at the foot of the stairs outside. I'll leave it there on my way out. Just in case you come home and I'm not here."

"Okay, Nan, thanks." I hugged her. Happiness washed over me. It was good to be here with her. "I'll see you later."

A few minutes after Nan left, there was a knock on the front door.

I opened the door, and my jaw dropped; it was Justin, looking well...hot. His clothes clung to his toned frame as rain cascaded down his chiseled features.

"It's raining - can I come in?" he asked.

"Er, sure," I opened the door wider to allow him to enter.

I couldn't breathe. He was standing so close. I could smell a slight hint of pine and rain. His eyes held mine, and I couldn't look away from them.

"What are you doing here?" I asked.

"I'm here to pick you up. Scott and Taylor were busy with the baby's room, so Scott asked me to come instead." He shrugged nonchalantly.

Retreating to the kitchen to get a glass of water and quench the dryness in my throat, I could feel his eyes on me as he followed.

"Why are you looking at me like that?" The second the words poured out of my mouth, I regretted them. It was a stupid question.

A smile spread across his gorgeous face. "Where would you like me to be looking?"

My eyes slid to his mouth. He had very kissable lips, and I was sure he knew how to use them in a way that would curl my toes.

He chuckled. "See something you like?"

He took a step closer, and I backed up, hitting the counter. A laugh escaped me. "Are you always so....so..." I couldn't find the words as his gaze swept over me.

"So?"

"So.... intolerable." I hissed. I needed to stop staring at him. "I would say some would say I am much more than tolerable."

He looked smug. "You didn't answer my question. Do you see something you like?"

Heat infused my cheeks. I wasn't sure what to say, "Let me grab my shoes, and we can leave." I pushed past him and sprinted up the stairs. I stared at the disarray of the clothes and remembered the dresser in the other room. Damn. I'd have to ask Justin for help or wait until I could get someone else to do it. I peeked my head out the door.

"Justin?" I called down.

"Yo!" he called back.

"Hey, would you be able to help with a dresser?"

"Yeah, be right there."

I went into my childhood room to the dresser and ensured it was empty. I pulled out the drawers and started bringing them into the other room. I ran into Justin in the hallway.

"Let me take that." He said.

"I got this one. There is more in there." I motioned with my chin.

I put the drawer on my bed and returned to the other room. He was standing in the center of the room, looking around. When I entered, his eyes landed on me.

There was an unsteady tug in my chest. "What is it?" I asked.

The quiet that followed was overwhelming; his beauty took my breath away. His soaked shirt clung tightly to his toned body, emphasizing his muscular frame. His face looked like it had been crafted by an ancient Greek sculptor or showcased in an art museum. His hair was so black it shimmered whenever he moved. A clap of thunder sounded in the distance, like an alarm bell. My throat felt dry again, so I swallowed hard to moisten it.

He stepped closer, and I stumbled back a fraction as he registered my reaction.

I took another step away, and he asked: "Are you scared of me?"

"No... not at all." My words came out stuttered, betraying my anxiety. Then, I felt a light touch along my back, causing me to inhale sharply.

He laughed softly and replied, "Let me guess - you've heard about my reputation?" His query was met with a nod from me; I didn't trust myself to speak.

"Well," he began with a wicked smile, "It's all true."

This time, I did speak up, "And you're proud of that?"

The coldest jade eyes stared into mine as he answered icily: "No, not really. But I'm defined by my life experiences."

"We make our own choices."

"Really?"

"Do you have a say in who your parents are? Do you get to choose when you're born? How about those toddlers in the hospital with cancer, desperately fighting for their lives, or crime victims – do any of them have a choice in what happened to them? Did you have a choice to come here?"

I barely moved, unable to even shake my head in response.

"That's what I thought," he said, turning on his heel towards the dresser.

Before I could stop myself, I whispered, "Sometimes there is a choice, and we must do the right thing."

"Like running away?"

I stumbled, stammering, trying to find my words. "I...I..how?"

Did everyone in this town assume the worst about me? I felt the tears well up in my eyes, but I bit them back. I would not give him that satisfaction.

I went and grabbed another drawer, and he was back. He reached for the last one and stopped. Then he paused; his phone was buzzing from his pocket.

"Yes, NOOO. I'm bringing her now. I was just helping her with a dresser. Whatever."

He hung up and looked back at me before speaking again. "Your cousin is anxious to see you. Let's get this done."

The storm was raging outside as we bolted down the steps to the car. My wet hair was clinging to my face when I opened the door. Great. I'd been trying to straighten it earlier, but now it would be a mess of waves. I glanced at Justin out of the corner of my eye. He was also soaked from the rain, but somehow, it made him look even more handsome. Raindrops gathered in the middle of his eyelashes, sliding down onto his high cheekbones. His wet hair shined like a black diamond. His fingertips reached for the volume on the radio; they were long and lean, the type of fingers that seemed they would move gracefully over a guitar.

Or skin.

I wondered what they would feel like if they reached out to touch me. Wait. What was I thinking? He was a jerk with a capital "J." No way did I want him touching me.

Justin drove through town, avoiding the main streets. He seemed more at ease now, although still not quite happy. Switching stations on the radio, he glanced over at me, and I gave him a small smile.

"Is this your car?" I asked.

"Yep," he replied shortly.

I continued admiring his vehicle, reading the wording along the dashboard. "A Cadillac? Really?"

He shot me a stern look, "What is so funny about a Caddy?"

"Nothing, I guess," I tried to hide a laugh. "I just pictured you in something different."

"Well, it's not my only car. It has a 500-cubic, 400-horsepower engine, V8, plus some other modifications I did myself. Nothing will beat it, not even your cousin Steve's car. I also like the space in the back." A sly grin spread across his face.

His attitude had changed back to flirting again, and I tensed up instinctively as my fists tightened in my lap.

"I'm sure you get lots of use out of it."

"What kind of car do you think would suit me?" he asked.

I paused for a moment to consider his question. "A red 1968 Mustang." Of course, he would have no idea what I implied or what I meant from the conversation I had with Steve. "Sleek, powerful, and draws attention wherever it goes."

"Interesting choice," he replied with a smirk. "I've never driven one, but there's always room for new experiences. I like variety." The glint in his eye was unmistakable, and I felt myself shudder involuntarily.

"Are you cold?" he asked with a raised eyebrow. "I have a jacket in the back if you want to borrow it." He reached behind the seat, retrieved a leather jacket, and tossed it casually at me.

"Thanks," I said as I pulled the jacket on.

We drove in silence while the rain pelted the windshield and a song on the radio played softly. We stopped at a pale yellow house. It was an older bungalow-style home, light yellow with brown and green trimming, and a big porch out front.

"That's their place," he said. "Just go up the stairs, and the door with number two is on the right."

"You're not coming in?"

He smiled, his jade-green eyes sparkling. "Why? Would you miss me?"

He leaned closer to me, and my breath caught. I swatted at his hand as it brushed a lock of hair behind my ear. "No, I thought since you picked me up, you'd help," I explained, feeling tense.

"I'll be back soon," he chuckled. "I have some stuff that needs taking care of."

I tried to take off his leather jacket, but his hand on my shoulder stopped me, "You don't have an umbrella, and it's still pouring out there."

I continued to struggle to free my arms from the jacket's grasp.

"Now you are being ridiculous," he said, reaching across me and opening the door.

"Alright, alright," I scrambled out and slammed the door shut. I didn't bother to look back as I rushed up the stairs, but I felt his eyes on me the whole way.

Chapter Six

I rapped on the heavy wooden door. It was an old house with many original features still intact, including the brass knocker resembling a lion.

Taylor yanked open the door in a state of alarm, which quickly dissolved into relief when she saw me. "I had Scott ready to go look for you two," she said, eyes searching past me for Justin. "Where is Justin?" Her tone carried a hint of irritation.

"He said he had some things to take care of," I replied, looking down at my soggy socks and shoes. I bent down to remove them before entering.

Taylor's eyes fell on the jacket, and she asked, "Is that Justin's?"

"Yes," I answered while trying to free myself from the oversized jacket. "He made me wear it. He didn't want me to get any wetter than I already am."

"Oh....how unlike him."

"Are they here yet?" Scott's voice floated in from another room.

"Rhi is," Taylor called back, a slight edge to her tone. "Your brother took off."

"He did say he'd be back," I added quickly.

Taylor pursed her lips and asked suspiciously, "What kept you two so long?"

"I needed help moving a dresser from my old room into my mother's room. I'm using hers since it has a bigger bed."

She nodded. "That's what he told Scott. Justin didn't give you any trouble, did he? I really didn't want him to go get you, but he was insistent, and Scott was in the middle of hanging wallpaper."

"No, Taylor. He didn't give me any hassle. I can manage him." I at least wanted to believe I could.

"If he ever does give you an issue, Rhi, let one of us know, okay?"

Scott stepped into the room then. "Let us know about what?"

"If Justin gives Rhi any trouble." She answered him.

"He won't, I talked to him." I couldn't see Justin's fiercely independent attitude listening to anything his polar opposite brother had to say. Nevertheless, I was tired of people speaking for me.

"Somehow, I don't see him listening," I said.

"What did he do?" Scott asked.

"He helped me with moving my dresser, lent me his coat so I wouldn't get drenched, and told me all the rumors about him were true," I answered. I wasn't lying; I simply left some details out.

"It's more serious than I suspected," Scott tried to hide a smile.

Taylor turned to him, her eyes wide. "What do you mean by that?"

"Don't worry about it." He smiled sweetly at her, his face and hands covered in glue and wallpaper pieces. Then, he touched her cheek tenderly and kissed her lips lightly. The gesture was sweet, and I could see why she loved him.

Taylor pulled me towards the newly decorated room for the baby. It was painted in the palest shade of blue. A large window overlooking the front yard had white curtains pulled back to show the rain still splashing against the glass pane.

A crib was situated against the far wall, lined with wallpaper. The crib was surrounded on all sides by a border of teddy bears.

"It's beautiful, Taylor," I said, admiring her handiwork.

"It's simple. It's all that can be done for now." She touched her belly tenderly.

"It's perfect."

"Come, I'll show you the rest of the house."

I trailed behind her as she navigated through the apartment, which had once been a single-family house but was now split into two residences. I admired its high ceilings, tall windows, and intricate woodwork. The kitchen was big, while the bathroom was tiny; Taylor wasn't pleased with that detail. Nevertheless, her bedroom was quite large, and she had painted it lavender; it looked beautiful combined with the dark wood floors.

"Scott hates it, but he deals with it for me." She giggled.

I noticed many unopened boxes scattered around their room. "Do you want help unpacking these?" I asked.

Taylor sat on her bed and propped some pillows behind her head and under her legs as she relaxed. "You don't have to, Rhi. I just wanted your company."

"No, no, I don't mind at all," I replied, already getting started on the nearest box.

"Fine, Rhi, have at it," she said and nestled down comfortably on the bed.

I quickly opened the box to find clothes inside, her clothing specifically. "Looks like shirts," I said.

"Bottom drawers," she answered, pointing at two large dressers in the corner. "That one over there is mine, and the other belongs to Scott."

I started folding her garments and putting them away. "So, what are you naming the baby?"

A huge smile crossed her face as she answered, "Ethan Scott." I could sense her pride in his name.

"That's pretty," I commented.

"Hehe, don't say that in front of Scott! He's not so fond of it.

Chuckling, I replied, "I'll remember that!" After folding the shirts, I moved to another box and asked about their relationship history. "How did you guys meet? You and Scott, I mean."

"We've always known each other," she replied without hesitation.

I frowned in confusion at the thought of Scott being around for so many years without me noticing him. "I don't remember you talking about him when we were kids," I said.

"Because I thought he was awful! He always teased me and pulled my hair! And honestly, he is still a bit of a brat," she replied with a laugh. "Steve and Justin became friends in school. One day, we were having a barbecue, and Scott came over with Justin. I think things just happened between us after that."

She gave a content sigh. "I don't need anything else. He's so loving and devoted to me and works hard to keep us supported."

A warm smile spread across my face as I basked in the joy radiating from her. My fingers reached for another box, but Taylor whispered for me to pause, asking me to close the door first. I carefully weaved my way through the maze of boxes, closing the door behind me before settling on the bed beside her.

"Scott's birthday is coming up soon, and I'm planning a surprise party," Taylor said, her bottom lip familiarly caught between her teeth. "Would you help me? You just moved back, so he won't suspect anything from you."

"Of course," I replied. "I'd do anything for you, Taylor."

"Thank you, Rhi," she responded, visibly relieved. "I've been so stressed about this being his last carefree birthday without any huge responsibilities."

"But..." I started to say as she scooted closer to me. "Isn't Justin's birthday the same day as Scott's? Are you leaving him out of this?"

"How did you know?" She raised her slim eyebrows at me in surprise. "Oh, never mind. Yes, his is the same day. But Justin won't want to be involved in Scott's birthday - he never does."

"What if we surprise Justin too?" I suggested.

"What? Are you joking?" Her brows creased as she let out a short laugh.

"Why not?" I pushed, unsure of why I was doing so. He may be arrogant and hard to deal with, but still, it was his birthday too.

"Because he won't appreciate it; because he probably won't show up anyway, making it all a wasted effort; because..."

Just then, the door swung open, and we both jumped.

Scott peered through the entrance. "Justin is back. He brought pizza if you two want any." His eyes moved between us before adding, "I won't ask what you're up to in here."

Taylor responded quickly. "Good. Don't. We'll be out in a second."

Scott shut the door, and I shifted my attention back to Taylor. "He brought pizza. That has to count for something," I joked.

"This party means a lot to me, Rhi; I want it to be special for Scott." Taylor rubbed her belly lightly as she spoke.

"He was okay at your shower. I'm sure he'll behave. If not, I'll kick him out."

"Like you could." She snorted.

"Taylor, it's his birthday too. I'd be pretty upset if I were him, and everyone focused on Scott, but no one acknowledged me," I told her honestly.

She sighed heavily, "Okay, Rhi. You win. You're right. It isn't right to exclude him. But his behavior isn't right either. He needs to act like he cares." She rolled over and hoisted herself up off the bed. "Let's get some pizza, and we will talk about plans later."

As we left her bedroom, the smell of the pizza hit me, and my stomach grumbled. We got to the living room and saw Justin sitting on the couch with a pizza box in his lap.

"What are you two up to?" Justin asked with a smirk.

"Nothing that concerns you," Taylor retorted.

Scott appeared in the doorway to the kitchen, a slice of pizza in his hand. "There's more pizza in here. Justin can eat a whole one himself." Justin smiled at his remark, raising a slice like a toast towards his brother.

I followed Taylor to the kitchen, grabbing a couple of slices before heading back to Taylor's room to continue unpacking the boxes. As we ate our pizza, we discussed the plans for Scott's surprise party. I could see the excitement in Taylor's eyes as she talked about it. I couldn't help but smile at how happy she was. We listened to music and talked about our childhood memories as we worked. Taylor shared funny stories about her and Scott, and I began to feel a bit envious of their relationship. I wanted that type of love.

I had never experienced a romantic relationship. Sure, I kissed a few boys and crushed on even more of them, but the way my life was, no one wanted to get serious with me.

Every so often, Scott would pop his head in and ask if we needed anything; each time, he had even more glue and wallpaper stuck to him than before. Justin stayed to help him, but he never ventured into the room. As night fell, I'd organized all of Taylor and Scott's possessions, flattened all the cardboard boxes, and learned what Taylor needed me to do for the party. She handed me a set of notes, which I tucked into my back pocket.

Taylor drove me home; Justin had gone off somewhere, and Scott had dozed off on the couch surrounded by wallpaper.

"Thanks for all your help today, Rhi. I couldn't have done it without you."

I smiled at her and opened the car door, but before stepping out, Taylor said, "We're all happy you're back, little cousin."

"Glad to be back, Tay."

She smiled at me as I shut the door. The smell of rain and damp earth filled the air. As I walked up the driveway towards the house, I couldn't help but feel a sense of accomplishment. I was going to help Taylor with the surprise party and even convinced her to include Justin. It may not seem like a big deal, but for me, it was a step in the right direction. Maybe I could help Justin, too, in some small way.

Chapter Seven

The week went by in a blur as I attempted to transform my mom's room into my own. I didn't have much at first, but I found an old TV in the basement along with a stereo and collected a few teddy bears from my old room to cuddle up with when night fell and sleep eluded me.

Taylor picked up things we needed for the party, dropping them off to me. I thought I might be able to find some great lights for the party in Nan's basement. Memories of Christmas came flooding back as I remembered how beautifully she decorated the house with thousands of white lights and covered the maple tree out front with ice-blue lights that twinkled like snow. She had to have them still somewhere. After rummaging around under the stairs, I located the boxes marked 'Christmas.'

"Aha!" I exclaimed to myself, kneeling down to pull the box out from under the stairs. I felt a chill crawl up my spine. Being in the basement gave me the creeps every time I entered, especially this past week. I often thought Nan's home was haunted; maybe Pop hadn't really left her. But I shouldn't be scared if it was him, right? If he were here, he wouldn't hurt me. Even so, the unknown of who or what was in the room made me uneasy, and my mind drifted to the night in the woods with Steve, the strange figure I had seen, and the voice I had heard.

That was why I had found the old television and stereo—to keep the silence from being too unsettling. I could have sworn I heard creaks, saw curtains move, or noticed a shadow lurking in the doorway. It was disturbing. I didn't really believe in ghosts, yet I felt something touch my shoulders in the woods with Steve and in my room with Justin. My heart had raced, expecting to see something there, but of course, nothing ever was. That would have been simpler and easier to rationalize. The touch had been soft—as delicate as the fall of snowflakes on my skin.

I scanned the area; nothing out of the ordinary—just as it always had been. The old pool table was in the center of the room, with a plaid couch and the washer and dryer tucked away in the corner. Sunbeams were streaming through the tiny window, highlighting dust particles in its rays. No one came down here often; that's why I felt so uneasy here. It was lifeless from lack of use, I concluded.

I opened the first box and scanned it quickly: ornaments. I moved it to the side and grabbed another one, which held exactly what I needed—string lights. They would be perfect if they still worked. I picked up the heavy box and slowly made my way up the stairs. As I ascended blindly, trying not to trip over my feet with how heavy the box was, I suddenly slipped and lost my balance.

I felt a pair of silky arms wrap around me and a voice whisper, *"I got you."* I almost collapsed in shock. I clutched the box to my chest and sprinted the rest of the way up the stairs, slamming the door behind me.

"Rhi?" Nan asked, her voice laced with worry.

I tried to steady my breathing. "What was that?" I whispered to myself. "It's nothing, Nan. I just got spooked. It's those scary movies you make me watch." I forced a smile, but she didn't seem convinced. She dropped the subject, though.

"Christmas decorations in July?"

"Yes, they're for Scott's party. Decorating duty has fallen to me." My heart rate began to slow down.

"I'm sure it'll be something special then." She walked into the kitchen and shouted back at me over her shoulder, "Some packages have arrived for you."

"Packages?"

"By the door."

Two boxes sat by the door. I glanced at who they were from, and my mom's address was scrawled across the top.

I lugged the large boxes up to my bedroom. The first one I opened overflowed with clothing. My old, comfortable clothes. Underneath them were CDs. I was ecstatic—my music! I found my small CD player and headphones at the bottom of the box.

As soon as I put them on, the lyrics of my favorite songs filled my head. I sighed, realizing my whole life had fit into two boxes. Reaching the bottom of the second box, I found a card signed by all my friends with wet rings where tears had fallen. That was when I realized how much I missed them, and my own tears spilled freely as I hugged the card close to my chest. Suddenly, something cool and soft brushed against my ear.

"Don't cry, Rhiannon."

My body went rigid. It seemed friendly and familiar, but it definitely wasn't Pop's voice.

After a moment of searching, I found my voice and asked, "Who are you?"

"Rhi?" I nearly leaped out of my skin with shock.

"Nan! You scared the hell out of me!" I exclaimed breathlessly.

"You don't have to curse Rhiannon." Her brows furrowed as she scolded me gently. "I heard you crying, so I came up to check on you."

"I'm so sorry, Nan. There was a card in the box from my friends...I miss them so much." My shoulders slumped in resignation.

"Oh, Rhiannon. I'm so sorry, but you'll see them again."

Flashes of frowning faces, heated arguments, and harsh words that were thrown around thoughtlessly all played like a nightmare in my mind. His words had cut sharper and deeper than any physical wound ever could. I knew Nan and my mother had spoken about me coming to live here. I just didn't think it would be so sudden.

Nan's hand rested gently on my shoulder, grounding me in the here and now. "I don't know how much you were told...."

"Shhh..."

"But Nan..."

"Sometimes we make decisions in the best interest of those we love. Decisions that are difficult to bear. Your mother..."

I put a hand up to stop her. "Please don't make excuses for her, Nan, and especially not that step-monster."

Her eyebrows wrinkled in confusion. "Monster?" she asked.

I lowered my chin, shaking my head. "Yeah, Nan. He really is. And mom is like in some kind of weird trance of his." My voice trembled with suppressed emotion - sorrow or anger or both. "I really don't want to talk about this anymore."

Nan studied my face for a long moment. "Okay, Rhi, but we really should talk more about this when you're ready."

Sighing, I nodded.

Chapter Eight

It was Saturday before I knew it, and I'd spent the day decorating for the surprise party at the Legion Hall.

Allowing Steve to help me had been a good choice; he was tall enough to string the lights along the ceiling and wouldn't tell anyone what I was up to. We laughed and joked with each other through most of it. I hoped Taylor would love it.

Steve dropped me off at home so I could take a shower and choose something to wear. Black was the obvious choice - it was both mysterious and allowed me to hide from anyone I didn't want to notice me. I put on my favorite black dress. It was in the clothes that Mom had shipped to me. It had delicate lace around the hem and spaghetti straps. It was the one I always wore when I wanted to feel pretty. I put on some silver hoop earrings I had borrowed from Kacey and Nan's bracelet she had given me. I was almost ready.

I deliberated over what to do with my unruly hair. I had already tried blow-drying it, only to find that the humidity had left it in a mess of frizz. My hair was naturally thick and wavy. So, I plugged in the curling iron and went with curls. When I was done fussing with it, I admitted to myself that it didn't look half bad. My pale cheeks had some color thanks to blush, and I'd found some mascara and lip gloss at the store with Nan. Pleased with my makeover, I stared at myself in the mirror, turning around to examine myself on all sides. I smiled a bit at the mass of curls that fell down my back and the strawberry lip gloss accentuating my mouth, not that anyone was going to taste it but me.

I heard a knock at the door. I rushed to it, opening it for Steve. He would drop me and Kacey off and then get Scott and Justin under the premise of a boy's night out for their birthday. If Steve could manage to get Justin to come with us, we'd be set. When everyone was picked up, Taylor would rush over to the hall. I knew they'd figure it out when they saw all the familiar cars parked up and down the street, but there wasn't much we could do about that. People had to park somewhere, right? It still would be a surprise. But no matter what happened, Taylor was going to be happy. And that's all that mattered.

"All black?" Steve remarked as we left the house and headed towards his car.

"Well, we're decorating the hall like a night sky, so it's fitting. Besides, you're wearing all black." I replied nonchalantly.

"True." He shrugged and opened the car door for me.

Steve dropped us off, and Kacey and I headed up the stairs to the air-conditioned hall. The cool air felt nice on my skin, and I was beginning to feel nervous about our plan coming together.

"Oh, Rhi! It's incredible!"

"The lights aren't even on yet, Kacey." I laughed.

"Yes, but all the lights! It must have taken you forever to hang them from the ceiling! I can imagine how it will look once they're on!" She beamed as she skipped around the room, admiring the work Steve and I had done.

"Kace, snap out of your trance and get to making the punch while I set out the chips. We only have half an hour before everyone else shows up."

"Don't worry, Rhi. It will all be grand!" She spun on her toes to make the punch.

My anxiety butterflies had turned into bees swirling around in my chest. Suddenly, I felt sweaty even though the room was really cool. A queasy feeling settled into my stomach. Taking a few deep breaths, I headed for the kitchen.

"Kace, is there some of the 7-Up left over from the punch I can have?"

"Hey, are you alright? You don't look too good," she said, handing me a cup.

"I'm just nervous." I sipped the soda, which seemed to help settle my nerves.

"It'll be okay, Rhi. You worry way too much." She flashed that brilliant smile at me as she returned to stirring her punch.

"Hello?!" Taylor's voice echoed from the adjoining room.

"We're in the kitchen," Kacey yelled back.

"Oh my gosh, Rhi! It looks unbelievable! Everything is perfect - thank you so much for this!" She gave me a joyous hug.

"There are people parking now. With all the RSVPs we should have about seventy-five people."

"Well, they'd better all get here in the next fifteen minutes. Because Steve said he would be back in half an hour when he dropped us off." I said.

At those words, Kacey got on her phone and started calling people frantically.

Taylor put a hand on my shoulder. "It's alright. Keeping it a secret this long is the surprise, and what matters is Scott enjoys it!"

Voices from the main room soon caught our attention, so Taylor left to greet them. I downed the rest of my soda and grabbed the punch bowl to stay busy.

The main room was filled with people. Walking into the loud room, my brain screamed to find a quieter place to hide. As I swerved through the crowd, trying desperately not to spill the punch, I felt nausea wash over me, along with a growing headache.

Suddenly, Kacey was at my side. "Let me take that from you. Are you sure you're alright?"

"Yes, I'll be fine." We made our way over to the food table when her phone rang. She answered it quickly, then hung up, eyes wide, and shoved it in her pocket.

"They're right around the corner, looking for somewhere to park! Everyone! They're here!" Her panic mounted as she looked to me for help. "What do we do, Rhi?"

"Just have everyone move to the back of the room. I'll manage the light switch." To my surprise, Kacey's tiny voice carried through the entire room.

"Move it!" she yelled as the guests cleared a path away from the door.

I flicked on the black lights, and all the white tablecloths glowed purple. We had strung up sheets along the ceiling to look like clouds, and I let some of them drape down for extra dimension. The main lights were off, so only the moonlight filtered through the windows. The moon was bright tonight and lent itself perfectly to the atmosphere.

I flattened myself against the wall and peered out the window, watching for the three shadows to walk up on the porch. I didn't have to wait long. I heard them before I saw them. I couldn't hear what they were saying, but they were obviously arguing.

"Great," I mumbled to myself.

Suddenly, the door flew open, and Justin flew in.

"Damn it!" Justin cursed.

Steve and Scott were quickly behind him, slamming the door behind them. I turned on the white twinkle lights, and Taylor's voice rang out with "SUR-PRISe!" as she ran into Scott's arms. Everyone echoed her with surprise and cheers as well. Then, the conversations started flowing, and someone began playing music. In seconds, the party was in full swing.

The absence of light was comforting to me. I had the brilliant idea to bring the night indoors, which was perfect for tonight's party. Taylor and Scott's love was palpable, and their eyes sparkled like stars whenever they were together. The darkness brought a sense of romance as they danced among the glittering lights. But, the shadows and darkness also allowed me to hide from curious onlookers.

The speakers pumped out music, and the dance floor came alive. I watched as people laughed and greeted each other. They held drinks in their hands and talked about their summer adventures. I wondered if they noticed how out of place I felt. I clutched my cup and stood awkwardly to the side. I hadn't been to a party in ages and didn't know how to act.

Kacey was showing off her dance moves. Taylor was laughing. And Scott was smiling. It was all so perfect. I couldn't help but feel proud of myself for making this party theme a reality. As I watched the people mingle and dance, my nerves settled.

I felt him before I heard him. "Why are you hiding?"

"I'm not hiding, Steve. I don't like big crowds. I don't dance. And someone needs to keep an eye on the food."

"You're unbelievable. You did all this work and won't even enjoy it."

I looked at Steve with an irritated expression.

Then, a melodious voice interrupted us. "Steve?"

"Trina," he grumbled.

She stepped up and hugged him around his waist. Ah, I thought to myself. This must be his mysterious not-girlfriend girlfriend.

"Who are you with?" she asked.

"My cousin, Rhiannon," he said, motioning towards me. "Rhi, this is Trina."

Trina was slender, of medium height, and had dark hair. Her gaze shifted towards me, her blue eyes swirling with an uncanny blend of curiosity and suspicion. She released Steve from her grip but still remained close, like an annoying moth flitting around a flame.

"Rhiannon?" She repeated my name, as if to assess the weight of it on her tongue. "Pleasure to meet you." Her voice was syrupy, sweet, dripping with feigned warmth.

I gave her a tight smile, "Same."

A faint smile danced on her lips as she turned back to Steve, her arm loosely draped over his waist.

"Steve told me a lot about you," I said. It wasn't entirely untrue. Steve's vague descriptions of Trina had painted an image of her in my mind.

"Oh really?" Trina's eyebrows rose slightly. Whether it was out of surprise or trepidation, I couldn't tell.

Steve seemed to grow stiffer by the second, his muscles tightening under the weight of Trina's affectionate arm wrapped around him. His jaw clenched in irritation.

"I love your name; it's different," She seemed to be trying to get me to like her.

"Thanks. It's a lot to live up to. There are many myths about Rhiannon."

A silky voice spoke into my ear, "I would like to hear about those myths."

Justin.

I glanced at Justin. My discomfort must have been a signal for Trina to drag Steve off.

His gaze swept around the room before eventually returning to me, his eyes seeming to pierce through me.

I shifted against the wall, and he mirrored my movement, casually placing himself beside me.

"So, what is Rhiannon's story?"

His question caught me off guard; did he mean me or the legend? By the look in his eye, it seemed like he had meant me, but I wasn't ready to go there yet. Instead, I began regaling him with what I knew about my namesake.

"There are different variations to the myths, but basically, Rhiannon was a Welsh fairy queen."

"Fairies, hmmm? Interesting..." He crossed his arms in front of his chest and leaned in closer to me.

"Yes, well, I told you it was a myth. Anyway, Rhiannon was promised in marriage to a man she found repugnant."

"Repugnant!" He chuckled.

I shoved at his shoulder playfully. "Do you want to hear the story or not? Yes! She found him unattractive, and he was much older than she was, and her family was forcing the marriage on her."

"Well, that is understandable, I suppose." He was still laughing.

"Her heart instead belonged to Pwyll, a young mortal prince. When he saw her for the first time, he became enchanted by her beauty."

He started twirling a few of my curls around his fingers, and my sudden nervousness made my heart flutter in my chest.

"Now, that is something I can understand."

My heart pounded so hard that it hurt; was he talking about me? My throat felt dry as a desert, so I cleared it before I resumed with the story. "Rhiannon was on a white horse, and it galloped so quickly that no one could catch up to her. Pwyll dispatched his swiftest riders, but they couldn't keep pace. Disheartened, he returned to the same spot where he had seen her alone the next day. And again, she outdid him in speed. He pleaded with her to stop, and eventually, she conceded- telling him all he had to do was ask." I giggled then. "She was a bit of a flirt...she told him she had come for him. She was seeking his love."

"If only it were that easy," Justin whispered.

I felt the now familiar soft hands on my shoulders, softly tugging on me again. I tried to ignore them as tendrils of fear crept along my skin.

Justin studied me, his brows coming together as if trying to figure something out. "So, the fairy queen and the mortal prince didn't live happily ever after?"

I smiled at him. "Eventually, they did, but Rhiannon had to suffer so much for her choices."

"Are we still speaking of the story?" He whispered to me.

My gaze met his. "Yes, of course," I said a bit breathlessly.

He was still playing with a curl in my hair, causing me to shiver. "There are other stories about Rhiannon. One is that she is a goddess, also referred to as the lady of the lake, who gave King Arthur the Excalibur sword."

"I know of King Arthur."

"You do?"

"I saw the movie." He mumbled, "Another messed-up love story."

I laughed again. "There are loads of movies based on King Arthur. The story is like rumors, you know. The person who starts out telling the story has it correct, but as it gets passed on, new elements get added or taken away, which changes the original tale completely."

I could feel his breath on my neck as he leaned in closer. "So, tell me your story, Rhi."

My heart beat unsteadily as I turned to face him. "What story?" I asked, my voice faint.

"Your story. The one that's not a myth. The one that's real."

His voice was like velvet.

I swallowed hard, knowing exactly what he was asking for. "I don't think I can..."

He brushed his lips against my ear as he spoke, sending shivers tiptoeing down my spine. "Please. I want to know everything about you."

I took a deep breath, feeling his hand on my waist. "Well, there's not much to tell..."

We stood there for a few moments, just looking at each other. I could feel the tension between us. I didn't know what would happen next, but I couldn't deny what I was feeling.

I wanted him to kiss me.

The music around us seemed to get louder, pounding through the speakers, and my head began to throb along with it. I lightly massaged my temples with my fingertips, trying to ease the growing pain in my head. "Crystal castles, magic gardens, and enchanted love are much more interesting than I am." I decided to change the subject. "What about your name? What does it mean?"

"What it says...Just. I'm just and good, or so I should be, but, like you said about your name, it's not very fitting, is it?"

"Only because you choose not to let it be," I replied tentatively. I was fearful I would upset him again, like I did the day at my house.

But instead of being offended, he asked if I was okay. "Does your head hurt?"

"What? Oh yes, a bit." I dropped my fingers from the side of my head. "Maybe I need some air."

"I'll come with you."

When we step outside into the rain-kissed evening, a fresh breeze sighs across my face and rustles through the leaves overhead.

We seat ourselves on a bench on the front porch together; our bodies close enough for our shoulders to touch. I steal a glance at his profile. His eyes are set forward, looking out into the dimly lit streets where lamplights flickered sporadically. Taking in a deep breath, he turns to look back at me with an encouraging smile, "Do you feel better?"

"Yes," A lie escaped effortlessly from my lips as I tugged nervously at the ends of my hair. I wasn't sure if it was my head or my heart that throbbed wildly now. The cool night air felt warm compared to the icy fear that gripped me internally.

I had never been in this position before, under the gaze of someone so alluring, so close to me.

His eyes set forward again, oblivious to the uneasiness waging within me. A wave of chastising thoughts floods my mind. *'You're being foolish,'* they taunt, *'he's just being polite, nothing more.'* Yet another part of me was daring to dream, a dream where he and I were more than just acquaintances.

Ripples of raindrops began to hit the wooden roof above us, each droplet a reminder of my pulsating heartbeat.

"I'll go see if anyone has any aspirin for your headache. I'll be right back." Justin leaves me alone with my thoughts.

Silken arms wrapped around me, startling me, and goose bumps exploded up my arms. A humming drifted into my ears. A soothing lullaby of the presence who cradled me; its whispered tones now clear in my mind. The arms, ethereal in their touch, seemed stronger now, their embrace more tangible. I could feel it—its cool breath against my skin, its feathery touch upon my exposed arms. It was there. Yet when I turned to look around, there was nothing but the inky night.

The humming became more like a melody. I closed my eyes and played this serenade in my mind. I listened to its vibrational poetry filter through my being. What could it be? What was this entity that kept coming to me?

The front door squeaked open, and Justin returned with a glass of punch and two aspirins in his hands as the presence and the melody left me. I took the pills and punch from him. He smiled, sitting on the bench and scooting closer to me. Instinctively, I curled tighter into myself. I could feel the heat radiating from his body where our legs touched. We were both quiet as I drank. He didn't say anything, but every now and then, I would catch him glancing at me.

Cautiously, out of the corner of my eye, I studied his profile. A beautiful cross with a shimmering stone in its center hung from his neck. His skin was perfect, smooth, and tanned, with high cheekbones and full lips. Said lips were pressed together tightly, a crease between his eyebrows. I wanted to trace my fingers along his face and ease away the ache, which now, in this quiet moment, was so plain to read. He was in pain. That was so obvious. It should be obvious to anyone who took the time to really look at him.

Suddenly, he turned to face me. "What are you looking at?"

I was tempted to tell him the truth, but instead, I lied. "Your hair. You always have it tied back; I wondered how it looked down." I bit my lower lip, hoping I was convincing. Okay, it wasn't a total lie. I did want to see his hair down. It was so shiny and dark. I was jealous.

"Seriously?"

I nodded.

"Then go ahead and take out the tie and see," he said with a mischievous smile on his face.

"I..um.." I stuttered.

He took the cup from my hands, placing it on the bench beside him. He took both of my hands in his, and their warmth filled me with sudden nervousness as well as something else.

"Tell him to leave Rhiannon."

It was back. I tried to remain still, but Justin noticed the tremor running through me, causing me to shake.

"Am I scaring you?" he asked, looking genuinely concerned. "You're trembling."

"No," I lied. But right now, it wasn't him that had spooked me-it was that voice.

"I'm begging you, Rhiannon...tell him to leave!" the voice echoed once more, and I jumped at the sound of it, looking around us frantically.

"Did you hear something?" I asked Justin.

Justin shook his head. "If you're worried about your cousins coming out here and finding us together, I can leave."

"No, it's not that," I said hastily, waves of panic rising in my chest. "I just thought I heard... never mind."

I turned to Justin, seeing the worry etched across his face. His brows were furrowed, eyes filled with confusion.

"You are freaking me out a bit," he said. He put his hands on my face and tilted my chin up to stare into his eyes. His touch was gentle, and for a moment, I forgot everything else around us. Until I felt it again - the soft hands on my shoulders and back, trying to pull me away from Justin. As the hands tightened around my arms, I realized I had felt it other times in my life.

A presence of some sort.

It never had a voice before, but it was a gentle pull that guided me when I felt lost. It would come when I sat crying in my bed, hiding from my stepfather's rage, or when I lay awake at night, wishing my mother would take me and leave. It would wrap around me like a soft, unseen blanket, filling me with calmness.

I always thought it was my subconscious mind trying to calm me. But, never had it been this close or felt this tangible. Its voice spoke clearly, just as if it were a human being sitting close to me.

"I don't understand what's happening," I whispered as my mind raced. This wasn't a hallucination or a bout of paranoia. The voice was real.

"What?" he asked, an odd expression etched onto his face. "Rhi... What's wrong?" Justin moved closer to me. His presence was reassuring, his broad shoulders supportive. His emerald eyes sparkled under the porch light. He didn't utter a word and instead wrapped his arms around me.

I started to move away, but he pulled me closer. "I think you are a little bit crazy, but I think I'll keep you around." He whispered.

His head dropped until our foreheads touched. My heart began to flutter violently. His lips were so near.

I felt those silky hands pulling at me again. The urgency in them suggested danger. Was Justin in trouble? Or was he the danger himself?

I ignored it. I felt safe in Justin's arms, and I didn't want to let go.

My fingers strayed through Justin's locks until they reached the band, holding it back. Gently, I pried it loose, releasing his hair to cascade over both of us like a veil. His hair smelled fresh like rainwater had been poured into it from the heavens above.

Justin sighed contentedly, "I like you too much, which is something I don't like at all." He pulled his face away from mine, and I wanted so much to pull him back. "I don't know what it is, but I feel like I'm being pulled to you." He admitted. "It's so strange."

I looked down at my lap, but I couldn't stop myself from running my fingers through his hair again.

Justin ran a finger along my jaw. "It's like the electricity I feel going on between you and me is...is..."

He was feeling it, too, this electricity that had filled the space between us. I didn't know why I couldn't resist him, "I don't know. I honestly don't. I have been warned to stay away from you, but I see something in you, something that draws me to you like you would understand me. Because honestly, Justin, no one really does." I was tempted to tell him that I saw his pain, too, but he wasn't ready for that; he worked hard to keep it hidden.

"I told you, you're crazy." A smile pulled at the corners of his mouth. "Maybe that is why I like you. I still don't know about all this, though." His tousled hair fell into his eyes as he looked at me through thick lashes. I gently brushed away the hair that covered his eyes so we could see each other clearly. "I'm not good with people," he whispered.

"That is an understatement." The voice said. Maybe it was just my subconscious. Maybe I was going crazy.

"I'm not good with people either," I confessed.

"You've been so good with me." His fingers grazed my cheek like a feather.

I could read the vulnerability in his eyes, and it struck a chord in me. Fear and vulnerability were a constant to me, too. It danced on the edges of my consciousness. The fear that letting Justin see who I truly was would result in rejection or regret.

These thoughts swirled inside me like a turbulent ocean. I chewed my bottom lip anxiously until I managed to say in a low whisper, "Maybe we should go back in."

Justin stood up to go, but he seemed hesitant about leaving. He then sat back down next to me. "Would you come to my parents' house for dinner tomorrow? We always eat together on Sundays."

I gulped nervously. "You want me to eat dinner with your family?"

He laughed. "Yes, that's what I said. Taylor will be there, too. Come on, say yes."

The air had left my lungs as his face hovered close to mine. "Alright," I breathed.

"Good." He ran his fingers through my hair and taking one of my hands in his; he laid a quick, chaste kiss on my knuckles and then turned my hand over. "What's this?" He asked, touching the scar on my palm.

"It's just a scar."

"Hmm, it looks like a star." He placed his lips gently against the tiny star-shaped scar. Taking my hand in his, he led us back into the party, leaving the ghost to themselves in the rainy night.

Chapter Nine

We all spent the night at Taylor's apartment. It felt like old times when we had slumber parties together. Scott came in with donuts and coffee from Sal's. I dug my hand into the box, pulling out a chocolate donut, savoring each bite.

Justin mentioned in passing how he had invited me to dinner. Steve scowled at him and me, but Taylor seemed to like the idea. Taylor volunteered to pick me up, but Justin quickly interrupted her, saying he was already taking care of that. They bickered about it back and forth until Scott finally said they all would pick me up. They argued so passionately that it almost felt like my opinion didn't matter. I just sat in the corner of the table, eating my chocolate donut.

Steve and Kacey had dropped me off close to noon. I showered and put on cut-off shorts and a green top. I again tried to tame the waves in my hair before giving up and putting it all up in a messy bun. I felt so much better than the night before. However, my stomach was flipping at the prospect of dinner at the Rizzos.

"You're going to wear a hole in the floor," Nan remarked, looking up from her knitting needles. Her keen eyes surveyed me over her glasses. "What has you so wound up anyway?"

My heart quickened in anticipation - Justin would be there. Justin, who had flirted with me last night. But instead of telling Nan that was the cause of my energy, I replied, "I'm just really hungry. I wish they'd get here already," as though summoned by my words, Taylor's car pulled up outside the house.

"They're here, Nan. I will see you later!" I called as I flew out the door. Somewhere behind me, I heard Nan say goodbye.

Taylor had a four-door compact car, which Scott was driving with Taylor in the passenger seat. That left the back for Justin and me. I looked up to see Nan in the house doorway, waving at me with an odd look on her face. I waved back and then hopped in the back seat with Justin.

Taylor turned around to smile at me. "Mrs. Riz called and needs us to go to Sal's to pick up some bread to go with dinner. She also said to pick up something for you to drink because she didn't know what you liked."

I felt embarrassed by all the attention, so I responded quickly: "Oh, that was nice of her, but don't go out of your way for me."

"I hope you're ready to eat." Scott piped in.

Justin's smile was deliciously wicked. "Do you have room after all those donuts you ate this morning?"

"Leave her alone, Justin," Taylor quipped at him as she adjusted herself in her seat. "Before I knew I was pregnant, I swore it was all the Sunday dinners finally catching up to me."

Justin gave my hand a reassuring squeeze and remarked, "Don't worry; whatever you can't eat, I'll finish for you."

Taylor appeared to have noticed Justin's gesture towards me, but she turned away and hid any reaction. I rapidly pulled my hand back and clasped them both together in my lap. I glanced sideways at Justin and saw he was still smirking.

You could feel the tension between us in the car like a thick blanket. Taylor's shoulders seemed tense as well. It seemed like Scott was the only one who hadn't noticed the strained atmosphere.

Scott parked the car in front of Sal's Bakery, nestled between a hardware store and a dry cleaner on Main Street. The area bustled with people coming and going. The bakery had patio seating with a few tables pushed under a shade umbrella, while people had pastries and coffee out on the sidewalk. The shop's exteriors were brick with apartments above. I treasured this area of town with its historical elements and personality; compared to the giant supercenters built outside the city, downtown held genuine hidden gems. These were Mom-and-Pop establishments that had been passed down for generations.

We all eagerly got out of the car, Scott offering **assistance** to Taylor, who was moving more and more slowly with each passing day. I followed them all into the bakery, pushing open the green door with the hand-painted sign on the glass that read "Sal's Italian Bakery" since 1904. The door creaked, and a tiny bell signaled our arrival.

There were a few small tables for people who wanted to dine in. The air was thick with the smells of sugar, butter, chocolate, and spices. There was a large cake display with lavish designs for weddings and parties. The shelves were heavy with wonderful confections and sweets of all varieties. There were abundant breads, bagels, rolls, and an array of other baked goods. The smell was intoxicating, and I was in heaven.

"Hey!" A boisterous voice boomed from behind the counter. "The Rizzo boys! Your Momma sending you in for some bread for her sauce, eh?"

"You guessed it, Arnie," Scott replied, grabbing the thick man around the shoulders and giving him a quick pat on the back over the counter. The bakery's owner was a big man. He looked like an Italian Santa Claus. His hair was white and curly, and his meaty forearms rested on a wooden table behind the counter with a white and red checkered tablecloth. He had on an apron that read "Sal's."

His radiant smile was contagious. "And how are you doing today, Miss Taylor? How is that little baby of yours?"

"I'm just fine, thank you for asking, Arnie," Taylor said with a warm smile.

"Here, have these cookies for your beautiful boy. And you..." He jabbed his pudgy finger at Scott, "You better marry this girl—she's one in a million."

"I'm not going to argue with you about that."

Arnie handed Taylor a small brown bag full of cookies before finally laying eyes on me. "Well, Justin, when were you going to introduce me to this young lady?" Sal's dark eyes twinkled at me.

Justin opened his mouth to speak, but Taylor spoke up before him, "She is my cousin, actually." I felt her hand on my shoulder protectively. "Rhi..I mean, Rhiannon, this is Arnie. He owns Sal's now. What are you, the fourth generation of Carinnnos?"

"Fifth, actually...and it's nice to meet you, Rhiannon, Taylor's cousin." His eyes flew back to Justin. "Here I thought you had found someone special, Justin...Ah well." He reached for another small paper bag. "So, for Miss. Rhiannon. What would be your favorite cookie?"

Before I could answer, Justin answered for me. "She likes chocolate."

Arnie raised a bushy eyebrow. "Hmmm. Maybe I wasn't wrong after all. I have a sense about these things, you know." He tapped a chubby finger against his temple. He reached into the display case and grabbed two chocolate cookies, plopping them in the bag and handing them to me. "Here you go, sweetie. A present from me to you. When you need something...anything...always remember us at Sal's. Okay?"

"Yes, thank you."

The familiar sensation of silky hands returned to my back again. They were becoming more solid. At first, it had been like an ethereal brush across my skin. Now, it was strong enough for me to feel its grip on my body through every fiber of my being. A chill raced up my spine. I hadn't sensed the presence since last night, but something must have triggered it to return. Or maybe it had never left at all. It just felt like letting me know at this precise moment it was here. "Go away!" I screamed in my head over and over. But it either ignored my request or couldn't read my mind.

Fine. I would have to ignore it again. Suddenly, I felt it leave, but it pulled gently at my hair as if it wanted me to look in a particular direction. As I turned, my eyes fell on one of the small tables. A young man sat at a table near the window. He had honey-colored hair that fell in waves to his shoulders like an angelic halo. He wore a faded black concert t-shirt and old, worn jeans. There was no food in front of him. He looked absolutely normal except for his eyes. They were a stormy silver filled with anger, sadness, worry, and love, all wrapped in endless pools of gray ice.

He was looking right at me. He knew me. I could see it in his eyes that he did. I could not explain how because I had never seen him before. Yet somehow, I felt as if I knew him too. He raised one finger to his eyes and then pointed it toward me. All the air seemed **to** leave my body, and stars filled up my vision.

"Rhi?" Justin said suddenly, his face appearing in front of me. "What are you staring at?" He glanced behind himself, and I followed his gaze. I saw nothing; the stranger had vanished. Was he even there to begin with?

"Rhi, are you okay? You look a bit pale...or paler than usual," he joked gently. "Is your head bothering you again?"

"No, I'm fine," I lied quickly. "Just hungry." I jumped slightly as I felt the silky hand touch mine. I quickly shoved my hand in my pocket, hoping no one had noticed. Justin looked at me quizzically, but I gave him a small smile and turned to Arnie, "Thank you for the cookies, Arnie. I can't wait to eat them," I said.

"Ah, you're welcome, sweetie. I'll make sure to have more waiting for you next time you come around," he replied, waving from behind the counter.

"Let's get out of here," Scott said, slapping Justin on the back. "Mom's waiting for us to bring the bread."

We all nodded, and I followed them out of the bakery, trying to shake off the strange feeling that had settled in my gut. The guy at the table, the hand on mine, the presence that never seemed to leave me fully. It was all too much. I needed air.

I took a deep breath, put on a cheery expression, and pretended to look around the streets as we drove. Really, though, I was searching the faces of strangers for him—for his golden hair and silver eyes. I couldn't feel him near me, but somehow I knew he wasn't far. Before long, we reached the Rizzo's house, located at the end of Main Street, before it curved toward Hayden Township on the southeast side of town.

We circled around several times but couldn't find anywhere suitable to park. Scott offered to drop Taylor and me off in front of his parents' house while he and Justin looked for a place to park on Main Street. All the houses here were on postage-stamp-sized lots and were more tall than wide, offering very little parking.

I sheepishly looked up at the tall house with a neatly trimmed lawn and white picket fence. "We should wait for them, right?" I thought. Please let her say yes.

"We can. However, Mrs. Rizzo is expecting us. Although...Rhi, I wanted to ask you something...".

Oh no, here it comes. Maybe I did want to go in before the inevitable what is going on with you and Justin questions started.

"It seems that you and Justin are becoming friends," She ventured.

Just as I thought. "And your question would be....is that all we are?" I raised an eyebrow at her.

She shifted her feet on the pavement. "Yes, I guess that is what I am getting at."

I rolled my eyes at her. "How can I answer that, Taylor? I hardly know him. I don't even know if he is interested in me that way."

"Oh, trust me, he is interested, so the question is...are you?"

Luckily, Mrs. Rizzo called to us from the doorway before Taylor could press further. "Girls, come in! Taylor, get off your feet, dear, and out of the heat! Come, come." She waved us into the house.

The comforting aroma of garlic and tomatoes wafted into my nostrils when we stepped through the door, causing my mouth to water. Mrs. Rizzo led us through the clean, lightly furnished living room, past the dining area, and into the brightly lit kitchen. Taylor flopped down in one of the chairs at the kitchen table, so I took up the chair next to her. I really wasn't sure what to do with myself, so I offered to help with dinner, but was quickly denied by Mrs. Rizzo.

I had seen Mrs. Rizzo at Taylor's baby shower, but I took the time now to study her more closely as she glided through the kitchen, stirring this and that and adding pinches of assorted things to the simmering pots. She was of average height, with wavy hair clipped short just above her shoulders. It was obviously dyed professionally as she had perfect highlights surrounding her round face, while her green eyes were identical to her sons'. Not much else of them seemed to have passed on in terms of looks, except maybe their flawless skin; she had skin so smooth and tan it almost looked ageless. I was distracted from my observations by the noisy arrival of the guys.

"Ma, it's a thousand degrees in here," Justin complained. "Turn up the air."

"Hush, and get the plates down and set the table. You have guests." She scolded.

"Taylor isn't a guest. She's family." He teased.

"Can I do something?" I asked tentatively.

"No, no, dear. It's all done." She said over her shoulder as she poured the sauce over the pasta. "Go take a seat in the dining room. Make yourself at home."

I took the seat closest to Taylor as Scott, Justin, and their mother brought plates and bowls full of food out, arranging them neatly across the table. My stomach growled embarrassingly loud, making Taylor giggle.

"Go get your father, Scott. He is out back tinkering in the garage." Mrs. Rizzo was passing out wine glasses as she spoke to him. She left and returned from the kitchen with a bottle of red wine. "Oh, I forgot the bread." She fluttered back to the kitchen again.

Mrs. Rizzo returned, followed by Scott, and who I could only presume was Mr. Rizzo. He was a stout man with grey, wavy hair. He had a round face with chubby cheeks and light blue kind eyes. I liked him instantly. I could smell motor oil mixed with sweat and cologne as he entered the room.

"I hear we have a guest!" he laughed heartily and slapped Scott on the shoulder. "I'll have a glass of wine, son, please."

Taylor reached out with her slender hand and patted my back. "Yes, Rick, this is my cousin, Rhiannon."

"I thought I knew everyone in your family, Taylor. Where have you been hiding this cousin?" He joked.

"She just moved back here from Colorado."

"Colorado?" Two bushy eyebrows shot up. "You know how to ski?" Excitement flickered in his eyes.

"Not at all," I replied. Sports weren't exactly my strong suit; every time I tried to play a game, it seemed as if I always ended up tripping and falling over myself. I had some pretty close calls, but managed to always catch myself right before crashing into the concrete or any other hard surface.

Everyone took their seats and passed around the home-cooked meal. The food smelled and looked exquisite, and although I did my best to control my portions, I wanted to overflow my plate with all of its deliciousness.

"So, what do you like to do?" Scott asked while five pairs of eyes shifted their focus towards me.

"I mostly like music," I responded while taking another sip of wine. "Listening to it, going to concerts; I write and can play a bit too." I quickly popped some more pasta into my mouth, hoping that was enough information about me for now.

"What instrument do you play?" Mr. Rizzo inquired.

Quickly swallowing my mouthful of pasta, I responded, "I can play a bit of guitar."

"Really?" Justin seemed taken aback; he had already finished his first round of food and had started filling his plate with seconds.

I squirmed in my chair, feeling the heat of everyone's stares. Taylor must have noticed how uncomfortable I was and filled up the awkward silence with details about her latest trip to the obstetrician. Everyone in the room leaned forward in their seats, eager for every detail.

I shoveled the last morsels of food into my mouth, hoping to help with clean-up duty and avoid more of the twenty questions with Rhiannon game.

Justin must have read my mind. "Here, let me take care of these dishes. Come on, I'll show you around the house."

His mother looked appalled. "Justin. I have dessert."

"Yeah, Ma, I know. You guys finish up, though, while I show Rhi around. Just call us when you are ready for cake and coffee."

He grabbed my elbow and guided me towards the kitchen, then swept his arm out theatrically and announced, "This is the kitchen!"

I rolled my eyes exasperatedly and replied, "Oh yeah? I never would have guessed!"

He pointed towards a door near the cabinets and said, "That door leads to the basement with a storage area, a washer, and a dryer, but nothing much else down there, so we'll skip that part of the tour. The back door over there goes to the backyard and a garage." As we made our way out past the dining room table, Justin waved at everyone as they stared back at us.

"Living room, hallway, and my parents' bedroom." He guided me down the short passageway to a closed door with 'Scott' painted in baby blue on it. "Scott's old bedroom. My parents still keep it here for him, like a shrine." He rolled his eyes.

"I heard that, Justin!" His mother called from the dining room.

He never lost stride or bothered to show me any of the rooms he referred to as we traveled down the hallway. At the end of the passageway was one more closed door. "The attic or my room, whichever you want to call it."

I stared at Justin, surprised at the sudden shift in the atmosphere. As we stood before the door, I saw his hand lingering on the doorknob, his eyes darkening with unspoken words. He was attractive and charming, with a mischievous glint in his green eyes that had caught my attention from the moment we met. But now, I felt uneasy thinking about going into his bedroom.

"Is something wrong?" he asked, breaking the silence.

He smiled at me in a way that made me feel all sorts of nervous. "No, nothing's wrong," I said.

His fingers were still wrapped around the doorknob. "I was just thinking maybe you'd like to see what's inside."

I hesitated, unsure what to do, but finally gave in to temptation and nodded. We scaled the narrow, creaky stairs.

"Please close the door behind you." He must have noticed the surprised look on my face. "It messes up the air conditioning if it's left open. It's brutally hot up here without it."

I did as he asked and followed him the rest of the way up the stairs.

The attic was massive, stretching the full length of the house. The floors were wood and a bit worn, but still shining clean. Sunlight streamed in through the window, showing off the tiny backyard beneath. A large air conditioner was humming happily, snug inside the window frame. On one end of the room housed an old dresser with a mirror, some photos with cars in them, and a calendar. The bed in the center of the space grabbed my attention immediately. It had an unusually carved headboard and footboard; it was rustic yet delicate in places, while other sections looked like they'd been hacked away viciously. I shuffled closer to get a better look. Intricate carvings adorned each pole—spiders, dragons, and more. Ranging from menacing to beautiful.

Justin flopped down on the monster bed, and I opted to sit cross-legged on the floor. Suddenly, Justin flipped over and hung his head over the edge of his bed to watch me. I glanced at him to try to interpret his emotions, but couldn't make them out. I leaned closer to examine the closest bedpost. This one was completely distinct from the others; it looked as if fire and flames had been etched into the entire length of the wood.

He broke the silence. "Well, this is a first."

I drew my attention away from the carvings. "What is a first?"

He flashed me a devilish smile. "The first time I've ever invited a girl up here who paid more attention to my bed than me."

I forced myself to remain calm as I asked, "Is that why you brought me up here?"

"No," he said nonchalantly. "I just find it interesting."

My heart raced against my chest like a jackhammer. He seemed intent on playing games with me, and I knew it. Taking a deep breath, I tried to even out my voice before speaking again. "I think the artwork on your bedposts is quite impressive."

"Really?" One corner of his mouth turned upwards as he raised an eyebrow skeptically. "I don't think anyone's ever noticed before."

Once again, I trailed my fingers along the pole, marveling at its beauty. "They're beautiful," I murmured.

"Beautiful?" he scoffed. "Please, it just does what it's supposed to - keep the mattress off the floor. I just carve on it when I'm bored."

"You did this?" I asked and lifted my gaze from the wooden storybooks to his piercing green eyes, just inches away from mine.

"Yes," he says, his lips so close to mine. "If you think my silly carvings are beautiful, you haven't looked in the mirror lately." Heat slams through me at his words as his scent wraps around me. He smelled like the scent of the forest after it rained.

Suddenly, he was off the bed and by my side. His speed and how close he was now scared me a bit. He lifted one hand and brushed the strands of hair away from my face. My gaze was downward, but he tilted his head so our eyes were level. His expression was serious, but still, I could see he was unsure of something. He didn't move forward immediately but lingered there for a moment. His warm breath blew onto my cheek, and I nearly forgot to breathe, feeling utterly dizzy. His other hand cupped the back of my head firmly as he spoke in a gruff voice: "If you want me to stop, tell me now."

I couldn't speak. I didn't want him to stop. My chest felt like it was going up in flames and could explode at any moment. I was paralyzed.

The voice was in my ear suddenly, *"Tell him NO!"* The beautiful and angry guy I'd seen in Sal's. Somehow, I knew it was his voice. He was here with us, which confused me and scared me.

I shut my eyes tight. If you don't see it, it isn't there. It can't hurt you. But the voice was not a sound. It was a presence inside my mind. Was I going insane? I wanted to keep going, to let Justin melt the fear out of me.

Justin slowly placed his hands on my cheeks and softly whispered into my ear, "I understand."

As he pulled away, I exclaimed, "No!" And clung onto him so hard that we both fell backward. I was lying awkwardly, half on top of him. He had a most bemused expression on his face.

"Does 'no' mean yes or no?" He laughed lightly.

"You've ruined the moment," I huffed out a breath.

"I ruined the moment?" He laughed out loud. "You yelled at me and threw me on the floor!" His eyes glittered with mischief. "You still haven't answered my question." He moved my hair aside and stared deeply into my eyes as if seeking my reply within them.

"No.....I did not want you to stop." I answered in a shaky voice.

"Then the moment is back," he whispered, and then his hands were tangled in my hair, pulling me in closer, our faces mere breaths apart. He didn't rush to kiss me. Instead, he caressed my cheek with the softness of his lips while whispering sweet, tantalizing words into my ear. "The feelings I have..." His hot lips left a blazing trail down my neck before journeying to my other ear. "Help me make sense of this, Rhiannon."

Then he swept me up into his arms and swung us around so I was pinned beneath him - his muscular body a heated blanket over mine. I traced lazy circles over his brow and cheeks with my fingers until I reached his lips; he kissed them gently before taking my hand in his and entwining our fingers together. "This is the last chance for you to tell me no."

"Say NO!" The other's voice screamed at me.

"Why?" The question had left my mouth without me realizing it.

"Why what?" Justin asked, confused.

"Why do you want me to say no so badly?" I replied, trying to save the moment.

He scowled at the question. "I don't want to hurt you—it's obvious I'm not everyone's idea of a nice guy. Don't you get it?"

"Kiss me, Justin, please."

He didn't need any further urging; his lips brushed against mine gently and softly. The kiss deepened, his tongue exploring my mouth, and I felt a fire start within me. My fingers knotted in his hair, pulling him closer to me. He tasted like wine and something else, something wild and untamed.

"Justin!" Scott's voice echoed from the bottom of the stairs, making Justin pull away quickly.

"Damn it." He whispered. "Yeah, Scott?" He shouted back.

"Mom has dessert ready."

"We'll be right down." He reached out his hand to help me to my feet. I smoothed down the tangled locks on my head. He spun me around to face him and softly ran his fingertips down my cheekbone. "It seems like I still owe you a moment," he said quietly.

I couldn't stop smiling as I took his hand. "I think our moment was perfect the way it was," I said, my heart still racing.

"Come on, you two, coffee is getting cold!" Scott called again.

"We're coming!" Justin called back, a hint of annoyance in his voice.

He turned back to me, leading me out of the room and down the stairs. As we made our way to the kitchen, I felt a mix of excitement and nervousness. I had just kissed Justin, and it had been amazing, but now we would have to face Taylor and his family. I couldn't believe I had let myself be so vulnerable and open with Justin. I was drawn to him in a way I couldn't explain, and I knew I wanted to explore that connection further.

Mrs. Rizzo beamed at us when we walked in. "Justin, Rhiannon, come join us! I made this cake from scratch, and it would be a shame if you missed out on it."

"Thank you, Mrs. Rizzo," I said sheepishly, trying to hide that my cheeks still felt flushed from the kiss with Justin.

"Just call me Mary." She said sweetly.

I took a bite of cake, savoring the rich chocolate flavor. We chatted and joked over dessert, but I couldn't shake the feeling that I was being watched again.

I had to figure out who or what that silver-eyed guy was.

Chapter Ten

I watched the rain flow down the window, forming streams and patterns along Justin's car window. Somehow, we made it through dessert. Taylor looked exhausted, so Scott kindly told us he was taking her home. She gave me a look, indicating she knew something had happened between Justin and me. I stayed silent, trying to avoid having to answer any questions, keeping my mouth occupied with cake and coffee. She kissed me on the cheek goodbye and whispered in my ear to call her when I got home. I returned to listening to the rain outside, soothing my anxious mind with its gentle lullaby.

"You are awfully quiet. Did my family freak you out that much? Or was it me?" Justin asked.

I turned from the window and looked at his beautiful face. His lips were curved up in a smile, but I could see the anxiety behind his eyes.

"I like your family," I said with a smile. "Your father especially." I bit my tongue, remembering what Steve had said. Mr. Rizzo wasn't Justin's real father.

Something flashed across his features that I couldn't quite decipher. He laughed lightly. "Well, you haven't spent much time with us yet...you may change your mind."

I knew he was waiting for more of an answer from me. "You don't freak me out...*much*," I added with a wink.

"Do you want me to?" He raised a sleek black eyebrow as our eyes locked.

"What?"

He didn't bother answering my question. He drove a few more blocks, pulled over onto the side of the road, switched off the engine, and jumped out of the car, the rain pouring down on him. After running around to my side of the car, he flung open the door and grinned at me.

"Come on." He opened his hand to me as an invitation.

"What? Where are we going?"

"Just come with me." Taking hold of my hand, he pulled me out of the car into the chilly rain pouring down hard from the sky. We sprinted along a sidewalk before turning onto a path that led to Cherry Creek Park, a place I was familiar with since it was close to my grandmother's house. His grip never loosened as we strolled around the duck pond, illuminated by street lights, the rain creating captivating designs in the water. We crossed over a small bridge, which opened up to an area filled with swings and slides.

"Freaked out yet?" He grinned at me mischievously. Both of us were drenched from head to toe, our clothes sticking to our skin; his hair was plastered to his head, and his shirt clung to his muscular body.

"Not a chance! I love the rain!" I took off running away from him, hopping onto one of the swings before he could catch up. He came up behind me and pushed me through the air with all his strength, laughing as I soared high above him into the night sky. My own laughter filled the air - loud and cheerful.

"Jump!" Justin shouted.

"I can't," I replied with a giggle as I kept pumping my legs, swinging higher and higher.

"Yes, you can. I'll catch you!" He stretched out his arms to me. "Come on!"

So, I took a deep breath and released my grip. I slammed into him full force. We both lost our footing and fell to the ground into the mud.

"Had enough?" Justin asked, leaning over me with rain clinging to his long lashes.

"Not yet; we haven't gone down the slide."

"To the slide then."

He helped me up again, and we slipped and slid through the mud to the slides. I picked the tallest one and scurried to the top, Justin behind me. His wet body pressed against mine, warm and hard. "Can I slide down with you?" his lips tickled my ear.

In response, I grabbed his arms, wrapping them tightly around my waist. We slid down together and splashed into a giant mud puddle at the bottom, laughing like little kids.

"You're filthy." He said.

"So are you."

"You have no idea," he whispered.

I couldn't breathe. His body was pressed against me as his eyes held mine. I couldn't look away.

Then he kissed me. Sensation rippled through me like crashing waves. Thunder boomed around us as he pulled his lips away from mine. He grinned at me, water dripping from his hair, and I laughed up at him. We both sat up, and I leaped to my feet, pushing him back into the mud, and took off running towards the stone bridge. However, the joke was on me when I tripped on the curb and fell to my knees.

Justin came to my side and helped me up. "Are you okay?"

"Yeah, I'm fine."

"Here, let's go up under the light and take a look."

He put his arm around my waist and led me up the bridge to where a large lamp hung. Baskets of flowers along the bridge smelled of fuchsia. He crouched to examine my knees, and the rain slowly let up, turning to misty droplets.

"It's just a scrape, nothing to worry about." He tilted his face up to meet mine, the lamp light illuminating the perfect angles of his chiseled features. Our eyes locked as he slowly ran his hands up my legs and settled them on my waist. He picked me up effortlessly and placed me on the bridge so we were eye to eye. His fingers moved across my rib cage and up to my shoulders, sending hot sparks through my body. I remembered how warm his lips had felt, and I wanted that warmth back now.

His eyelashes were heavy with raindrops, making his green eyes look like emeralds. His fingers caressed my shoulders and then lightly touched my collarbone. He moved closer, and then suddenly, when I thought I couldn't take one more moment of the anticipation, his head dropped to where his fingers had been.

My shoulders relaxed, and a shaky breath escaped me. His arms wound around me, his head dropping on my chest as his warm breath kissed my cool skin. My own arms circled his back as I lay my cheek against his damp hair. This was our moment, and it was perfect. The first kiss we shared had been special, but this beat that by far. It was in the rain, under a lamplight, on a stone bridge, and completely romantic.

I clung to him tighter, taking the time to engrave this beautiful surrounding into my memory, and then I saw him. I had a feeling he would be here, watching us from the other side of the bridge to ruin our moment. He was untouched by the light drizzle that fell around us and appeared worried rather than angry. I blinked away a few raindrops, and when my vision cleared, he was gone.

I clamped my eyes shut and concentrated on my feelings and the sensations that consumed me. The smell of the flowers, the sound of the raindrops on the pond, the warmth of Justin's body.

I wanted him closer.

I had no experience with this, but the sweet smell of the rain mixed with his hair made me want to kiss his head. So, I did. Gently. So gently that I wasn't sure he felt it until I felt his breath stop briefly.

He had felt it.

Unsure whether this was good or bad, I kissed him gently on his brow. He rested against my shoulder until he seemed to melt into me. I let out a small moan, so he turned towards me and moved his hands through my hair, tucking it away from my neck before placing gentle kisses over my exposed skin, kissing and licking away all the raindrops.

"I won't mess this up," He said against the hollow of my neck.

I clung to him, silently begging him to come closer. His grip on me tightened for a moment before his arms dropped, and he stepped away from me, taking away the warmth of his embrace and leaving a cold void in its place.

He stood rooted to his spot for several agonizing moments. His eyes roamed over my face with an intensity that shot straight down my spine. In those green depths were raw and powerful emotions. He looked torn, as if he was battling an internal war.

"If you want me," he began, his voice suddenly filled with a desperate edge. "Then come to me."

My chest tightened at his words. I could hear my heart pounding in my ears, suspended in the heavy silence that fell over us.

His eyes explored my face like they were committing it to memory. For a moment, I caught the gleam of something vulnerable, fleeting across them before disappearing completely behind a wall of hardened jade. But I had seen it - a flash of fear that mirrored my own insecurities.

I swallowed hard against the knot forming in my throat, my hands clenching into tight fists at my side. It was that vulnerability that I had seen that finally caused me to break free from my self-imposed shackles of indecision.

With a shaky breath, I gathered my courage and began walking slowly towards him. I looked up at him as I stood before him, my shoes touching his.

His gaze never left mine as translucent fog enveloped us in a mystical ambiance. As I shivered, I understood what he wanted; all I needed was the courage to do it. Just the thought of initiating something with this beautiful and broken boy had anxiety snaking across my skin, and it was taking everything I had to be brave and not run away.

I brought his hand to my face and clung to it, not letting go. With my other hand, I stroked his cheek gently as he watched me warily. I was shaking, whether from the chill or my nerves, I didn't know. There was something in this boy that called to me. Like something broken in him, mirroring what is broken in me. Slowly, I pulled his head down to meet mine. I curled my hands around the back of his neck and said in my head to the ghost, *"Don't ruin this moment for me."* I then brushed my lips against Justin's.

That was all it took, the simple light touch of my mouth on his, and he folded his arms around me and pulled me hard against his body. The electric shock that went through me was frightening, and I tore my mouth away. His glorious face filled my vision as I tried to comprehend what was happening between us.

"Are you done then?" he asked with a laugh. "You look confused."

"I am. I mean...no, I'm not done, but yes, I am confused. Come here." I tugged him back and kissed him ardently, continuously running my lips over his mouth and exploring them. He responded with equal fervor, crushing my mouth against his as heat blazed through me.

The rain began getting heavy again, and he swept me off the bridge and onto the ground. I didn't want to let go of him. "I could kiss you all night," he said gruffly. The night sky lit up with a strike of lightning and a boom of thunder. "I should take you home, though. It looks like it will downpour again, and you are a soaking, wet, muddy mess."

We raced back to his car. He spread an old blanket across the seat to prevent it from getting wet. It was not a far ride, but I shook and shivered the whole way home. We pulled up in front of the neighbor's house. I didn't want to wake Nan if she was sleeping.

Justin drew me close and hugged me tightly against his chest. I felt his heartbeat thundering against his ribs. His soft breath hovered near my ear, "I don't want this to be goodnight."

I was shaking uncontrollably, which had nothing to do with the cold and everything to do with Justin. I didn't think I wanted the night to end either, but I knew it had to. "I have to go in; Nan will worry."

"Can I come up?" he asked hopefully.

"I don't think Nan would want you in my room at ten o'clock at night," I replied, my teeth beginning to chatter.

He smiled wickedly. "She doesn't have to know."

I searched his face. He wasn't kidding. "You want me to sneak you in?"

"I can sneak myself in. But only if you want me to." He leaned back against his seat, searching my eyes for an answer.

I wanted to spend more time with him. What if Nan caught us, though? I was torn.

He seemed to read the indecision on my face, and he reached down and kissed me gently. "Another time, then."

"No!" The word tumbled from my mouth. What was I doing? "I want to spend more time with you. You can come up for a little while. Just be careful, please."

He smiled and gave me one more kiss. "I'll see you in a little bit then."

I hurried up the stairs, inserting the key in the door and opening it as silently as possible. The house was pitch black. I crept up the steps to my room and snatched my PJs.

I sneaked back down, wincing whenever a stair creaked beneath me. I needed to shower as I was plastered with mud. The bathroom was right across the hallway from Nan's room, though. Her door was partially closed, and I was almost to the bathroom when she called out my name.

"Rhi? Is that you?"

"Yeah, Nan, it's me. Sorry if I woke you."

"You didn't. I had been listening to the news. Did you have fun?"

Please don't ask too many questions, and please keep Justin away until she's asleep.

"Yes, the food was great, and everyone was very kind. Just gonna jump in the shower now." I hoped she wouldn't come into the hallway and see me covered in mud.

"Okay, Rhi, goodnight."

Relieved, I dashed to the shower and stood under the steaming hot water, defrosting my freezing skin as quickly as possible. Justin could be upstairs at any moment. After toweling off and brushing my teeth, I changed into my pajamas. I tiptoed back up the stairs and opened my bedroom door. Flipping on the light switch, he was sitting on my bed.

Instinctively, I opened my mouth to scream.

Chapter Eleven

It wasn't Justin. It was the stranger—the ghost or whatever he was. The scream never escaped my mouth. He moved at an impossible speed and covered my mouth with his hand, addressing me in a gentle, tranquil voice. "Please don't scream. I would never inflict harm upon you. I am here to protect you. I've always protected you, Rhiannon." His voice was melodic and soothing. "I am going to remove my hand. Now don't scream because it will frighten your grandmother, and she can't see me anyway. Do you promise not to scream?"

He was right. No one else ever saw him but me, and I certainly didn't want Nan to wake up with Justin sneaking in here at any moment. I nodded in agreement, and he removed his hand.

He strolled back over and perched himself on my bed, cross-legged. I hadn't seen him up close yet; he was so beautiful, so perfect. His skin was flawless, and he looked like he had been carved from a block of marble. And his eyes, oh his eyes! They were a mesmerizing shade of silver. His long, honey-blonde hair fell gracefully over his shoulders, and his lips were full and inviting. Despite the fear still pulsing through my veins, I couldn't help but feel drawn to him.

"Who are you?" I whispered. My voice was barely audible.

He smiled at me, a warm and comforting smile that made my heart skip a beat. "I suppose under these circumstances, I can allow you to know my name. It's Kiran."

His movements were strange. He was too fluid and graceful—unearthly. He moved, unlike any human being I'd ever seen. When he spoke, his hands gestured almost like sign language.

My voice trembled as I asked him another question. "Okay, Kiran. What are you?"

A magical laugh escaped from his lips. "What do you think I am?"

"A ghost?" I questioned quietly.

"Not even close."

His words gave me a jolt of fear. What could he possibly be? "I have no idea," I replied softly.

"I've been with you since the day you were born," he said, holding my stare. "I held your hand when you were in the hospital with a fever at five months old and kept you safe as you learned to walk and explore the world around you. I remember a time I kept your head from hitting a rock when you were about nine." His eyes locked onto mine with such intensity that it made my heart race faster as I pressed myself against the door behind me.

"What are you saying?" My voice shook with anxiety, and I felt a cold sweat break out on my forehead. "I'm your Guardian, Rhiannon."

I licked my dry lips. This wasn't real. He wasn't real.

"I assure you, Rhiannon, I am real." Before I could blink, he was in front of me. He picked up my hands and held them between his. "Your hands are like ice."

My hands warmed as he ran his thumb along my wrist.

That was very real. He was tall, his shoulders broad. He looked effortlessly perfect. He still wore a faded band shirt, which I now saw was The Beatles' iconic 'Abbey Road' album cover.

The four members crossed the street, their figures slightly cracked and distressed on the well-worn shirt. Something weird spread through me, a feeling of familiarity. "How is this possible?" I asked him, barely managing to keep my voice steady.

"Energy transformation. We are beings of light and energy. I can condense my energy into my physical form." His eyes were gentle and kind as he spoke, "It is easier this way when we interact with humans."

My mouth was agape. "Why are you here?"

"I told you. To protect you."

"I could have used protection many more times in my life than now." The words left my mouth harsher than intended.

He held onto my hands softly. "We don't always know what is best for us. Perhaps you had to go through all of those experiences so that you could get here now."

"But you show up now when I'm with Justin?"

His gaze turned stony. "That's one reason why I'm here, yes. You should stay away from Justin Rizzo." He let go of my hands and walked toward the bedroom window overlooking the backyard.

"But, you just said everything happens for a reason. Shouldn't Justin and I be happening for a reason?"

He spun around to face me. "No."

"No?"

"Rhiannon, please trust me." His expression was so honest, his eyes beseeching me for understanding.

"Why should I?" I scoffed.

"I have never failed you before. You are under my guardianship, but I cannot manage each detail of your life. You have your personal autonomy. But in this scenario, I cannot stand still. He took a deep breath and took a step closer to me. "We rarely reveal ourselves for what we truly are. We live among you, but we normally stay hidden. I am not playing by the rules here, but I must do what I feel is right. I care about you too much. I have been through so much with you already." His eyes were overcome with emotion. "You don't understand what peril you were facing in the hospital room as an infant. Your mom had no clue, nor did the medical team. However, I knew. You don't know what would have happened if your head had smashed against that rock while playing with your cousins near the creek—you could have drowned, and they wouldn't have been able to save you. I saved your life then, and I'm trying to save you now." He came to me again, gripping my shoulders in his hands. "Please stay away from Justin."

Tears pooled in my eyes as I pleaded for an explanation. "But why? I care about him."

His lips formed a tight line, "You're at a critical juncture in your life where this relationship could lead to long-lasting consequences."

His head suddenly snapped up. "Justin is outside. He should be here in a few seconds. I've already said too much; I can only offer guidance and protection. You must choose your own path."

"But...."

Before I could finish my thoughts, there was a quiet knock on the door. Kiran was gone. I opened the door with shaky hands to find Justin standing with a paper bag in one hand and a bottle of water in the other.

"What's wrong?" He asked, concerned.

What could I say? "I thought you changed your mind and wouldn't show up." I didn't know what else to tell him; I couldn't share the truth.

He pulled me into his strong embrace, stroking my wet hair soothingly. His human presence was calming. "No, silly girl. I just went home, took a quick shower, and changed. It looks like you had the same idea." He kissed my brow.

"Maybe this will make you feel better," he said, offering the paper bag filled with my cookies from Sal's and a bottle of water.

I turned and locked my door. Justin went and sat on my bed, taking off his big shoes and quietly placing them on my floor.

"Turn on that little lamp, please," I asked.

He illuminated the tiny lamp beside my bed, and I switched off the overhead light. I then quietly walked over to the old TV and turned it on.

"What are we watching?" Justin asked.

"Nothing. I keep it on for background noise when I sleep. It's just too quiet up here. So quiet that I think I hear things." Only now did I know I was hearing a real thing, and his name was Kiran.

"The reception is horrible. Don't you have cable?" He reached over and messed with the antennae of the old TV.

"Nan does on the main television downstairs. I don't up here. Like I said, I don't really watch it. I just need the voices to keep me company."

"What about those CDs of yours? Do you have a CD player?" He gestured to my pile of CDs scattered across the floor.

"Yes, I have an old stereo that I can plug my portable one into." I rubbed my hands up and down my thighs. "I never thanked you, by the way." He glanced at me over his shoulder. "For leaving your party to stay with me."

He shrugged and finished messing with the antennae, and the reception was a little better. You could sort of make out the show behind the static. "I know how to splice the cable box so you can get cable up here," he offered.

"No, no. Don't mess with Nan's stuff. I appreciate the gesture, but she would freak out."

"I get it."

I shifted until I sat beside him, propping my chin on my knees. I still couldn't believe he was here. In my room. And he'd kissed me.

I thought of myself as plain. Boring. I didn't stand out in a crowd. Justin, however, was tall and muscular. Not bulky, but lean and cut exquisitely. His hair was dark and glossy, like black silk, and his eyes were a dazzlingly unique color of green. I felt insignificant in comparison.

His gaze flicked to mine. "Why are you staring at me?"

"I'm sorry. I'm just trying to figure you out." I mumbled to my knees.

He examined me closely before speaking. "What is there to figure out?"

"Why are you interested in me?" I uttered quietly.

He paused for a long moment before he replied, "Do you remember the first time we met?"

I nodded. "You came off as a little full of yourself."

He laughed at that. "Well, I am. You didn't misjudge me there." He scooted back again, making my bed creak beneath his weight. He looked off when he spoke. "I know everyone in this town. Hell, everyone knows everyone in this town, and everyone knows everyone's business, too. I hate it. I saw you and thought, 'This is someone who doesn't belong here.' You looked so lost, not fitting in at all. But Steve obviously cared a lot about you. I was curious." He shrugged his shoulders. "I was playing the game. Seeing what you knew, seeing how much I could find out about you. It was obvious by how your cousins protected you that you were important to them, but it's futile to even attempt to try to protect anyone against me." He said smugly.

I squirmed and thought about Kiran's earlier statement, "I am your Guardian."

Justin continued. "It quickly became obvious that you didn't need their protection, although they still believe otherwise," he added with a laugh. "I decided to go to the baby shower because I was very intrigued. I got the speech from Steve and my brother." He rolled his eyes. "Honestly, Rhi, I have been with lots of girls, just like they have said. I won't lie about it. But, I wasn't out to hurt them or use them like they think." He paused for a long time. He let out a deep breath. "It just was better that way. No strings attached. They always want something I am not able to give. Anyway, I was messing with Steve and my brother at the baby shower by flirting with you, but you didn't react like I thought you would. Again, I got curious. I asked about you. I found out the stories about why you were here."

I drew in on myself, my body tensing up.

He turned to me and grabbed one of my hands, rubbing it tenderly. "Relax, Rhi. I know most were rumors, but I also knew some had a grain of truth. So, I asked my brother if he knew what the truth was. I thought Taylor would have told him. He was reluctant to tell me, though. My brother and I aren't very close anymore."

He was massaging my hand now, kneading the little muscles in my fingers and working his way up to my wrist. "He talked to Taylor about it, and they called me over one day to talk."

He tugged me closer to him, and the rough material of his jeans against my bare skin caused goosebumps to erupt on my skin.

"Taylor loves you very much. She asked me to please be kind to you. She knows this move is hard for you in your senior year. She didn't want me to pursue you. She wants you to be happy here, and she thinks I will break your heart." He was massaging my arm now, and I was feeling more at ease from his physical ministrations and how he was opening up to me. "She told me to think about my own family problems. That I should understand family trauma."

"She was right on one point. I understand how messed up family can be. She was very wrong about me leaving you alone." His voice trailed off, the words lingering in the air between us. His hands were on my shoulder now, and I looked down at where they were touching my skin.

The silence was deafening. I had to break it. "Are you here out of curiosity or pity...or both?" My voice barely reached my own ears, but he heard me. He abruptly stopped his slow-burning touches and grabbed hold of me, causing me to flinch as his fingers dug into my skin.

"Curious?! Yes, I'm curious," His eyes never left mine, intense emerald orbs that held a dangerous glint. "I was curious how you tasted, and I found out, but I want more."

I tensed. "More?" I whispered.

"Yes, more," he echoed, his voice a husky whisper in the stillness of the room. His grip on my shoulders tightened even further, and I could feel his fingers burning into my skin as if searing an unseen brand upon it. "I want to know what makes your heart race and your cheeks flush with that innocent shade of pink; I want to know what angers you and what coaxes laughter from your lips."

His dark gaze caressed me as heat pooled in my belly. "I want to know what makes your heart race," He continued, his gaze dropping from my eyes to my mouth and then slowly trailing down to where my heart thrummed wildly against my chest. "What are your dreams at night? Are they filled with starlit skies or dark nightmares?"

He moved closer, the distance between us shrinking until there was nothing left but our shared breaths. "And what about the sadness in your eyes? What shatters you? What are those fears lurking in your soul that you keep hidden from everyone else?"

"Justin...." My voice sounded frail.

"Rhi, I'm so sorry," he sighed, his eyes heavy with sadness. He reached his hand out to me, but quickly pulled it back again, "I'm just frustrated." He ran his fingers roughly through his hair.

"You're frustrated with me?"

He pulled his legs up, copying my pose. "Yes, I'm frustrated with you. But I'm also frustrated with myself."

He let his toes touch mine, and I smiled at the small gesture. "There's something special about how you look at me – like you can see more than anyone else. Like you understand me." He offered an affable smile, a seeming attempt to lighten the weight of his confession.

The echo of past pain resounded within me, the phantom sting of harsh words and violent outbreaks from my stepfather, who should have loved and protected my mother and me. Instead of feeling safe in his presence, it was pure fear that seized me whenever I thought of him - a cruel tyrant ruling over my young heart with an iron fist. That fear had woven a shroud around me; mistrust threaded through every fiber of my being. Justin must feel similar about trust. He was lied to about his own father.

"My father isn't really my father," he confessed, his voice heavy with resignation. "Not biologically, at least. He is in every other respect." I could see the hurt etched into his features, feel it radiating from him. "I didn't know until a few years ago."

"I'm so sorry," I said quietly, squeezing his hand in an attempt to offer comfort.

His shoulders rose in a deep breath. "My real father is not a good person. He's never been one to follow the law. And I look just like him, which only adds to the stigma. No matter how hard I try, there's no denying he's my father, and that dark mark will always be on me."

Justin's eyes were clouded with a familiar pain as he opened up to me about his past. "And my mother. I just don't get why she would cheat on my....on Rick. I'm judged in this town not based on who I am in here." He placed his fist on his chest for emphasis. "But instead, based on circumstances beyond my control."

His words struck a chord with me, reminding me of my own struggles with my family. I retreated into my mind, trying to make sense of the conflicting emotions swirling inside me. Boys had always been a foreign concept to me, never noticing me or whispering flirtatious words in my ear. I certainly never expected a beautiful boy like Justin to open up to me in this way.

"I don't know my real father," I whispered, staring at my feet. "I don't even have a photo of him."

Justin's hand moved from mine to gently rest on my knee, "My stepfather drinks," I confided. "He gets mean."

"Did he hit you?"

I shook my head. "No, no. He was just cruel with his words. Sometimes, I wish he had hit me. I think I could take a punch better than being told what a horrible person I am."

"I understand that, Rhi," Justin said, his voice full of empathy. "I really do."

"And my mom....I just don't understand her. She would never be with someone like that. She used to be strong, but now she is just a shadow of her old self." I took in a shuddering breath. In that moment, Justin and I were two wounded souls finding solace in each other's pain. Our shared wounds had torn apart pieces of our hearts, leaving us both searching for something or someone to help mend them.

A single tear trickled down my face, and he wiped it away with his thumb, his large hand lingering on my skin. "I understand how you feel when the people closest to you have betrayed your trust."

I said nothing. I just leaned into the warmth of his palm. He knew my pain. From the moment we met, we seemed to have a deep connection. Maybe all things do happen for a reason. Perhaps we were kindred spirits.

"My heart is destroyed," I stated sadly.

"As is mine," he echoed.

"If both of us combine our broken pieces, maybe we'll start to feel whole again," I suggested cautiously. I didn't know what I was asking from him—or myself. Could he let me into his wounded soul? Would I be brave enough to let him close enough to touch the fragments of mine?

"Come here then." He reached for me and pulled me onto his lap. "You need to be closer." He spoke softly in my ear.

"How close?" I whispered back.

"Until our hearts collide," he murmured as he wrapped his arms around me, crushing me to him. I felt his heartbeat hammering against me as I leaned into him, resting my head on his shoulder. We sat there for an interminable length of time, lost in each other's arms.

Eventually, he broke the silence. "When we're like this, it's like everything falls perfectly into place." He said quietly. "I won't let you go now, Rhiannon. You are my girl."

I steeled myself and raised my chin to meet his gaze. I wanted to ask him what he meant, but never got the chance to speak; his lips were on mine before I could utter a single word. He kissed me tenderly at first, then with more intensity.

I couldn't help but respond, wrapping my arms tightly around him.

He spoke my name softly against my mouth before moving down to caress my neck. Every nerve in my being sparked with electricity.

My hands wandered along his face, committing it to memory. His hair was pulled back, but I untied the band that held it at the nape of his neck and let it fall across our faces. The strands were soft and brushed against us like delicate butterfly wings.

He put his hands on either side of my face and pulled away slowly. "We have to stop," He panted.

I was confused. I thought he liked my kissing.

"I don't want to stop, but if I don't do it now, I don't think I'll be able to, and I won't screw this up." He said.

"But I don't want you to," I replied, grazing his bottom lip lightly with my finger.

He let out a slight laugh. "Rhi, if this continues, I'm going to struggle to keep us from crossing the line." He lifted me up without effort and put me next to him. "It's too warm in here, not just because of our chemistry." He smiled at me. "You need an air conditioner."

"And you are changing the subject." I challenged.

"Right again." He grabbed the bottle of water off my nightstand and took a long drink before handing it to me. I accepted the offering, taking a sip while still watching him intently. He then pulled out two of Sal's chocolate cookies from earlier. "Cookie?"

I turned my nose up at him.

He just laughed, shaking his head in amusement. "Your loss."

Peeking at him out of the corner of my eye, I saw him break off a piece of the cookie and stick it in his mouth, licking the bit of icing that stuck to his fingers.

"You know you want some, so quit being so stubborn." He held out a piece of cookie to me, and the delicious smell almost made me cave in.

"You don't play fair," I said accusingly.

He smiled wickedly at me, "Never said I did."

I took a bite of the chocolate cookie. It was the best chocolate cookie I had ever tasted. Icing was left on his fingers, and he quickly stuck them in his mouth.

"Hey, that isn't fair! The icing is the best part," I scowled at him.

He ran his long finger over the rest of the cookie, gathering up any remaining icing on its tip. "Here you go. Never say I didn't share."

"They were my cookies to begin with!" I said, still smiling.

I took his finger in my mouth and bit down.

"Ouch, you brat!" he exclaimed, but there wasn't any anger in his tone.

"Oh, come on, it wasn't that hard, you baby." I giggled like a little schoolgirl.

He gave me a dirty look, but I could tell he wasn't mad.

"I love chocolate. I think I could live on it," I said, popping another piece into my mouth.

"It's the color of your eyes," Justin said as he ran a finger along my eyebrow. "They are the first thing I noticed about you. Very sweet."

"Very plain," I murmured.

"Why would you say that? I love your eyes. They're beautiful."

Wow, had he really said that? How did I even get this boy into my bed? I thought to myself. He is well....perfection. I was a five-foot-nine awkward mess. "Well, you...you are just gorgeous." Even more so now, as his thick black hair has fallen forward along his face. He looked wicked and wild and sexy as hell.

"Oh, come on now." He scowled. "Gorgeous? You are exaggerating a bit there."

"Is hot a better word?" I said sarcastically, "Come on, Justin, you can't tell me you don't know your appeal."

"And you can't tell me you don't see yours."

"No, I honestly don't."

He lay down beside me and stroked my arm with his fingers. He snagged an unruly curl, twirling it around his fingers. "I like your wild waves." A swarm of butterflies fluttered up into my throat as he kissed my stomach softly. "I think you're hot."

I almost passed out. I'm hot?

He sighed and said, "I gotta go, Rhi."

"Why?" I asked, disappointed.

"It's Monday tomorrow; work calls. I don't think your grandmother would want to see me coming out of your room in the morning."

I let out a long sigh. "No... I guess not."

He laughed softly and lay his head on my stomach. "I honestly would stay until you fell asleep, but I don't trust myself anymore tonight." He jumped up and began to put on his shoes. He pulled a silver key out of his pocket.

"Don't forget to put this back under the rock outside." He placed it in my hands.

"Wait, how did you know that's where the door key is kept?"

"The first day I picked you up, I saw your grandmother put it under the rock. When I got here, it was the first thing I tried. If that hadn't worked, I would have tried a window." He grinned, flashing his straight white teeth.

He ran his hands through his hair, pulling it to the nape of his neck. "Where is the rubber band?"

I felt around the bed for it and found it near my pillow. "I like your hair down," I said.

He raised one eyebrow at me. He took the rubber band and stuffed it in his pocket. "Come here," he said, extending his arms towards me.

I sat up and scooted to his side. He took me tenderly in his arms.

"Yes, I like how much my heart feels when you are close to me....because it actually feels something." His lips pressed warmly against my forehead before he pulled away. "I'll see you tomorrow."

And then he was gone.

I looked around my room, searching for Kiran to give me any indication he was there. There was nothing. Had I even seen him tonight at all? Or was my head so far in the clouds that I was imagining a guardian angel?

Chapter Twelve

I woke up feeling blissful. It was another hot day, and with all the rain we had last night, I was sure it would be equally humid. But today, I wouldn't complain about anything.

Had it all been real? Rolling to my side, I breathed in deeply as I registered the lingering scent of Justin on my sheets. It was fresh and smelled of pine, most likely his soap or shampoo, but still uniquely him. My fingers grazed over my tender lips. They were swollen from his passionate kisses. God, his kisses had been exquisite. My knee had a slight ache from where I fell in the park during the rain- that glorious rain where we laughed and played like children. That was when I felt a spark of electricity in my heart, which brought it back to life. No doubt - it had happened. I was so full of happiness that I actually giggled out loud as I swung my legs out of bed.

"That wonderful, was it?" A smooth voice asked.

I gasped, "Kiran!"

So, he, too, was real.

"I thought angels weren't supposed to be scary."

He pushed himself away from the wall where he had been leaning. "Is that what you think I am, an angel?"

"Are you going to tell me you aren't?"

"No, I'm just curious. Do you genuinely believe I'm an angel?" He took a graceful step closer to me and added, "And I'm not scary."

"Well, you scared me." I huffed.

"No, I just took you by surprise. Scared...well, I sincerely hope you never find yourself frightened by something from my realm."

"Nan's not here, is she? She'd think I was crazy...talking to myself." My eyes flicked to the clock on my nightstand to check the time - nine o'clock. She would be at work.

"I wouldn't do that to you; I would let you know if someone were able to hear us...well, you. They can't hear me unless I want them to."

"I think I'm completely losing my mind," I said more or less to myself than to him. "I'm seeing things...go away."

Fuming, I yanked open my door and stomped out of my room. I took the stairs two at a time and headed to the kitchen. Kiran was already there, perched on the counter. "Stop doing that to me! You are going to give me a heart attack."

"So it isn't a matter of believing in me as much as you don't want to believe." He tapped his finger lightly against his temple. "Would it help if I looked more like this?" He jumped off the counter, vanishing only to reappear an instant later wearing white, flowing robes with gold edging.

Stunned, my feet stumbled backward, causing me to trip over them and tumble against the wall. His face glowed with an ethereal light, but that was not the most astonishing thing about his appearance. It was the enormous wings that fluttered behind him. Feathers, brilliant white feathers, cascaded down his back to the floor. I could hardly breathe, hardly think. Kiran was an angel! An actual, real-life angel. A slight smile crossed his lips before he reached out his hand to help me up. As he did, the wings flickered in the sunlight like diamonds so dazzling that stars suddenly appeared before my eyes.

Everything went black.

I heard the most beautiful voice. It was singing my name— no, not singing. It was a voice so melodic that it was like listening to the sweet sound of a lullaby when you are on the edge of sleep.

"Rhiannon, open your eyes. I know you can hear me," the melodic voice hummed. But I didn't want to open them; it was so peaceful here in the dark, with this overwhelming comfort surrounding me. I felt cherished and safe.

"Rhiannon..." the angel crooned. Angel.... "Angel.." I murmured.

"Yes, Rhiannon...open your eyes," he said gently.

"I don't want to."

He chuckled lightly, "Would it be easier if I turned myself into a cat?"

That made me flutter open my eyes, and when I looked at him, he had returned to his human form, no iridescent wings or silver glow, just his golden hair framing his face and his sparkling silver eyes staring back at me.

"Wait, what?" I asked incredulously. "You can take the form of a cat? I might faint again. This is all too unbelievable."

He grinned at me, his eyes alight with amusement, "I can take any shape I desire." He shifted my weight in his arms.

I narrowed my eyes, scrutinizing him more closely. "What are you really?"

He pulled me closer to him, and I felt inexplicably calm in his presence. "I'm very sorry. My little exploit must have really upset and confused you. I will try to explain myself better."

He placed a gentle hand against my head. I looked into his sparkling silver eyes and felt an immense calm come over me. "Feeling better now?" He asked. I had felt this before. All the times I was hurt or sad, the warmth that enveloped me was him.

His voice soothed me, making me feel like I could trust him. "Yes, thank you." I got up from his embrace and found a glass to pour myself some orange juice, letting the sweet flavor slide down my throat. Turning back to face him, I noticed he was watching me anxiously. "Explain then," I demanded.

"I am your guardian angel," he said smoothly.

"I got that part."

"I assure you, I am real. I am not your mind playing tricks on you." He stared at me intently.

"Okay, let's assume that is true. Why are you telling me this? Why appear to me right now?" Anxiety bloomed in my chest. "I mean, am I dying? Have you come here to take me away?"

He was suddenly in front of me, taking my hand in his. "Oh no, no, Rhiannon! I am here to protect you while you are here on earth."

My eyes turned into slits. "So, again, I ask...where have you been these past few years and why are you here now that I am finally feeling happy?"

"Why don't you have something to eat so I can explain?"

"I'm not hungry."

"Don't lie to me, Rhiannon." He said. "I can tell when you are lying."

I huffed as I grabbed an apple from the bowl on the counter, washing it quickly before taking a large bite. "Satisfied?" I asked.

He nodded gracefully. "You may not feel like it, but you are more vulnerable now than ever." His intense eyes searched mine for understanding.

"Vulnerable to what?"

"To forgetting who you are, forgetting your heart, and losing hope." He searched my face for understanding.

"Hope? I have never felt so hopeless as I did before coming here to Nan's, yet...."

He cut me off. "I was there, Rhiannon, and you have no idea what troubles I kept you from."

I took another bite of my apple, trying to disguise my uneasiness. I had a million questions I needed to ask him.

"How long have you been with me?"

"Since the day you were born."

"But you barely look older than I am. Or is that just one of your imaginary forms? Are you actually a two-hundred-year-old lady?"

He chuckled quietly. "I am only eighteen and very much a male. This is what I truly look like, except I'm keeping my wings and angel light concealed."

"I don't understand. How did you become my Guardian?

You're just a teenage angel. They didn't think I deserved someone older and wiser?"

"It's hard to explain because age doesn't factor into my realm like it does on Earth. I remember being held in a warm light and then just enlightened all of a sudden. None of the knowledge I have requires physical growth like humans need. It's all stored within my soul." He ran a hand through his hair. "When my soul was matched with yours, I took the form I needed when I needed to, to protect you."

"What do you mean our souls were matched? Do they hand out numbers, and you got mine?"

He laughed. "No, not at all! Have you ever heard of soulmates?"

"Yes..."

"Angels and humans have something in common regarding love. We write about it, sing about it, and feel it deeply. But for us angels, we can actually hear our souls singing all the time. It's a beautiful sound that is beyond what human ears can comprehend." He smiled wistfully as if lost in thought. "Anyway, when a soul is meant to be with an angel, their song will be unmistakable. Even among thousands of other voices, a distinct voice, which is your intended partner's song, will stand out. I heard yours on the day you were born," he finished with a glimmer of pride in his eye. "From there, I took a blessed vow to protect, support, and comfort you...and that sacred covenant can never be broken or abandoned."

"So, does that mean you don't have any choice in who you are supposed to protect?" I asked.

He furrowed his brows as his forehead creased together, pondering my question. "You can choose to ignore it, but it is very difficult and even a bit maddening." His eyes grew more intense as he spoke. "You always hear your soulmate's song in your heart."

I let his words sink in, twirling them around in my brain. I tried to comprehend how hearing the songs he spoke of must feel. He watched me, gauging my reaction to what he told me.

Finally, I asked, "You protect others, though, if they need it?"

"That's complicated," he replied with a smile. "It's just that when someone's song resonates within you, there's no escaping it." He leaned back against the counter, crossing a foot over the other, "You are my primary concern, Rhiannon. Others have their own angels to protect them."

We sat silently for a beat as I tried to wrap my mind around everything he'd shared. "So everyone has a guardian angel to protect them?"

"Sadly....no. Some level of belief is required for that to be true."

"But I had no sense of belief as an infant."

"Ah, but your family did." His eyes were vibrant with enthusiasm. "And because of that, someone requested protection for you. Despite your hard exterior and doubts, deep down you believe....you have always believed."

"So, you are with me until my dying day? The idea of someone being with me until my last breath was both comforting and daunting.

He nodded his head in response.

"Then what? Do I become like you?"

"No. You will go where you belong, depending on what path you go down. I travel between realms. I am a servant. I was chosen for this course."

He fell quiet, giving me time to reflect on his words, absently drumming his fingers against his leg. He seemed so completely human now that I would never know he wasn't if it weren't for his bizarre transformations.

Before I could stop myself, the words tumbled from my mouth. "Do you wish you were mortal?"

His gaze shot up to meet mine. "What?"

"I mean, being human," I said, my voice trembling a bit.

He stopped his idle finger-tapping. "I was created as I should be."

I apologized quickly. "Sorry, I didn't mean to be offensive." He waved off my apology. "I understand the question. Or at least, I think I do....you want to know if I envy human life?" He turned his head to look out the kitchen window. The sun glinted off his honey hair, showing its many faceted hues. "Things like having a family, eating ice cream, playing baseball?" His gaze met mine once more.

"Yes, that is what I am asking."

He let out an amused chuckle. "I told you I can mingle with humans if I choose to show myself. I can play sports all I want. As far as food...I don't need it, but I can eat it and like it. Especially pizza. There's a place on Main called Mario's. It's like heaven in pizza form."

I giggled at that before he continued.

"But as for family.... that's not possible." The room fell quiet once more. Somehow, I knew he was holding something back.

I sighed. I guess it was okay for him to know all about me, but not for me to know him. Well, he would have to learn that things didn't work that way...not in my world.

"So, what is it like...on the other side?"

"There are no human words to describe it. Now, enough about me...I am here about you."

I was filled with instant suspicion. "But I thought you already knew everything about me."

"I have been with you your entire life, but cannot read your mind. I can pick up on your feelings. When you are sad, I feel it; when you are anxious, I am also; and when your eyes overflow with tears...I cry inside."

"The soul connection again?" I asked.

"Exactly. I have my own feelings, but I also have yours, and I feel them just as strongly as you do. So, even though I cannot read your mind and know what you are thinking," His voice became serious and thoughtful. "Most of the time, I can make a pretty accurate guess based on your emotions because I feel them simultaneously with you."

"You feel every emotion then?" I asked. My cheeks burned, and I could sense my blush deepening. He couldn't have known what I had felt last night, right?

He cleared his throat and shifted his gaze around the room, avoiding me while he spoke. "Yes. I can feel your strong emotions for Justin. Do not confuse passion with love, Rhiannon."

Rage replaced the blushing heat. "Don't assume I don't know the difference! And stop spying on us when we are together!"

He took a deep breath and jumped back up on the counter, sitting casually. "I don't spy, and I don't watch."

Tears pricked at the edge of my eyes, and I fought back the urge to cry.

"There is no need to watch anything. As I said, I can feel what you are feeling."

"Oh, yeah, like that is any better." I threw away the rest of my apple and stormed out of the kitchen. My fists were clenched as I marched to my bedroom, and with a loud bang, I shut the door behind me.

I paced back and forth for a brief period, unsuccessfully trying to let my temper cool down. The heat in my room only made me more aggravated. So, I quickly changed into a white tank top and denim shorts before grabbing my music player and heading back downstairs.

Everything was silent on the main floor, and Kiran was nowhere to be seen; all that remained was an oppressive heat. So I hurriedly closed all the curtains, hoping it would keep the scorching sun from coming inside. I turned up the fans, but hot air kept circulating around me.

I was desperate to get my hair off my neck. I washed my face with cold water and brushed out my wavy mane. It was even wilder because I let it dry naturally last night and fell asleep with it still damp. I pulled it up into a bun on top of my head. There was so much of it that it pulled heavily on my scalp. I knew I would pay for this later with a headache, but the heat was more imposing right now.

I headed toward the old tree in the backyard and sat down on the cool grass, letting my toes play through the blades as I listened to music to find some peace. The air was still hot, yet I welcomed a slight breeze with open arms. Music always helped me express emotions I could not express and swam through my veins, carrying the notes of rhythmic therapy.

So, was this what Kiran felt? A melody that twisted through his being, calling to him? My soul sang to him. That is what he said. I wondered what my soul sounded like. Was it screaming like I felt like doing so much of the time? I would have to ask him. I wondered if he would tell me. I imagined having someone else's soul singing to yours must be an incredibly beautiful experience. Almost as beautiful as love itself.

The breeze brushed against my face, and then he was there, kneeling by my side. "You are much calmer now," he said; his voice was in my mind, blending with the music in my ears.

"Music has that effect on me," I replied.

"Yes, I can certainly understand that."

I pulled the plugs out of my ears. "So why Kiran? Why not leave me in the dark?" I searched the perfect lines of his seraphic face. "I have heard of people seeing angels or what they think are angels, but whatever this is between us is beyond anything I have heard of before."

He shifted himself into a more comfortable position and crossed his legs. "You'll come to see that what we have is too sacred to share with others."

"Awfully sure of yourself, aren't you?"

"Indeed, I am." He played with a few strands of my gathered hair. "Well, and I could potentially erase any memories we share together since I am breaking a few rules right now." He smiled halfheartedly.

"Can you really do that? Erase my memories?" I whispered in disbelief.

"Not all...just those that include me, and being that I am breaking some rules, I may just have to."

I clutched onto the front of his shirt, not sure what I expected, but he felt completely human and reacted accordingly, jumping slightly at my abruptness. "Promise me you will never do that!" I cried. "Never erase my memories!"

"I can't promise that or else I would be lying, and I don't lie." He said, his voice steady and even.

I shoved at him in frustration. "There you go again! You are infuriating! You are here to protect me, but you talk in riddles about why. You supposedly live by some code of honor, and yet you are breaking the rules? You can perform supernatural acts, but don't want the world to know about them! I don't understand any of this!"

Kiran's silver eyes fluttered shut for a moment, a flicker of something - Pain? Regret? It flashed across his face before he opened them once again. His wavy honey-blonde hair rustled in the warm summer breeze. "Being an angel is both a blessing and a curse." His voice was low, a melodic tone that echoed the murmur of rustling leaves above us. "I apologize for seeming... cryptic. There are just things I can't tell you as easily as you'd like." His jaw clenched tightly, and he looked down, his hair shrouding his face.

Frustration swirled inside me like a stormy sea. "But why?" I snapped, impatient, knotting my words into a tight ball. "If you're here to protect me, don't I deserve to know why?"

"You do," he murmured quietly. For a moment, silence hung heavily between us.

"I am your guardian angel," he said as if reciting well-learned lines from a play. "And yes, there are rules that bind us. Rules I am breaking for you because..." He swallowed hard; something that looks suspiciously like fear flickers across his expression just briefly. "Because your happiness matters more to me than the rules I'm bound to follow. And if I can spare you even a fraction of the hurt this world can bring... it would be worth it."

My gaze didn't waver, urging him to continue.

"You're entrusting your heart to someone new, and I couldn't stand idly by if there was even the slightest chance that Justin might cause you pain."

"You think he's dangerous?"

He hesitated, seeming to choose his words carefully. "Not in the way you might think. But people can be unpredictable. Their intentions aren't always as pure as they seem."

My brow furrowed. "You mean to protect me. But why now? Why didn't you show yourself all the times I cried myself to sleep? If you've always been with me, then you know. You know how my step monster called me a waste of life, how he belittled me!" Tears stung my eyes.

"I do know, and I'm sorry, Rhiannon," He exhaled slowly, his inner turmoil evident in his eyes. "It was the combination between your mother's Guardian and myself that led to you being here."

"What?" I breathed.

His voice lowered to a tender murmur as he continued, "I intervened to bring you here because it's where you need to be right now. Safe and surrounded by love, but I didn't know.... I... I couldn't. I just..." He stammers, searching frantically for the right words. The confidence I saw earlier was replaced by something different altogether; he seemed vulnerable.

"You just what?" I press on, desperate for him to continue.

His gaze is steady as he swallows painfully, shaking his head as if his confessions were physically painful for him to utter. There was something in his eyes that made my heart hurt for him. When he noticed me staring at him, he disappeared.

Chapter Thirteen

I let music fill my head for a while until the sun shifted in the sky, causing my legs to burn. I stood to go inside, casting a glance at my faded swing set by the fence that I played on as a child. My eyes roamed to the overgrown shrubs along the back end of the yard and a statue of the Virgin Mary. The yard had always been immaculate when Pops was alive. It was still beautiful, just overgrown a bit. I thought I would try to manicure it before school started.

A faint memory from earlier that morning returned to me as I entered the kitchen. Had he been real or just my imagination? My knowledge of angels came only from brief mentions in the Bible. I knew Nan had several Bibles in the house, but I wasn't sure where she kept them, aside from her antique family Bible. Nan mentioned keeping it in the old curio cabinet, which stood against the dining room wall. She had inherited it from her parents as a wedding gift and said it belonged to her grandmother before that. The brass hinges creaked as I opened the door, revealing the Bible alongside other keepsakes, including Nan's wedding album and an antique rosary made from bone and wood that had also belonged to her grandmother.

I gently touched the rosary with my fingers. The idea of a bone rosary struck me as creepy, but Nan once told me it was a common practice centuries ago when wood and bone were plentiful. I carefully removed the rosary from atop the Bible and pulled it out of the cabinet.

The Bible's leather was worn thin from the hands that had held it over the years. The pages were old and yellowed, and the cover creaked like an old woman with arthritis when I opened it. I intended to research the birth of Jesus and any references to angels. That was the only story I could remember mentioning an angel, although I was aware of other biblical stories that had them.

The book's inside cover held records of births, deaths, and marriages going back to the mid-1800s. I scoured the fading names until I spotted mine near the bottom. Pop's death entry stood out to me with its fresh ink. My finger lightly brushed his name - Robert Tobias Crandall - and I felt a pang in my chest. Then something else caught my eye. My parents' marriage date, but no divorce date listed. That struck me as odd. That's when I noticed his middle name, Jared Michael Flynn. A piece of information I'd never known before.

Jared Michael Flynn. So that was his full name. I was still a Crandall, though. I was never given his last name and was never told why. For years, I had thought my father wasn't real; I believed perhaps I had been adopted until, one day, I heard my mother on the phone. Her tone was seething as she exclaimed angrily to the caller, "No, absolutely not! I won't allow it!" She was distraught, and curiosity got the better of me. I crept to the edge of her room in the hallway and listened to what she was saying to the caller.

I pressed closer to the doorway, and then I heard it: "Jared, she is not yours! You are nothing but a liar and manipulator, and I will not have her know you or anything about you."

That was when I knew she was talking to him, my father.

All I knew was his first name, and from the anger coming from her voice, it couldn't be anyone else. I had choked back a sob in the hallway outside her door. Anger burned in me - at him for leaving and at her for hiding the truth from me. He had called, which meant he wanted to know how I was doing, yet she refused to let him have that information. But he had called, which led me to believe he wanted to know at least how I was. How could she keep him from me? What did he do that made her so fearful of letting me know anything else about him?

My anger grew over the next year as I asked more and more questions, and I was refused an answer every time. The more I was denied, the more my rage intensified. I should at least have the right to speak to him on the telephone. My hostility towards my mother's refusal to allow me contact with my father only increased, and alongside it, so did my rebellion against her.

My thoughts went to Justin. He understood at least some of what I felt, even though I didn't share this information with him. He, too, had been lied to about his father, yet now he at least knew him and had some relationship with him. This made me determined to continue searching for my father - especially now that I had obtained his full name.

The deep, resonating sound of the grandfather clock caught my attention, and I glanced up at the time. Nan would be home soon. My eyes darted back down to the Bible, and I quickly flipped to the page I was looking for. I knew it was somewhere in the Book of Luke. I scanned quickly for the word angel when a white feather drifted onto its pages. Kiran was suddenly standing behind me.

"And, lo, the angel of the Lord came upon them, and the glory of the Lord shone round about them: and they were sore afraid. And the angel said unto them, Fear not: for, behold, I bring you good tidings of great joy, which shall be to all people." Kiran quoted.

I gazed at him in awe. "So I guess that means you're real," I croaked out.

He nodded and smiled reassuringly at me. He took the feather gently, and it vanished into his palm. "Can't leave this lying around."

"Why not?" I asked.

"It's like a fingerprint for angels," he explained. "If someone—or some-thing—was searching for me or any other angel, they could use this to track us."

I placed the Bible on the table and spun around to face him directly. "What else should I know about you and your kind?"

He laughed lightly. "Know? Is that why you were going through your grand-mother's Bible?"

"It's actually the family Bible, and it will be mine one day," I replied, closing the cover with care.

"That it is. Did you find what you were looking for?"

"No, I was looking for passages on guardian angels, and all I could recall was the angel at Christmas who visited the shepherds. I played it once in a church play." I placed the Bible back in the cabinet, carefully laying it just as it was with the rosary on top of it.

"I believe I felt sadness from you and a bit of anger?" He questioned.

I gave him a suspicious look. "Maybe."

"You still don't believe me, do you? That I'm who I say I am."

"If I told people I had a guardian angel that looked like a teenage boy that I could see and speak to and who likes to wear vintage band shirts, they'd think I'm insane." As I walked past him into the kitchen, my arm grazed against his.

He sure felt real.

"What is so different about that than believing in ghosts, vampires, fairies, unicorns, or dragons?" He asked, a small smile tugging at the corners of his lips.

I leaned against the counter and shot him an intense gaze. "You're telling me vampires and unicorns are real?"

He stepped closer to me until our noses were almost touching. "In a manner of speaking, yes."

I couldn't help but laugh out loud. "Okay, now I know this must be a dream because that's the most ridiculous thing I've ever heard!"

"I told you I can take any form I choose." He raised an eyebrow at me. "So, yes, we can be those mythical creatures." He crossed his arms over his chest as he spoke. "Go look in that Bible. Dragons are mentioned thirty-five times. You will also find mentions of them in almost every culture on earth. Do you not find that curious?"

"I think those are just metaphors," I replied as I grabbed a glass and filled it with water.

"Maybe, but maybe not." He said.

"So you're saying the stories about vampires, werewolves, fairies, and dragons are true?" I asked incredulously.

"No, not all of them. Just like not all stories of angels are true." He gazed into my eyes intently as he continued. "Vampires are usually demons. Most angels don't want to take that form. I guess I should mention that demons, too, can take whatever form they want. Have you ever seen a werewolf like you see in movies? Probably not....but legends may arise from people spotting angels or demons transforming from human shape into wolf form; I know plenty who prefer that guise."

I shook my head in disbelief. "I feel dizzy." I placed my hands on my head, and suddenly, the sweet scent of vanilla filled my senses. I opened my eyes to find myself in my bed.

I jolted upright, my head swimming. "It was just a dream," I whispered to myself.

"No, not a dream," Kiran said from near the window.

I slumped back onto my pillow and began slapping myself on the cheeks, yelling for myself to wake up. Then, suddenly, Kiran's hands were in mine. They felt so soft and warm.

"You feel real," I said in an unsteady voice.

"Yes," he replied with a gentle smile on his face. "Because I am."

I delicately touched his face, and he looked slightly surprised before tenderly pressing his hand against mine. His skin was unusually soft. "You have to tell me what lotion you use on your skin. It's incredibly soft." I said.

He chuckled at that, and I saw amusement in his eyes. "You always make me smile, Rhiannon."

"Tell me more about the world you come from."

"Our worlds are intertwined, with only a veil between them."

"Can I see the other realm?" I asked curiously.

He shook his head, "No, I'm afraid not. Not until you pass over."

"Is my grandfather there? Can you speak to him?" My heart tightened at the thought. "Tell him I love him."

The gentleness in his voice made me tear up. "He is there, sweetheart, and he already knows you love him."

Filled with curiosity, I asked, "Can you talk to God?"

"Yes, and so can you."

I leaned back against my bed and looked up thoughtfully at the ceiling. "He doesn't seem to answer me."

"Well, maybe you need to listen with your heart instead of your ears." He tapped his chest gently where his heart sat.

"How many of you are there?"

"More than your mortal mind can comprehend."

I pondered his words for a moment, trying to understand the vastness of heaven and the countless beings that inhabited it. "Tell me more about your kind."

He seemed to think about this momentarily, rubbing his chin as he pondered. "There are different types of angels. Hierarchies of our kind," he finally said. He shifted on my bed to get more comfortable. "The highest is the Seraphim; they are God's closest companions, and you can easily tell them apart from others because they shine so brightly it's blinding, and they possess an extra set of wings. Then there are the Cherubim and Thrones. The Cherubim are in charge of worship, and the Thrones are pure humility, peace, and submission. They are unique as they can dispense justice with perfect objectivity. Below them are the Dominions, Powers, and Authorities."

I nodded, trying to take it all in.

"We all have different tasks to perform, but they are all important in the grand scheme of things. We work together."

My gaze wandered over him. God, he was beautiful. He let go of my hand, his fingers trailing across my palm.

His eyes flicked to mine as he continued. "Then there are Principalities, Archangels, and Guards - like me. I'm the lowest of the angels apart from the Fallen Ones."

"Fallen Ones?"

Kiran's features contorted with what seemed to be bitterness warring with sorrow. "They're the ones who refused to submit to God's will. They were consumed by anger, envy, and pride. Some left of their own accord, some were...cast out." His voice dropped, "They're not all monsters. Some just... made a different choice."

The air around us seemed to shift, as though the memory of their rebellion hovered. I realized I had never once thought of angels as being capable of refusing anything, especially God.

"Like Lucifer?" I whispered, remembering Sunday school stories and oil paintings of falling, burning wings.

Kiran nodded, gaze averted. "Yes, like him, but there are others....legions of them. Some are lost, some have purpose. Some are here, in this world, trying to sow the same misery that damned them."

I was speechless; all I could utter was, "Wow."

He smirked. "Just wow? Honestly, I hoped for more than that." He chuckled lightly. "We have work to do. But when we're not serving, we can take on different forms and explore this mortal realm. We can experience joy, love, and happiness in our own way."

"I thought you weren't supposed to interfere with mortals."

"We aren't supposed to interfere with free will, but we can guide and protect. and sometimes we need to give a little push." He winked at me.

"I think I'm in shock. I think I actually believe this is real."

He grabbed my hands and said, "Yes, Rhiannon, it is real, and I am your Guardian, your soulmate." His eyes glowed slightly like a bottomless pool of silver surrounded by some of the longest lashes I have ever seen.

"What about the Devil?"

He glanced away for a moment and then gazed back at me again. "Ah yes, the Morningstar. What a beautiful name for probably the most beautiful-looking angel... But you should know that his beauty only applies to his physical form—not his heart." He inclined his head and said, "Stories of the Fallen and the Watchers are for another day because your grandmother just pulled in the driveway."

"But..." I protested.

"I'll just be on the other side of the veil." He said and was gone.

"Thank you for being with me," I whispered to the empty room.

"Always," Kiran whispered back.

Chapter Fourteen

We drove into the high school parking lot, spotting an empty spot near the main building. The fact that there were very few cars meant fewer people were there, which was a relief. It was orientation week, and it was time to pick up our schedules and get our locker numbers.

Steve got out first while Kacey glided gloss across her perfect pouty lips. I was gazing at her in the rearview mirror when I saw a silver car pull up behind us. A pair of tan, shapely legs swung out of the driver's side door, and then a cascade of raven black hair. A pair of sky-blue eyes met mine.

"Trina is here," I said to Kacey.

Kacey spun around towards me with a start. "Really?" "Does she have some sort of tracking device on Steve or

something?"

Kacey snickered. "I wouldn't doubt it. She freaks me out sometimes, but Steve is a big boy. He can take care of himself." Kacey snapped her purse shut and opened the door. "Come on, Rhi."

I jumped out and walked up to Steve and Trina. Kacey was already there.

"Let's get this over with," I said. "I just want to see what classes we have."

"What's the rush?" Trina asked. "Hot date?"

Before I could respond, Kacey jumped in. "Just me," she snickered.

Trina looked between us before her eyes landed on Steve. "Well," she said, looking away from us, "then we should go out, Steve, and let the girls have their girls' night."

Steve shook off Trina's grip from him. "Trina, I promised I would BBQ for them. Besides, I have some work to do on my car. Come on, girls." He motioned us forward and began walking confidently across the parking lot to the school's front steps. Kacey and I trailed behind him and left Trina alone, staring at Steve in disbelief.

The school was old. It harbored a lot of nostalgia for my family, the same school my mom and uncle had graduated from. This was the original spot where the first school was built, and Nan had gone there before it burned down. Now, I would graduate here. I took a deep breath before pushing through the heavy metal entrance doors.

"Come on, Rhi." Kacey grabbed my hand and directed me down the corridor. Steve was waiting for us at the end of the hallway, slouching against the countertop.

"I've got all the paperwork ready for vocational school already," he said to an older woman with wispy white hair seated behind the desk. "Just need my math and science credits."

"Yes, Steven, I see that." She replied.

He shifted uneasily as she glanced up at him. "Yes, well, Mrs. Shift. My cousin Rhiannon Crandell just moved here, and I was wondering if you could place us in the same classes. It might help her adjust. I poked my head around his shoulder and waved at her shyly.

Mrs. Shift flicked her eyes to me. "I presume this is Ms. Crandall?"

I nodded.

Kacey popped around Steve's other side. "C'mon, Mrs. Shift, they should be able to be in the same classes."

She tapped a button, and a flurry of papers began spitting from a printer. She took out a hefty folder and grabbed the stack of white papers. "Hmm," Mrs. Shift said as she flipped through the documents. "I'm afraid you can't have the same classes as your cousin, Ms. Crandall."

Kacey and Steve both protested at precisely the same time. "Now, now, you two. From what I can tell here," she continued while scanning more papers, "you've already taken most of the classes needed to graduate in Colorado. Except...hmmm," her eyes narrowed on the paper before her. What did my old school send over? "Ms. Crandall, you'll need to come with me to speak with the principal so we can figure out where you fit in. You're quite an anomaly." She came to the door and pushed it open. I turned around to see both Kacey and Steve staring at me, as well as four more students who had formed a line behind us. I felt the heat rise into my cheeks.

"Come along now, Ms. Crandall," Mrs. Shift said kindly, "I'd like to get out of here on time and have some summer break left."

I followed her obediently. We wound our way between desks and filing cabinets until we reached a large wooden door with gold lettering: The Principal's Office. It was slightly ajar, so Mrs. Shift knocked lightly before pushing it open.

"Mr. Wendal," she addressed him, handing over my paperwork. "This is Rhiannon Crandall, the girl from Colorado. Her schedule is going to require some special organizing."

Mr. Wendal had a friendly face with short, salt-and-pepper hair and gentle eyes. "Take a seat, Rhiannon," he said as he gestured to the chairs across from his desk.

He flipped through the folder Mrs. Shift handed to him. "So, you excel in language arts, science, and history, but barely passed math. So, you really don't need any language arts, science, or history classes to graduate. You've already taken our highest classes for high school. However, we have college courses you can take online in study hall. It's really worth it. You get college credit without having to pay for college. Only our top students are offered it. Your problem is math; you're at the sophomore level right now."

I sat quietly. As far as I knew, they didn't offer college courses for seniors back home. This was more than I could ask for.

"Are you interested in this option? All you need to do is pass math to graduate, but we want to make sure you make use of these other classes." He smiled warmly at me.

"What kind of college classes am I allowed to take?" I asked tentatively. He handed me a list to review, and we went through the task of creating my school schedule.

When I left the office, even Mrs. Swift had gone home. Searching for Kacey and Steve, I hurried down the hallway and flew out the doors to my waiting family. Steve drove us to Nan's. When we pulled up in front of the house, Justin was leaning against his car with his dark hair glinting in the setting sun. He flashed a devilish smile when he saw me.

"What is Justin doing here?" Steve asked as he parked behind him on the street.

"He said he had something for me," I replied.

"I bet," Steve muttered under his breath.

As we approached, Justin stepped away from his car, his dark hair falling in front of his eyes. He had left it down, which caused my heart to do a little dance.

"Where have you guys been?" He asked.

"School. Getting our classes and showing Rhi around," Steve said, shutting the car door behind him.

"Rhi's a genius." Kacey piped in.

"Hush, Kacey. I am not." My cheeks reddened with embarrassment.

"Oh, don't be modest. She could graduate now if she had one more credit in math. So, she is taking college courses this year! Isn't that cool!"

"You're going to college?" Justin's brows shot up.

"No, it's all online during study hall, but I still need Nan's permission."

Justin looked relieved. "I have your present in the car," he said, thrusting the key into the trunk. It popped open, and he wrestled out a heavy square metal box and started up the stairs. I scrambled to grab my keys from my pocket and rushed ahead of him to open the door. With a determined stride, Justin walked up the stairs towards my room with the box.

"Where does he think he's going?" Steve gaped at Justin. "To install Rhi's new air conditioner," Justin shouted over his shoulder.

Just then, Nan came through the door, bumping into all of us. "Oh, I'm so sorry, kids!" she said apologetically.

"It's okay, Nan," I assured her. "We shouldn't all be crowding in the doorway."

"We were heading out anyway. We still have food to pick up! See you soon, Rhi!" Kacey said, pulling Steve with her out the door.

"OWWWW!" I heard Justin's voice echoing down the stairs. I ran up to check on him.

I swung my door open. "What happened?"

"I pinched my finger, and it hurt!" Justin's face was twisted in pain.

"Here, let me see," I reached for his hand.

"Nah, just wait until I get this thing in. It isn't steady." He adjusted the air conditioner until it was snug in the window frame. Then he shot me a mischievous smile. "Now, plug it in."

I reached down to plug it in. Justin flipped the switch on, and we were immediately greeted with cool air on our faces. I closed my eyes, enjoying the cool air caressing my skin.

"Amazing." I sighed blissfully before turning back to Justin.

"Tell me you love me."

My eyes widened in surprise. "What?"

"I just meant..." His jaw tightened. The air blew his hair across his face, shielding his eyes from me. I reached up and brushed it back.

"Thank you," I whispered, placing a light kiss on his lips. "Let me see your finger." I pulled his hand into mine. His right index finger was swollen and purple, but not cut. "It needs ice to bring down the swelling."

"No, it will be fine."

"Rhi." Nan's voice floated up from the bottom of the stairs.

I hurried out of my room to the top of the stairs. "Yes, Nan?"

"Your clothes are in here. I just finished taking them out of the dryer." She held a basket out for me. "Thanks, Nan." I accepted them with a humble smile. "You didn't have to go through all that trouble."

"Is that Justin Rizzo up there with you?" She asked in a hushed voice.

"Yeah, he brought me an air conditioner to use. I had mentioned it was hard for me to sleep in this heat." I looked down at my feet, a bit embarrassed. "He hurt his finger putting it in."

Nan looked towards my bedroom door before responding. "Well, that was very nice of him. I'll get some ice for his finger."

"Thanks, Nan."

I returned to my room and found Justin seated on my bed. I dropped the clothes basket next to him. "Nan is bringing some ice for your finger."

"Cool, thanks." He leaned forward and quirked a brow at me. "So you're some kind of genius, huh?"

I shook my head adamantly. "No, I already told you Kacey's exaggerating; I just didn't have much of a life where I used to live."

Justin studied me as I shifted uncomfortably.

"Is it some sort of problem?"

He rolled his eyes playfully at me. "No, Einstein... It's not a problem."

Nan appeared in my doorway with a small towel filled with ice. "Here, Justin." She said, handing him the towel. "It really does make a difference with the air conditioner up here... Thank you for doing this for Rhiannon." She said gratefully.

He seemed embarrassed. "It was no trouble; we have loads of them down at the shop from customers who traded for service, so I thought I might as well put them to good use."

"You never told me you weren't sleeping well, Rhi," Nan remarked, her dark eyes locking onto mine.

"It really wasn't that big of a deal."

Justin eyed me suspiciously. "Did she tell you she is taking college courses this year in high school?"

Nan raised her eyebrows in disbelief. "Justin!" I glared at him. "Not now."

"Really, Rhi? Why didn't you tell me?" Nan asked, intrigued.

"I just got home and haven't had time to explain yet; I'll go over it tomorrow when I get back from Uncle Nick's," I replied as I went through my clothes basket and began packing my bag for the night.

Nan stayed by my side as she probed further. "Why didn't your mom say anything about you being in advanced classes?"

I shrugged my shoulders.

"Are you going to one of the college campuses?" She persisted.

I finished packing what I thought I needed for the sleepover with Kacey.

"Um, no. I do it online. I communicate with the teachers over the internet. It's good because I get some college credits without having to pay for them.

Nan smiled brightly at me. "Oh, Rhi! I'm so proud of you!"

I tensed up and glanced at Justin, who intently watched our interaction.

"Thanks, Nan. I'll explain more about it to you tomorrow."

"Tomorrow, I'm taking you shopping to celebrate." She declared.

"No, I don't want you spending more money on me." I protested.

She gave me a gentle look and shook her head. "Rhiannon, your grandfather left me plenty. Let me take care of what you need."

I could only nod my head in agreement. Then I looked over at Justin and asked: "Ready?"

He hopped off the bed quickly. "Let's go." He handed Nan back the towel with ice still in it. "Thank you."

Chapter Fifteen

Pulling in front of Uncle Nick's house, I noticed a silver car gleaming in the driveway behind Steve's Gran Torino.

"Is that Trina's car?" I asked.

"Yep."

"I don't understand why she's always around. Steve told me she's too clingy, and it drives him crazy."

"Presumably because they're still together because he doesn't have the guts to break up with her," he said, eyeing the house. "So, where are your aunt and uncle again?"

"At some police ball. Kacey said they won't be back until late."

"Well, you could blow it off."

Shaking my head, I replied, "They are all expecting me, and this is where I told Nan I would be."

"Okay, then. Come on." Justin squeezed my hand and opened the car door.

Justin never left my side throughout the evening. Trina finally left because she had a curfew to meet. The guy I met at the reservation that Kacey introduced me to was also there, but only for about an hour. Justin left shortly after Trina because I was falling asleep on his lap. On his way out, he whispered that he would call me tomorrow, planting a soft kiss near my ear.

I dragged myself up the stairs to Kacey's room, quickly changing into my pajamas before flopping onto the bed and feeling sleep tugging at my eyes.

"Oh, no, you don't!" Kacey leaped on the bed beside me. "Get up, get up! I need details about you and Justin." She twirled a spoon in front of her, taunting me. "I've got ice cream."

Groaning in protest, I flipped over and asked, "What flavor of ice cream?"

"Chocolate chip cookie dough."

She waved the carton before me, knowing that was my weakness.

"Oh, you play hardball," I grumbled.

"Yeah, pretty much," Kacey answered with a mouthful of ice cream.

"Fine, give me a spoon," I said, taking her bait. "What do you want to know?"

Kacey's eyes lit up. "The obvious....is he a good kisser?" Stunned, I stopped mid-spoon and looked at her.

"Seriously? That's what you want to know?"

She nodded eagerly and shoveled another spoonful of ice cream into her mouth. "Well, that's not the only thing, but I am dying to know the details of the kissing."

"How do you even know we kissed?!"

She rolled her eyes at me and said assuredly, "Oh, please, Rhi. You can just feel the chemistry between the two of you."

"You can?" I asked, shocked.

She nodded vigorously. "Yes. Give me that carton of ice cream and spill it."

I sighed. "Kace, I'm not the kiss-and-tell type."

"Are you serious? Oh, no, you are not doing that to me! Are you two a couple or not?"

"Well, he told me I was his girl. So, does that mean yes?"

"Oh, most definitely!" she exclaimed enthusiastically. "So, that must mean he kissed you."

"You aren't going to give up, are you?"

"Nope." She answered, licking her spoon.

"Okay, okay. We've kissed a few times. He kissed me on a bridge in Cherry Creek Park, and then he asked *me* to kiss him...in the rain. It was absolutely magical." I could almost feel his lips on mine again.

Kacey raised an eyebrow skeptically. "He asked you to kiss him?"

"He said he wanted to make sure I really wanted him."

"So it looks like you do," she concluded after taking another bite of ice cream. "Are you sure about this?"

"Kacey, honestly, I don't even know what to think anymore. He tells me to believe all the rumors about him, but when we're together, he doesn't act like any rumors I've heard."

"Huh." She said, scrunching her eyebrows together.

"Huh, what?"

"It's just really out of character for him."

I wanted to ask her more about what she meant, but she changed the subject before I could.

"So Trina..." She began. "Has she said anything weird to you?"

I scrunched my eyebrows together, "Like what?"

"She's pretty jealous and possessive, if you haven't noticed." She rolled her eyes and scooped another spoonful of ice cream into her mouth.

I did notice.

"She really hates when anyone takes Steve's attention away from her...even us."

"So you think she doesn't like me because he's been spending time with me?"

"I know it, and because Justin is spending time with you, too."

"What? What are you talking about, Steve and Justin? Why would she care I was spending time with them?"

"She told Steve. He told her she was crazy, of course. I thought that would have been enough to break them up. But, she cries, and they have make-up sex, and then they are back together."

"Kacey!"

"Oh, don't look so shocked. They have been together for almost a year and only started sleeping together three months ago. Trina became even crazier after that, though. Maybe that is why Steve doesn't break up with her. She is the first girl he has ever been with."

"Kacey, that is really personal. I don't need to know about Steve and Trina's sex life."

"I'm not gossiping. He would tell you himself. Anyway, Trina is jealous of your relationship with Steve."

"Okay, well, what about Justin? They don't seem to like each other very much."

"Not now, but they did." Her eyes glinted with the knowledge she knew.

"Oh no, you can't be serious." I groaned. "Of course you are- Justin has been with everyone! So, why not Trina?"

"It's a little different with Trina. Trina's mom and Mrs. Rizzo are best friends. They live on the same street, a couple of houses away from each other. Both their moms work at St. Mary's Hospital. Trina was born only six months after Justin; they grew up together."

"I don't think I want to hear this." I flopped back against the pillow.

"It's really not bad, Rhi. They played together like we used to as kids. The Rizzos had BBQs, and the Delroccas were there, and vice versa. Justin took Trina to school dances when they got older, and they were a couple in junior high school. That was when Justin was still the perfect child. They had broken up but stayed close. Then, something changed in him, and he pushed everyone away - including Trina. It hurt her, and it hurt their families, too."

I was almost afraid to ask, but I had to know: "Do you know more about the affair his mother had with his biological father? All of these things must have contributed to why he said he only has half a heart..."

"He told you about that?"

"Steve told me first, and then Justin did after we had dinner at his house. Neither gave many details, though."

"I know as much as Steve does. Scott told Taylor, and she told Steve and me. I don't know how Justin found out. I know he went home to confront his mom.

Justin wouldn't relent until his mom told him the truth and insisted on knowing who his biological father was."

"And now he works for this guy...Vince Moretti?"

"Yes, Vince Moretti. He's been arrested a few times in the past, but always gets off. I can't imagine why Mrs. Rizzo would have an affair with him, but there's no denying Justin looks just like him. They look identical except Justin has his mom's eyes, Vince's are brown."

I couldn't help but blurt out, "He's been in jail? What for?"

"I don't know precisely; something to do with drugs and theft, I believe," she replied.

"Then why would Justin go and work for him?"

"It could be he wanted to find his place in the world, develop a relationship with his father, or maybe because he loves cars. He felt like everyone lied to him except Scott. Scott didn't know about it either. Vince welcomed him with open arms. From what I've heard from Taylor, Vince adores Justin, yet Justin keeps him at arm's length."

"Oh, Kacey." I settled down in the bed and draped the quilt over me. "Why is life so complicated? Why do those who are supposed to love us end up hurting us most?"

"Are we still talking about Justin?" She studied my face for an answer, her chocolate-brown eyes searching mine.

"No, I'm not speaking about Justin anymore, but I am too exhausted to talk about myself tonight."

She frowned, "You can talk to me, you know, or Steve, or Taylor."

I let out a giant yawn, "Yes. I know."

"Alright, then, sleepy head. I'll see you in the morning." She scooted off the bed, and my eyes were closed before the light was out.

I woke up cold, more than cold, freezing. My eyes fluttered open to an unfamiliar place. I blinked away the obscuring snowfall and looked around at where I was. I shivered, my breath visible in the frigid air. I tried remembering how I got here, but my mind was foggy.

I stood up, began to walk forward, and examined some of the trees. I realized they were made of crystals. They had thin branches that caught the wind gracefully, reflecting a full spectrum of colors from their glittering surfaces. It was more beautiful than any other place I'd ever seen. I followed a path that led through the trees, my arms wrapped around my body, trying to conserve heat. The terrain began to incline, and I started to slip on the wet ground as panic set in. That's when I heard voices shouting nearby, giving me pause. Did I really want to walk into a possible altercation? But with no other option to turn to for shelter, I moved toward the voices. The wind howled around me, and my limbs began to ache as I came to the top of a ridge, and there, not twenty feet from me, was Justin.

His face was a mask of rage. His clothes were in tatters, and his hair was wild about his head. He had yet to notice me. I watched as his chest heaved, his gaze fixed on the snow-covered ground below him. I moved my eyes to follow his stare and gasped at what I saw. Kiran lay there; his beautiful angel wings splayed out beneath him; his features were marred by bruises and cuts, and a pool of dark red had begun to soak into the pure white blanket of snow.

I screamed, causing Justin to jerk his head in my direction. As soon as our eyes met, recognition flashed across his face. As he took a step towards me. I took a step backward, only for me to trip over the edge of the ridge. I wanted to scream again, but a set of luxurious black feathery wings enfolded me like silk.

"Rhiannon." A soft voice spoke in my ear. "Rhiannon, please wake up." There was a light brush of softness against my cheek.

"He killed you; oh no, no, he killed you." I screeched.

"Rhiannon." The voice was stronger now and seemed to echo inside my head. "You're dreaming. Now wake up—it's Kiran."

I forced my eyes open, hoping it had all been a dream; I was still so cold. Kiran knelt on the floor beside the bed, our faces just inches apart.

"It's cold." I managed to say.

He silently moved to the closet, pulled out a blanket, and returned. He tucked the messed-up quilt at my feet around me and then spread the new blanket over that. "Better?" he asked softly.

I shuddered and replied, "No, not really." I was still shivering. "I had a terrible dream."

"Yes, I thought so. I felt it, your fear, then your sorrow, and then your fear again. Then I saw the tears. You were crying in your sleep." He knelt again on the floor and whispered quietly, "What happened in your dream to make you cry?"

I peered over at Kacey, who seemed to be sleeping soundly. It had all seemed so real, yet everyone else was calm, and nothing here had changed. Kiran was staring at me, waiting for a response.

"Well, it was snowing, and I was freezing."

"That was your subconscious mind reacting to how cold you were."

"The place was so beautiful, even though I saw the most horrifying thing there."

"It was just a dream, though, Rhi."

"I saw you dead, Kiran."

A slight shock passed over his face, but he quickly composed his features. "Like I said, you were just dreaming. I am right here and can't die." He took a long, shuddering breath.

"I know, but it felt so real and was so frightening. The thought of not having you with me is unimaginable now that I know you exist." I didn't think I should mention Justin in my dream or that I had fallen to what I thought was my death, either. Kiran would see it as a justification for me to stay away from Justin.

"Aw, sweetheart, you never have to worry about being without me. I am dedicated to you forever." He lifted his arm and reached out to touch my face, but then he stopped himself and gave me a warm smile instead. "Rest now, sweet girl. I'll stay right here with you." He shifted back against the wall, and I suddenly felt warm again.

Taking my hand from beneath the blankets, I gently touched Kiran's shoulder. "Thank you."

He tenderly gripped my hand in his own, and I fell asleep with our hands still intertwined - never wanting to let go. I wouldn't find myself wandering lost in that dreadful forest alone ever again.

My slumber was filled with Kiran's calming presence. The chilling, uncanny woods from before had now changed into a wondrous and vivid fairy tale forest. I meandered through the trees in sheer amazement, absorbing the glistening snowflakes cascading around me. I could feel Kiran's hand tightly grasping mine with every step I made. I felt absolutely safe and secure.

Kiran tenderly turned towards me and softly said, "You are cherished, Rhiannon. As long as you embrace that love, there is nothing to fear."

Chapter Sixteen

I squinted at the world around me, one eye slowly opening at a time. The faded quilt on the bed assured my mind that I was not in a crystal forest at the bottom of a ravine as I had dreamed. Kacey was nowhere to be found, and the digital clock told me it was 9:15 AM. My gaze shifted to the floor beside me, and my eyes widened. His honey-colored locks of hair were splayed across his sleeping face. Or at least, I assumed he was sleeping. Angels never truly rest, he had told me, so maybe he was daydreaming. Our hands were still intertwined, and I smiled to myself, feeling a tightening in my chest.

His eyelids fluttered open, and he glanced in my direction. "You're happy this morning." He wasn't asking a question; rather, he had sensed my joyfulness through our bond. " I'm glad; I was worried about you last night." He rubbed my knuckles soothingly.

"I apologize for worrying you."

"Well, I always worry about you. It is my job, but I am more concerned about why you were dreaming about me."

"What do you mean?"

"Most often, dreams carry some significance. They could be our brain trying to solve a problem we can't figure out, or it could be someone like me trying to influence you."

"You mean angels put dreams in our heads?"

He lifted his chin, his eyes gentle. "Well, angels appear to humans in dreams all the time. Sometimes they appear as angels, and sometimes they send messages in a dream. I can assure you, I didn't send you a dream about my death last night."

"You think another angel did?"

He shook his head. "No, not an angel. I don't believe anyone influenced your dream last night, apart from yourself."

"At first, I thought you dreamt of snow because you were cold, and it was just your body reacting to it, but as I thought about it, snow can mean other things."

"Such as?" I probed.

"Many things, depending on the context of the rest of the dream," he said. "It can mean unexpressed emotions that have been repressed for a long time."

I dropped my head. "Sounds like me. Though I'm not sure how that fits."

"Snowstorms can represent obstacles in your life. Snow is also a good omen. It is pure and reflects positive changes."

"But...I saw you lying in it. Your wings were broken, and there was blood." Tears welled up in my eyes, cascading down my cheeks.

He tenderly cupped my face with his hands, chasing the tears that had fallen with his fingers. "No, sweetheart," he reassured me softly. "That's not going to happen. I am here to keep you safe. You are not to be having nightmares and worrying about me. Do you understand?"

I nodded weakly in response, and he reluctantly released me.

"I recognize your insecurity and understand why you feel this way. However, I can't leave you even if I want to because I'm bound to you by something more powerful than anything you can fathom. You must trust me." His gaze penetrated mine, compelling me to believe him. I didn't like deceiving him. I thought I should tell him everything about the dream. As if he could read my mind, he asked. "Was there more to your dream?"

"I was in a forest, and the trees were like crystals. it was so striking. It was snowing so heavily. When I found you, I screamed and fell backward off a cliff." I still felt that I shouldn't mention Justin.

A scowl crossed his face. "Falling is often a sign of insecurities, instabilities, and anxieties as well." He stood up and sat beside me on the bed.

"Come here, Rhiannon," he said softly, his arms invitingly open. Uncurling myself from the sheets, I went into his embrace. "This is very unorthodox, to say the least, but you know now that I exist and am not going anywhere. You are not alone."

His whisper was soft against my ear, and his breath was warm as he spoke, sending chills skittering up my spine. I felt the now familiar softness of wings envelop my whole body. I opened my eyes to peek as I had in my dream, but these wings were glowing pearlescent and the purest of whites. Not black.

I did not want to leave this feathery embrace. I felt no pain, either physical or mental. I wondered if this is what angels did to prepare you for death. If, when they wrapped you in their arms, you forgot everything else except this sweet bliss. I let myself indulge in the feeling, taking deep breaths and inhaling a scent I had never noticed before. It was an aroma I could not quite identify—not entirely floral, but still intoxicating. Warmth spread throughout me, and then I heard it...a melody so faint that it might have been a figment of my imagination. I closed my eyes to focus more on the sound, and there it was, sweet and gentle. I hummed along with its hauntingly beautiful tune.

Kiran's head shot up. His wings were gone, and our tranquil moment vanished. He stared at me with an expression that was locked in awe.

"What is it?" I asked nervously.

"You were humming." His voice was no more than a whisper upon his lips.

"Yes. I heard a song within the warmth, the light, the softness, and the serenity of everything else you were doing."

He began to shake his head violently from side to side as I spoke.

"I'm sorry, Kiran. I didn't mean to upset you. It was so beautiful—everything was so..."

"Rhiannon, that song...it is our souls singing. You should not be able to hear it! Even with me bringing you into my angel light, you still should not be able to hear it!"

He trembled.

"I didn't mean to. I'm so sorry, Kiran."

"No, sweet girl, don't apologize." He said as he ran his long fingers through his hair.

"I just don't understand how it's possible."

"So, the song that brought you to me....that was it?" I asked.

He raised his eyes to mine and gave me a single nod.

"It's beautiful," I whispered.

He let out a deep breath. "It's more than that; it's the connection between us, our light and essence, and the heartstrings that bind me to you."

"I wasn't trying to trivialize it, I..."

He silenced me with a wave of his hand. "We have company coming. We're not done here." And with those words, he vanished just before the door opened.

Kacey burst into the room in a dazzling yellow dress. Her hair was still wet from her shower.

"Finally! I was beginning to worry about you! Taylor brought bagels-you have to see her; she looks like she has doubled in size since last week!" She pulled me out of bed and onto my feet.

I grumbled as I started towards the door. "Okay, let me jump in the shower. I'll be right there."

She hopped back out the door, and I shuffled through my bag to find my clothes for the day. I didn't feel Kiran around and wondered if he was upset with me. Between last night's dream and this morning's bizarre experience, I felt frazzled.

I got in the shower, letting hot water massage my stiff muscles. But unease crept over me again as I thought of him. Where was he? He seemed so upset and almost angry. He wouldn't leave me, though. That was what he was trying to convey in the first place.

I hurried through the rest of my shower and quickly got dressed. As I ran the comb through my hair, I tried to shake off the feeling that had settled in my chest.

A frantic knock came at the door; "Rhi! Quick! Taylor's water just broke!" Kacey shouted from the hallway.

I opened the door to see my two cousins' worried faces.

Kacey had been right; Taylor looked like she was about to burst with her swollen stomach.

"Rhi, I need you to drive me to the hospital. The contractions have already started, and they are only three minutes apart....this baby wants out now." Taylor gripped her belly and leaned against the wall for support.

"Where is everyone else? Where is Scott?"

"I called him, and he said he would meet us there. It will take him too long to get here from work. Do you know where St. Francis is? We need to go now." Taylor wrung her hands as a contraction hit her, and she began panting through it.

"Yes, yes, I know where it is. let's go." I wrapped my arms around her, her round belly pressing into mine. "It will be okay, Tay."

We all lingered in the pastel-colored waiting room in the maternity ward. Racing thoughts seemed to consume everyone as their glazed eyes fixed on the cityscape beyond the windows. Scott had arrived shortly after us, face ashen and fear radiating off him. The hospital staff took him to Taylor while we continued to wait.

The wait was agonizing, as minutes turned into hours, and we all tried our best to keep our minds occupied. Kacey was frantically flipping through magazines. The soon-to-be grandparents were all sitting together on one side of the room, whispering amongst themselves, and I was staring at the clock, willing time to move faster.

Justin shifted his weight uncomfortably as he sat beside me. "I'm gonna go grab something from the cafeteria. Want anything?"

"Yeah, that would be great. I haven't had a chance to eat yet today," I smiled at him.

"Call me if you hear anything," he smirked.

Justin was only gone a few minutes when Scott entered the waiting room, and his family gathered around him.

I fished out my cell phone to call Justin, but it went to voicemail.

I stood up and joined the others who were huddled around Scott. His face was slick with sweat, and his eyes were bright red—you could tell he was shaken up by whatever happened.

"Yes, she is fine," Scott told our group. "I don't think all of you can come in at the same time. I'll take you back four at a time."

The new grandparents were the first to go, led by Scott down the lengthy white corridor as the rest of us returned to our seats.

Justin returned, and I relayed the news to him. He handed me a sandwich wrapped in plastic, some chips, and a bottle of water.

"I tried calling you. Scott took the parents back first to see Taylor and the baby." I twisted open the cap of my water container before taking a sip from it.

"Hmm. I didn't feel it vibrate." He sat beside me. "You owe me half that sandwich, you know." He grinned at me crookedly and snatched the sandwich from my hands. "It's no East Side Deli, but it will do. I hope turkey is okay."

"It's great; thank you," I replied as he ripped the sandwich in half and handed me one side.

The parents were elated when they returned, beaming with happiness from the newest member of their family. Scott took a few at a time until Justin and I were the only ones left.

Kacey skipped up behind me and squeezed me tightly, enthusiasm radiating from her as she said, "Oh, Rhi! It is so exciting! I'm an Aunt!"

Following Scott, we arrived at the last room at the end of the hallway.

"Hey there, hun." Scott walked to the side of Taylor's bed and stroked her hair softly. "This is the last of our visitors." He let out a small chuckle.

Taylor looked tiny in the hospital bed, like a child herself. She was wearing a pale yellow hospital gown, and her hair was tied back in a ponytail. Held against her heart lay a tightly wrapped bundle with light blonde curls popping up from above the blanket.

"Looks like he got grandpa's curls," Justin said. "Actually....he is a she." Scott corrected us, one side of his lips kicking up into a half smile.

Justin looked surprised. "You guys said you were having a boy."

"We thought we were, Justin," Scott replied. "Taylor only had one ultrasound. They must have been wrong." He tenderly ran his fingers through his daughter's soft curls as she rested quietly.

Taylor remained focused on the infant in her arms. "So what is her name?" I looked directly at Taylor, but

Scott answered.

"We never settled on a name for a girl, so for now, she doesn't have one." He kissed Taylor on the top of her head and then leaned down to kiss the baby, too. "Taylor, sweetie, I'm going to run home, grab your things, and shower. I'll be back soon."

I watched Scott leave and then felt Justin step up behind me. "May I see her, Taylor?" I asked.

She raised her sky-blue eyes to meet mine. She glanced towards Justin briefly before turning back to me, and she pulled back the blanket tenderly so I could see the endearing face of the newborn.

She was beautiful. Her pink cheeks overflowed with chubbiness, her little button nose barely visible beneath it all. Her eyes were closed in peaceful contentment, pale lashes resting like tiny angel hairs on her face.

"She is perfect," I said in admiration.

Justin lifted his palm from my shoulder and reached for his phone. He muttered a few rushed words into it before closing the call. "Rhi, I gotta go pick up a car for work. It won't take long. I'll come right back and get you." He looked genuinely sorry that he had to leave.

I turned to Taylor. "Is that okay, Taylor?"

She nodded her head slightly. "Yes, please stay, Rhi." She murmured softly.

Justin ran his hand through my hair and peered over my shoulder at his niece. "She is perfect, Tay."

Taylor looked surprised at his remark. "Thanks, Justin. I think so, too."

I sank into the chair beside the bed, "She looks just like you, Tay." Unconsciously, I reached out towards the pink bundle nestled between us. The baby cooed and latched onto my hand with surprising strength.

I laughed and gently stroked the baby's hand with my thumb. "Look at the family you've created, Tay; it's beautiful."

Taylor regarded me quietly for a moment before answering. "Family," she began slowly, "Family is complicated. It's messy with tangled emotions and unsaid words; it is joy and sorrow intertwined...but above all, it's love." She stroked her daughter's cheek and continued, "Remember that you are part of our family too."

My heart ached at her words, knowing how complicated the concept of family had become for me. Yet, here, in this moment, I felt a glimmer of belonging. A flicker of warmth I hadn't felt in ages. It was as if I had been wandering through a fog and finally found a place where I was seen. Where I was loved and cherished. Would it last?

I dared not hope too much, but right now, it felt like home.

Chapter Seventeen

J ustin came back for me. Taylor hugged me tightly and whispered *'thank you'* in my ear. I returned her hug and promised I'd come by her house when they were released from the hospital.

We stopped for gas, and when Justin returned, he said, "Check out who I ran into." He gestured behind him, showcasing Mia. She looked alluring in an all-black outfit with a gold chain around her neck and bracelets that adorned most of her left arm, which looked like they were made of stones.

"Hey, you!" Mia knelt to peer through the open window at me. "Are you still up for heading to Witches Well with me? There will be a few other people there, too."

I glanced at Justin, who shrugged his shoulders in indifference.

"Sure." The words slipped out of my mouth before I could stop them.

Mia smiled at me before slipping on her sunglasses and saying, "See you at the res, Lady Bug." She spun around and approached the vehicle I assumed was hers, a small green car covered in rust.

Justin scooted into the seat beside me and handed me a soda. "Are you sure you're up for this?" he asked.

"Yes, I'm fine." I twisted open the cap of my soda and took a long sip, "Besides, what could possibly be scary about wandering through a haunted forest with rumors of an evil witch's well lurking somewhere within?"

He grinned, and his deep green eyes twinkled with excitement. "Don't worry about it, Rhi," he reassured me. "I'll protect you."

We followed Mia to the reservation through the forested roads. As we traveled through the trees, the road became more like a path until we couldn't drive anymore. The sun had just begun to set, casting an orange glow through the forest. I felt a sense of unease as we got out of the car, my heart pounding in my chest.

Mia got out of her car and greeted us with a grin, ushering us towards a group of people. "These are my friends," she said, "Sam and Sophie."

Sophie had a neat pixie cut dyed an eye-catching red. "Hi, I'm Sophie. Mia's girlfriend."

My gaze landed on the boy standing by her side. He was nearly as tall as Justin. His skin was dark, and he wore a baseball cap. He looked shocked when he saw us, his black eyes studying us.

We exchanged pleasantries, and I felt myself relaxing a bit.

They all seemed like friendly people. Sam seemed to ignore us, but I caught him looking at Justin and me out of the corner of his eye.

Kiran's voice whispered in my mind. *"Sam isn't what he appears to be."*

I furrowed my brow, wondering what Kiran meant. I glanced sideways at Sam, and our eyes locked, but he quickly looked away.

I tried whispering quietly to Kiran what he meant about Sam, but Mia spoke up before I could ask. "Alright, let's get going!" She led the way down a winding path that led deeper into the forest. The trees grew taller and denser as we went along, and the light was quickly fading. I shuddered, feeling goosebumps erupt over my arms. "This used to be a real road up to the deserted village," Mia said, taking a flashlight from her pack and illuminating the way forward.

"Thirteen Witches Road," Justin whispered to me. "Are you scared?" He asked, taking my hand.

I shook my head, trying to put on a brave face. "Of course not," I said, my voice trembling slightly.

As she walked backward, Mia talked to us, her flashlight in hand, moving from side to side. "Thirteen Witches Road was the home of several witches long ago, but before they came, it belonged to the Lenape tribe." She stepped around a large tree that had fallen across the path. "My grandmother is Lenape," she added. "We should be coming up on the first witch soon!"

The trees towered above us, their branches twisted into gnarled shapes that seemed like claws. I shuddered as a cold sensation crept down my spine. I looked around, trying to see if anyone else felt it, too, but they all seemed excited and eager to explore. I gritted my teeth and tried to push through my fear.

"There it is!" Mia shouted. A bump across the path was clearly visible. Reaching into her backpack, she took out an apple and set it on the small hill. "A tribute to whoever is buried here, so if anyone steps on top of it, this offering will make amends." We watched as Mia gracefully hopped over the bump, and we all followed suit, hopping over the mound one by one.

The darkness slowly engulfed us as we kept walking forward, my heart beating faster with each step. Kiran's whispers in my mind grew louder and more urgent, trying to convince me to turn back. I wanted to stay with everyone else, so I tightened my grip around Justin's hand and continued on. My palms were damp as fear crept through me.

We continued climbing over twelve more mounds in the path as Mia left offerings at each one. As the trail widened up the hill, I could make out some buildings perched on the ridge. Kiran's voice kept ringing in my head: *"Turn back now!"* But I kept walking, not letting myself waver.

"It's just ahead on the right," Mia said enthusiastically. A few moments later, we reached the Witches Well—a small clearing with a stone well at its heart.

Mia busied herself by unpacking her bag and setting up candles around the stone wall. A yellow glow filled the air as match after match lit up, casting long shadows and painting everything in shades of gray and black.

I felt a sudden surge of energy course through me, making my heart race. I heard Kiran's voice in my mind again, urging me to leave, but I ignored it, instead taking a deep breath and peering into the well. It was made of stone and rose about two feet high. In its center was a deep hole surrounded by tree roots and vines. As I looked into the darkness, I felt something soft tug on my shirt. It was Kiran's wings urging me away from the edge. I saw nothing, but it felt like something was watching us from the depths.

Before I could even blink, Sam's strong hands whisked me away with a playful tug. "Careful now, you might fall under the witch's spell," he teased, his eyes sparkling playfully. Sage and lavender filled my nose, and smoke encircled us as I broke free of Sam's grasp.

Justin had come up behind me and held me protectively around the waist. "I got her, Sam; there's no need to be a hero."

Sam placed a dramatic hand to his chest. "And here I thought I might win Rhiannon's eternal gratitude," he said, winking at me as he turned back to where Sophie stood. Justin wrapped his other arm around me, pulling me closer to him.

"Welcome to the Witches Well," Mia said with a sweeping gesture. "We come here for spiritual guidance and to connect with the energy of Mother Nature. It is a powerful and sacred place."

"Man, it's kind of creepy," Sophie said from behind Sam.

"Don't be scared," Mia coaxed. "Everybody, make a circle!" Mia took her place near the well, tucking her long legs beneath her.

As we settled in around the circle, I noticed Sam move closer to us, and I felt Kiran's presence strengthen in my mind.

Mia led us in a chant to summon the spirits, requesting their help in our lives. Sophie joined in, their voices weaving together into an ethereal song. Sam's glance flicked wickedly to me, not even pretending not to stare. His grin lingered, and I looked away, heat rising in my cheeks.

The chanting quiets. Immediately, the air feels denser, tinged with ozone, like right before a thunderstorm. Justin's arms tighten around me, but my mind is stuck on the well. I can't shake the memory that for the briefest instant, I swore there were eyes staring up from below.

My head snaps up, and I lock eyes with Sam. There's this instant where I swear up and down he knows exactly what I saw in the well.

Justin leans in so close that his dark hair brushes my ear. "I don't like the way he looks at you."

"Relax," I say, elbowing Justin in the rib. "You're the one who looks like you'd throw him down the well if you got the chance."

"I might."

Out of nowhere, Sophie grabs my hand, her fingers icy cold. "Did anyone feel that?" Her voice has a tremor to it, but it's not fear so much as...excitement? "Like, I felt something down my back, I think I'm tingling."

"The veil is thin tonight," Sam tells Sophie, his voice all velvet and mischief, "and highly susceptible to beauty." He gives her a little toast with an invisible glass, but then his gaze flicks to me, and he winks, not even attempting to be subtle.

Justin glares at him, which only seems to amuse Sam more. I feel his chest vibrate with a low growl, and he suddenly stood up, interrupting the ritual. "None of this is real. It's all just a bunch of nonsense."

Mia shot Justin a look of annoyance, but her chanting dissolved, and everyone frowned at him.

Sam rolled his eyes. "Come on, man. You don't have to ruin it for everyone else."

"Sorry, Mi, I really should get Rhi home. We all had a long day." I nodded, grateful to escape the tension.

I slid my hand into Justin's, and his fingers curled around mine. "Sorry Mia," I manage to choke out, "I am pretty tired."

"It was nice to meet you, Rhi," Sophie shouted after us, and I spun around to give her a quick wave goodbye.

We continued on, and once we were out of earshot, Justin turned to me with a concerned expression. "Are you okay?" he asked, brushing a strand of hair away from my face. "You look pale."

"I'm fine," I said rubbing my fingers along his hand. "And I always look pale."

He gave a little laugh and tousled my hair. Hand in hand, we ventured through the forest. We circled around the mounds that the witches supposedly rested eternally under.

"Justin?" I asked nervously.

"Yes?"

"Did you feel like somebody was watching us near the well?"

He stopped and looked down at me. "No. Trust me. I've been to parties up there, it's kinda spooky, but I've never seen anything out of the ordinary."

He resumed walking as the leaves rustled from above, creating an eerie sound.

"Don't worry," he said with a reassuring squeeze of my hand. "I won't let anything happen to you."

I didn't really believe anything would happen. I had my guardian angel. Still, I felt like eyes were upon us, and it gave me the heebie-jeebies.

We walked silently until finally emerging into the clearing where Justin's car was parked. As we reached his car, he wrapped his arms around me again and held me close. "I mean it. I promise to take care of you," he whispered against my ear.

Chapter Eighteen

J ustin gave me a tight hug before saying goodbye. "I'll call you later. I have to do some late work tonight," he said, planting a swift kiss on my lips.

"I'll talk to you later, then, Uncle Justin." I smiled up at him.

"Yeah, it is pretty cool, isn't it?"

His cell phone buzzed in his pocket. "That's probably work looking for me. I've got to go." He gave me a hasty kiss, leaving me lightheaded before he took off.

I jogged up the stairs and pushed open the door. As soon as I stepped through the doorway, the aroma of warm chocolate filled my nostrils. My stomach growled as I followed the scent into the kitchen, where Nan stirred a pitcher of iced tea on the counter.

"Hey Nan, I'm home."

"Hi, sweetie, I made brownies. Help yourself."

I grabbed one and followed Nan to the table, where she was pouring tea into glasses for both of us.

We both nibbled on brownies, enjoying each other's company. I helped her with the dishes before we watched some TV until it was time for her to turn in for the night.

I kissed her goodnight and walked silently upstairs. Leaning casually against the far wall was my angel. He seemed calm and serene after today's unusual day. I studied his face and posture for any sign of anger at going to the Witches Well despite his warning. He seemed composed enough.

"Hi," I said quietly, walking cautiously past him to adjust the air conditioner.

"There's no need to act so timidly around me," he reassured me. "Everything is alright."

I turned to him with a questioning look, "Are you angry I went to the Witches Well with Mia and her friends?" I asked timidly.

He shook his head slowly, his soft hair floating silently around his face. I gazed at him doubtfully. "I am annoyed at you. You really should listen to your Guardian, you know. That place..." He seemed to try to come up with the right words. "That place is full of miscreants."

"Miscreants?" I scoffed, but then thought about something else. "What about this morning's incident when I was humming our song?"

His face changed and seemed to light up at the change of topic. "I thought about why you could hear it, and think I have some answers."

My curiosity was piqued. "Really? It isn't bad, is it?"

"No, not necessarily, sweetheart."

"Well, just don't stand there, tell me!"

He laughed his deep, throaty laugh, and I pulled him by his hands to sit with me on the edge of my bed.

"Explain what you've discovered, Kiran, because the melody is still echoing in my mind, and I need assurance that everything is alright." I released his hands and waited for him to speak.

He hesitated, his eyes locked on mine. "Can you hear it now?"

I closed my eyes, focusing on my thoughts. "Only when everything else is quiet."

"Hmmm," he pondered.

"What is it, Kiran?"

He sighed, running a hand through his hair. "Either our connection is stronger than I thought or..." He trailed off, a guilty look crossing his face.

"Or what?" I prodded, my frustration mounting.

He looked away from me, unable to meet my gaze. "Or I have allowed it to happen," he admitted reluctantly.

"Allowed? I don't understand."

He closed his eyes, shaking his head. "I can't explain it to you," he said quietly.

"What do you mean you can't explain it?" I asked, frustration bubbling up inside of me. "Is it that you can't explain it or that you won't?"

He sighed heavily. "Honestly, Rhiannon, I can't, and I won't — it would just be wrong."

I couldn't understand his hesitation and felt my anger rising. "What the hell is that supposed to mean?"

He got up and walked to the other side of the room, keeping his back turned to me. "Don't curse at me, Rhiannon," he said softly. "It means exactly what I said: It's wrong. What I've done is wrong, and it's entirely my fault. That's why I could never be angry with you — not that I ever could anyway." His shoulders slumped in defeat as he spoke; my heart filled with sympathy for him. I wanted to comfort him despite my frustration at his reluctance to tell me everything.

"Kiran, you're speaking in riddles."

He turned his head slightly to look at me over his shoulder, and there was something in his eyes that wasn't there before, something raw. "I guess you could say that, he said, his voice strained.

"It's a constant war raging inside of me." He turned to face me, but kept a distance between us. "You know I haven't been following the rules, Rhi. But I thought it was for your own good. Or maybe I was fooling myself, and it was really for my own selfish desires." His words trailed off into silence.

I struggled to understand what exactly he was trying to tell me. "What desires?"

He chuckled lightly, but there was no humor in his eyes. "You really are so naive."

My throat tightened at his words, a knot of hurt blooming in my chest. "Well, if you aren't going to tell me, then I will just go to bed," I said as I got up from where I sat and went to my dresser.

"Don't be angry with me," he said softly. "It's for the best."

"For the best? Always for my own good? How can you always know what's best for me? You may sense what I feel, but you don't know what's in my heart or mind."

His gaze found mine again. He sighed, massaging his forehead with long fingers. Then he looked at me, his silver eyes filled with anguish. "I'm so very sorry," he started, and there was something in his voice that made me brace for what was coming, "You are right. I am not in your heart, nor can I read your mind."

He vanished.

My heart stopped. I turned around and looked around my entire room. He was gone, and I couldn't feel him. "Kiran?" I whispered. "Oh, Kiran, come back, please. I didn't mean to hurt you."

Complete silence. My tears came from nowhere, streaming uncontrollably down my face. I wiped them away angrily.

"Dammit!" I cursed at the empty room.

"No more heartache. I thought you were supposed to take the pain away." I sobbed to myself, and I slipped to the floor. The pain washed over me like a tidal wave.

Abandoned again.

"I will always be alone." I sobbed into my hands.

He heard me, though. I didn't think he had. I hadn't felt his presence. I thought he was gone. He scooped me off the floor into his strong arms, encasing me in his velvet wings again, taking me back into peaceful nothingness as I listened only to the rhythm of his heart and the sweet harmony of our souls singing.

I'm not sure how long he kept us in this tranquil shroud, but eventually, I felt I needed to say something. "Kiran?"

"Hush." He whispered, sliding his hands through my hair.

"But, Kiran." I protested, arching my body upwards to meet his gaze.

He placed a comforting hand against my head to keep me in place. His thumb moved along my jawline as he spoke. "We don't need words when we are together like this." His wings fluttered around us both.

I considered his words. "This is sacred to you, isn't it?"

His chest heaved beneath me as he let out a heavy sigh. "Yes...it really is."

I could feel his warm breath against my hair as he dipped his head to lie between my neck and shoulder. "And it's also against the rules?"

Another sigh escaped him. "Yes....and no. It depends on the situation. I am purely being selfish now, so in this case- yes."

Then I felt him breathe....Long and steady breaths like he was breathing my soul into his.

"No, Kiran, you are not being selfish. I begged you to come back. I said that you are supposed to keep the pain away. I didn't realize you heard me. I thought you were gone."

His fingers caressed my face. "Oh, my sweet girl, I am always connected to you. I can never be away from you, even if you don't realize it. " His arms pulled me tighter against him, and I melted into him.

"I'm sorry I took so long to appear to you. It was hard to deal with your anger knowing that it was directed at me." He drew his hand up my back, leaving a trail of fire in its wake. "It has been a trying day."

"I'm sorry," I said as my eyes fluttered shut.

He shook his head. "Don't be."

"What did you mean when you said we don't need words when we are like this?"

He spoke slowly, "You are within my angel light. Our souls are not just connected as they are normally but woven together tightly. Think of it this way: You and I are always tied together like with a rope, but now that rope has been braided together."

His breathing became uneven. "Everything is stronger; I can feel you so much more clearly. You said I cannot read your mind or your heart, but this is the closest thing I can come to it. I am ashamed to say I enjoyed it way too much this morning. I swore I wouldn't bring you back into my light, but seeing you crumpled on the floor...how could I not? Or maybe I just needed an excuse for my own selfish needs."

I struggled to be free of his iron grip. I wanted to look into his eyes, to see what was going on behind those endless depths.

"What's wrong, sweetheart?"

"Nothing is wrong. I just want to look at you."

"Why?"

"Why not? What are you searching for when you keep me held close like this?"

I shifted my body and managed to free one arm. Then, I looped it around his neck and pulled myself up to look into the silvery depth of his eyes. I cocked my head to the side, examining him closely. He kept an iron mask on that hid his emotions. His eyes were such an unusual color of grey, but iridescent simultaneously. They had tiny flecks of silver. Like stars in the night sky and, they sparkled like diamonds, framed by long golden lashes that matched the color of his hair. I searched them for answers, but he had hidden away all of his feelings. I let my mind search back through everything he said, trying to determine what was happening in his head. Then it clicked, and I noticed minute changes in his eyebrows. He knew I had figured it out.

"You wish you were human, don't you?" I whispered as I brushed my fingers over the curve of his cheek.

He scoffed. "That's ridiculous! Human life comes with pain and suffering. Besides, I can do all that you do. In fact, we will have pizza tomorrow." He joked, attempting to lighten the mood.

I shook my head slowly in disagreement. "Not all that we can do."

His voice suddenly took on a note of seriousness I'd never heard before. "Rhiannon, you are wrong."

"I am right. I can see it." I said firmly.

He broke the connection. His wings were gone, and the shelter of our cocoon disappeared. The humming of the air conditioner suddenly seemed very loud. I still remained on his lap, staring at him intently.

"Why won't you admit it to me?" I asked softly. "Do you not trust me? Are we not soul mates, as you say? If you can't tell your soulmate, who can you tell?"

He tenderly cupped one side of my face, and I leaned into his palm, feeling his warmth. His sudden intake of breath startled me.

"There are some things that we cannot share, no matter how close we are. You must understand that nothing is black and white; all shades of grey lie in between." He let his hand drop. "Soulmate or not, some things must remain mine alone."

I examined his seraphic face, tracing a line from his brow to his jaw with my finger, and he clenched it tightly in response.

I wouldn't look away.

I leaned in even closer and took a deep breath through my nose, concentrating on the scent....yes, it was still there. I only had to make myself more aware of it now.

"Rhiannon, what are you doing?" He asked, but I chose to ignore him.

With my finger still tracing his face and his scent fresh in my mind, I allowed my mind, or rather my soul, to search for the melody, which immediately overcame me.

At once, his eyes grew large with shock, and he lifted us both so swiftly off the floor that I didn't realize what he had done until I was standing on my feet a few feet away from him.

A wave of dizziness made me stumble backward, but he was there in an instant to catch and steady me. He kept his distance, though, even as he studied me anxiously with concern in his eyes.

"Are you all right?" He asked.

The wave of dizziness had given way to a wave of nausea. "I think you gave me whiplash, moving me so quickly."

He looked contrite. "I'm sorry. I forget my own strength sometimes." His thumbs gently rubbed my shoulders, still supporting me. "Do you forgive me?"

I waved him away dismissively and went to sit on my bed. Concern still showed in his eyes. "It's fine, Kiran, but why did you do that?"

He didn't move closer to me. He stood in his place, stuffing his hands into the pockets of his worn jeans and shifting uncomfortably. He looked so human with his Rolling Stones t-shirt, the one I first saw him in at Sal's, and beat-up sneakers.

I wanted to see his back to see if it looked different from ours and to see where those powerful wings sprouted from. Great, now I was wondering what he looked like shirtless.

Idiot.

He nervously bit his lip before he spoke. "Your mind is full of curiosity, I can feel, and yet, I am the one with the questions now."

"What sort of questions?" I asked.

"How did you do that before?" His eyes got wide with wonder, and for a moment, I thought I detected fear.

"Do what?"

"You truly don't know? You didn't feel the same experience as when I pull you into my light?"

I felt my face twist in disbelief. Even though I heard our song, smelled his beautiful scent, and was acutely aware of him, wasn't this something always there under the surface when we were together?

"Rhiannon?" He pushed.

I said nothing, letting my mind wander through the possibilities of what was happening.

"Rhiannon, please," he begged.

My eyes rose to meet his gaze. "Why won't you come close to me now? Are you scared of me?"

"Of course not."

"Then come sit with me, Kiran."

Reluctantly, he moved closer and sat by my feet. "Speak to me, Rhi."

"Not until you speak to me first," I demanded.

His brows rose slightly at this command, but other than that, he stayed collected.

"Admit that you sometimes wish you were human."

"I will not say something which is untrue." He answered in a monotone voice.

I groaned in annoyance. "Say it, Kiran—admit that there are moments when you wish that you were human! You don't lie, remember?"

He rolled his eyes. "You are one of the most stubborn, obtuse..."

I cut him off. "Just answer the question."

"Fine, at times, I wish I could be human. Are you happy now? Can we get on with how you were able to do what only an angel can do?"

"No, I'm not done." I held up a hand to quiet him. "What times would those human moments be? I have my theories, but I'd like to hear them from you."

He stares at me for several long seconds, his silver eyes searching my face with an array of emotions that I couldn't comprehend. My skin heats up under his gaze as embarrassment washes over me. When he looked at me like that, all sorts of forbidden feelings bloom in my stomach. I shake my head to clear it.

"Why is this important, Rhi?"

"You are with me every moment of every day. You know more about me than I do, apparently, since I have no memories as an infant, and as far as I'm aware, you can even sense what I feel when I'm dreaming. You know all about me at those moments in my life. When I dream, you know if I am happy or having a nightmare, even if it is intimate, because you feel what I feel during my sleep. I can wake up and not remember, but you knew how I felt. So spill it."

He straightened his spine, his eyes growing icy. It was evident that this pained him. His silver irises flickered like moonbeams on a stormy night, revealing a private universe of discord hidden within him. I watched, my heart pounding, as he attempted to mold his angelic expression into a blank canvas, yet the brushstrokes of torment were too deep, too vivid.

"Do you understand what it means to be human?" he asked quietly.

I crinkled my eyebrows, unsure of where he was going with this.

"It's about feeling everything so intensely... unfiltered emotion slamming into you like an oncoming train." As soon as the words left his lips, I could see the anguish on his face. "I am meant to guide, to guard," Kiran's voice broke slightly, concentrating on some point beyond me. "I do not merely want to watch over you from a distance; I wish to share your every joy and pain."

His words hung in the air between us.

"Human emotions are not meant for me, but I cannot deny the attraction to them." His gaze dropped, and he looked at his hands. "So beautiful. So flawed. They can create, touch, feel... deliver both pain and pleasure."

His eyes locked with mine again. This time, there was a desperate pleading set in the cool silver irises, a raw need to be understood. "And love." He raked his hands through his hair in despair, "The love you share with each other is a beautifully chaotic sentiment." His silver eyes glowed brighter. "And here I am, an angel crippled by emotions intended for mortals."

I slid off my bed and put my arms around him. He let me, which eased some of my worry. He laid his head on my shoulder as a shudder passed through him.

"Are you crying, Kiran?"

"Angels don't cry as humans do. Our tears do not fall on the outside but rather burn us from within, and it's the most painful form of agony."

"I'm so sorry."

"Hush, Rhiannon. It is my fault. I love you unconditionally, as all angels love their humans. But if I had not allowed you to know of my existence and, worse, allowed you to bond with me, then you would not have grown any sort of attachment to me. Any consequences that come out of this completely lie on my shoulders."

"Some of those consequences are that you might get in trouble because of me," I said.

He didn't answer.

"I saw it, Kiran – and even more than that, I felt it. You wish you had a family of your own- a human family." He gently pulled my arms off his shoulders, and before he could pull away again, I rushed to say what was on my mind. "It's not only the fact that you're an angel that keeps you from achieving that dream - it's also the fact that you're bound to me. I'm sorry for everything you've given up because of me; I know this wasn't your choice, that you're stuck with me."

His face contorted in anger, and his hands balled into fists at his sides. "You are so far off base you cannot imagine how wrong you are." He menacingly clenched his teeth, making him look like an angel of death instead of a protector of innocents. "I am done discussing this! I could not just fall in love with some human and fall from grace to pursue them and leave my soulmate behind!"

I averted my gaze from him, unable to bear seeing the rage he directed towards me any longer.

He grabbed my chin between his fingers and brought me back around to face him. "Do not underestimate the power of the bond between soul mates. It is unbreakable." His startling eyes penetrated into mine. "Do you believe me?"

I nodded.

"Good." He released my chin as he stood up. "I will be back soon. Get ready for bed - your boyfriend should be calling shortly, and then it will be time for you to answer my questions." He left no room for further discussion. I had never seen him this angry before. Without looking back, he vanished from the room.

I crawled over to where my nightgown had landed on the floor when Kiran had pulled me into his winged sanctuary. Quickly removing my clothes, I threw them into a haphazard pile on the floor. Slipping the dark blue nightgown over my head, I thought of the first time Kacey took me to the mall with her. It was a clearance sale item, but I had instantly fallen in love with its softness and femininity—not something I would typically pick out for myself. I examined myself in the full-length mirror that hung on the door, admiring how well the dark shade complimented my pale legs. Letting my hair cascade down my back, it felt as if Kiran had returned, though he did not appear or speak. After searching the room and finding no trace of him, I left to brush my teeth and wash my face.

When I returned, he was back, sitting silently on the floor. The room smelled of something sweet, and my eyes fell upon a candle next to my bed. I turned and locked the door behind me.

"Why the candle, Kiran?"

"Do you recognize the smell?"

I stepped closer and inhaled. "Lilac?"

"A favorite of yours, is it not?" he raised one slender eyebrow at me questioningly.

I walked over to sit on the bed. I felt his eyes on me, and suddenly grew shy at how I was dressed.

"Yes, I always loved the scent of lilacs in the springtime."

"Good," he said as a smile finally crept onto his face. "Is it covering up the scent that I give off?"

I sniffed again before shaking my head. "Sort of, but not completely. I'm afraid I have become quite attuned to you. In fact, I think you have a bit of a lilac smell yourself, mixed with vanilla and with something else that I can't put my finger on." I tapped the side of my head in thought. "Pine, maybe? But not like the forests of Colorado. Different. It's hard to explain—I just know it's you." I said, exasperated. "You were here earlier, too, weren't you? Even though you didn't speak or show yourself, I could feel you."

We sat in silence for a moment. His stunned expression said more than words ever could. Then, my cell phone buzzed on my nightstand, causing the candle flame to flicker wildly.

"That would be Justin," I said as I scooted across the bed to retrieve the phone.

"Who else?" Kiran's voice dripped with disdain.

I grabbed the old phone and spoke into it. "Hello?"

"Hey, Rhi. What took you so long to answer?" Justin asked.

My eyes flicked to Kiran, who had an annoyed look on his face.

"What are you up to?" Justin asked.

"Just finished getting ready for bed and was thinking about everything that happened today." I settled back against my headboard. Kiran feigned disinterest in our conversation, his slender fingers absently picking at a fray on the end of his jeans as he surreptitiously peered up at me beneath his lashes.

I asked Justin, "Have you finished all your work?"

Kiran snorted, and I frowned at him in disapproval before continuing with my conversation.

"Yeah, I still have one more car to pick up. Deadbeats didn't pay Vince what they owed him for the vehicles. I have to repossess them."

"I thought you said you would be done by eleven?"

"I thought I would be, but the last car was harder to find than we thought, and I still haven't found this one." He paused and spoke to someone else besides me.

"Sorry, I'm at a drive-through, grabbing something to eat. I haven't eaten since that sandwich at the hospital. I'm starving."

"Sorry that you can't go home yet."

He paused for another moment, presumably to pay for his meal. "Yeah, it sucks, and I am supposed to be back at work at eight-thirty in the morning. Maybe I should just tell Vince I couldn't find the car and come over there instead." He laughed, and I heard him sip his drink.

I glanced down at Kiran again.

"I'm afraid that I'll be asleep by the time you get here. I'm so tired." I said with an exaggerated yawn.

Kiran looked at me with surprise and shook his head. Then he yawned and lay out on the floor. I scowled at him; angels weren't supposed to sleep. He ignored me.

"I miss you, Rhi; tomorrow night then, okay?" Justin asked hopefully.

"Of course, tomorrow I'm all yours," I replied reassuringly.

"I'm counting on it."

I heard a voice in the background. "Hold on, Rhi." Justin was speaking to someone else on the CB radio. His tone suggested annoyance, but I couldn't make out what he said. He obviously wasn't pleased with the conversation when he came back on. "The other guys found the car, and they're having some trouble with it. I gotta go - I'll call you tomorrow."

"Sure, just be careful."

I placed the phone back on my nightstand. Kiran was still lying down on the floor with his arm draped over his face. "I know you aren't sleeping."

"Well, I thought I would just make myself comfortable since you are *sooo* tired and you are just going to go to sleep." Sarcasm dripped from his lips.

"You are upset with me because I lied to Justin? You don't even want us together. What was I supposed to tell him?" I asked. "He wanted to come over."

"Tell him you didn't want him to come over."

"Oh yeah! Justin, it's not that I don't want you here tonight— it's just that I'm in deep conversation with my guardian angel and need to finish that first! That won't sound crazy at all..."

He rolled onto his side and propped himself up on his elbow. "A simple 'not tonight' would suffice," he suggested.

"Yes, but then he'd ask why — and you said yourself that not everything is black and white. Besides, I didn't lie. I am tired, but also, I know you won't let me sleep until you get your answers."

He pushed himself up to a sitting position and leaned forward. "Okay, fine - I'll excuse your lack of complete honesty this time."

"Hey, I'm only human, after all," I said, a playful smile tugging at the corners of my mouth.

"Yes, that you are. Which brings me back to how you are able to do the things that I do."

"Kiran, I think you're overreacting. I can't just vanish like you or sprout wings, and I certainly can't travel to the places you go."

He leaned forward and crossed his long legs in front of him. "But you inter-twined our souls."

"I did what?" Confusion poured into me.

With fervor in his eyes, Kiran explained further, "When I pull you into my light like I told you before, it's like our souls are intertwined together." He clasped his hands together to punctuate his point. "I knit them around each other and bind them tight. That's something only angels can do—humans don't have this kind of power, yet you just do it." He released his grip on his hands, reaching out as if to touch me, then pulling back.

Heat bloomed in my cheeks. "I didn't realize that›s what I was doing. I just... opened myself to you, focused on your essence. Then it hit me, this overwhelming wave." I paused,

Lost in the memory. "I always hear it, but this time, it drowned out everything but us." My voice softened. "It was similar to when you embraced me with your wings, but not the same. Definitely not the same."

Kiran moved closer still, now mere inches away. His honey-blonde waves caught the light, tempting me to run my fingers through them. "Tell me more," he murmured, his tone low and intimate. "Exactly how you did it."

I swallowed hard, hyper-aware of his proximity. "I didn't even know I was doing it. It just... happened."

"Well, tell me what led up to it then." His eyes were full of wonder.

I knelt beside him, my fingers trembling as they hovered near his face. The air between us crackled with an unseen energy, drawing me closer. I inhaled deeply, savoring the hints of vanilla and lilac that clung to his skin. My fingertips grazed his cheek, and a jolt of warmth surged through me, igniting every nerve ending.

"I was trying to see it in your eyes...they are the windows to the soul, so they say, but I could see you covering up your emotions. So I touched you and inhaled deeply—your scent was powerful and reassuring. Then, it was as if warmth emanated from where my fingers pressed against your skin, and this quiet suddenly became louder than anything else in the room. There was nothing but that gentle electric current and this tune running through my veins, and I had the strangest feeling...."

Kiran's gaze held mine, silver depths swirling with an intensity that made my breath catch. His lips parted slightly, and I found myself leaning in, drawn by an inexplicable force. "I felt...odd." I breathed out.

"Odd?" His brows drew together in confusion. "What do you mean by odd?"

"It was like watching a show on an old TV with poor reception—you can barely make out the pictures, and there's too much interference to pick up sound clearly. And before I could fully comprehend what it all meant, you broke away from me, and the moment passed."

Kiran's face was mere inches from mine. The air between us seemed to shimmer, charged with possibility. The electricity between us seemed to buzz. It was so intense it felt like my entire body pulsed with fire.

Suddenly, with a swift exhale that brushed against my cheek, Kiran pulled away. That jolting electrical current dissipated as the distance between us grew as he scooted away from me.

"Rhi... I..." He stuttered before shaking his head slightly as if trying to arrange his thoughts. "I'll figure out this mystery surrounding your abilities," Kiran said. "I'll leave you be for now."

Feeling awkward and exposed after all that transpired, I rose from my spot on the floor to sit on my bed. "This means you'll never wrap your wings around me again, doesn't it?" Even though I tried hard, a trace of sorrow crept into my voice.

He stood and came to sit on the edge of my bed. "Oh, sweet girl, I don't think it is the best idea."

"Are you leaving then?" I felt my eyelids getting heavy, and I shuffled under the sheets of my bed, wrapping them tightly around me. "Or will you stay here with me?"

"I'm always with you. When will you believe that?" he said softly.

My eyes closed again, and I felt his lips brush my forehead—but he was gone when my eyes opened again.

I reached over and turned off the light, so all that illuminated the room was candlelight, creating eerie shadows on the walls.

"Kiran?" I murmured. "When I'm asleep, please wrap your wings around me, keep the nightmares away, keep me safe.... just let me know I'm not alone." The last words came out in a slur as my consciousness drifted away.

Sometime in the night, I turned in my sleep. Soft, downy feathers tickled my cheek as I tried to open my eyes. They stayed closed, though, and part of me knew this must be a dream. I sighed in contentment as I embraced the feeling that Kiran had come to grant my wish and protect me from nightmarish terrors. I was no longer alone, even in the darkness of night. So, what if it was just in my dreams? It felt real enough, and it eased my mind.

I curled into a ball, yearning for every inch of my body to be touched by the satin-like feathers. Their gossamer softness ignited a warmth within me, spreading throughout my body.

For a moment, I thought I heard a heartbeat and a melodious song whispering in my ear, lulling me back to the dark recesses of slumber.

I tilted my head upward, brushing my lips against what I imagined to be the underside of Kiran's wing. A gentle moan vibrated through the air, sending a flutter through my stomach.

This dream surpassed all others, a tapestry of tender touches and unspoken devotion.

I beheld an eerie fog, the sort you would expect to find on dark Scottish moors with ancient castles looming in the background. It was impenetrably thick, dense enough that I wouldn't be able to see my arm if I stretched it out in front of me. Instantly, I knew I was dreaming again and longed to return to the dream where I was safe in my angel's arms. But instead, here I stood, in a foggy field, with dewy grass grazing my bare toes.

"What now?" I murmured to myself.

As in answer, a soft breeze blew through the meadow and stirred up ghostly spirals of fog. I heard waves crashing against some shoreline in the far-off distance and decided to follow their call. The soil underfoot was soft and spongy, and wet grass stuck to my feet as I walked. I reached down to wipe the bottoms of my feet and realized I was wearing my nightgown in my dream.

"I can't dream of wearing more appropriate clothes for the outdoors at night. I grumbled to myself. "Ugh, this is ridiculous!"

I furiously swatted at my feet to remove the clinging blades of grass, and when I lifted my head up again, I gasped in astonishment. In the mist, there was a figure crouching with enormous wings. Enormous black wings. My first instinct was to run away, but my feet wouldn't move because when the creature stood up, its wings spread wide to reveal human arms and legs.

Then, it leaped into the air, vanishing before my eyes. I ran to where it had been and knelt down to see the unmistakable imprints of human feet on the muddy ground. The sound of crashing waves was louder now, and I turned to peer through the thick haze to notice I was again on the edge of a cliff, as in my last dream about angels, only this one ending at the bottom of a raging sea.

The angel who had caught me in my last dream had black wings. Did I have another Guardian? Was that possible? I needed to find out - if I could ever wake up. Or maybe it was Kiran. Could his wings shift between various colors? In every painting or picture I have seen of angels, they have white wings, but maybe humans were mistaken about them. We seemed to make a lot of mistakes and assumptions when it came to the supernatural.

I wanted out of this dream. I wasn't scared; I just didn't want to be here anymore. I was getting wet from the mist and just wanted to return to sleeping soundly. More importantly, this place was so desolate and lonely, and that was exactly what I was trying to avoid.

Loneliness.

Even dreaming, I knew he was in my room watching over me. So I spoke aloud to him. Maybe he would hear me? "Kiran, take me away from here or wake me up. Please, Kiran, help me." But all that responded was the crashing of waves against rocks below.

Desperately, I pulled at my hair and slapped at my face. "Wake up!" I screamed.

Then I heard the whoosh of giant wings and felt the force of the air as they swooped above my head. My eyes strained to see through the thick fog, but I couldn't make out anything. I scrambled to my feet and stepped back in the direction I had come.

I heard the familiar ruffling of feathers and turned to my right. There he was - only a few feet away. His back was to me, his wings tucked in close against his body, with only his bare feet visible beneath the feathered tips.

"Kiran?" I asked uncertainly.

He didn't answer me. As I walked tentatively around him, I saw that his wings were sparkling with droplets of water.

He kept his face turned away from me. I could not smell the familiar scent I had come to know. I could not feel the presence I knew so well. This wasn't Kiran.

"Who are you?" I asked.

"You know," he whispered.

The misty ghosts engulfed us, and without thought, my hand rose up to stroke one of his large, glossy wings. It quivered beneath my touch.

"I'm sorry, I don't think that I do," I said softly, "Why won't you look at me?"

His movement was so swift I never saw a thing. I was entirely surrounded by the giant black wings, similar to when Kiran cocooned me against him, but now everything was pitch black.

"Rhi." He breathed urgently in my ear.

Then his lips were on mine, warm and demanding. I felt his mane of hair whisk around my face and knew it was him. His delicate locks had graced my cheeks before, and his soft lips were unmistakable. I wrapped my arms around his neck, pulled him close, and immediately felt the glossy wings caress me tighter.

"I love you, Rhiannon," he gasped. "Please help me."

He vanished. I was left alone in the foggy field, the sound of the sea in the distance. "Oh, Justin...." My voice sounded distant even to my ears.

My eyes shot open to find myself in my dimly lit room.

Kiran's presence was evident almost immediately, and I searched for him in the shadows. I found him by the window. He had pulled back one side of the curtain slightly and stared at something in the sky.

"You are up early." He commented without turning to face me.

"I guess I am," I rubbed the rest of the sleep out of my eyes.

"What time is it?"

"Just before dawn. I'm waiting for the sun to rise."

"Really? That early? I don't think I have ever been up that early."

He chuckled. "No, Rhi, you haven't." He did turn to look at me then. "Would you like to watch with me?"

I smiled amiably at him. "Of course, I would." I scooted off the bed and came to stand by his side. He wore new clothes today—black jeans with holes in the knees, a white tank that showed off the muscles of his arms, along with his usual sneakers.

"It's supposed to be hot again today," I said.

"Is it?" He gazed down at me.

"Do you get too hot wearing jeans all the time?" I asked.

"Hot and cold don't bother me. I'm comfortable regardless."

"Must be nice."

He shrugged his shoulders. "I suppose it is," He elbowed me in the arm. He was in an awfully good mood this morning. "Now hush; the sun is about to come up."

"But..." I protested.

"Hush or you'll miss it." He pulled the curtain back and pulled me in front of him so I could better view the sunrise. It felt so intimate with my back pressed against him, the rough material of his jeans rubbing against my bare legs. I felt pulled to him against my will, and in response, he wrapped an arm around my waist so we were molded together.

"I don't know if we can see the sun with all these trees and rooftops in the way," I said a bit breathlessly.

"Well, we aren't really, just the hues of light as it reflects off the clouds. It is still quite pretty. It's not as beautiful as watching it rise and set by the ocean. That is my favorite place."

A chill tiptoed down my spine as he spoke, calling to mind the dreams of the sea I had the night before. I was tempted to bring up all the questions his words provoked, but before I could say anything, he was speaking again.

"See, Rhiannon, the start of a new day," he said while pointing towards the sky where streaks of pink and yellow were beginning to peek between the trees. "Dawn's always been my favorite; it reminds me that there's hope for tomorrow and new beginnings."

"For me, it's the night when I can forget what happened during the day," I replied. "I like stars and the moonlight."

A soft chuckle escaped him, vibrating through me as a soft gasp escaped my lips. "Well, you can't have one without the other. I love the night, the dark. We would not have needed light if it weren't for the dark. I especially love the light of the stars, but nothing compares to watching a sunrise."

"I'd like to see it at the ocean too....with you." I turned to face him.

He let the curtain fall and stepped away from me. "Someday then." He promised.

"It's funny you mentioned the ocean because I dreamt of the sea last night."

He looked confused. "You did?"

"Yes, though not like the oceans here, more like the Pacific Northwest or how I picture Scotland. It was definitely not like any sea I had seen before."

"You seemed to sleep quite peacefully last night."

"I did, for the most part. The couple of dreams I remember were very different."

"Do you want to tell me about them?" he hedged.

"Yes, and ask you something as well." He waited for me to go on. "First, I was dreaming that I was back in your wings and that you held me while I slept. I thought at first that I wasn't dreaming and that you were really there. Then, when I couldn't wake up to check, I knew I must be dreaming." I smiled at him. "Even though it wasn't real, it comforted me to know you were there."

"But you do know that I'm always here for you." He said.

"It isn't the same as feeling you."

He sighed and leaned against the windowsill. His features were just dark shadows in the early morning light, and I couldn't see his expression.

"And your other dream?"

I bit my lip before I answered. "Well, I have a question. Can you change your wing color the way you change your appearance?"

His head whipped towards me. "Where did that question come from?"

"I had a dream of an angel with wings of a different color than yours."

"What color?"

"Black."

"Black....are you sure?" He seemed distressed.

"Yes, pretty sure. It was very foggy."

"Could they have been purple?" he inquired.

"Maybe, but I am pretty sure they were black." He was staring at me with watchful eyes. "Are you going to answer my question?"

He stared off into the distance before replying. "Um, no, we can't change our wing color. They are given to us depending on our importance or rank; we can also get more wings, or the ones we have can become....damaged."

"Well, what does black mean?" I asked curiously.

He gazed out the window again as he spoke. "Azrael."

"What is an Azrael?"

"Not what, whom. Azrael is the Angel of Death."

"What?!" I felt the air get punched from my lungs. Kiran was at my side, immediately holding me to him. "He is not evil, Rhiannon. He was banished from Heaven, but he isn't bad. He is an Archangel and helps mortals. He finds lost souls and brings them to the veil. Those who feel the need to cling to earth as ghosts or shades. He also fights off demons who would try to take them. He is a collector of souls. It is not a bad thing to have the Angel of Death on your side."

"But why was he thrown out of Heaven?"

"It is a long and complicated story. Basically, he got caught sneaking into hell to try to minister to the souls there and have them repent for their sins. As you can imagine, it didn't go over well. However, he believed he was doing the right thing. He never stopped worshiping God, so he remains his servant and continues his work. He just can never go back home because his job is too closely tied to the earthly realm of mortality to be allowed in the celestial realm. To us, that is a terrible fate. When you have been to peace itself, the embodiment of contentment, then being banned is well....torture." His lips pursed together in a sad line, and sorrow filled his eyes. "May I ask you something?"

"Yes, of course."

"Please be honest with me. Was I the one with the black wings?"

"No, Kiran, most definitely not. Why would you think that?"

He ignored my question, "Are you sure? You said my name in your sleep last night."

"Yes, when I was standing by the foggy sea and glimpsed the figure with dark wings, I thought it was you—but his face was turned away from me. That's why I called your name."

"Did you see this angel's face?"

I swallowed hard, my mouth going dry. I couldn't lie. "No...but he spoke to me and then enveloped me in his wings. It was completely dark."

Kiran left his shadowed sanctuary and came to me. He asked quietly, "Was it like it is between you and me?"

"Not at all." I paused, hesitating on whether I should continue.

Before I could answer, he stroked my cheek and asked, "What is it, Rhiannon? You can tell me anything."

"I asked him who he was, and he asked me to help him, and then he...he.."

"He what?" Kiran prodded with growing concern. "He kissed me."

Kiran sharply inhaled, and an odd light filled his eyes as he waited for me to go on.

"I knew who it was then." I continued, not meeting his eyes.

"Did you?" He asked again, still wearing that odd expression.

I nodded silently as I turned away from him. "It was Justin," I whispered the name softly as if speaking it louder would make it reality. "He told me he loved me and then disappeared."

Kiran's expression hardened as I finished speaking, but he was quick to compose himself. "Well, it was just a dream." He walked away from me to lean against the windowsill again.

I couldn't comprehend his strange behavior. "But, did you not say that dreams had meaning?"

He spun his golden head to glance at me. "Indeed, they do most of the time, but sometimes they're just dreams."

"You are impossible, you know that? I can tell it means something by your reactions to some of what I was saying." I raked my fingers through my tangled hair in frustration. "Why won't you be honest with me?"

"How am I not being honest?"

"Because you won't tell me what you're really thinking!"

He grunted as he pushed away from the window and began to pace back and forth with his hands tightly tucked into the pockets of his jeans. "The truth is, your first dream was not a dream at all. I told you that I cannot deny you anything, so when I returned, I held you while you slept. Of course, there were blankets between us- nothing improper."

He glanced at me under thick lashes and then resumed his pacing. "It could mean many things or nothing at all. Your mind may be confusing me with Justin." He gave me a sternly pointed look, and I glanced away.

Did I feel the same way about Kiran as I did about Justin? When I peered back up at him, he was watching me curiously. "What do you suppose it symbolizes?" I asked.

"You aren't going to like what it means."

I scowled at him. "Just tell me anyway."

Kiran raised one thin golden eyebrow, crossing his arms across his chest. "Fog in dreams usually signifies that you're not seeing things as they really are." He watched me warily, ready for my reaction.

I considered this for a moment before responding: "So, everyone, including you, sees Justin negatively. I see him as an angel—the Angel of Death, but an angel all the same, and he tells me he loves me." His body seemed to relax when it appeared that I had begun to understand.

"Maybe it's you and everyone else not seeing him clearly - perhaps I'm the one who knows who he really is."

Kiran's lips formed a tight frown. "No, Rhiannon, you couldn't see clearly in this fog, correct? That is what it means....You are not seeing clearly whatever was in your dream."

I balled my fists at my sides. "So maybe it meant I'm not seeing you clearly then, since Justin also happened to be an angel, and the only angel I know is you!"

Kiran was taken aback by the implication of my words.

"Are you doubting me?" he asked, his voice becoming pointed.

I sighed heavily and crossed the room to my bed, flopping back upon the mattress. "No, Kiran," I replied. "I don't doubt you. I know you'd never hurt me."

He sat down next to me and clasped my hand silently in his own. I gave him a half-hearted smile. When I woke up this morning, I thought I understood my feelings. Now, everything seemed so confusing. Was I second-guessing my-self about Justin? Was I starting to develop feelings for Kiran? One thing was sure—Justin had never told me he loved me in real life, while Kiran had said it many times before. But I also knew I could never be with Kiran the way I could be with Justin, and maybe that is what all these bizarre dreams meant. I needed to kill any feelings I was developing for Kiran, other than that he was my protector, the keeper of my safety; he could never be the custodian of my heart, but Justin possibly could.

Kiran jolted me out of my thoughts and wished me a pleasant day with Nan.

"What?" I shook my head. "Oh yes, Nan. She wanted to go shopping today. Thank you for reminding me." I stood and opened the curtains further, letting the sun in.

I turned from the window and glanced around my room, but he was already gone. His presence still lingered around me, though, and I knew if I called his name, he'd be there immediately. It was comforting to know that someone was looking out for me.

I returned to my bed to straighten it up. As I smoothed out the covers, I noticed light shimmering from a pearlescent feather. I picked it up tenderly and held it against my face, then quickly pulled it away, looking around my room and wondering if he saw what I had done. I again took the feather and let it glide through my fingers. It was not like a bird feather; it was smoother and softer, as if it were made of the finest silk. I closed my eyes and let it glide down my cheek, just like when I held my face against him. Then I slid it down my neck and let it come to rest where my heart beat hard and heavy beneath my chest. I swore I felt an electric charge where it lay. I placed the feather tenderly underneath my pillow.

Chapter Nineteen

I skipped downstairs and noticed immediately that Nan must still be asleep. Not a sound came from anywhere in the house. I crept into the kitchen and grabbed a glass of orange juice and some toast. Standing at the counter, I let the sun's warmth shine on my back. The birds' cheerful morning songs filled my ears as they hopped around outside. I gulped down the rest of my juice and headed for the shower, bumping into Nan in the hallway.

"You're up early!" she marveled, eyes wide like an owl.

"I slept like a rock." I shrugged my shoulders and smiled at her. "I guess I got all the sleep I needed."

I scooted past her and into the bathroom. I took a long shower because I could. I was in no rush today, and relaxing in the hot, steamy water felt good.

My thoughts turned to Justin, as he would be coming over later. I missed him when we were apart and began questioning what these feelings meant for me. Were these stirrings of feelings I had for him love? Were the butterflies in my stomach just nerves? Or was that how people felt when you were with someone you loved?

I rinsed out the shampoo from my hair and began working the conditioner through the thick tangles. As I rubbed it between my palms, I noticed a familiar scent. It was lilac. I never noticed before, but my conditioner smelled like lilacs. I inhaled deeply and thought of Kiran.

Now I missed him. As I closed my eyes and concentrated on him, I heard his voice whisper my name. My eyes flew open, and I threw back the shower curtain, expecting to see him standing there, but he wasn't. Had I imagined his voice? I pushed the curtain back and returned to slathering the conditioner in my hair.

The thing that was bothering me now was his humanness. Sometimes, he seemed more human than celestial, and I had to check myself every so often when I was with him because I felt tempted by human ways.

That was wrong on so many levels.

Justin assumed I belonged to him, whether or not I agreed with the idea. In any case, I wasn't exactly the type to play the field. But worse, Kiran was sacred; you can't have impure thoughts about a holy being. Couldn't he see how attractive he is?

I tried to push both of them out of my mind and finished my shower before throwing a towel around myself and heading upstairs to get dressed.

I ran a hair dryer over my hair to straighten it, then grabbed a pair of black shorts and a white tank top. I pulled my hair up into a high ponytail and headed downstairs.

Nan was in the dining room, sipping her tea. She looked up as I entered. "Would you like to go to the restaurant for breakfast before we head out shopping?"

I wasn't really hungry, but I did want to go by The Pier and beg cousin Jimmy for a job. I didn't want Nan to buy me anything else, and I really wanted to buy a car.

"Actually, Nan," I began hesitantly, "I wanted to talk about the restaurant. Do you think Jimmy would give me a job there?"

Nan carefully placed her cup on its saucer before motioning for me to join her at the table. "Rhi," she said sweetly, "You don't need to work for cousin Jimmy."

I opened my mouth to respond, but she silenced me with a wave of her hand.

"Please just listen to me, Rhiannon. When your grandfather passed on, he left me with quite a bit of money. Not only did he have a life insurance policy, but bless his soul, he had invested money since the early days of our marriage and had never touched it."

She took my hand in hers, patting mine gently. "We are in need of nothing. The house is paid for. My car is paid for. I don't even need to work, but I like it at The Pier. It is where I have worked for over forty years. What else would I do?" She leaned back in her chair and took a sip of her tea. "Now, please don't mention this to your Uncle Nick, your mother, or your cousins, for that matter. They don't know about it. I would like to keep it between us. I'd like to leave what I have left to each of you when the time comes."

My heart sank at the thought of Nan no longer being here. "Nan, don't talk about those things."

"Oh, Rhi, I had no idea that you were so advanced in school. Even if you weren't, I would want you to put your utmost effort into getting an education." She stared at me with watchful eyes. "It will make me happy if you let me do this for you."

I looked at her soft face, lined with age, and the soft white curls surrounding it. I didn't want to take anything from her. I felt guilty, but I couldn't deny her either because if the roles were reversed, I would want to do the same.

She seemed like she had something more to say. I watched from the corner of my eye as she slowly swirled the dark liquid inside her teacup. I was ready to escape this talk, quickly pushing my chair back and standing up. "I'm just going to grab my bag."

She grabbed my wrist before I could get away. "There isn't a rush to go. Sit for a minute. I want to talk to you about something."

It wasn't something good, judging by her tone. I settled back into my seat and said, "Okay then, Nan, shoot."

"It's about your mom," she started off in a soft voice.

I was taken aback. Of all the things I was expecting, it wasn't a conversation about my mother. My posture stiffened, and I crossed my arms at her words. "What about her?" I asked warily.

Nan spoke softly, "She called yesterday while you were out, and I talked to her. She asked how you were doing and said that she misses you." She paused briefly before adding, "And that she would like it if you called her back." My focus drifted past Nan out of the window into the backyard as her words sank in.

I had no idea where it came from, but I yelled in a sudden burst of anger, "She can just keep on waiting! I refuse to talk to her!"

"Rhi...you don't really mean that..."

"Oh, Nan, I certainly do mean it!" Mist grew in my eyes. "Her new life with her new husband...." I spat, the tears flowing uncontrollably now. "He is a monster! I have no idea why she stays with him, and worse, I don't know why she would allow him to treat me like he did. He'd come home drunk," I whispered, squeezing the scar on my hand as though it could keep my tears at bay. "And he'd look at me with these eyes... these cold, hateful eyes."

I swallowed hard, pushing down the knot in my throat. "And he'd call me names. Belittle me. Made me feel..." My voice broke off into a pitiful whisper. I pushed roughly away from the table and stood, turning on my heel to leave.

"Rhiannon, please," Nan begged. "I didn't mean to upset you."

When I looked back at her, I saw that tears were rolling down her cheeks, too. "I didn't know about any of the things he did. I know your mother loves you though, Rhi, and as a mom myself....I know we make mistakes, but there is no excuse for what her husband did." She wiped at her eyes with a napkin.

I bit down hard on my lip to keep from saying something harsh. After taking a deep breath, I said, "We all make mistakes, Nan, but knowing that everyone makes mistakes doesn't make the pain from them any less agonizing."

Without waiting for a response, I ran up the stairs and threw my bedroom door open. Kiran was there to greet me with sympathetic eyes. He opened his arms, and without hesitation, I fell into them.

Nan and I didn't speak much at breakfast; cousin Jimmy didn't show up at The Pier until it was almost time for us to leave. We bumped into him at the doorway, and he immediately scooped me up in a big bear hug and beamed at me. "Little Rhiannon!" he exclaimed.

Cousin Jimmy towered over me, nearly a full seven feet tall. He had played basketball all through school before suffering a severe knee injury in a ski accident in his second year of college. This ruined his professional aspirations and left him with a permanent limp. Nevertheless, he was as strong as an ox, and when his father passed away, he took over the restaurant. For all he had been through, he seemed content and happy at The Pier.

I stood there looking up at him, saying jokingly, "Compared to you, I am still little!"

A hearty laugh rolled out from his chest as he replied, "Where are you two going today?"

"I'm taking Rhi to get a computer for school," Nan answered.

Just then, my phone buzzed in my pocket. I yanked it out and looked at the caller ID. It read Vince's auto, "Justin?"

"Hey, Rhi."

"You sound tired."

"I am. I got in pretty late, but I did get all my cars, and I have a surprise for you."

Sighing heavily, I replied, "Oh, Justin, not another surprise. I can't keep taking things from you."

"No, it isn't that kind of surprise," Justin replied with a hint of aggravation. "So, can you meet me for lunch?"

"I just finished eating breakfast at The Pier with Nan, so I don't know if I can handle any more food."

"Alright then. I'll eat, and you can watch me. But I promise to bring you one of Sal's cookies to munch on. You know you can't resist those."

I glanced at Nan and cousin Jimmy quickly, who were both stealing glances at me as they talked to each other. "I have to go, Justin, but save me a cookie."

"Okay, call me. I'll come by and pick you up when you're done. I can't wait to tell you about the surprise....you'll love it." I groaned audibly and shoved the phone in my pocket.

As I made my way back over to Nan and cousin Jimmy, Nan was in fits of laughter. Cousin Jimmy's grey eyes met mine as soon as I stopped walking. "Who were you talking to just now?" He asked curiously.

"Justin Rizzo," I answered bluntly.

His expression brightened with recognition. "Oh yeah? I went to school with his cousin; she was three years younger than me...a cheerleader too; one of the best." A look of nostalgia crossed his face.

I wasn't particularly surprised when Jimmy told me he knew the Rizzos. "Well, doesn't everybody know everyone here?" I asked with a hint of sarcasm.

Jimmy quickly snapped out of his musing and ruffled my hair. "Yeah, kid, we do, and that's what makes it so great! It's nice to come home, isn't it?" he said before heading off to work at the restaurant.

As I followed Nan to the car, I scanned the old buildings, and the cars stopped at the intersection. I watched an elderly couple sit at the bus stop with their packages from the grocery store across the street, and a jogger turn the corner by the south side of the parking lot. Was this my home? Was it really preferable to have everyone know you so well, or would I be happier lost in a sea of unfamiliar faces?

We finished our shopping quicker than anticipated. We went into a mega electronics store with everything from laptops to refrigerators. There was a back-to-school sale going on, and I found the perfect laptop for what I needed. Just something for internet access and word processing programs, so I could write my assignments.

When I got in the car, I called Justin at the shop, plugging in the numbers from when he called me earlier.

"Yo."

"Yo?"

"Rhi?"

"I'm all done shopping. I got a new laptop. Do you want to meet for lunch?"

"Things got pretty hectic. Vince is ordering pizza for us. I'll still bring you cookies from Sal's, though. I promise." I heard the smile in his voice. "I can come over after work and help you set up the laptop."

"Okay, see you tonight."

Nan peeked at me out of the corner of her eye. "So Justin is coming over this evening?"

"Um, yeah, he is going to help set up the computer."

"Should I make dinner?"

I hadn't even thought of that. "Don't go out of your way, Nan. We can just make sandwiches or something."

She smiled sweetly at me. "Well, I'll see what I can whip up."

I decided to clean my room when we got home. It wasn't too messy, but it could have used a little work before Justin arrived. His bedroom seemed so neat and clean compared to mine. So, I put on some music and started cleaning.

I put away the clothing I'd washed the day before, changed my bed sheets, and alphabetized my CDs. I took the feather I had found this morning and put it in my nightstand drawer. When I opened the drawer, my eyes immediately fell upon the envelope I had stuffed in there from my mother. I had forgotten I even had it. I pulled the plain white envelope out and placed the feather carefully away. I sat down on my bed and flipped the envelope over in my hands, contemplating what to do with it. I had no idea what my mother had to say to me.

I made up my mind and hooked my finger in the crease and ripped it open. I sat for another moment. I did want to move on, so I pulled out the letter from its envelope and let it fall into my lap. The faint smell of my mother's perfume lingered on the paper. In her tiny, neat script, she had written:

Dear Rhiannon,

Sending you to live with your grandmother was the hardest thing I've ever done. I know it may have felt like I was pushing you away, but I need you to believe that I did it out of love. I was trying to protect you. There are things I haven't told you. Things I wanted to wait until you were old enough to understand and your heart was ready. There is strength in you, not born from me alone. A fire that cannot be taught. I see it when you stand your ground. When you care more than others dare to. When you dream of something beyond this world.

Your father, your real father, is the one who gave you that fire. I will never forget him as I see him in you. His presence was like standing in sunlight, and I still hear his voice sometimes in the quiet.

If you ever feel alone, close your eyes. You might feel something. A warmth that wraps around you, even in your darkest moments.

I love you more than my own breath. Always have. Always will.- Mom

I'd read it three times before I realized my face was wet. My hands shook uncontrollably as I held the paper. It offered no answers, just repackaged riddles.

Thoughts of my father swirled in my head. He was an enigma, elusive with nothing concrete to grasp unless I embarked on an investigation myself.

The letter left hollowness in my chest that seemed to echo with every heartbeat.

A warm, gentle hand settled on my shoulder.

Kiran.

He didn't speak, but the air around him softened, like someone had dropped a thick woolen blanket around my shoulders.

"Hey," he said, his voice gentle and cautious, as if he feared I might shatter.

I lowered my head, quickly brushing away the moisture from my cheek with the back of my hand. "It's stupid. I shouldn't even care." I hated that my own voice broke.

"It's not stupid," Kiran reassured, easing himself onto the bed beside me with a gentle nudge.

"Aren't your parents supposed to love you unconditionally?"

"You know the answer to that yourself," he replied, taking hold of my hand in his own and squeezing gently. "Parents are not infallible."

The room was filled with a charged silence until Kiran finally spoke again. "Rhiannon," he murmured softly, his voice like a caress against my roiling turmoil of emotions. "They have nothing to do with who you are. Not the man who raised you, and not the one you've never met." His breath stirred the air between us. "You are your own. Your choices make you, not your blood."

I shook my head, but the heat of tears threatened anyway. "You make it sound so simple."

"It is simple." His thumb swept away tears that caught on the edge of my jaw.

"You are the sum total of every brave thing you've done. Every time you forgave when you could have hated. Every time you stood up and said 'no,' even when your voice shook." His silver gaze pierced into mine, unwavering and fierce. "You have faced demons in human skin and survived. Your stepfather, Sorin, is a horrible creature."

Something unidentifiable swept across his face, and I moved closer to him in response, but he was up and gone before I could blink. He quickly picked up my mother's letter from the other side of the room and made his way back to me.

"You might want to keep this even if you don't look at it for years." His voice was low yet clear.

"No."

He sat down by me again, taking my face in his hands, and forced me to look into his eyes as he spoke again. "We don't have our families with us forever, Rhiannon."

"He'd say no one would ever want me," I confess, pain searing across my heart as I spoke. "That I was too insignificant...too worthless...to be loved." Tears flowed freely down my cheeks, hot and scathing.

He pulled me closer, his warm breath caressing my cheek. I gazed into his silver eyes, steady and unwavering, "I won't pretend to know the depths of your pain or the extent of the cruelty you've experienced." The sincerity etched on his face struck a chord deep within me. "But I can tell you this." He paused for a moment, collecting his thoughts. His eyes darkened just a shade - a hurricane of conflicting emotions swirling beneath their surface. "You are not insignificant. You are not worthless."

My eyes closed at the rush of more unwanted tears. "You are not just deserving of love, you are worthy of adoration," he whispered, an underlying intensity seeping through each word that left his lips that suddenly made my heart tight in my chest.

The silence lingered for a moment before he pulled away slightly, picking up my mother's letter. "Perhaps I will keep it safe for you. I'll have it if you ever want it." He stuffed the letter in his pocket. "I will see you later, Rhiannon."

I sat motionless, trying desperately to keep my emotions in check. "You're leaving?"

"I believe Justin will be here soon, and you prefer that I not be here when he is around."

I felt a burn in my throat as I spoke. "You can stay until he gets here, Kiran."

He raised one slender, perfect eyebrow at me. "You are a very complex human." He stood and smiled at me, though it didn't touch his eyes. "Later, Rhi," he said.

And with that, he vanished.

I drenched my pillow with my tears until I felt my eyelids grow heavy.

The scene changed around me, and I was suddenly back in the snowy forest with the crystalline trees. My body was clad in a white gown and thick white robes. My bare feet ached from the chill of the snow beneath them. The wind was viciously whipping my hair around my face, and I pushed it repeatedly away, only to have it blow back into my eyes. It was a total white-out. Frantic, I wrapped the thick robes tightly around me, desperate to find shelter fast. I lifted my feet to walk and saw they were crusted with blood. I screamed, but the wild howling of the wind concealed it.

Suddenly, I was lifted off the ground, surrounded by darkness, and soft black feathers were embracing me.

"Rhi?" Justin's familiar voice swept over me like a wave. I opened my eyes to find him hovering above me.

"Justin?" I said groggily as I blinked heavily.

He brushed the hair away from my forehead. "You took a nap? You know you're going to be up all night now." His throaty chuckle made me smile before he leaned down and kissed me. "Not that I'm complaining."

"I don't remember falling asleep. I got up earlier than usual; I guess I was just a bit tired." I sat up and tried to arrange my sleep-disheveled self.

"Your grandmother is apparently making a meatloaf. She told me it was about done and to run up and get you. Don't worry; I remembered the cookies from Sal's." He smiled widely at me with the familiar bag in hand. "Before we go down, though, I want to tell you about my surprise."

"Oh, Justin, I don't think I can take anything else from you." My voice sounded raspy as I rubbed my sleepy eyes.

"It isn't so much as taking something from me as coming with me somewhere." Excitement shone in his eyes. "Vince is going to Florida for a wedding next weekend."

"You want me to go to Florida with you? I don't think I can, Justin. I mean, I would love to because I've never been there before..."

He shook his head while laughing. "Let me finish. Vince is going to Florida because his cousin is getting married or something. Anyway, he has a house down in Point Pleasant Beach, so I thought you might want to spend one of the last weekends of the summer down the shore with me."

The surprise I felt must have shown on my face because he quickly added, "We can bring Steve, Kacey, Taylor and Scott if they're up to it."

I could tell that wasn't initially part of his plan, but he was willing to do what it took to make me feel comfortable and maybe even get Nan to agree to the idea.

"I would love to go to the beach, and I know Kacey would want to go. I'm not so sure about the others. Is there enough room for everyone at Vince's?"

"Yeah, it's a four-bedroom house, and one of the bedrooms has two double beds so that everyone will fit comfortably. Think your grandmother will let you go?"

"I'm sure she will if my cousins are there. I don't know how she would feel if it were just you and me."

"I'll work on my brother, you invite your cousins, and then we tackle your grandmother."

He pulled me close and hugged me tightly against his chest. His warm skin felt comforting against mine as his strong arms held me. "Anything for the chance of spending more time with you." He placed a kiss on the top of my head, and tiny chills ran along my skin.

Nan's voice floated upstairs, summoning us to dinner. Justin chuckled in my ear, "We will pull off this weekend; I can't take any more interruptions."

We savored Nan's delicious meal. I was always amazed at her superior culinary skills, which just proved she was superhuman. Justin had three helpings. How he ate so much and still remained slim and toned was beyond me. When I questioned him, he just smirked and kept eating.

Justin set up my computer while we shared Sal's cookies in my bed. I didn't care that we got crumbs all over when the cookie sharing led to kissing, leaving me breathless.

Justin finally left when Nan wasn't going to bed at her normal time. It was hard to let him go; I was desperate for him to stay. He said he would return when Nan had gone to sleep.

I made my way downstairs to find her knitting and watching TV. I brushed my teeth, washed my face, and changed into comfy pajamas before strolling by her nonchalantly. "Wow, Nan, you are never up this late."

She glanced up at me over her glasses. "They're playing two of my favorite movies back-to-back. I haven't seen them in ages. I'm going to stay up late and watch."

Of course. The night my skin was practically begging for Justin to be near me, and Nan's classic black-and-white films were on.

"Cool, Nan. Thanks again for the new computer."

"You're welcome, honey." She said, returning her attention to the TV screen.

I flopped onto my bed and called Justin first. He sounded disappointed that we wouldn't be able to hang out, but he promised he'd come over no matter when Nan went to sleep. I sighed inwardly and said I would try, but I might fall asleep myself. I decided to call Kacey next. When I explained that we could use Vince's house for a weekend, she screamed with excitement.

"Do you know how much money Vince has? I can only imagine how big that house is! Eeek!"

"Kacey, he said it was only four bedrooms."

"Rhi, a three-bedroom with walk-in closets and their own bathrooms, I bet. Bet me, Rhi! The man is loaded! I will make Steve go, or I'll tell Mom and Dad all his dirty secrets. I am not missing this."

After hanging up with Kacey, I turned on my laptop and decided to look for anything I could on guardian angels.

The screen flickered to life, casting a bluish light around me. "Guardian angels," I type into the search bar. The results are largely predictable. Web pages full of religious scripture, the occasional forum thread speculating on paranormal encounters. An entire online community dedicated to sharing stories of divine guardianship. Websites filled with prayers and rituals, alleged signs, symbols, and sensations that hint at angelic presence.

A particular phrase caught my eye: *'angels breeding with humans'*. I clicked on it. Page after page loaded with theories and accounts detailing these supposed relationships between celestial beings and mortals. I felt an electric current course through me. Tales from multiple cultures spoke of heavenly beings descending from their lofty realms to consort with humans. They talked about producing offspring that straddled dimensions, belonging neither wholly to Heaven nor Earth. The more I read, the deeper I spiraled into a rabbit hole of forbidden love.

I scanned through each line, each paragraph. *'Angels falling out of heaven for forbidden love'*

'Celestial beings and mortal women creating children of both worlds'

'Guardian angels breaking their vows....' Kiran's face flashed in my mind's eye.

I closed my eyes for a moment, pressing the heels of my hands into them until stars danced behind my lids. I shifted uncomfortably, feeling overwhelmed by the thoughts whirling in my mind. I saw flashes of stolen moments, a lingering touch here, an intense look there. Each one leaving an imprint on me.

I shut my laptop abruptly, the sudden silence in the room deafening. I glanced at the time on my phone. It was just shy of midnight, and I got up to check if Nan was asleep yet. I peeked out my door, and all the lights were off in the house except for a dim light from my old room across the hall.

A cold sweat broke out on the back of my neck, and a scream bubbled up my throat. Immediately, I whispered for Kiran, and the door crept open as a hand clamped over my mouth.

"Hush! Do you want to wake up Nan?"

I clamped my teeth around the fingers held over my mouth and yanked on his shirt, bringing him into my bedroom. "Don't you ever scare me like that again!"

"You bit me!" He accused, sucking on his bruised finger.

"What are you doing in my childhood room?"

Kiran pulled his finger away from his lips. "Giving you space."

My eyes narrowed suspiciously. "Don't you think Nan will find it odd that there is a light on in there?"

"Don't be absurd, Rhiannon; I didn't turn the light on until she went to bed." He was watching me through thick lashes, rubbing his bruised fingers.

"You don't need a light." I huffed.

"Yes, but I prefer the light to the dark." He grinned, one corner of his mouth turning up into a crooked smile.

My eyes narrowed at him. "You still haven't explained why you scared me."

"I didn't mean to scare you. You called out to me." His bright silver eyes twinkled in the low light.

"You infuriate me! You know that?" Infuriating, annoying, and insufferable...that's what he was. My chest began to burn. Other words echoed in my mind. The kind of words that would make me admit there was something else driving my sharpness besides just being mad.

"Do I?" He shook his head as a little laugh escaped him. "But if someone else had been here instead of me—maybe ready to hurt you—you would be singing a different tune right now, wouldn't you?"

He let one slender finger trace my eyebrow. It's not just tracing my eyebrow ....no, it's sliding down my cheek in reverence, like it's mapping out every inch of my face to memory.

He smirks, and my stomach clenches. "It seems like you only want me when it's convenient for you," he murmurs, his voice low and dark.

His breath brushes against my lips, and I can feel the heat of them and the overwhelming presence of him.

"That isn't true. You are twisting things all around." I say, but my voice is shaking, trembling like a leaf in a hurricane.

His finger lingered on my chin, and I swear, it's not just an electric current anymore—it's a firestorm, burning me alive from the inside out.

He watches me curiously as an odd warmth creeps over my body. "Can you feel that?" I ask, my voice barely audible, like I'm afraid of the answer.

He moves his arm, but I grab it and hold it in place. He's stronger than me. He could throw me across the room if he wanted to, but he doesn't. No, he stays there, his hand trapped against my face, his breath coming faster and hotter.

"You do, don't you?" I challenge him, "That is why you did that. Am I some sort of experiment for you?"

The shocking heat intensified, and I squirmed like my body had already surrendered to him, even if my mind was still fighting it.

I felt him tremble like he was the weak one, not me. "I would never hurt you or use you like an experiment. But sometimes, when I push my own boundaries, you get caught up in them too. I apologize for that." His voice was pleading, and he tried to remove his hand again, but I kept it there. "Forgive me, Rhiannon."

"Tell me what this is then," I demand, pressing his hand tightly against my face as the energy surges through me, crackling like lightning, like it's alive. Instantly, his other hand was on my cheek, and the force of it nearly knocked me off my feet. He must have sensed me faltering because almost immediately, he wrapped his arm around my waist and pulled me so close I could feel every inch of him. My hands landed on his chest, and there was a moment when I wasn't sure if either of us was breathing.

His hot breath glided along my face as he spoke. "I'm sworn to protect you and don't want any other path," he growls. "But you are the one thing that can weaken me, Rhiannon. How can I guard you when I'm not strong around you?"

My heart is threatening to burst out of my chest at his words.

"And there's the added problem of your supernatural powers." He continued as his body shook in my embrace. "Even as a baby, you could see me even when I didn't show myself. You followed me around everywhere." His hand moved across my face in a tender caress, leaving behind trails of electricity in its wake.

My mind wandered back to when I was a child, trying to recollect a guardian angel, but when he was near me like this, all I thought of was being closer to him. My senses returned, and I stood up straight again, but his arm remained on my waist.

"No." I leaned forward, pushing him against the wall with my body. While I was tall for a girl, my head only reached just below his chin. "How am I making you weak? Am I hurting you somehow? Do I affect your power? Because it seems to me I am the one who feels weak, and you are the one holding me up. It always seems that way." Every breath I took felt like it was burning a giant hole in my chest. "Please tell me," I begged.

He shifted closer, shaking his head slowly and biting on his lower lip, "How come you can't see what's right in front of you? You're so intuitive in other ways."

I didn't know what to say as we stared at each other. Something real and intoxicating pulled me closer to him. I wanted to kiss him. The pull I felt overcame me.

"Rhiannon," he whispered, my name- a prayer on his lips, and I know it's coming. I know he's going to kiss me, and I'm ready for it.

I'm craving it.

I slowly turned so our lips were almost touching, our breaths mingling. The only sound in the room was the air conditioner humming away in the background until my phone buzzed on the nightstand, jolting me out of my trance. Kiran took advantage of my distraction and moved off the wall and back towards the window.

My phone vibrated again, the vibration moving it across the glossy wood of the stand.

"Grab it before it falls." Kiran's voice broke the silence between us. He stood motionless by my window, my bed separating us.

Another buzz came, and I grabbed the phone before it dropped onto the hard floor.

"I'm around the corner." It was Justin, of course. I looked up and met Kiran's eyes. I had one beautiful angel in my room, my heart still straining against my ribs. I begged him with my eyes to tell me what to do, to tell me what I needed so badly to know.

What was this between us?

"Rhi?" Justin's voice pulled me back, and I tried to catch my breath. "Is it safe for me to come up now?"

"I'm sorry, Justin. Nan was up late watching movies," I whispered into the phone, glancing back at Kiran. He held my gaze silently. "I'll come down and meet you."

Part of me knew that I couldn't let Justin up here, not now. Even though I knew Kiran would leave us, it didn't feel right.

"I'll be parked across the street." I hung up abruptly.

"You're going to meet him," Kiran stated firmly, his silver eyes sparked with a bright intensity as they locked onto mine.

"I promised earlier that I would see him," I muttered, grabbing my shorts from the floor. Kiran turned away discreetly. Without bothering with a bra, I threw on the top I had worn earlier. I wasn't planning on being gone long.

"Don't go," he begged quietly. He seemed to reach for me without moving.

"Are you going to give me a reason not to?" I asked him pointedly.

He didn't answer. I waited for him to come to me, wrap his arms back around me, and give me the reason I yearned to hear. But he remained where he was.

Taking a deep breath, I slipped on my shoes.

Well, I guess not.

He was at the door when I turned to leave, and I gasped. "I'll be there to protect you." He seemed like there was more he wanted to say, but he didn't.

"I know that, Kiran," I said in a shaky voice.

I walked past him, my arm brushing his, and electricity jolted through me again. I touched the chilled brass doorknob and opened it to inhale the cool evening air. I saw the familiar car waiting for me across the street.

"You can't protect my heart," I spoke in a low voice to myself. I had no idea if he heard me or if he would know that my heart needed protecting from him, also.

Chapter Twenty

I sank into the Cadillac's plush leather seat, and Justin pulled me close. "Hey Rhi, I missed you," he said, kissing my forehead.

"It's only been a few hours," I replied with a laugh.

"Yes, but I didn't want to leave you. I never want to leave you, not when you're warm and soft in my arms like this."

I pulled away from him, feeling guilt wash over me. I was just pressed against Kiran, wanting desperately to kiss him.

I was such a mess.

"What did I do?" His perfect eyebrows knit together with worry.

"Nothing. Where should we go?"

"We could always go to my house." The thought of being alone with Justin in his bedroom made me nervous.

"I don't think I should be out too long," I said. "I'm really tired."

"How about we just head down to the res?"

"That works." I smiled awkwardly up at him.

Justin threw the car into gear, cranked up the radio, and settled his arm around me as I leaned into him.

The drive wasn't far, and when we reached the reservation, I was shocked to see how many cars were there. "Don't the people in this town have anything better to do than hang out at the reservation?" I murmured as we drove by the parked vehicles.

"Not really."

Justin drove us out of the crowd and further into the forest. He pulled off onto a side road and shut off the car, leaving only the radio softly playing in the background. A sense of déjà vu overcame me. It was like the night I was out here with Steve and felt the gentle touch on my shoulder and the voice in my head. Back then, I didn't know it was Kiran. Now I knew it was my flesh-and-blood angel. I shivered.

"You're cold?" Justin asked.

"No, no. It's just so dark out here." I scanned the encroaching forest around us.

"You're scared?" he chuckled mockingly at me.

"It's not funny!" I punched him lightly in the shoulder. "Rhi, there are at least half a dozen other cars out here; we just can't see them....which is the point." His emerald eyes fixed on me again like a cat's.

"You have such interesting eyes," I said.

"Interesting, hmmm?"

His fingers drew my hair back away from my ear, and he kissed me softly near the base of my jaw.

"Beautiful like emeralds, but so watchful like a cat's." I stuttered out.

He nuzzled my ear. "I like the beautiful part."

I shivered involuntarily.

"You are the beautiful one though." He whispered against my ear, and my heart did a little skip.

I glanced outside the window, not knowing how to accept his compliments. My mind went to Kiran. I had just been with him, and now I was here with Justin. What was I doing? I was so conflicted as I thought about Kiran begging me not to go.

His plea not to leave him had been so fraught with emotion that it was impossible to ignore. But what did he mean exactly? Was it an unguarded moment confessing his feelings for me?

"Earth to Rhi." Justin teased. "Where did you go?"

I looked up into his emerald eyes, staring at me with concern. "I...well..." I stammered. "I just don't think you really know all about me." I hesitated, thinking of Kiran again.

He hummed thoughtfully. "I know enough," he said, smirking at me. "And I like what I see." He leaned in for a kiss, slow and deliberate, as if he had all the time in the world and wanted to spend it all kissing me.

God help me, I was weak when it came to boys. Human or angel.

I wrapped my arms around his neck and breathed in his earthy scent. I felt his silky hair against my cheek when I saw a strange light out of the corner of my eye. I squinted to try and make out what it was. It was a person with a foggy glow around them. It was definitely not Kiran. I strained my eyes more to try to get more detail, and then it hit me.

It was Sam. It was Sam with tattered grey wings! My stomach flipped. This was impossible. It couldn't be Sam. I could hear a whispering voice that sounded familiar yet distant. The fog swirled around him, and it began to crawl along the ground closer to the car. I squinted harder and noticed the wings looked almost transparent, as if made of mist themselves. The whispering grew louder, and I realized it was coming from Sam. He spoke in a language I didn't recognize. It had a soothing, but eerie quality to it.

A gasp escaped my lips, and Justin chuckled. "Don't worry, Rhi, my hands will stay on your back."

"It's not that! Look!" I said, pointing out the window to where Sam stood in the increasingly thick fog.

Justin turned to look out the window. His expression seemed intent as he squinted his eyes. "It's just the fog. That's no surprise around here."

"No, not the fog, Justin." I persisted, pointing towards Sam, who was standing in the distance. The fog seemed like it was coming directly towards me, causing goosebumps to erupt over my arms. "Sam is over there."

He swiveled in his seat to take a better look. "I don't see anyone, Rhi."

I blinked hard to clear my eyes and looked again, scanning the trees around us, and I couldn't spot a soul. He was just right there!

Suddenly, Kiran's voice filled my head. *"Tell Justin you need to get home."*

Justin grinned at me slyly before speaking. "Ready to pick up where we left off?"

The sense of dread remained, and I believed Kiran was trying to keep me from something other than Justin. "I...I think it's time for me to go home," I stammered nervously.

Justin eyed me with uncertainty and turned on the ignition of the Cadillac. "Then I'll take you home."

I sank down into the seat as we drove, leaving the mist behind and passing all the kids hanging out in the parking lot. I couldn't shake off the feeling that something was watching me. I turned to Justin and asked, "Do you ever feel that there is something out there that isn't right? Like, there's something out there that's not human?"

Justin let out a chuckle. "You've been watching too many horror movies, Rhi. There's nothing out there but animals and trees."

"But what if there's more than that? What if there are things out there that we can't explain?" I persisted.

Justin rolled his eyes and groaned. "You're starting to sound like Mia. Maybe it wasn't a great idea bringing you out on Thirteen Witches Road." His arm had been sitting snugly over my shoulders, and he pulled me closer so my head rested on his chest. "Trust me, I've been exploring these woods for years, and I've never seen anything out of the ordinary."

I wanted to believe him, but the feeling of unease in my stomach wouldn't go away.

As we drove up to Nan's house, Mia sat on her porch and waved at us as Justin slid the car into the park. Sitting beside her was Sam.

I gasped, and Justin turned to face me. "What's the matter? You look like you see a ghost."

Searching my eyes, he turned in the direction I was looking. "Well, look at that. Sam is right here, so he couldn't have been in the forest."

"I guess you're right," I replied hesitantly, yet the feeling of unease only intensified within me.

Finally tearing my gaze away from Sam, I looked up at Justin. He had a slight grin on his lips as he gently kissed my forehead. "I had a great time tonight." His searching gaze met mine, silently pleading for any hint at what was going through my mind.

"I did, too," I replied, forcing a slight smile that barely masked my inner turmoil.

Without hesitation, Justin leaned in and pressed his lips against mine in a tender kiss. It was a gentle and lingering touch that made my heart melt.

Stepping out of the car, a rush of cool night air enveloped me, carrying with it the scent of dew-covered grass and the distant sound of crickets. Trying not to be noticed, I glanced over at Mia and Sam on the porch as I walked by them. Sam held my stare, and as I sped up my pace towards the door, I swore that he winked at me.

I was quiet as a mouse as I slid the key into the lock and gently pushed open the door. I took a deep breath and let it out slowly. The house smelled like Nan's perfume, and I felt like the walls welcomed me back home.

Kiran appeared at the base of the stairs that led up to my room. He held his hand out to me. "Come."

I locked the front door behind me and reached for his hand. We walked up the steps silently, and he pushed my bedroom door open with a reassuring smile. The candle he had brought me was lit, and the scent of lavender lifted from its flame, glazing over the wood of my nightstand in a pool of yellow light.

My curtains were closed, and I turned a questioning eye to him as he shut my door gently. "Kiran, I..." My voice trembled as I spoke. The questions burned in my mind. He took my hand gently in his own and pulled me towards the bed.

"Sit," he insisted, his voice like velvet.

I could hardly move, but I did as he said. I crossed my legs beneath me and leaned against the headboard. "Am I going insane?" I asked, my voice trembling in fear.

Kiran shook his head slowly and replied softly, "No, you are not."

"But I saw Sam in those woods; I saw him! What is he?" I blurted out.

Kiran placed a finger against my lips to silence me. "I know what you saw; that is why I was so insistent on getting you out of there." Kiran sighed heavily before continuing to hold my gaze with his own. "He is an Ancient One, one of the Watchers."

"The W-what?" I stammered.

"The Watchers were the original sons and daughters of the Creator - some confuse them with the fallen angels. Yes, they disobeyed orders, but they are not the same."

My head was spinning. "Why can I see his wings?"

He sighed heavily and took one of my hands, gently rubbing my palm. "I'm not sure." His face had looked heavy with emotion as he spoke. "I again have done something I shouldn't."

"I hope you didn't do this something because of me," I said.

My eyes focused on him in the candlelight.

"I will do anything for you." He said with conviction. He touched my cheek as his silver eyes searched mine and seemed to caress my soul. "You know this, don't you?"

I did.

"Let me continue about the Watchers, and then I will get to the rest." The silence swelled between us until he spoke again. His thumb continued a rhythmic massaging of my hand.

"Their name is what they were charged to do- watch. They were to watch humanity and report back what they observed." The candlelight danced along his striking features, and I felt that need again, that pull to be as close as I could to him.

"You see, Rhi," he said softly, "Angels have free will, just like humans." He glanced down to where our hands were entwined. His lashes fell against his cheeks like gentle wings, and he sighed quietly.

"Kiran. What is bothering you?"

He shook his head slowly. "Hush, Rhi," he said quietly, "you did nothing. It is my own actions." He glanced back up at my face. "As I was saying, the Watchers were the first of our kind to have any contact with humanity. They were supposed to just watch, but they started to feel protective of their humans. So, instead of just observing them, some decided they would appear to the humans to whom they had a particular affinity." His eyes searched mine for understanding.

"You mean they fell in love with humans?"

He swallowed thickly before nodding. "Some, yes. In the beginning, it was more like lust," he murmured softly as his gaze slid away from me for a second. "We angels don't..." He seemed to be searching for words again before finally settling on ones he thought appropriate for what we were talking about. "We don't engage in physical acts with each other." His cheeks seemed to blush in the low light.

I tentatively touched his head and slid my fingers through his silky hair as I said, "I'm sorry." All I could think about was how sad it must be to never even get to hug someone you cared about or receive any physical affection that most people take for granted every day. "It must be hard on all of you. It doesn't seem very fair."

Turmoil swirled within his eyes. His voice was barely a whisper, yet it felt like a hammer against my soul. "Yes, it is hard to fight, and I have lost that fight with you."

He squeezed our intertwined fingers, pressing them so tightly that his knuckles went white. "I don't think I could ever go back to not feeling your touch," he said, desperation filling his voice, and that electricity sparked between us again.

My hand reflexively lifted to his face in a caress of comfort. "Same."

He pulled my hand away from his cheek and rested it next to my other one in his grasp. His firm grip held both in place as he spoke, "Rhi, the Watchers, they married humans and had children with them. Those children are called the Nephilim, half angel, half human."

I lowered my eyes, thinking of what I read online.

"It's in many holy texts, but humanity doesn't like to teach those stories." He hesitated before adding, "When I told you in the woods that Sam was not what he seemed, it's because he is a Watcher."

My voice cracked with emotion. "Oh no! Mia! Do you think he wants Mia that way?"

"No, Mia is not interested in him that way, and regardless of our transgressions, no angel would force a human into anything they didn't ask for."

"How do you know this?"

"I knew who Sam was the minute I saw him. We have a sort of aura that only other supernatural beings can see. I knew about Mia and her family's origins since I watched over you when you lived with your grandmother before." He stopped massaging my hands and moved to sit closer to me. His voice was low and serious. "Mia practices witchcraft. Sam and other Watchers have taught humans sorcery and charms for thousands of years. They also taught humans how to use herbs, make weapons, use astrology, and many forbidden things. That knowledge was only meant for angels."

"But that doesn't seem so bad; why was it forbidden?" I asked, confused.

"Because having that knowledge could be used for good but also for evil." He paused before continuing. "In the end, the Watchers are the ones responsible for evil in this world."

I couldn't help but scoff in disbelief. "Wait, what? I thought Eve eating an apple and all that was the cause of evil in the world."

His eyes burned with conviction as he replied. "There are many stories from all over the world about the cause of evil, but I can assure you it does not fall solely on one act by Eve."

I stared at him, aghast. "So, witches and magic are real?"

"Don't let the name fool you. Sorcerer, wizard, witch - it's all the same." He let out a quiet laugh and leaned in even closer to me. "Witch is a human term. Those who are taught how to speak to spirits, heal with plants, and have knowledge of the future terrify some people. Whatever name you want to use, they're all people who've been taught by the Watchers or had the knowledge passed down from previous learners. Mia is one such person."

"Does she know what Sam is?" I asked urgently.

"No," he sighed. "She believes him to be no more than a classmate who shares similar interests."

My shoulders slumped, and my eyes drifted shut as a million thoughts raced through my mind. Was it really true that witches existed - or at least people who could cast magical spells? The idea seemed surreal, but so did angels to me until Kiran.

Kiran continued to speak. "Some Watchers became a great warrior race. Those who still believed in protecting the human soul stood together in a battle against the Watchers that sided with demons that sought to devastate humanity. Their skills in magic and combat were unmatched. They had no respect for human life, divine power, or any other angelic being; they only desired to make earth their kingdom and enslave its people. The first battles were long ago, but they still fight each other to this day.

"Which side is Sam on?" I asked.

"That is something I cannot answer," came his reply. "There is nothing that marks them as on the side of good or evil. I would have to engage with him to know and well..." He paused, leaning away from me slightly. "I want to watch him for now and see if I can gauge his intentions."

"I saw him in the forest; his wings were grey and tattered."

"That doesn't reflect what side he is on. It only indicates that he has not seen the other side of the veil in many years and has been tarnished by this side. He could still be a warrior for good. He will reveal his intentions when he chooses to, but, for now, stay away from him."

"I don't get the feeling he is trying to hurt me or is bad," I said.

Kiran got up and stood next to the window, which bathed him in delicate moonlight. God, he was beautiful. I stared at his slightly curved lips and began to think about how they would feel in other places besides my hand or my forehead.

The conversation we had earlier came back to me, and I felt I needed to talk to him about it. "Kiran?"

He turned to face me fully, his expression a mixture of understanding and anticipation. The room seemed to hold its breath as I grappled with finding the right words to express myself.

"Kiran," I began, my voice echoing slightly in the silence that had engulfed the room. "About earlier tonight...your words... I'm confused." My gaze held his, unblinking. His eyes were a well of emotion, a tumultuous ocean that was both alluring and terrifying.

He didn't respond but continued to look at me. A shaft of moonlight illuminated his face, casting a surreal glow on his features and highlighting the contours of his sharp jawline and tousled hair.

"I can't help but wonder," I continued slowly, "if there is something more you haven't told me." A hesitant pause followed, "About Justin. About....you..and... me."

The moonlight dancing in his eyes seemed to hide secrets beneath their surface. "Rhi," he finally spoke, "It's complicated."

"I can handle complicated," I encouraged him.

Kiran clenched his hands tightly at his sides as if grappling with an unseen force. "My feelings for you...they exist in a realm beyond my duty as your Guardian," He said after what felt like an eternity.

His admission hung in the room like an invisible tapestry. He had feelings for me, and as my heartbeat thundered in my ears, I knew deep in my soul that I had feelings for him as well. "I have spent countless nights watching you sleep, wondering about your dreams, mulling over your fears," he confessed, his voice strained. "I have seen inside your heart, and it has made me yearn for something I should not - cannot - have." His gaze flickered to mine momentarily before dropping to the floor.

A heavy sigh escaped him as he confronted something within himself. "But I am bound by my duty. My responsibility is to guide and protect you," He said softly but firmly. "For now, that is all I can be...all I should be."

"But—" I began, my voice tinged with a mixture of confusion and frustration. My hands reached out instinctively to touch him as I got to my feet.

He raised a hand gently, halting me mid-way. "Rhi," he interjected softly, his voice carrying an undertone of pain. "It's better this way."

The words hung heavy between us. His expression was one of profound sorrow. It was heartbreaking. There was a vulnerability about Kiran that shattered my heart and ignited a burning desire within me to soothe his torment.

"Kiran," I whispered his name like a sacred chant. His gaze immediately riveted towards me. "I know there is more to this than you are letting on." I gathered up my courage and spoke again. "I felt it before I left with Justin. We were so close to...." My voice began to shudder with emotion.

Kiran's face became an indecipherable mask as he processed my words. When he looked at me, his eyes flashed with an intense determination as he stepped forward with an armor of resolve.

"Rhiannon," he began resolutely, the softness in his voice replaced by a steely note that hinted at what was to come. "I have sworn to protect you... and I will continue doing so whether you accept it or not."

His words echoed around us in the quiet room, reverberating off the walls and wrapping themselves around me like constrictive vines. I knew better. What was I thinking? My face felt hot, and the back of my eyes burned.

"I'm going to the shore for the weekend," I said abruptly, my voice a soft tremor against the weighty silence that pervaded the room. "With Justin." The words came out far too quickly, like a hastily fired arrow.

"Justin," he echoed the name bitterly, "Rhi, you don't have to—"

"I know I don't have to," I interjected, my voice sounded more firm than I felt. "I want to."

"Alright then," he conceded, his tone carrying an ache that rippled through me. His hands were clenched, and for a brief moment, his guard slipped, allowing me to see the storm raging within him.

The emotions of the day were taking their toll on me. I returned to my bed, shoved my feet under the sheets, and plopped back against my pillow.

Kiran's voice broke through the silence once more, "Rhi?" The tenderness in his voice made my heart flutter uncontrollably within its cage.

"Yes?" I responded without turning around.

"I'm so sorry...my Ahavah." his voice was a hoarse whisper, and his words trailed off into the evening air like a promise sealed in the echoes of time, and I knew he was gone.

My dreams were scattered and confusing. I dreamt of kissing Justin in his car and then being yanked out and dragged up to the Witches Well. A bubble of panic rose up in my throat when our lips parted, and I lost sight of him.

Things began to swirl again, blurring into each other, and then I saw a group of people standing in a circle. The fog was thick, and I couldn't make out any of them except Sam.

I took a tentative step towards them when Sam suddenly came up behind me, putting his hand on my shoulder. "I wouldn't." He said, turning me to face him. His eyes were hollow even though his grin stretched across his face.

"Sam...what are you doing here?" I asked, not taking my eyes off him.

He put a finger to his lips as if to tell me to stay quiet. As close as he was, I could get a better view of his wings. They weren't beautiful, strong, and healthy like

Kiran's, nor were they the way Justin's had appeared in my dream. They looked weak and frail.

"But.." I protested.

"You are a stubborn one, aren't you?" He said, but did not wait for an answer before dissolving into the surrounding fog.

The next thing I knew, I was lying on the sand looking at a grey sky, unsure how I got there. The waves crashed against the shore, emitting a mesmerizing hum as they curled along the beach and into oblivion. Faintly in the distance, bells chimed. In front of me, the sun was rising, and the figure of an angel was silhouetted on the horizon.

I got up and sprinted towards Kiran, calling out to him as I ran. The sun crested over the horizon, its golden hues illuminating his enchanting beauty. His gaze locked onto mine, and he opened his arms in welcome. I leaped forward into his embrace, feeling his strong arms wrap around me.

"Do you remember how much you loved this as a child?"

He asked me, grinning as he spun me around like a top.

My smile widened, and then everything went dark. The world spun chaotically as freezing fear coursed through me. I screamed for Kiran, and his wings wrapped protectively around me, but a powerful force ripped him from my side.

Suddenly, Sam's voice echoed out of the abyss, "You can save him; you have the power."

I woke up to my heart pounding in my chest. Kiran was back with his arms protectively around me. I lay heavily upon his chest. The steady pace of his heart, strong against mine, comforts me. I looked up at the beauty of his face, his eyelashes softly grazing his cheeks.

"You're alright, sweet girl," he said, giving me a reassuring hug.

"Kiran?"

"Hmm?"

"Can you be taken from me?"

His eyes flew open. "Why would you ask that?"

"I had a dream—it was complex and all over the place, but in the end, we were falling into an endless darkness, and then someone ripped you away from me. I can't be one hundred percent sure, but I think it was Sam's voice saying that I could save you; I had the power."

Kiran shifted and positioned me tighter against his chest. I drew in a breath, smelling the scent of vanilla and flowers that was unique to him. Then I heard it, our souls singing to each other, humming at a single pitch. Peacefulness fell over me.

"Oh, Rhi," he sighed against my hair, "you saved me the second your soul called to mine, and that bond will forever save us no matter what the circumstance."

With that, all the anxiety about my dream fell away. A stronger emotion took its place, something deeper than simple happiness or satisfaction. Belonging settled into my bones, and I bathed in the feeling of it.

Deep primal feelings coursed through my blood. Whether I wanted them or not, they were there, and it scares the hell out of me.

Chapter Twenty-One

"Evangeline, her name is Evangeline." Taylor smiled down at her baby daughter.

"We can call her Eva for short," Steve said.

Taylor nodded and brushed a strand of hair from the baby's face. She spoke quietly, "Or maybe Eve."

"I like Eva better, though," I said, and my cousins turned to stare at me. "What? It just sounds prettier that way." I explained hastily.

The baby was snuggled in a swaddling blanket with tiny hands and feet peeking out. Her skin was cream colored, and her eyes were a dark blue.

"Come here, little Eva." Kacey reached for the baby, and Taylor carefully handed her to her sister.

Taylor had dark circles under her eyes, her golden locks twisted into a messy bun.

"Tay, why don't you take a nap? We'll watch over Evangeline." I said.

Heaviness seemed to be lifted from her shoulders. "Thank you, Rhi; I think I want to take a shower, though, if you are all okay watching her."

Kacey was gently rocking little Eva and answered before the rest of us, "Yes, yes... go shower, sis."

Steve plopped down in the corner chair, his eyes twinkling with mischievous-ness. "So, you two have been hatching a plan without me?" he said with a wide smile.

"What are you talking about?" Kacey asked, pausing her focus on her niece.

I rolled my eyes at him, remembering our conversation on the drive here.

"He wants us all to go?" Steve had asked while we were in the car, studying me skeptically.

"Of course he does," I replied nonchalantly.

"Mhmm hmm."

"What?" I said innocently.

"Let me guess. Justin wanted you to go away with him for the weekend, but you knew that would never fly with Nan. So then you thought of bringing us along?" Steve said wryly.

"Ugh, whatever." I groaned. "I want to spend time with all of you, and Justin said there was plenty of room..."

"Mhmm hmm," Steve replied again.

"He is teasing you, Rhi." Kacey had chimed in from her seat, "I already told him about it."

I laughed, feeling slightly embarrassed that my attempts at subtlety were not as sly as I thought they were. "Well, it's not just about Justin, you know. I want to spend time with all of you, and a weekend away seems like the perfect opportunity to do just that."

Steve shifted in his chair, leaning casually against his arm. "Okay, Rhi, I'm in."

Kacey gave me a warm smile before asking, "So, does this make it official?"

"What official?"

She sighed heavily. "That you and Justin are a couple, Rhi."

We heard Taylor coming down the stairs, looking refreshed and relaxed after her shower. "All right, I'm feeling much better now. How's my little Eva?" She turned towards me. "And Rhi, out with it about Justin."

I could hear Taylor's curiosity and concern as she approached. I took a deep breath, "Apparently, there's a rumor going around that Justin and I are dating, Tay."

She raised an eyebrow, intrigued. "Oh, really? And is there any truth to this rumor?"

I glanced over at Steve, who sat in the chair with arms folded across his chest; then my glance flitted to Kacey. Her smile was all teeth. They were all waiting for my answer. My cheeks felt red hot. I tried to keep my expression neutral, but inside I was freaking out.

Before I could say anything else, Justin himself appeared in the doorway with Scott at his heels. "What's all the talk about me and Rhi?" he asked, glancing back and forth between all of us.

Kacey chuckled as if she thought his question was hilarious. "That you two are a couple."

He just shrugged his large shoulders.

"Wow, you two are full of answers," Taylor said, taking Eva back from Kacey.

Scott and Justin made their way to the kitchen with the bags of groceries they had brought. As I sank into the couch, Taylor settled in beside me.

I glanced at the baby, whose eyes were shut, her tiny fists held close to her face. Justin and Scott returned from the kitchen. Justin nudged Kacey over so he could sit down beside me, putting an arm around me as he did so.

"So, you guys are all interested in our love life?" He said to everyone in the room.

"Love life?" Taylor snapped her attention to me and then back to Justin. "You better not be taking advantage of my cousin Justin."

"Look, Taylor, it's none of your business, but no, I'm not taking advantage of her. I care about her, and I think the feeling is mutual." His arm glided down my back, making small circles as he moved along my spine.

I quickly looked around at Kacey and Steve before answering. "Tay, I honestly don't know what this is between Justin and me. We spend time together and go out occasionally, but I wouldn't call it dating."

"Yeah, I wouldn't really call it that either." Justin agreed with a smirk.

Scott entered the living room and surveyed us all. "Whoa, it's like Antarctica in here. Um, what is up with all of you?"

Justin removed his arm from behind my back. "So, apparently, there's this rumor that Rhi and I are together. Neither of us would use those words, but we hang out a lot, and she seems to like it." He flashed me a smile. "Did I get it right, Rhi?"

I wanted to sink into a crevice in the couch. "Yeah, pretty much," I muttered without looking up.

Scott burst out laughing. "And that's it?"

Taylor glared at him. "That's enough," she said sharply.

Scott put up his hands in defense. "Okay, Mama Bear. I know how protective you are, but, honestly, sweetheart, it's not that big of a deal."

My eyes flew to Scott, and he winked at me.

Taylor shook her head and rolled her eyes. She jumped up from the couch, cradling Eva to her chest, and stomped past Scott to her room.

My conscience tugged at me for not telling them more about what was happening between Justin and me, but I couldn't explain it myself.

"Guess someone will be stuck on the couch tonight," Justin joked to his brother.

"I'm already on the couch, Bro. Taylor is up every couple of hours to feed the baby, and I need to get up for work, so it's just easier that way." His shoulders shrugged similarly to Justin's.

"Well, all the more reason for us to go away for the weekend, right, Justin?" Kacey elbowed him in the ribs, and he swatted her away like an annoying mosquito.

"If I had my way..." he started to say, but I cut him off.

"But you don't." His gaze met mine, and there was a hint of a smile on his lips.

I stood and made a beeline for Taylor's room to talk to her and escape the attention.

I tapped lightly on her door and twisted the knob, leaving the others still chatting. When I poked my head into the room, Taylor was rolled up into a tight ball on her bed with the curtains drawn. She looked like she was asleep, so I turned to leave, but then heard her muffled voice: "Rhi, why Justin?"

I stepped inside and sat down at the edge of her bed.

Fiddling with the strings of my cut-off shorts, I sighed before answering. "The truth is, I feel like he understands me."

She lifted her crystal blue eyes to meet mine. "And we don't?"

"I didn't say that," I stuttered out. Taylor's eyebrows creased together.

"Rhi, I understand what Justin has been through, and I feel for him, but everyone can use their struggles as an

opportunity to push themselves further. He hasn't done that—he lets it consume him instead."

"I see him differently than you do, Tay," I said softly, feeling a deep ache in my chest. "But don't worry; I'm careful with my heart. I learned long ago to protect it and keep it safe."

Taylor sat up on the bed and reached out to hug me.

There was a gentle rapping at the door, and Scott stepped inside. "I made lunch. You need to eat something, sweetheart."

Taylor stood to follow Scott. I called out before she made it to the door. "Oh, and Tay," I paused momentarily, my eyes locking with hers, their sky-blue depths tinged pink by lack of sleep. Her expression remained unreadable as I mentioned going to the shore next weekend and staying at Vince's. She smiled slightly and nodded, following Scott out of the room.

I waited patiently for Kacey to finally fall asleep. I saw a figure out of the corner of my eye pass through the beam of light streaming in from the door that I had left slightly open after I knew Kacey was sleeping. Seconds later, Justin opened the door and stepped in. I had started to reach for my flip-flops next to my bed, but he gestured for me not to bother and waved me over with his hand.

My palms felt clammy as I joined him. We sneaked outside, past the pool area, and towards the beach. The air was cool, and I shivered, thankful for my t-shirt over my swimsuit.

Justin was wearing his trunks but had no shirt or shoes on. I wasn't sure what he had planned, and curiosity gnawed at me.

Being on the beach in the dark felt strange, with only moonlight around us. Off to my right, I could make out the shimmering lights from down by the boardwalk and some of the other nearby houses whose balconies lined up along the shoreline. Vince's was by far the largest on this stretch of beach, though.

"Keep an eye out for jellyfish." Justin's voice was subdued, like it was swallowed by the night. He sounded younger than i'd ever heard him before.

"How can I watch when I can't even see where I'm going?" I said with a hint of sarcasm.

"Your eyes haven't adjusted yet? Hmm, I guess I'll just have to carry you, then," he replied before swinging me onto his shoulder.

I let out a squeal. After a few moments, he stopped and carefully slid my body over his bare chest before my feet touched the warm water.

"Oh! It's so warm!" I exclaimed.

"Of course it is. The sun's been heating it all day." He put his arm around my waist and kissed me tenderly.

"I guess it's been too long since I've gone to the beach." I sighed when he kissed my neck. "That, and it is a bit chilly out now."

"I will keep you warm," he said as his arm snaked around my back and scooped me off the ground. I had to cling to his neck as he twirled us around and around.

Justin lost his balance, and we both tumbled into the water with a loud splash.

He started laughing. "Sorry, I got dizzy. See what you do to me?"

The waves came in and out, lapping at our legs. Whenever the tide receded away from us, a tiny chilly breeze would send shivers across my skin.

Justin stood up and offered me his hand. "Well, this isn't what I had in mind. I was going to take you for a romantic walk on the beach, but instead, I just dropped you in the ocean. Sorry, babe."

The moonlight showed off the angles of his face and how at peace he seemed to be. I pushed Kiran out of my mind. This night was about me and Justin.

I smiled and placed my hand in his as he effortlessly lifted me off the sand, and I threw myself into his arms with abandon. His lips met mine, and I could tell he was surprised at first, but soon enough, he was kissing me back as feverishly as I was kissing him. His hands slid over my drenched t-shirt, which clung to my body. He pulled away from me, breathing heavily.

"I did have some other stuff in mind for tonight besides a walk. I still have time not to screw that up." He kissed my forehead. "Come on. You're freezing and wet, and I did promise to keep you warm."

My eyes had gotten used to the darkness by now, and we held hands as we returned to the house. His thumb was tracing circles over my knuckles in a calming rhythm. As I peered at him curiously, his silky hair blew gently in the breeze. Steve remarked that he rarely wore it down until recently. I knew he did that for me.

Just before reaching the house, I noticed a large blanket on the ground with numerous items atop it.

"I'll build you a small fire - sit," he said, handing me another blanket to keep warm. "Take off your t-shirt."

"What?" I asked in surprise.

"Relax, Rhi," he said with a contrite smile. "You won't get warm if your clothes are wet. Take it off and give it to me. I'll hang it on the fence."

Nervously, I did as he asked. I was wearing a bikini that Kacey had picked out for me, and although I was comfortable wearing it around everyone else at the pool, being alone with Justin made me feel exposed. I grabbed an extra blanket and pulled it tightly around me from neck to toe.

Justin got a small fire going in the circular pit next to us. He reached behind me and returned with something in his hands before sitting beside me. He offered me a white box tied with a slim golden ribbon.

"Justin, not more presents."

"Relax, it's just the box it came in. You eat it."

That piqued my interest. I untied the knot of the ribbon and opened up the lid of the box to find four huge chocolate-covered strawberries, fancily decorated.

"Ohhh."

"Did I do good?" He asked with a boyish grin.

I picked one up by its stem and bit into it. It was divine. "They're amazing, Justin," I said with delight.

"And they say the way to a man's heart is through his stomach. Maybe that goes both ways?" He teased.

I nodded in agreement and finished the strawberry, licking my fingers of juice and chocolate. "Did you happen to bring water?"

"I did." He leaned past me to search for it in the dark, his body pressing against mine and radiating warmth through the blanket around me. His arm reached back up, presenting me with a water bottle.

"You have some chocolate on your lips." He swept his thumb across my mouth.

"Justin I...."

"Shhhh." He hushed me. "I didn't bring you out here for that, although I wouldn't mind it at all." He winked at me. "When or if that happens, it will be your move."

That took me back to our kiss on the bridge in the rain. He wanted to make sure I wanted our relationship to begin; now, he was leaving it in my hands to see where it progressed.

"Don't couples usually make those decisions together?" I asked.

"I'm ready. I'm just waiting for when you are." His jade eyes glittered in the orange light of the fire.

A knot formed in my throat. Justin wasn't one for being tactful.

"I didn't mean to make you nervous." His thumb moved from its place at the corner of my lip, tracing along the contour of my face. He cupped the back of my head with his hand, and I thought he would kiss me again, but instead, he started to massage my neck with gentle strokes, kneading away all of the tension that had built up there.

"Rhi, relax, please. I won't do anything you don't want me to do."

My mind reeled, and muscles low in my stomach clenched tightly. This was real. He wasn't an angel. He was human. That made sense. Having anything romantic with Kiran did not.

His fingers continued to move up and down my neck. I let out a low groan when he hit a particularly sore spot. "You're wound tighter than a top," He said.

I leaned back into his touch even more. "That feels so wonderful," I breathed, "So this is what getting a massage feels like."

A hint of surprise flashed across his face. "You've never had one before?"

"No."

"Never?"

"No, Justin, never."

"Unwrap yourself from this thing."

My eyes flew open, and I stared at him.

"I can do it better if you move this blanket and I sit behind you." He wiggled his fingers in front of me. "Two hands work better."

I pulled myself free of the blanket. I felt a bit self-conscious as I realized his eyes were on my nearly bare flesh. He smiled reassuringly and patted the ground between his legs.

I sat down obediently and crossed my legs in front of me.

He reached over and threw the discarded blanket over me.

"Snuggle up. I'll keep you warm from back here."

My gaze stayed fixed on the flames of the fire burning near us. Justin's experienced hands moved my hair over my shoulder, but he lingered there, gliding his fingers across my skin so softly it was like the touch of a butterfly wing. His hands worked over the muscles in my neck and then made their way down to my shoulders. He didn't speak, and neither did I.

The fire suddenly popped and threw sparks into the night sky; he paused to throw another small log into the burning embers before resuming his manipulations on my shoulders. I held my breath as his fingers slipped over the string that tied at my back, holding my bikini top in place. His fingers dipped lower, kneading the muscles that lined my vertebrae.

His chin was suddenly resting on my shoulder. "Breathe, Rhiannon," he said in a gentle voice.

He never called me by my full name, and I glanced over my shoulder at him. "Are you trying to seduce me, Justin?" I exhaled shakily.

He fixed his gaze on me, his eyes serious. "Can you think of no other reason why I would do all this for you? Why I would bring you here tonight like this?"

"I'm sorry, Justin," I whispered.

He lifted his head from my shoulder and pulled me closer to his chest. His skin was hot and hard against my back, prompting a gasp from me at the sudden intimacy. He tangled his fingers in my hair, resting them on either side of my head while caressing my cheeks with his thumbs.

"I know that everyone wants you to stay away from me, and maybe you should. I'm not what anyone would call a nice guy."

I wanted to say something, but the look on his face suggested I remain quiet and let him speak.

"When I want something, I get it, and I want you," he said.

"I don't give a damn about a lot of people in this life, not even myself half the time, but I meant what I said out there." He motioned with his head towards the ocean. His voice dropped lower. "About my heart."

My own heart skipped a beat.

"It feels like my heart has been trapped in a vice for years, with an indescribable ache that sometimes turns into emptiness and desolation so intense that I can barely leave my bed in the morning." He said as he caressed my face. "But since you were dropped in my life by some sort of angel, the pain is getting better. I meant it when I said you make my heart whole."

Why did he have to say, angel? My eyes closed at the rush of unwanted tears.

"I'm no angel, Justin."

He kissed me lightly and whispered against my lips, "Well, you're mine. I love you."

My heart stuttered, the words rebounding in my head like a pinball.

Love.

That four-letter word felt heavy, sinking deep into the pit of my stomach like a stone in water. His fingers linger on my cheek, the heat of his touch making me shiver.

I want to believe him. Want to lose myself in his declaration and drown out everything else from my mind. But my heart's been broken too many times before and threaded back together with shaky hands, only to be torn apart again.

I was no angel that could save him from his trauma, no balm for his wounds. Yet, as Justin held me close to him, his heartbeat thundering in our shared silence seemed to say otherwise. Could a broken girl like me genuinely ease the torment of someone bruised by life's harsh realities?

Chapter Twenty-Two

I stirred awake. I was pulled from a deep slumber by the caw of seagulls outside. I flipped over to cover my ears from the annoying sound and caught a glimpse of the clock on the nightstand shining at me.

"Darn it." I moaned, realizing I had slept half the day away. Closing my eyes for another moment, I thought of last night. I hoped I hadn't hurt his feelings by not responding to the "L" word. My emotions were still so confusing. We fell asleep next to the fire until the sky grew lighter. In the dark, predawn hours, a silhouette of angel wings stood out against the colorful sunrise like a pillar of light.

Kiran.

I groaned to myself again. That was precisely what Kiran was to me. He was a pillar of light and strength for me. I had carefully removed myself from Justin's embrace while he snored lightly, wrapped tightly in the blanket in the sand.

Walking down to the water's edge, where Kiran stood. Sparkles of light bounced off his wings as though they were brilliant diamonds. I reached out and touched them with care. He turned, letting his wing sweep over me.

I looked up to meet his gaze. His silver eyes were always intense, but now they held something new, an emotion I hadn't seen before. A flicker of something smouldered underneath that familiar devotion of his. The rawness in his eyes felt surprisingly real, human-like in their sincerity.

"I've always loved the mornings and the sea," he said, eyes scanning my face as if reading something written there.

The water swirled around our feet as the tide came in, yet it was not the cold that chilled me. The sun rose over the waves, glaring into my eyes; Kiran noticed my squinting and spread his wings to full glory. I had never seen anything so beautiful. I felt myself being pulled closer to him as he averted his gaze.

"Kiran," I whispered, "What's wrong?"

"I'm fine," he replied, although his voice sounded strained.

"I wish you would let me in," I said softly, locking my gaze with his.

His eyes softened then, and he gazed at me quietly for a long moment, "Please just take it slow with Justin," and then he was gone, and I could feel the sun burning my skin where he'd stood just moments before.

I ran my fingers through my hair with a long sigh. "God, why am I so confused?"

"Confused about what?" Kacey asked from the doorway, holding a sandwich in her hand.

I threw the blankets off and stumbled out of the bed. "Are you going to eat that all, or can you share?" I asked with a voice hoarse from a night in the salty air.

Kacey stepped away from the doorway and tore off a piece of her sandwich, holding it out for me. "I'll share if you tell me where you went last night and why you're so confused now."

I took the sandwich and gobbled it down as fast as I could. "I don't know what you mean," I mumbled through a mouthful of ham, cheese, and mayonnaise.

Kacey strode past me and reclined on the bed. "Don't try to play innocent with me, Rhi. I knew the second you left and the second you came back."

I sighed as Kacey continued to stare at me. I knew she wouldn't let it go until I told her where I had been all night.

"Alright, alright," I said with a groan. Justin and I went for a walk on the beach. I fell into the ocean. He made a fire, and we fell asleep. nothing happened."

"And..." She said with an eyebrow raised in suspicion.

I tossed my head back, gazing out of the window. The sky was a pastel blue canvas dotted with sporadic fluffy white clouds. The air smelled of the beach – of salty breeze and coconut-scented tanning lotion.

I swallowed hard, "And he...he said that he...loved me."

Kacey let out a little squeal and plopped down on the bed beside me. She motioned for me to continue. catching onto this, I added hastily, "But you can't just go blabbing about it." She stuck out her lower lip, pouting prettily. "I mean it, Kace; please don't say anything to anyone, especially Justin."

I felt a flush creep up my face as I recalled the beach under the moonlight, the rhythm of the waves resonating with our heartbeats. Justin's confession still echoed in my ears: "I love you, Rhi."

"You're blushing!" Kacey exclaimed. She rolled onto her side, staring at me intently. "It sounds so romantic!"

"I guess so."

"Wait, you guess so? What is that supposed to mean?" Kacey poked me in the arm, and I turned to look at her.

Just as she opened her mouth to say something else, we were interrupted by Taylor breezing into the room. Her sun-bleached hair was pulled into a high ponytail, and she wore an airy sundress over her bathing suit. "What are you two up to?" Taylor inquired suspiciously.

"Nothing," I lied quickly before Kacey could blurt out what I had just told her.

Taylor's eyes narrowed as though she knew we were hiding something from her. "Nothing? Really? Would this nothing have anything to do with the fire pit made last night?"

My throat felt dry, and my tongue seemed stuck to the roof of my mouth as I stammered, "What fire pit?"

"Rhi..." Taylor said my name softly but with an undertone of disapproval, like a parent scolding their child for misbehaving.

"Fine, Justin and I had gone for a walk by the ocean. As always, I tripped over my feet and found myself in the water. He built a fire. End of story. Like I was telling Kacey...."

Kacey's eyes lit up with excitement. "Justin told her he loves her!" she blurted out.

Taylor's head snapped towards Kacey. "He actually said love, Rhi?"

I buried my face in my hands, groaning into my palms. "Ugh, yes."

My cheeks felt hot and flushed as I peered out between my fingers nervously at my two cousins staring intently at me.

But before Kacey could start her next unwanted sentence, I whispered solemnly: "I didn't say it back."

Once again, both heads snapped in my direction, and they exclaimed in unison: "What?!"

Taylor moved to sit beside me on the bed, pulling my hands away from my face. "Why not, Rhi?" She asked softly.

"I don't know," I answered truthfully.

Kacey huffed. "Trust me, you do. You've had a thing for him since the moment you laid eyes on him; you just don't want to admit it."

I let out a deep sigh, feeling emotional and vulnerable. "I don't know if I do love him. I mean, I care about him so much, and we have this connection, but I'm scared. What if I say it back and it doesn't work out? What if it ends badly and then there is always this weirdness between us?"

Kacey put a hand on my arm. "Rhi, you can't live your life in fear. Sometimes, you must take risks and put your heart on the line. Otherwise, you'll never know what could have been."

Taylor looked worried.

"What Tay?" I asked.

"Listen to me," Taylor said, taking my hands in hers. "If you don't love him back, it's okay. You don't have to force yourself to feel something you don't. I mean, I can't say for sure, but I don't ever remember Justin saying he loved any girl. But, and that's a big but, he may just be saying it to get what he wants."

I felt a lump form in my throat. Taylor's words may have been valid, but they still stung. I shook my head, trying to clear the thoughts from my mind.

"Thanks, Taylor. I appreciate the concern, but I don't think Justin is trying to use me in any way."

Kacey sat on the bed beside me, throwing an arm over my shoulders. "She is right, Rhi. As excited as I am for you, you still should be careful with him. He's had a lot of trauma in his life, and he may not know how to handle his emotions properly. You don't want to get hurt."

"I know, I'll be careful," I said, trying to sound convincing.

They both wrapped their arms around me and gave me a giant bear hug, and it warmed my soul that they cared so much for me.

Chapter Twenty-Three

The sun was beginning to set as we packed up our belongings and prepared to head back home. The gentle breeze carried the salty scent of the ocean, and I knew I would miss it. Justin hadn't uttered those three little words again, but his touch and lingering glances spoke volumes.

The traffic was surprisingly light as Justin and I drove home. The beach trip had been a refreshing escape from reality. It was also the first time a boy had told me he loved me-well, besides Kiran, but I wasn't sure if that counted.

With the windows rolled down, we sang along to songs on the radio. Every so often, I would steal a glance at Justin and find his lips curved into a small smile. He seemed genuinely happy. As we approached our exit on the highway, he turned to me and said he needed to stop by the shop and drop off the keys to the beach house. "It won't take long," he reassured me as he reached for my hand once again. "It's on the way."

We had taken the exit three down from mine, venturing into a part of town I had never been to before. The neighborhood was grimy and neglected—graffiti marked nearly every wall, and a few homeless people huddled under sparse trees that lined both sides of the street. "You work around here?" I asked him hesitantly.

Surprised at my question, he quirked an eyebrow in surprise before responding with an amused grin. "Yep...are you scared?"

Shrugging nonchalantly, I replied honestly, "Not really. I know how it feels to be sleeping on the streets." Turning again to take in our surroundings, I added, "Most people on the streets are just in a bad place in their lives, trying to survive."

His face softened with compassion. "You slept on the streets? Rhi, I didn't know that." His words were laced with genuine concern as he reached out to squeeze my hand gently.

"It was only a few times. Mostly, I ended up on a friend's couch or floor when my stepfather was drunk or in a particularly bad mood." I glanced downwards at my hands, twisting them in my lap. I felt the heat of embarrassment radiating from my skin. "I guess that's part of why I ended up here."

Justin's emerald green eyes flickered with an emotion I couldn't quite place as he spoke in a soothing tone, "You're safe now. No more sleeping on the streets or floors." A small smile tugged at the corners of his lips as he added, "I've slept in some pretty sketchy places myself."

We stopped in a parking lot outside an imposing industrial building with a bright neon sign reading 'Vince's Automotive.' On one wall, covered by years of weathering, were faint words proclaiming, 'We Do Repossessions!'

"I was so angry when I found out about Vince being my biological father," Justin confessed. "First, I was furious with my mother for cheating on Rick, who will always be my father to me. Then I was upset with Rick for forgiving my mom and letting me believe he was my dad. And then...well, then I just wanted to hurt Vince for tearing my family apart." His gaze drifted towards the building, his jaw tense with unresolved resentment.

"But you work with him now," I said.

He merely shrugged in response while still gazing at the building. "I thought about seeking him out and punching him in the face. But when I finally mustered up enough courage to walk into the shop and saw him, it was like looking in a mirror. He was my father; there was no denying it. He accepted me, but despite being a physical twin to him, I had no desire to turn into the kind of man he is."

He turned to me then, his eyes meeting mine. "Anyway, it was during this period that I felt like an outcast, and I would stay in abandoned buildings with the homeless and drug addicts, so I get how you feel. Vince saw me one day coming out of one of the abandoned buildings. He jumped out of his car while it was still running, slamming me against the brick wall."

My heart pounded in my chest as I gasped in shock and concern. "Did he hurt you?" I asked, my hand instinctively reaching out to touch his arm.

His laugh was like velvet, soft and rich. "No, he didn't hurt me," he explained, his voice tinged with amusement. "But we did exchange a few punches." He was right in my face, saying if I wanted to hate him, my family, and the world, that was fine, but he wouldn't let me destroy myself. He offered to let me come live with him, and when I refused, he said I could sleep on the couch in his office at the shop. At least I would be safe. I took him up on his offer and got to see how his business ran, and eventually, he gave me a job. I did eventually return home to my mother's house. It was Scott who convinced me that I should. I think he was the only one who was even close to as angry as I was, but because he loved our parents and our family, he wanted to try to mend the bridges."

Our conversation was interrupted as someone burst out from inside the garage and quickly climbed into one of the tow trucks parked outside. "I'll be back soon." He kissed me quickly before leaving the car and disappearing inside the building.

I waited, listening to the radio and studying the surroundings. The radio was playing an old classic rock song, and I tapped along with the beat of the music with my foot.

I had been to the police station Uncle Nick worked at, and if I recall correctly, it was also somewhere around here. His stories of the horrid things he encountered as a detective were all set close to this area.

Suddenly, I felt a gentle touch on my shoulder, breaking me out of my thoughts. "It's okay, Kiran," I reassured him. "I was just remembering Uncle Nick's stories. But I'm not afraid."

"Anyone would feel uneasy and afraid here, Rhi," Kiran replied, his voice full of understanding. I peered around at the buildings and tiny homes surrounding us. In some buildings, windows had been shattered, but there were also houses where people sat outside laughing while children played. It couldn't be that bad.

"They're just people, Kiran," I said, continuing to tap my foot to the music.

"Well, I see more than you."

I swiveled in my seat to face him, my eyes narrowed in intense curiosity. "What do you mean?"

Kiran's hand reached out and gently rested on my shoulder. The touch brought a strange warmth, spreading like a comforting embrace. His silver eyes seemed to glimmer with knowledge and experience beyond my own understanding, peering into unseen corners of the world invisible to my own sight.

Before he could elaborate, I caught movement in my peripheral vision. Justin's arm lifted in a lazy arc through the doorway, motioning me forward.

He stood just inside the scarred wooden door, hair falling into his eyes.

I smiled at him, grabbed the keys, and climbed out of the car, Kiran's gentle presence at my back as he hurried to catch up.

As soon as I walked inside, the scent of oil hit me. The front room was small but neat: magazines were spread out on a table, a coffee machine hummed in the corner, and an empty desk stood nearby, facing large windows that opened up into the garage. Several car lifts were scattered throughout the space, with mechanics covered in grease working away at them.

Justin's hand found my elbow, steering me with a gentle pressure. "Over here," he said, angling toward a door that opened up onto the shop floor. The workers didn't pause at the sound of the door, but one man with grey hair and a long braided beard that hung down to the middle of his chest glanced up from beneath the hood of a battered Honda.

"Yo, Taz!" Justin called, "Meet Rhi."

The man called Taz wiped his hands on a red shop rag and tipped his chin up at me. "Hey," he said, voice gravelly.

"Sorry, Rhi, I got held up discussing Taz's newly fixed Harley with him, and I thought I might as well bring you in and introduce you.

I noticed a group of guys huddled around a car, their hands coated in grease as they tinkered with its engine. Justin led me over to them, beaming with pride as he introduced me as his girlfriend. A chuckle reverberated from beneath the car, and then a loud screech pierced the air as someone on a creeper rolled out from underneath the vehicle's frame. It was a girl with a ponytail sticking out of her cap, her face streaked with dirt but still managing to look effortlessly cool.

She raised an eyebrow at Justin's introduction before grinning mischievously. "Girlfriend, huh?" she teased, her voice carrying a hint of amusement.

Justin rolled his eyes, but couldn't stop the corners of his mouth from twitching into a slight grin. He shot her an exasperated look before turning back to me. "Don't listen to her, Rhi. They all probably hear way too much about you, including Blue."

Blue was a fitting name for her as her eyes were like two brilliant sapphires, only made more dazzling by the smudges of grease that adorned her cheeks. "Nice to meet you, Blue," I said timidly, turning to include the rest of them in my greeting as I added, "All of you."

The door to the back of the shop opened, revealing a tall man with broad shoulders. He wore a black shirt under a blue work shirt printed with the words 'Vince's Auto.' This had to be Vince. The striking resemblance between him and Justin was unmistakable—they had the same dark hair, Vince's just sprinkled with grey, and the same exact face.

His dark eyes met mine, and a sly smile spread across his lips as he strode confidently towards us. "So this is the girl that stole my son's heart," he said, extending an enormous hand to me.

I felt Kiran tense up behind me. It was hard not to respond to him.

I reached out tentatively and placed my hand in Vince's, feeling the power of his grip as his fingers closed around mine. A strange pulsing sensation erupted in my palm. My scar throbbed terribly, causing me to flinch. Vince's eyes seemed to bore into my very soul as he examined me closely, and I realized I wasn't breathing.

My throat felt dry like a desert sandstorm had just swept by. I finally spoke up nervously, "I wouldn't say I stole his heart exactly."

A laugh erupted from Vince's chest, and he released my hand, which I quickly shoved into my pocket. He seemed to be examining me intently, but then I noticed how his gaze seemed to flit past me. He was looking behind me, where I knew Kiran invisibly stood.

Vince's piercing gaze flicked back to me with a curiosity I couldn't place. "Why don't we all grab some dinner, son? I'm starving."

"I'm in." Blue piped up eagerly.

"Another time, Blue. I meant just Justin and Rhi," Vince replied coolly as he again looked beyond me.

Before Justin could answer, I spoke up hastily: "We've been gone all weekend. My grandmother is expecting me home."

"Maybe another time?"

"Another time then," Vince said quickly. "How about dinner at my place tomorrow?"

"I think we can make that work," Justin said smoothly with a smile that didn't reach his eyes. "Right, Rhi?"

I tried not to let my nerves overwhelm me as Kiran's presence filled my senses. He did not seem happy, and I felt fear radiating from him...or something. Whichever emotion it was, it was making me anxious. I needed to change the subject quickly. "This is a great place you've got here, Vince," I said, forcing a smile so fake it hurt.

He smiled, and his eyes sparkled with pride. "Thank you. I've been running this garage for over twenty years now."

"That's impressive," I said.

"Yeah, he's been around as long as these old jalopies." Blue gestured towards the cars on the jacks.

Vince let out a hearty laugh. "I've seen it all." His eyes narrowed slightly, and I wasn't sure he was talking about cars.

I noticed Justin staring at me, and I could tell he noticed I was changing the subject. "Rhi," he asked again with more insistence. "Will tomorrow work for you?"

"Um, sure," I replied enthusiastically, trying to mask my inner turmoil. "We should really get going, Justin," I added quickly before turning towards the door, eager to escape Vince's presence.

Blue piped up one last time as we were about to leave: "Nice meeting you again, Rhi! Looks like I'm your dinner date, after all, Vince!" His bellowing laughter followed us out the door into the late summer evening air, where I finally released my breath and tossed Justin his keys before slipping into the passenger seat next to him.

Unease crept over me. Justin must have noticed my unease, his cat-like eyes studying my face inquisitively.

"What's the matter, Rhi?" He asked, his voice laced with concern. "You look like you've seen a ghost."

I forced a smile onto my lips. "Nothing. I'm fine."

On the ride home, Justin and I were both lost in thought. The excitement of our beach trip was gone; all I could sense was Kiran's nervous presence around me. What could possibly make an angel feel nervous, I thought as we turned onto my street.

I couldn't take the silence between us anymore. "Justin?"

"Hmm?"

"Do you want to go to Vince's tomorrow?" I asked hesitantly. "I mean, I thought you didn't do things like that with him."

He turned his jeweled gaze on me. "I haven't before, but maybe this time will be different."

"Why now?"

He shrugged his large shoulders. "It's just dinner. What's the harm in that?"

He pulled up in front of the house. Nan's car was in the driveway, and I noticed Mia was again sitting on her porch reading that giant book.

Justin took my hand into his. "Listen, if you don't want to go..."

I cut him off. "I'll go if you want me to."

He smiled his lopsided grin, "I want a lot of things from you, Rhi...dinner at Vince's is nowhere near the top of that list."

I could feel myself blushing. My heart fluttering in my chest, but I squeezed Justin's fingers tightly. "I know it's up to me when," I said softly, looking down at our clasped hands.

He grinned broadly with a twinkle in his eye now. "And I like your thinking, but I wasn't referring to that."

My eyes flicked to meet his. God, he was so gorgeous, like a finely sculpted piece of art. My heart rate increased, and I became breathless, and that pull came over me. My hands slid slowly over his arms until they reached his neck, touching the soft strands of dark hair that lay there. I kissed him hard and pulled him against my body. His hands slid up the back of my shirt, tickling my skin. I could feel his heart beating in rhythm with mine, and his mouth was warm, soft, and inviting against my own. It had never been like this, as if I could not get close enough to him or the feeling was never satisfying enough.

My body wanted him like I had never wanted anyone before, but then my mind drifted to Kiran, and I felt myself pulling away. He must have felt it because he became more demanding and pulled me tighter against him. His lips pressed against mine with a rough passion that took my breath away. I finally managed to pull away, panting for breath.

There was a mixture of shock and desire on his face. "Well, that was unexpected," Justin said as he cradled my face with his hands. "If you kept that up, our first time might have been in the front seat of my car."

My eyes widened in shock. "Justin!"

He replied with a smirk. "I am only human, Rhi. And you started it, remember?"

It was true; I couldn't help that strong pull to him. My body and my mind were in constant battle. "I know," I said simply.

He chuckled. "I'm not complaining." Then he brushed his lips against mine again, and it took all of my willpower not to grab him and kiss him with abandon again. "But before we got so...side tracked... what I was talking about though..." His hands left my face and brushed my hair behind my ear. "What we talked about on the beach..." He trailed off.

I put a finger to his warm lips. "I have such strong feelings for you, Justin," I began. "No guy has ever said those words to me, and it sort of shocked me."

Justin took my hands in his, kissing them gently. "I'm sorry I didn't say it back...." I whispered.

He brushed his lips across mine and whispered, "I know I shocked you by saying I loved you. Honestly, I shocked myself." A shuddering breath left him. "I can wait, Rhi, it's fine. I know you have been through a lot, and so have I. I understand you want to protect your heart from getting broken."

A shuddering sigh escaped my lips. "I have a place for you in my heart, Justin," and I did.

I just didn't know if my whole heart belonged to him.

He enveloped me in his arms, resting his chin on top of my head. "That is the best thing I've heard in a long time."

Justin and I carried my luggage inside, where Nan was watching one of her classic movies, her thick glasses perched on the brim of her nose as she knitted in her favorite chair, "Hey, Mrs. C." Justin said to Nan before he gently kissed my forehead and whispered that he'd call later. I watched him disappear out the door before turning to grab my bags.

But before I could take more than two steps, Nan's sweet voice beckoned me to her side. "Rhi, before you go upstairs, come sit with me a moment," she motioned for me to join her in the armchair opposite hers.

My feet felt like lead as I trudged across the room and plopped on the chair across from her. I could feel her eyes upon me, but said nothing, awaiting her first word. She put her knitting aside, carefully folding it into her knitting bag. Taking off her glasses, she fixed her gaze on me and asked, "How was the beach?"

I shifted uneasily under her scrutiny, tucking a stray strand of hair behind my ear before answering, "Um, very nice. Vince has a huge house right on the beach."

"Yes, I suppose he does," she replied softly as she lowered the volume of her movie. Turning to look at me again, she said, "Did you know I was acquainted with Vince's father? We were schoolmates, and they lived a few blocks away from us."

"No, I didn't, but it doesn't surprise me. Everyone seems to know everyone around here."

She laughed a little. "That's true. He actually took me to a school dance."

My face must have given away my shock as she said, "Don't look so stunned, Rhi. I had other suitors before I met your grandpa."

I glanced at a framed photograph resting on the mantel behind her. It showed my grandparents in their youth. Pops looked handsome in his Navy uniform; Nan was wearing a gorgeous dress, leaning into him with a content smile playing across her lips. She followed my gaze and spoke again, "I know you've heard the story of how your grandfather and I met."

I had heard the story many times. Pops had come home after he was injured in World War II. He went into the first restaurant he found near the room he was renting from a widow. Nan was waitressing at The Pier then, and he sat at her booth. They had been together ever since.

"I figured you probably dated other boys in school; I just didn't know it was Justin's grandfather." It took me a moment to take it all in. "He's never mentioned him."

Nan's eyes twinkled as she spoke: "I wouldn't think he would. He died many years before Justin was born."

"How did you end up at a dance with Justin's grandfather?" I asked, full of curiosity.

"During World War II, the US Navy used some unconventional means to help protect the seaports both here and in New York." She said.

"Unconventional?"

Nan peered at me intently. "The Mob Rhi."

I was taken aback. I knew, well, I should say I had heard about the Mob. The news frequently talked about the crime bosses around here, and then all of the movies that were made about the Mafia. "I'm confused, Nan. What does the Mob have to do with World War II or Justin's grandfather?"

"Frank, Justin's grandfather, frequented The Pier; many mobsters did."

"Wait, what? Justin's grandfather was in the Mob?"

"Yes, Rhi. He was very handsome. I really loved his eyes. They were dark brown with long black lashes and were always full of mischief. Both Vince and Justin look so much like him. He was also very charismatic. The girls all swooned over him when he came into the restaurant."

Nan seemed to be lost in the memory. "My dad was a very strict police officer and even more of a strict Catholic. I knew what kind of things the Mob was into, so I stayed away from Frank at first. But he kept requesting my table at work and asking me out, so I finally said yes." She blushed. "I didn't tell my parents."

"Nan!" I giggled. I couldn't picture my saintly grandmother lying to her parents.

She gave a light laugh, her eyes showing me the teenage girl who had been smitten by love.

"Frank was always a perfect gentleman with me, and I thought I had fallen in love with him for a while. We were strolling on the dock one day when a Navy officer approached us. They stepped away, and I could tell their discussion was quite heated. When Frank returned to me, he was obviously agitated. I asked him if everything was alright. He said he really shouldn't tell me, but he and his family were helping the US Government and the Navy in particular. The order had come down from the highest of the Mob bosses, securing the ports in secret for the allies during the war. I felt a bit over my head when he confirmed that his family was part of three of the biggest Mob families around here. I didn't want to break up with Frank, but I felt I needed to. Especially with my father being in law enforcement."

She sighed then and continued. "A few years later, my dad told me that he knew that I was secretly seeing Frank. He told me that not everything is black and white. Shades of grey were where most things existed. He had known Frank's family; he knew what they all did, but, at the time of the war, well...everyone turned a blind eye to it so the Allies could have every advantage against Hitler."

"That's an interesting story, but why are you telling me this?" I asked.

She sighed heavily and continued, "Because Rhi, I think Justin is a good kid. Mary and Rick are decent people; they raised him, not Vince. But Vince – he still has ties to the criminal side of his family."

"What about his shop?" I wondered aloud.

"He does legitimate work out of his shop, but...." She drew out the word. "He also does illegal things out of his shop." She replied.

I wondered if Justin knew. I wondered if half the people who worked there knew. How could they not? I thought to myself. However, I remained determined to defend Justin until proven otherwise. "Nan, I don't believe Justin is a part of any of that."

"He may not be Rhi." She conceded before adding, "However, your Uncle Nick knows Vince is very active in illegal activities. I'm not going to ask you to stay away from Justin...."

I let out a breath of relief.

"Do, however, stay away from Vince and that shop."

"But, you let me go to his shore house."

"Because you told me Vince wouldn't be there. I love you too much to see anything bad happen to you."

My heart quickened as I thought of Vince's invite for tomorrow. I felt guilty just considering it, but I didn't want to deceive Nan. I decided to tell her about meeting Vince earlier instead. "I actually met Vince today," I said, lifting my gaze from under my lids to gauge her reaction. She remained silent, forcing me to continue with my explanation. "I got a weird feeling from him when he spoke like he could see right through me."

Nan cleared her throat. "How did you meet him? I thought he had left town?"

"It was unexpected," I replied quickly, squirming in my seat. "Justin stopped by the shop to drop off keys, then he asked me to come in for a minute. That's when I saw Vince."

"Oh," Nan murmured before an abrupt knocking sound cut off our conversation. We both whipped our heads around simultaneously, and before she could stop me, I jumped out of my chair to answer the door, thankful for the interruption.

I opened the door to find Mia and Sam standing on the front porch. Mia smiled large enough to light up the entire city, while Sam had a mischievous glint in his eyes. "Hey, Lady Bug! I saw that you got home from the shore. How was it?"

"Um, nice. It's been a while since I went to the ocean." I glanced at Sam looming behind Mia; the corner of his lip turned up into a smile.

"Anyway, school is just around the corner, and I love going thrift shopping when it's back-to-school time. Let's go check out some stores together before school starts. It'll be fun!" Her eyes gleamed with excitement, and she seemed to genuinely want me to come. She might be my first real friend here besides my cousins and Justin.

Suddenly aware that I had been staring between them both, my cheeks flushed with embarrassment as I stuttered out an answer. "Sure."

She practically glowed with anticipation, "Great! I'll text you the details. We can make a day of it tomorrow. How does that sound?"

I nodded, "Sounds like a plan."

"Sam," her voice took on a teasing edge as she nudged him with her hip, "wants to come too."

Sam's lips thinned into an almost invisible line, but he didn't deny it. "Mia exaggerates," he said with an air of nonchalance.

Rolling her eyes, Mia giggled and slapped him playfully on the shoulder. "Oh, stop pretending. You know you love thrift stores."

She turned back to me, her smile warm, "I'll text you later."

As they turned to leave, I watched them from the doorway. Sam glanced back over his shoulder at me. His brow furrowed as though he were trying to solve a particularly complex puzzle. He offered me one final half-smile before disappearing down the steps with Mia.

My back pressed against the smooth, cool wood as I closed the door. The house's silence enveloped me, and I took a deep breath to calm my racing thoughts.

Nan's voice broke through the stillness. "So that should be fun tomorrow," she said, a small smile playing on her lips.

"Yeah, I suppose," I replied half-heartedly. My mind was elsewhere, thinking how I would get out of dinner tomorrow at Vince's. Retrieving my bags, I turned to head back to my room. Just then, my phone chimed in my pocket. I pulled it out, thinking it might be Mia. But instead, it was Justin: *"I miss you."* Those three simple words brought a smile to my face and warmth to my chest.

"Well, that brought the smile back to your face," Nan remarked. I looked up to meet her gaze and felt overwhelmed by all the love and support she gave me.

I quickly shoved my phone back into my pocket and headed upstairs.

Chapter Twenty-Four

My phone chimed in my pocket again. I pulled it out, and there was another text from Justin, *"Still missing you."*

"Ugh, how am I going to get out of this dinner at Vince's tomorrow?" I huffed.

My fingers danced nervously over my phone screen as I typed out a reply. *"Miss you too,"* I finally sent, accompanied by a smiling emoji. *"By the way, I asked Nan about tomorrow, and she said I can't go."* My heart sank as I hit send and waited anxiously for a response.

My phone pinged again, signaling a reply from Justin. *"It's okay, I get it. I didn't really want to go anyway."*

I started to unpack when my phone chirped again. This time, it was Mia. *"Hey, girl! I can see your light on in your room. If you want some company, come on over. A few of us are just hanging out."*

I bit my lower lip and punched in a response to Mia. *"Sure, be there in a sec."*

The phone chimed again. *"Just let yourself in. The door is unlocked."*

Where was Kiran? I hadn't seen or heard from him since we were at Vince's garage. I tried to feel him and felt.... nothing.

I pressed my hand to my chest, the cool fabric of my shirt doing nothing to soothe my mounting panic. I felt...hollow and empty like I was missing a vital part of myself. Kiran, where are you?

My phone chirped again, and I yanked it out of my pocket with agitation.

Mia: *"Are you coming?"*

I left my empty feeling room and descended the stairs; the faint glow of the television illuminated the living room. Nan was seated in her favorite chair, eyes glued to the screen. Her voice broke through the silence as she noticed my presence. "Where are you off to now?" She asked.

"Mia has some friends over and invited me to join them," I replied, pausing at the door and waiting for her response.

"It's okay to go, Rhi, I'm glad you've made friends." With a click, she turned off the television and began making her way down the hallway. I headed out the door into the warm night air, quickening my pace as a light drizzle began to fall.

Mia's house mirrored Nan's layout, but her house had a larger front porch. I hesitated as I approached the front door with my hand on the doorknob. Before I could decide, the door swung open, revealing Mia's beaming face.

"What took you so long?" She asked eagerly and pulled me into the house.

Mia's house was dimly lit. A soft orange glow illuminated the corner of the room, where a short, stocky woman sat with a headlamp atop her curly mass of hair. Her petite frame was barely visible in the darkness.

"Gran, you remember Rhi? Mrs. C's granddaughter," Mia said, ushering me forward to greet her grandmother.

The woman turned towards us, her face illuminated by the light atop her head. She appraised me with sharp eyes before nodding in greeting.

"Hello," I said, extending my hand for a shake. Her small hand was adorned with multiple turquoise rings. Her grip was firm, surprisingly so for a woman of her age. "Ah, Rhi," she murmured, squinting at me as the tiny light atop her head glared into my eyes. "Nice to see you again."

"Y-yes, likewise, ma'am," I stammered, momentarily taken aback by the intensity of her stare.

"Well, don't just stand there, child," she said, waving us off towards the stairway. "The spirits are lively tonight, and I have a line of them waiting to chat with me." She waved her hands in a shooing motion. "Off you go."

Mia took my hand and led me up the staircase, the walls lined with faded family portraits that grinned back at us. The hallway was eerily silent, save for the distant murmurings of Mia's friends, and I couldn't help but feel like there were eyes on me.

"Don't mind, Gran," Mia said as we reached the top of the stairs. "She can be quite forward, but she means well." I smiled in response, unsure how to react to a woman who claimed to converse with spirits. Who was I kidding? I had regular conversations with an angel. The thought occurred to me about Sam. Mia's grandmother must know what he is. My thoughts were interrupted as we entered Mia's room, and laughter greeted us. Inside Mia's room sat Sophie and Sam. Their faces were animated, lost in delightful chatter.

"Rhi! We were wondering when you'd show up," Sophie called out. Her bright red hair fell over her eyes in messy strands. She waved me over, patting the empty space next to her. I obliged, sinking into the softness of a plush bean bag chair.

Sam's dark eyes flicked up as I sat a smirk on his lips. He pretended to listen to Sophie, but every other second he'd dart me a glance, like we had some secret joke between us. A flutter danced in my belly. I had to admit, he was unnervingly good at the quiet art of flirting with no more than his eyes.

He leaned back, propping his feet on a small battered table. "You missed the good debate," he said. "We nearly came to blows over whether Justin is a future serial killer or merely a run-of-the-mill narcissist."

I shot Sam a sharp look, and he leaned further back, palms up. "Relax," he said, his mouth all teeth.

Mia stepped in. "Sam, lay off," she said, kicking his foot off the table with her heel. "Sam's teasing, Rhi. He's a dork."

I nervously twirled a strand of hair with my fingers and quickly changed the subject, "So, what happened after Justin and I left you guys at the Witches Well the the other night?"

"What if I told you that we may have encountered spirits?" Mia exclaimed. She drew her knees up to her chest and wrapped her arms around them, her bright eyes gleaming excitedly. She stood up suddenly and moved towards an old wooden chest at the corner of the room and pulled out the book she was always reading on her porch.

"I found an incantation that, if done right, lets a person speak to those in the veil," she explained.

"In the veil?" I whispered.

"Yes." Sophie answered solemnly as she explained, "The souls of those who are waiting to get to their final destination, whether it is heaven or hell."

My mind conjures an image of a great waiting room with souls lined up shoulder-to-shoulder, each shrouded in fog and expectation. "But, why do they have to wait?" I ask.

Sophie's lips press into a line. "Because most souls aren't ready to be judged. They have unfinished business. Old wounds. Things they can't let go of." She looks pointedly at me, "Mia's mother and grandmother have seen the souls themselves, waiting in the void for their final judgment. It may seem unreal to you, but what we have witnessed is all too real to us." Sophie said.

"You really believe all of this?" I asked, my skepticism creeping into my tone.

Before Mia could respond, Sam cut in. "Belief has nothing to do with reality when dealing with the supernatural." His gaze never left my face, his eyes twinkling with something I couldn't quite interpret.

"We know it sounds crazy," Sophie chimed in, pushing thick black glasses up her nose. "We tried contacting the witches again through Mia's book of ancient spells after you left. And trust me, the voice we heard was not something of this world."

I turned to Sam, feeling a slight flutter in my stomach. "Did you hear it too?" I asked.

His eyes didn't leave mine as he let out a low hum of confirmation. "I did."

His confession hung in the air between us, "So, how long have you known each other?" I asked.

Mia sank down on the floor beside me again; the book now sprawled across her lap. "Oh, Sam's family and mine have been close friends for generations," she said nonchalantly.

"How many generations exactly?"

Mia turned her head to look at Sam, her expression curious. "How long has it been, Sam? At least as far back as our grandmothers," she mused, furrowing her eyebrows together.

"Much farther than that," he said. "Our families are bound by blood and magic—since the dawn of time, perhaps."

Mia lightly knocked his shoulder with hers and laughed. "Dawn of time, Sam," she giggled, "I don't think it goes back that far." The corners of her eyes crinkled with genuine mirth.

Mia reached for the aged book in her lap, flipping through its pages with practiced ease. Her fingers danced over the yellowed vellum as she searched for something specific. A glimmer of excitement sparked in her eyes when she found it, and she eagerly pushed the book towards me.

"This is what we used to attempt communication with them," Mia explained, pointing to an intricate diagram of a ritual circle filled with cryptic symbols and unfamiliar words. "I heard something. Just a whisper, but it was undeniably a voice from beyond."

I trace the diagram with my fingertip. "So this happened after me and Justin left you at the Witches Well?

"Yes, around midnight, actually. That's the thing; spirits are heard more easily during the witching hour. Gran says the veil is thinnest then."

Sam adds, "You should know, those woods are very old. The circle is more of a conduit than a shield. It opens the door, but there's no telling what might come through."

I exhale, trying to seem casual. "So what did you hear? Something actually spoke back?"

Sophie nods. "It was like static at first, like a radio not tuned all the way. We were about to give up, but then everything in the woods just... stopped. The crickets, the wind, everything.

Mia's eyes sparkle with unspent adrenaline. "We heard this voice. it said that the twin souls hide among you."

"Creepy," I say as my eyes scanned the page with intense curiosity, my lips moving silently in an attempt to decipher the spidery handwriting. It wasn't English. However, one word stood out to me, repeated several times throughout the text.

Samyaza.

"What is this language?" I asked, tracing the words with my fingers. "Greek, Latin?"

"Lenape. It's my ancestral language," Mia explained, flipping back to the beginning of the book and running her fingers over the intricate symbols. "My grandmother can speak our language fluently, and both my mother and I have learned from her."

I pointed to a sentence containing that same name again. "This seems like a name. What does it say here?"

"It roughly translates to call on Samyaza, for he possesses the knowledge of the Creator and can ascend to the spirit world at will," Mia replied.

Sam's lips curved upward as he leaned against the wall, his sharp features illuminated by a nearby lamp.

Sam....Samyaza. This book talks about Sam!

"You look spooked, Rhi," he said quietly when I caught his eye, a hint of teasing in his voice.

"N-no, just...find it interesting."

"Are you okay, Rhi?" Mia asked. You're paler than usual," she teased.

I tore my gaze from Sam, forcing a laugh that sounded hollow even to my ears. "Yeah, I'm fine," I replied with a weak smile. "Just...this stuff is kind of disturbing, you know?"

Sam chuckled under his breath, the sound low and throaty. All the while, that damn smirk remained on his face.

"Were you able to make out anything else the spirit said to you?" I asked Mia, trying to ignore Sam.

"Not really. I did hear the word away pretty clearly. Not sure what came before it. It might have been 'go away' or 'gone away.'" She shook her head in frustration.

"This is the first time I've ever heard a voice like that. I've only ever seen images of spirits in my mind." A spark of excitement lit up in her eyes as she added, "But Gran was just as thrilled as I was that I could hear something."

"Why is this Samyaza person's name in here so much?" I asked.

"Samyaza was one of the Watchers," The voice near me said silkily. It was Sam, his gaze now on the sketch on the vellum. Anxious energy flowed through me like a swarm of bees. "He was the badass leader of a group of angels who interacted with humans, imparting their angelic knowledge to humanity."

"Isn't it fascinating?" Mia exclaimed with enthusiasm. "To be able to communicate with spirits and bridge the gap between our world and theirs!"

"Indeed..." My voice was barely audible over the pounding in my ears. Mia began to read aloud from the old book, an invocation that ended with, 'Samyaza, guide us to wisdom.'

The air in the room seemed to hold its breath momentarily before Mia let out a laugh. "I remember trembling as I said those words," she said, shaking her head and smiling at the memory. But her smile quickly faded when she noticed the expression on my face. "Hey, Lady Bug? Are you okay?"

"I... I just need some fresh air," I gasped, rising hastily from the bean bag chair. The surprised looks on everyone's faces blurred together as I hurried towards the door.

As I stumbled down the stairs, my mind raced with what I had just seen in that book. But Mia's grandmother stopped me in my tracks before I could escape into the cool night air. The wrinkles on her face seemed to deepen as she leaned closer to me, her raspy voice whispering, "Girl, you keep running, you're gonna trip right into your destiny." She cackles, clutching my arm with a grip surprisingly strong for someone who looks like a breeze could topple her. "You got Watchers now, sugar. All up in your business."

I gazed at her, my heart racing as I heard the door to Mia's room creak open behind us. Mia emerged from the room and stood on the landing above us, her eyes filled with concern. "Rhi, I'll walk you home," she said softly. "You look like you're going to be sick."

Her grandma let out a cackling laugh. "Yes, yes, Mia. You help your friend find her way." With a small smile, she stepped aside and motioned for me to pass.

"Did you speak to anyone tonight, Gran?" Mia asked as she came up beside me.

"Oh yes, yes," the old woman replied, scratching her chin absentmindedly. "I heard some most unusual stories."

Mia's face lit up with excitement. "Oh, yay! I can't wait to hear them. But first, let me get Lady Bug here home."

"It's okay, really," I assured them as I grasped the doorknob and stepped outside.

The streets were quiet and dark, enveloped by the veil of night. My feet faltered with every step as I walked towards Nan's house, my heart beating wildly in my chest. As I turned into our yard, I sprinted toward the front door. My trembling hands fumbled with the key before finally pushing it into the lock and turning it. With a sigh of relief, I shut and locked the door behind me, leaning against it for support.

I headed to my room, and he was waiting for me as I entered.

Kiran appeared from the shadows and enveloped me in his arms, his presence a source of comfort and security. "Kiran,"

I whispered, my voice shaking with emotion. "Sam is not just any Watcher."

"I know," he replied soothingly against my ear.

"You know?" I pulled away from him, confusion etched on my face. "I don't understand."

"I know you don't. When the Watchers decided to teach mankind what they knew, one of the things they taught was spells and magic." His eyes flicked to mine. "I'm guessing you know which Watcher this was?"

"Samyaza." The name slipped from my lips like a curse.

"One and the same," Kiran confirmed.

I stepped closer to him, taking his hands in mine. "Mia's grandmother stopped me as I was leaving," I began, "She said something about I have Watchers now."

He studied me intently; a faint crease appeared between his brows.

"It wasn't just that. She looked at me like she knew everything about me. My God, Kiran! Sam, he knows for sure that I know who he is."

He squeezed my hands gently, his eyes filled with concern. "I'm pretty sure he meant to show himself to you in the woods."

I studied him, taking in every detail of his tense muscles and strained expression. He gently touched my cheek, causing me to lean into his touch. "Kiran, I didn't feel you earlier."

"I know." He looked away from me, his sculpted features hardening under all the unspoken things hanging in the air. "I'm trying to... distance myself."

"Why?" The question, raw and unfiltered, surged past my lips before I have the chance to hold it back.

Kiran's mouth opened and closed in silent contemplation before he finally forced out an answer. "I need space...space to fulfill my duties without distraction."

"Distr—," I start, struggling to swallow against the lump forming in my throat. "Is that what I am to you? A

distraction?"

"My purpose is to protect you, not to wrap you tighter into this dangerous world. But every day..." He swallowed hard, "Every day I'm around you, I feel myself getting more....involved." There was vulnerability in his confession, an admission of human-like emotions that warred against his celestial duty.

I felt a choked sob rising in my throat, threatening to spill out. Fear like I'd never known grips me. No, this surpasses fear. This is a crippling dread ripping through me; a nightmare where I'm reaching out for him only to find thin air; a world where he isn't there when I wake up, where I no longer see him each day, nor feel him by my side.

His beautiful face is etched with pain, guilt maybe, but his words are steel. It's clear he doesn't mean to hurt me...but he does. "Rest now, Ahavah. I will take care of everything."

My knees felt weak, and I let myself fall against him. His strong arms wrapped around me protectively. "That's the second time you've called me that, Ahavah. What does it mean?"

His eyes softened as he gazed down at me. "Love."

Then he was gone, and I stifled a sob, but the tears came. Hot wetness spilled down my cheeks. My fingers shook as I curled them against my temples.

I knew what this was. My heart breaking.

Chapter Twenty-Five

A knock on my door jolted me out of sleep. I groaned, pulling the covers tighter around me. But then I heard Mia's voice and immediately felt grateful for her presence after a long night alone.

She walked in, her movements full of energy. "What's going on, Lady Bug?" she asked, gesturing towards me with concern.

I sat up, meeting her gaze. "What do you mean?"

Her scowl deepened as she took in my appearance. "You look terrible," she stated bluntly. "Did Rizzo do something to upset you?"

I shook my head. "No," I muttered.

"Well then, get your butt out of bed! We have some retail therapy to do!" Mia declared with determination, pulling me out of my self-pitying bubble.

After showering and getting dressed in a black miniskirt and t-shirt, I couldn't shake off the weight of Kiran's words from the night before. I didn't want to be the cause of any inner conflict he was feeling. It was selfish of me to always want him around, but the thought of being unable to talk to or see him every day was unbearable.

I would deal with it, though, the way I dealt with all my pain. I would throw a wall up and make it like nothing bothered me. I would have fun today with

Mia. I'd survived worse, after all. I whisper to myself, "You don't need Kiran to be happy."

As I climbed into Mia's car, I admired its unique charm. Unlike the cars Steve and Justin drove, Mia's car had a cozy, lived-in feel. The faded cloth seats were adorned with patches covering holes, and strands of beads hung from the rearview mirror.

Sam wasn't in the car. Curious, I turned to Mia and asked where he was. With a flick of her wrist, Mia pushed her heart-shaped sunglasses up onto her head as she casually replied, "He had some family obligation that he couldn't get out of."

I wondered what family business he could be doing. The thought of Sam being with other Watchers left me feeling unnerved. How many were there, and were they all close to here? That could be the only family I could think of that Sam would have.

"So, your grandmother mentioned something about having visitors last night? I mean...spirits?" My words came out hesitantly, and I watched for Mia's reaction.

"Yes, she did," Mia replied, her eyes flickering with a hint of admiration under the rose-colored glasses. "She said a group of spirits came to her in need of her help last night." Her voice trailed off, and I wondered what kind of aid they could have possibly needed from her grandmother.

"What kind of help?" I asked as we came to a stoplight.

Mia turned to me, her eyes alight with enthusiasm. "Most of them are lost," she said. "Some don't even realize they're dead."

The light changed, and Mia turned left, leading us towards the historic art district. We passed by old industrial buildings that had been transformed into vibrant and eclectic shops and galleries. The walls were adorned with colorful murals, and the air was filled with a sense of history and creativity. "Things have certainly changed in the valley," I remarked, taking in the sights.

"I absolutely love it here now," Mia replied, a smile spreading across her face.

"Wait, isn't the Star Tavern somewhere around here?" I asked, scanning the streets for the familiar restaurant.

"You bet it is, Lady Bug! Just a block or so over," Mia replied.

"I could totally use a slice from there later." Comfort food always made me feel better.

"Then it's a date," Mia laughed and pulled up in front of a small storefront with charming brick walls and flowers lining the windows.

"This is Retro Revival," she announced, grabbing her bag from the backseat. "My absolute favorite place to shop."

"I already love it," I gushed.

Mia and I entered the quaint little boutique, the jingle of a tiny bell announcing our arrival. As we browsed through the rows of vintage clothing, I noticed some retro-looking band t-shirts near the back.

"I think I'll check out the stuff in the back," I said, turning to Mia.

"Tell me if you find anything good," she said as she continued flipping through a rack.

My fingers ran over the fabrics as I pulled out a random shirt and examined it. My attention shifted as the tiny bell chimed again, signaling someone else had entered the store. I glanced up and saw Trina walking in.

"Hey there, Trina," Mia called out to her cheerfully.

Trina walked towards Mia with genuine warmth and affection, embracing her in a hug when she reached her.

The muffled sound of their conversation reached my ears, but I couldn't make out the words. They seemed to enjoy each other's company, laughing and nodding in agreement. I turned my attention back to the shirts in front of me. I selected two that were well-worn from bands I loved.

Suddenly, I heard my name being called and looked up to see Mia waving me over. Trina's eyes met mine in surprise, which she quickly masked. I made my way over to them, clutching the shirts in my hands.

Mia beamed at me, "Rhi, this is Trina."

"We've met," I replied, forcing a smile on my face.

"Where's your boyfriend?" Trina asked.

"He's at work," I answered simply. "And yours?"

That seemed to ignite something in her, as I saw a flicker of anger in her eyes.

Mia stepped in, sensing the tension between us. "What's going on with you two?" she asked, her mouth slightly agape.

"Nothing," I responded quickly.

"Oh wait, wait, wait," Mia said quickly, grabbing one hand from each of us. "This isn't about Rizzo, is it?" She looked back and forth between us.

Trina scoffed dismissively.

"Trina, don't you 'tsk' me," Mia retorted. "I know- well, everyone knows how much you loved that boy."

Trina's head snapped towards Mia, her eyes narrowing. "Forget Justin Rizzo." She spat.

"You need to," Mia said sternly.

Trina tried to pull away, but Mia tightened her grasp on both of our hands.

"This is just stupid," Mia exclaimed, her voice filled with frustration.

"You don't understand what she did." Trina hissed, her eyes blazing with anger.

"What I did?" I said in astonishment. "I did nothing! I don't know you. But what are you doing with my cousin if you're in love with Justin? Who, by the way, was pursuing me."

"I don't care about Justin," Trina snapped, turning her wrath towards me. "But I love Steve and you...you turned him against me!"

I was taken aback by Trina's accusation. "What on earth are you talking about?" I asked, genuinely dumbfounded.

"Everything was going great between us until you showed up. Then he dumps me and won't return my calls or texts."

"I did nothing to turn him against you." I defended myself, not really feeling the fight within myself. "Your actions are what led to Steve breaking up with you. Not mine."

"My actions? My actions?" Trina's voice cracked as mist filled her eyes. She roughly wiped it away with the back of her hand.

I let out a deep sigh and addressed Trina again. "Look, Trina, I'm truly sorry that Steve broke up with you. But I swear I had nothing to do with it."

Her tear-filled eyes met mine, and I could see the pain and hurt behind them. There was something raw about her gaze, like a wounded animal backed into a corner. A part of me wanted to reach out, to comfort her, but the other part of me was utterly consumed by sadness. The emptiness in my chest clawed at me, trying to consume me from within. But I pushed it back into the farthest corners of my heart.

"Rhi, Lady Bug?" Mia's voice broke through my daze.

Startled, I turned to face her. "Sorry, what?"

Mia rolled her eyes playfully. "Girl, you have a habit of spacing out like you're in another world."

I chuckled nervously. "I know, sorry. My mind tends to wander."

I turned towards Trina, her delicate features still displaying traces of distrust, but she was noticeably calmer. "Trina," I said, "I know Steve cares about you. Maybe try not to act like he's your possession and give him some trust." I reached out to touch her shoulder, but she flinched away. "I swear you can trust him."

Her response was a slight nod, almost imperceptible. Despite the smudges of makeup around her eyes from tears, Trina still looked like a goddess.

"Would you like to shop with us for a bit?" I offered, trying to diffuse the tension. "We're planning on getting pizza afterward."

"Sure," she agreed, sweeping her dark locks over her shoulders.

I slowly walked away from the girls as we browsed through racks of clothes and shoes.

As I ran my fingers over the rows of shoes, my eyes caught a bright orange, chunky, heeled ankle boot. The color was bold and eye-catching, and I couldn't resist picking it up to admire it. Suddenly, Mia's voice chimed up from behind me, startling me out of my contemplation.

"Lady Bug! Those shoes are amazing! You should get them."

I hesitated, knowing they weren't my size and thinking about how clumsy I was. "Um, no, they aren't my size, and I'd probably end up in the hospital wearing them," I laughed, handing her the shoes. "You would look incredible in them, though."

Mia gratefully took the shoes and plopped down on the floor to try them on. "Oh, these are AH MAY ZING!" she gushed, admiring how they looked on her feet.

I smiled down at her, surrounded by her finds like a little pirate surrounded by their loot. Trina had joined us with a few shiny shirts draped over her arms.

"What did you find?" I asked Trina, trying to be friendlier towards her.

She shrugged a slender shoulder. "Just a couple of blouses. They have that vintage seventies vibe."

"Nice." I complimented.

Mia jumped up from the floor, donning the orange shoes. "Oh, yeah, these are my new favorite shoes!" She twirled around proudly, showing off her new footwear. "Oh Rhi, I found this." She suddenly bent down to shuffle through the pile of clothes at her feet. Peering up at me with excitement in her eyes, she handed me an army green utility jacket covered in different types of buttons and adorned with a large peace sign patch above the front pocket.

"Try it on," she urged eagerly.

I obliged, slipping into the well-worn jacket that felt like it had been made just for me. Some of the stitching was frayed, and the sleeves had a couple of small holes, but I loved it.

Mia stepped back to admire me in the jacket. "Now look at that," she mused with a grin, noting how perfectly it fit me.

"It will go perfectly with these band t-shirts I found," I remarked, thinking of Kiran and the band shirts he loved to wear.

"Are you two ready?" Trina asked, her eyes darting between us, waiting for our response. "I could really use that pizza."

We quickly paid for our items and made our way out the door, the sound of rain pattering against the roof. The sky was a dark gray, heavy with water, and the streets were slick with puddles.

Mia turned to Trina, "Where did you park?" she asked, trying to shield her face from the rain.

"Just a block down."

"Why don't we all just go in my car? It'll be easier, and we can drop you off afterward." The three of us huddled under the overhang, shielding ourselves from the rain before making a run for Mia's car parked nearby.

The Star Tavern was just as I remembered it as a child, with the familiar smells of rich tomato sauce and melting cheese filling the air. My stomach growled loudly as we found a cozy table by the window. As Mia and I eagerly ordered a pizza, Trina opted for a side salad and mozzarella sticks.

We were quiet for a while, lost in our thoughts as we watched the rain pouring outside until Trina finally spoke up. "So, Rhi," she began, "Steve told me that you were born here."

I took a deep breath before responding, not wanting to get into this with her. "That's correct," I replied curtly.

Trina's eyes studied me. "Why did you move away?" she probed, causing an uncomfortable knot to form in my stomach.

I lowered my gaze to my plate, "I guess my mom just wanted to start over somewhere new."

If only she knew about the dam within me, threatening to burst at any moment. if only she knew that every time I breathed, it hurt.

I frowned at her, shoving down the pain in my chest, "I assume you heard some things about me." I stirred my drink with my straw, trying to remain calm. "Not that any of it is anyone's business, but my mom married a controlling, drunk monster, so I was sent here to get away from all that."

Mia's sharp gaze didn't miss a beat as she watched our exchange. "You know what I think?" She said after a moment. "I think people say many things about others, but only a fraction is true." She casually propped her foot up on an empty chair next to her. "Don't you agree, Trina?" She turned to face Trina, who stared at her with wide eyes. "I mean, I've heard some things about you and Rizzo, but you told me yourself they weren't true, so..."

I saw Trina choke back a cough, and I felt some satisfaction from seeing her squirm. "Well, yes, they weren't true," she admitted finally, her cheeks turning pink with embarrassment. "I just find it hard to believe..."

We were interrupted by a deep voice behind us, slicing through the chatter of the bustling pizza restaurant. "Best pizza in town, isn't it, ladies?" The tone was familiar, and I turned to see Vince towering over us. I hadn't even heard his heavy footsteps approach from behind. It was surprising for someone of his size to move so silently.

"Ah, Rhiannon," Vince said smoothly, his voice like warm silk. "My son is just parking the truck; he should be in any minute." His dark eyes were fixed on me with an intense gaze. "I hear you can't make it to dinner tonight." His hand landed on my shoulder, causing a cold shiver to run down my spine. "I do hope you can join us soon. I'm eager to get to know the girl my son is so in love with."

I almost choked on my drink at his words. I closed my eyes and tried to count to four before letting out a long exhale. "Yes, well, I don't know if I would go so far as to say love."

Vince chuckled, "Oh, my dear," he crooned. "I saw how he looked at you in my garage. He is most definitely in love." Vince looked at me with an odd expression as if he knew something no one else did.

I glanced around the busy street outside, trying to see Justin somewhere. Mia and Trina stared at me with curious expressions, making me want to shove Vince's hand off my shoulder.

The front door creaked open, and Justin walked in. His shirt was drenched from the rain outside, clinging to his muscular frame as he shook drops of water out of his hair.

"Look who it is, son," Vince said, patting Justin on the shoulder.

Justin stepped forward, his intense stare fixed on the three of us. "Rhi?" he said in disbelief, his eyes scanning our faces before landing on Trina. "And Trina?"

Mia chimed in, waving her hands at him. "Hello! I'm here too, you know."

"Well, of course, Mia." He chuckled. "Who could miss you?"

"Not many." Mia giggled, taking another slice of pizza.

"I was just telling Rhiannon that we should still do that dinner sometime soon since she can't make it tonight." Vince interrupted.

Justin frowned. "Vince, just leave it alone."

But Vince didn't seem to like being told what to do by his son, his gaze hardening as he stared back at Justin. I watched how Vince moved like a giant, predatory cat. He caught me staring, and his expression softened slightly.

"Just trying to be polite," Vince replied calmly.

Justin rolled his eyes and leaned down to give me a quick kiss on the cheek. "Have fun with the girls, Rhi," he whispered near my ear, sending delightful shivers over my skin. Then, turning to Trina, he said, "And behave, Trina."

"Whatever," she huffed, turning her attention back to her salad.

"What can I get for you, kid?" Vince asked Justin, clapping him on the back as they walked towards the counter to order.

Trina leaned in closer to Mia and me and whispered, "Justin's dad, I mean Vince. He gives me the creeps."

"That's because he is a creep," Mia stated matter-of-factly.

I couldn't shake off the chill that Vince had left behind. "I'm full," I announced, dropping my napkin on my plate. "Are you both ready to go?"

"I'm all set," Mia replied cheerfully. "Let me just grab a box for this leftover pie."

Chapter Twenty-Six

Nan and I chatted over dinner. I told her about the cool jacket I had found at the thrift store and how we ran into Trina.

As I looked out the window, something caught my eye. Little lights blinked around the yard in a mesmerizing rhythm. "Lightning bugs!" I gasped, feeling a rush of nostalgia for my childhood summers spent chasing them.

Nan turned to look over her shoulder into the yard. "I remember how you used to catch them in jars during the summers when you were little," she reminisced.

I rose from my seat and carried my plate into the kitchen. As I rinsed it off in the sink, I watched Mia chase after the fireflies in her yard. A memory surfaced of us doing the same thing together as kids. With a smile, I called to her through the open window, "How old are you again?"

Mia's head snapped toward me before breaking into a wide grin as our eyes met. "Lady Bug, you're never too old to play with fireflies." She said, holding up a jar of the critters. "Come see." She waved for me to join her.

The air was thick with humidity, and a gentle drizzle continued to fall from the dark sky. I could smell the earthy scent of wet grass and soil mixed with the sweet aroma of flowers that lined the fence. It was foggy, and the mist, rain, and glow of the lightning bugs gave the yard an otherworldly look.

"I love the rain," I whispered to myself as I felt my lips turn up into a smile. *"And how much fun I used to have catching lightning bugs."*

I wonder if Kiran would feel the same? An angel, touched and moved by something as common as rain? Blinking hard, I half expected to see him standing there in front of me. A surge of longing rippled through me for that familiar ethereal face.

I followed the stone path to where our yards joined. As I approached, I saw Sam sitting quietly on the back steps of Mia's house, fiddling with some small object in his hands. He looked up as I stared at him, and his lips turned upward. He stood, crossing the yard to where I stood by Mia.

I returned my attention back to Mia and the jar she held in her hand. Lights blinked behind the glass, and it looked like it was filled with magic.

"How many do you think you have?" I asked, peering into the jar but unable to count the rapidly moving creatures inside.

"A few dozen at least," Mia grinned mischievously.

"Did you know some cultures believe fireflies are spiritual messengers or even souls of deceased ancestors? They bring good omens and messages from the spiritual realm."

"Interesting," I commented as Sam walked closer to the fence. His eyes darted behind me into my yard. I followed his gaze and saw he wasn't looking at my yard; he was looking at Kiran.

A voice from Mia's back porch broke the silence. It sounded like her grandmother calling her to come inside. Mia turned on her heel and headed towards her house. "I'll be right back," she called over her shoulder.

As the screen door slammed shut, Sam spoke. "Guardian." Instantly, Kiran stood beside me. "Watcher," he said emotionlessly.

"Kiran," I breathe out, not daring to trust myself to say more. I want to reach out, to touch him, let my fingers trace along the chiseled lines of his face, and tangle themselves in the wavy strands of his hair.

Sam twirled a small object in his hand, and I strained my eyes to make out what it was, but Sam's grip on it remained tight. My gaze flickered to Kiran, who stood motionless beside me like a stone sentinel, his intense gaze never leaving Sam.

"At last, we get to chat," Sam said, his gaze sliding towards me. "I would have preferred to do so alone, but it seems you never leave this one's side."

Wait? He never leaves my side. But, he had. Did Sam not know this, or was Kiran there all along, not allowing me to see or feel him?

Kiran shifted by my side, crossing his arms over his chest, "It's my duty."

"Ah yes, your duty," Sam repeated, his words tinged with amusement.

"Yes, duty. You remember what it is like to have a purpose?" Kiran retorted.

Sam laughed, a genuine sound rising from deep within him. "I've found my purpose," he said, his eyes darting between us with interest. "And it wasn't blindly following orders." Sam's eyes raked over me. "Not that I blame you. She's quite a beauty."

I could feel the anger simmering beneath my skin, and looking at Kiran, I knew he felt the same.

"What do you want with me, Samyaza?" Kiran asked in an unnervingly calm voice.

Sam caught a lightning bug that fluttered in front of him. Reaching for Mia's jar, he unscrewed the lid and placed the glowing insect inside.

"I want nothing from you," he said casually.

"Lie." Kiran snorted.

"You wound me, Guardian," Sam mocked. "The Watchers have only ever helped humanity."

"By teaching them witchcraft and war?" Kiran snarled.

"Come now, Guardian. Why is that a bad thing?"

Kiran stepped closer to the fence, his body tense with anger. "You disobeyed the Creator."

"We did no such thing!" Sam snapped back, his voice rising. "There were never any rules bestowed upon us forbidding us from helping when needed."

Kiran scoffed. Clearly not believing him.

"Our orders were to watch over humanity and assist when needed," Sam said, leaning closer to Kiran. "When humans were sick or injured, what do you think happened to them before we intervened?"

Kiran stared at him, not blinking.

There was a palpable tension in the air as Sam responded coolly. "They either died or suffered from disease," he stated matter-of-factly. "You call it witchcraft, while we call it educating these weak beings for survival." He looked pointedly at me.

Kiran's disbelief was evident as he challenged him. "Do you truly believe that you are without sin? That you were justified in your actions?"

Sam closed the gap between them with ease, his face close to Kiran's, but he simply chuckled. "You have no authority to judge me," he raised a dark brow before stepping back. "I apologize," he said, placing a hand over his heart. "It's difficult to constantly be portrayed as the villain since... well, since the beginning."

"Enough of this." Kiran's voice rose. "Mia will be back any minute, so I ask you again, what do you want, Samyaza?"

"I need you to deliver a message for me," Sam replied calmly.

"And why would I do that for you?"

"Because I have information about your ward," Sam's gaze flicked towards me briefly. "She is in danger."

I felt a chill like my body was plunged into ice water. "What?" I breathed.

"You both heard me. Your precious soul mate is in danger."

"I will protect her," Kiran stated firmly, his back straightening and his eyes blazing with determination. "From anything."

Sam chuckled playfully. "Ah, how long have you been playing Guardian? Just a few fleeting years? Meanwhile, I've been around since the dawn of time." He straightened with a twinkle in his eye. "You are not as strong as you think, Guardian."

"You're weak and full of corrosion from your years roaming the Earth." His tone was laced with venom. "Do not threaten me or my Ahavah."

My eyes darted between the two powerful beings, feeling overwhelmed by their intense energy. Sam's wings suddenly sprang from his back. They were larger than Kiran's, and they twitched behind him. The feathers were marked with scars and tears, yet there was a certain roguish charm to his divine yet slightly rebellious appearance.

Kiran's sharp and angular features contorted with rage as he glared at Sam. But what could Sam possibly know about any danger I could be in? I nervously stepped between the two. "What exactly do you want Kiran to do?" I asked boldly, causing Kiran's head to whip towards me.

"Do not—" he began, but I cut him off.

"Hush!" I snapped, glaring at him before turning my attention back to Sam.

Sam snickered. "She really has you wrapped around her little finger, doesn't she?" he taunted.

"You shut up, too!" I snarled, unable to control my temper. "How do you expect any help from Kiran when all you do is provoke him?" My heart raced as I stood between the two fierce beings.

Sam's penetrating gaze settled on me, searching my face for something. I could feel the heat rising in my cheeks. But then, his expression softened, and he spoke. "You're so much like your father," he said with a hint of sadness in his voice.

I gasped, opening my mouth to ask him how he knew my father, but he held up a hand to silence me. "Like I said, I've been around from the beginning."

Like that answered everything.

He plucked a hollyhock flower from its stem growing against the fence. "Did you know I still do the Creator's bidding?" he asked as Kiran's features twisted in confusion.

"I do. Go ahead and ask your Power angels if you don't believe me. After all, I am one of them," Sam continued, a sly smile playing on his lips.

"You are no Power," Kiran spat, anger flashing in his eyes. "You're a..."

"Yes, yes. I'm a Watcher now, but did you know that all Watchers were among the first angels? I also happened to be a Power before I was sent to Earth."

A muscle ticked in Kiran's jaw, but he remained silent. "I did as I was told. I watched as humans multiplied and grew in number, but they did not thrive." He twirled the flower between his fingers absentmindedly. "I couldn't help but feel pity for them. Humans are weak and vulnerable. So we showed them how to protect themselves." Sam's eyes narrowed as he continued. "But our intentions went beyond mere survival tactics. We showed them how to use plants for medicine and conjure spells for protection out of love for them."

"Love?" I gasped in surprise.

"Yes, keep up," Sam scoffed, still playing with the flower in his hand. "Despite the many hardships and challenges humans faced, what set them apart was their capacity for love. They could love even complete strangers, animals, and the world around them. It was inspiring to witness acts of compassion, generosity, and selflessness that surpassed individual interests." He paused, no longer twirling the flower as he met Kiran's gaze. Sam's eyes lit up with an intensity that caught me off guard. "That is what we wanted, to love. We craved it."

"What you wanted was to feel lust, not love." Kiran retorted bitterly.

"Oh no, young Guardian. Lust was merely a side effect. It stemmed from our growing feelings towards mortals. Not the other way around."

Kiran's face twisted in anger as he spat out the words, "You showed them how to create weapons!"

"So?" Sam said nonchalantly. "It's not like they didn't harm each other before we did that. Rocks, hands, sticks. all weapons." Sam's lips ticked up on one side, "Remember how Cain killed his brother? A rock."

I thought Mia would return at any moment, and I really wanted to know what Sam wanted from Kiran and the answer to my question about my father. "For someone who has barely said anything since I met you, you sure are chatty," I interjected, unable to take the tension any longer. "Can you get to the point, please?"

"It's just the part I play, the quiet, brooding teenager," Sam replied. "I actually am very chatty and adore a good conversation."

I glared at him, but he seemed unfazed.

"Learn some patience, girl."

"Mia..." I began.

"Mia will not return until I will it," Sam interrupted smuggly.

"He froze the moment," Kiran said, keeping his eyes on Sam.

"I'll get to the point," Sam said with a huff.

"Finally," I muttered under my breath.

"How do you put up with her?" Sam said, curiosity dancing in his eyes. "She's so bossy."

Kiran took a step forward, a hint of irritation flickering across his face.

"Oh, right...I know why." Sam's eyes were positively dancing with merriment. He turned to Kiran. "You can cross into the veil. I have someone there I would like to get a message to."

"Who do you want me to give a message to?"

"My daughter," Sam said simply.

I gasped.

Kiran scoffs, his silver eyes narrowing. "You have a whole family of witches at your beck and call, and you're asking me? This smells like a trick."

Sam folds his enormous wings back in with a noisy snap. "Mortals are useful for some errands, darling Kiran, but not for this." He leans closer, conspiratorial, voice low. "It's private. The kind of private a father reserves for his only child."

"If I do this – and I am not saying I will – who will protect Rhi while I am there from this danger you speak of?"

"Me, of course," Sam replied confidently.

"I can take care of myself, thank you," I interjected, slightly offended by the assumption that I needed protection.

Sam rolled his eyes in response, clearly not convinced.

"Tell me then," Kiran pressed on. "What is this danger Rhi is in?"

Sam clicked his tongue impatiently. "That is not how this works," he stated. "You do what I want, and then I tell you."

Kiran growled under his breath, clearly less than pleased with this response. "You are such a...."

Sam cut him off. "Now, now, Guardian," he chided. "That wouldn't be very angelic of you."

Kiran's expression darkened. "Fine, what is her name, and what do you need me to say for you?"

Sam lifted his hand with a theatrical flair, and a glowing, delicate scroll seemed to materialize from thin air. "It's all in here," he said, handing the parchment to Kiran.

I watched Kiran carefully examine the parchment, its luminescent presence almost seeming to whisper secrets. The note unraveled, thin lines of text glowing like veins of fire. I leaned forward and saw that the words weren't words at all—they were symbols shaped from light, shifting and rearranging in quicksilver flashes. The parchment began to smolder with a sublime inner heat, curling at the corners but never burning away. It lifted from Kiran's palm, hovering just above it, and contracted into a glowing sphere.

Kiran fixed his jaw and pressed the ball of light to his sternum. He grunted and gritted his teeth as the sphere bored into his chest.

I step closer to Kiran, searching his face for signs of pain. "Did it have to be a solisgram?" Kiran asked in a ragged voice.

"I don't trust postal services. Not even celestial ones." Sam quipped. "Besides, it's tradition between celestial beings. Otherwise, how's she to know it's truly from me?"

"Does it hurt?" I ask Kiran softly.

He shakes his head and gently touches his chest. "The message is secure."

"Wonderful!" Sam exclaimed, clapping his hands together. "Her name is Azura."

"Azura?" Kiran repeated, clearly surprised. "Not the daughter of Eve?"

"The very same," Sam confirmed. "She is my daughter as well."

"She isn't your daughter!" Kiran retorted, growing more exasperated by the minute.

Sam raised a dark eyebrow. "I can assuredly say that she is," he stated confidently.

"She's..." Kiran began.

"Adam's?" Sam said. "That is what has been taught in old writings, but I am her father."

Kiran shook his head as if trying to make sense of it all. "It doesn't matter," he whispered, more to himself than anyone else. Turning to me, he grasped my hands in his. His touch was warm and comforting, and I could feel our song filling my ears. "I won't be gone long," he reassured me, brushing his fingertips over my knuckles. "Stay home." He turned to Sam. "And don't leave his side."

"I have your word," Kiran directed at Sam, his voice firm. "You will protect her as a Guardian and let no harm come to her."

"Cross my heart..." Sam began before being interrupted by Kiran's growl.

"Lighten up, Guardian," Sam teased. "I'm only joking."

"She is the most important thing in this world and the next one to me," Kiran whispered fiercely.

Sam rolled his eyes yet again, but this time, his gaze showed a hint of understanding. "Fine." With a slight wave of his hand, delicate tendrils of glowing mist left his fingertips.

Startled, I jumped away from him as Kiran's hand tightened around mine. I could feel the moonlit slivers of light wrapping around my arm. They glowed with a soft, ethereal light and seemed to pulse in time with my heartbeat. "It's okay," Kiran whispered, his voice soothing and reassuring. "It's a part of his soul. An unbreakable vow." I flinched, but Kiran held my hand tighter, grounding me.

"I expect it back," Sam said as I watched the light curl around my arm like a snake before disappearing into my skin. It left behind a cool sensation like snow falling on my skin.

Sam stuffed the stem of the flower he had been playing with into his shirt pocket. "I think it's time Mia joined us again," he said, raising his hand, but Kiran grabbed it firmly.

"One more thing," Kiran said, staring intently into Sam's eyes. "Who told you about this danger Rhi is in?"

Sam looked down at Kiran's hand digging into his arm. "Isn't it obvious?" he asked with a small smile playing on his lips.

"It isn't to me," Kiran pressed.

Sam lowered his chin, meeting Kiran's gaze head-on. "If you were not so blinded by emotion," he explained. "You would see the danger yourself." His words hung heavily in the air between them as Kiran released Sam's arm and stepped back.

Sam snapped his fingers, and Mia bounded out of her back door. I told her I had some chores to do before excusing myself and leaving her and Sam.

As I entered the house, my mind was racing with questions for Kiran. Stepping into my room, I immediately bombarded him with all that was on my mind. "What is this in my arm? How is it possible for someone to freeze a moment? Why is Sam's daughter in the veil? And where have you been until now?" My mind raced with confusion and curiosity.

"I promise I'll explain, but right now, I need to run his errand for him and come back as soon as possible to find out what he knows about you." Kiran's tone was serious, causing a knot to form in my stomach.

"You've been in the veil before," I said.

"I have." He responded with a heavy sigh.

"Then why are you so worried?" I questioned, still feeling confused. "Can't you still sense me while you're there?"

"The veil exists all around us, intertwined with this world, but it's invisible to most beings. You may have heard of piercing the veil."

I nodded, recalling hearing the term in movies and during Halloween when it was said that the veil between worlds was at its thinnest. I also remembered reading about the origins of Halloween and some of its traditions, such as wearing masks to ward off spirits who might try to capture you from the veil. Who knew there was truth behind those stories?

"So, if it's just an invisible plane within our world, why do I need Sam to guard me? And why can't he just go himself?" I pressed.

Kiran walked over to the window and pulled aside the curtain. I joined him, peering at Mia and Sam, who were still playing with lightning bugs in her back-yard.

"Because time moves differently within the veil," Kiran explained. "It's sort of like a waiting room for souls." He scrubbed a hand through his hair. "I usually just pass through it, not stay there. No one wants to stay there." He closed the curtain, shifting on his feet. "If I were to enter the veil, time would pass faster on this side. I might only be gone for five minutes, but it could feel like five days here."

He turned to face me fully, his expression troubled. "I will know if you're in pain or feeling fear, but the difference in time may prevent me from getting to this side fast enough." He began to pace.

My gaze traveled over his face, and I could tell he didn't want to do this. "I'll be okay," I reassured him, touching his arm. "Why do you believe Sam knows anything about me?"

"Because he was right when he said he has been around since the beginning," Kiran answered, his jaw clenching tightly. "He is eons older than I am and pos-sesses knowledge I may never fully comprehend." His tone became even tenser. "Watchers are unique in that they are still angels but have been cast out of Heaven. They have known and interacted with humanity for centuries, giving them an extraordinary understanding of humans. They also disobeyed the Creator even if Sam said they didn't, and that made them welcome among demons."

"What?" I whispered in disbelief. "Demons?"

Kiran's gaze bore into mine as if grappling with how much to reveal. "It's possible he heard something about you from a demon."

My pulse kicked up at the mention of demons. "Why would a demon want anything to do with me?"

"Why do any of them want what they want?" Kiran's voice was filled with bitterness. "Above everything else, demons want power. After all, that is what their master wanted, the Creator's power."

I suddenly felt chills, causing the tiny hairs on the back of my neck to stand on end. "I'm just a girl, an average one at that. I don't see why...."

His gaze burned into me as he moved forward, cupping my face between his hands and leaning in close. He pressed his forehead against mine, and I was overwhelmed by his sweet vanilla scent that seemed to surround me like a warm embrace. "You're not just any girl," he murmured. "You're extraordinary in ways you can't even begin to imagine." There was a moment I thought he stopped breathing because I couldn't feel his chest move beneath my palms. "Sam cannot go because he is forbidden." His warm breath caressed my skin. "That was one of his and the other Watchers' punishments for disobeying God. They are bound to Earth and cannot enter the veil or Heaven. The only other place they can be besides Earth is Hell."

My hands instinctively curled into the fabric of his shirt, feeling the steady rhythm of his heart beneath them. His breath mingled with mine, and the temptation rose up in me to kiss him. That electric pull stronger than ever. God! What was I thinking? This beautiful creature was an angel, and I had Justin to consider.

He pulled back slightly, confusion evident in his silvery eyes. "What?" I asked, my breath catching in my throat.

"You have conflicting emotions," he said softly, searching my face.

Oh, no, no, no! I screamed in my head. I prayed that he wouldn't be able to read my thoughts to understand why I felt so torn.

"I have to go," he finally said with a pained expression. "The longer we wait, the longer it will take to find out what Sam knows."

My fingers brushed against the cool, invisible band around my arm, a physical reminder of Sam's soul. I looked back up at Kiran, overwhelmed with the desire to wrap my arms around him and never let go. I closed the gap between us and enveloped him in a tight embrace. At first, he tensed up, but then slowly relaxed into my arms. I breathed in deeply, committing his unique scent to memory.

I felt the softness of his wings surrounding us, and my heart hummed with our soul song. Pressing my cheek against his chest, I whispered. "I want you to freeze this moment. I never want to leave it."

His chest rose and fell beneath me as he inhaled deeply before letting out a small chuckle. "I don't think that's what that power is meant for," he said, gently stroking my head. "But if I could, I would hold onto this moment forever, Ahavah."

Chapter Twenty-Seven

He disappeared in the blink of an eye, leaving behind a sudden void that felt like a punch to my gut. I turned around to find Sam lounging on my bed, nonchalantly filing his nails and sucking on a cherry lollipop. My brows furrowed in annoyance as I crossed my arms over my chest.

"Now, now. Don't give me that look," Sam said with a smug grin. "I'm just trying to be helpful." He motioned for me to come closer and patted the bed beside him. "Come sit, and I'll do your nails."

I raised an eyebrow at him as I slowly uncrossed my arms.

"I won't bite," he teased. "Well, not until we know each other better." He let out a low chuckle.

"Where's Mia?"

"I didn't want her here. I'd much rather have some alone time with you," he replied, winking suggestively.

I rolled my eyes at him, unamused. "Does she know where you are?" I finally asked as he persisted in patting the bed next to him.

"Oh, come on, Rhiannon! You have a piece of my soul within you. I'm not going to hurt you," he reassured me.

I suppose this was true. Having a piece of his soul bonded to mine did give me some sense of security. But then again, maybe he didn't care about his own soul.

Sighing, I crossed the room and allowed him to take my hand in his surprisingly soft touch.

"Now, let me see those nails." He took my hands and examined them.

"Girl, do you bite your nails?" he asked as he examined each finger thoroughly.

"Sometimes," I admitted sheepishly.

"Well, this is not acceptable." With a snap of his fingers, a small table materialized before us. On top were an array of colorful polishes and shiny nail tools.

I couldn't help but jump at the sudden appearance of the table. "What?" He asked, raising an eyebrow. "Your Guardian has never manifested anything for you?"

I shook my head, mesmerized by the table magically appearing in my room. "Um, no. I don't think he's ever felt the need to.

A soft laugh escaped from Sam's lips. "That boy," he shook his head in mild exasperation before picking up a file from the table.

"What?" I asked curiously as he began filing my nails. "That one does not take full advantage of his powers." "Well, maybe because he's kind and doesn't feel the need to impress me."

"If you believe that, then you truly are foolish," Sam replied, his gaze meeting mine.

I pulled my hand away from him, irritation bubbling up within me. "I am not foolish," I retorted sharply. "And he is kind."

Sam reached for my hand, but I pulled it away. "I apologize," he said softly. "I tend to be...well, blunt."

"Bluntness does not equal truth," I shot back bitterly.

He tipped his chin towards me in acknowledgment. "Touché," he conceded with a slight smile. "But I stand by what I said. Your Guardian is young and naive, and so are you."

I frowned with irritation, but curiosity got the better of me. "What kind of powers does Kiran have that I don't know about?"

"Well," Sam began, tossing a glance my way as he continued to meticulously file my nails. "Guardian angels hold an arsenal of gifts that can both protect and conceal."

"Like?" I prodded.

"Take this table, for instance; it's conjured out of thin air - a product of celestial manifestation. It's one of all angels' most basic abilities."

He paused for a moment and then continued, "Angels can manipulate matter." His eyes flickered towards me. "All of us can create a storm in the middle of a desert or grow flowers from barren soil. Guardians will use this to alter reality to protect and help those they're assigned to."

"He told me once that he could erase my memories."

"Did he now?"

I swallowed nervously, "You don't think he has done that to me already, do you?

"No, no. I don't believe he has."

I sighed with relief. "What else can angels do?"

"Do you remember me freezing the moment before?"

I nodded.

"Time," he added nonchalantly as if he was discussing weekend plans and not some superhuman ability. "We can slow it down, speed it up, or even stop it entirely like I did.

Though messing with time does have its consequences."

"Consequences?" The word slipped out before I could stop myself, but Sam merely shrugged without elaborating.

A confused frown creased my forehead. I chewed on my lower lip as I pondered over his words, wondering what else he wasn't sharing with me.

As Sam finished with the last nail, he reached for a bottle of pink polish. "I think this color suits you," he said, undoing the cap, and the scent of the polish wafted up from the open bottle.

He meticulously painted each of my nails. "Can't you just snap your fingers, and my nails would be done?" I asked.

"Well, yes, but where's the fun in that?"

I watched his hands move gracefully over mine, marveling at how effortlessly he wielded the small brush. As he worked, a thought suddenly struck me. He had mentioned my father earlier, and I wondered how much he actually knew about him. "You said I'm like my father," I blurted out.

His hand paused, and I saw him take a deep breath before answering. "You are," he confirmed.

"You know him then?" I pressed on.

"I do," he replied simply.

I studied his profile as he continued to work on my nails. "How?" I prodded.

"How what?" he asked, feigning ignorance.

"Don't play stupid, Sam. How do you know my father?"

He stopped his movements again and raised his dark eyes to meet my gaze directly. "Like I told you."

"I know, you've been around from the beginning," I said, exasperated.

"Does that mean you remember and know every human that has ever lived?"

He stopped again, and his dark lashes lifted so that he could look directly into my eyes. "No. Not every human."

He snapped his fingers, and the table and polish disappeared. "There. Pretty in pink."

"Wait, you still haven't answered my question," I protested.

A faint smile tugged at his lips. "Rhi..." His voice trailed away as he lowered his gaze, "Your father was...is someone special."

"Special?" I questioned, my heart pounding in anticipation.

"Yeah," Sam confirmed quietly as he rubbed the back of his neck, "Very special."

"But you can't tell me where he is or why he left my mother and me?"

Sam clenched his jaw and fixed me with a long stare. "I can tell you this. Your personality, your strength, your resilience... I see those qualities in you that mirror his."

A brief smile flitted across his lips, "That's all I am allowed to say. You'll know in time. And that's all I'm going to say about it."

"But you can't tell me where he is."

"Rhiannon, don't push me." Sam's eyes are like twin barriers of obsidian guarding the answers I seek.

I want to know more about my father; I want closure from all the nights I lay awake, wondering why he left my mother and me. I want to scream at him, stomp my feet, and demand answers about the father I've never known. But I don't. Instead, I tamp down my frustrations, pushing them to the back of my mind.

"You opened that door, not me," I finally say in resignation.

"I suppose I did." Sam sighed.

I stared down at how pretty my perfectly manicured nails were. "Maybe you should give up your day job and become a nail tech," I joked.

"Honey." He drawled. "Who says I haven't? I have been around...."

I cut him off before he could finish. "Yes, yes, since the beginning of time," I quipped.

He let out a hearty laugh and gracefully leaped off my bed. "What shall we do now?" He inquired with an excited spark in his eyes. "Perhaps a makeover? I can give you a glamorous new hairstyle!"

I glared at him.

"Now, I promised to protect you, but that doesn't mean I'll be cooped up in your room with you while your Guardian is away."

"He has a name, you know," I reminded him.

Sam let out an exasperated sigh. "Yes, I know he does. Now let's go out." His gaze swept over me before adding, "Put on something more alluring."

"Alluring?" I repeated with a raised eyebrow.

"I don't have the patience for this," he huffed before snapping his fingers once again. Suddenly, I stood in silver heels that sparkled under the light and a green sequin dress that hugged my curves perfectly.

"Hey!" I protested.

"You're right, that's not really your style," Sam conceded with another snap of his fingers. This time, I was dressed in a black leather miniskirt, a t-shirt that boldly claimed 'Half Angel Half Devil,' and thigh-high boots that made me feel well, powerful, and seductive.

"That's more like it," he grinned wickedly. "We're going dancing."

"Whoa, whoa," I stumbled slightly as I approached him. "I can't dance, especially not in these things." I lifted one of the boots up to show him.

He rolled his eyes and snapped his fingers for a third time.

"Better?" he asked.

The outfit remained the same, but the boots were now flat and easier to walk in. I made my way over to the mirror, admiring my appearance. Despite never owning anything like this before, I couldn't deny that I looked good. My eyes landed on the t-shirt again, and I raised an eyebrow at Sam.

"Really?" I questioned, pointing to the words emblazoned across it.

His grin grew even wider. "Oh yes, really."

With another snap of his fingers, we suddenly stood outside in front of a large motorcycle. Sam's attire had also changed; he wore designer dark blue jeans, a fitted black t-shirt, and a black leather jacket. "Get on, sweet cheeks," Sam said with a mischievous grin.

I narrowed my eyes at him. "Sweet cheeks?" I retorted, not amused.

"What? It suits you," he chuckled as he swung his leg over the seat of his bike and started the engine, the loud roar filling the air. My heart raced with excitement at the thought of riding on it.

"Wait, what about Nan? I need to tell...."

He put a hand up to stop me, "I took care of it, so stop worrying."

"How did you..." I began again, trailing off into uncertainty.

He rolled his eyes dramatically. "We can nudge human minds toward certain trains of thought or away from others. Your Nan won't realize time has passed; she'll think you're still upstairs." He grinned at me, eyes twinkling under the dim light filtering down from the streetlamp. "Think of it as being camouflaged."

I sighed heavily with resignation, "Let's go then."

Sam motioned for me to get on behind him. "But I'm wearing a skirt," I protested over the noise of the powerful pipes.

"Live a little," he egged me on, revving the engine even louder.

Rolling my eyes, I muttered, "What the hell" to myself before finally giving in and swinging my leg over the seat.

"Hold on," Sam instructed and gunned the gas, causing us to lurch forward. I quickly wrapped my arms around his waist, afraid of being thrown off by the wind rushing past us.

As we weaved in and out of traffic, I felt a rush of adrenaline. Sam seemed to have complete control over the bike, effortlessly maneuvering through the streets. I was slightly disappointed when we stopped in front of a club with loud music blasting from within. The line of people waiting to get in stretched around the corner, making it clear that this was a popular spot.

I was unsure of our location or if we were still in my town. Sam helped me off the bike, and I ran my fingers through my wind-tangled hair. "You look fine," he assured me with a grin as he led me towards the entrance.

A tall man with aviator sunglasses stood outside with a clipboard in hand. When Sam tapped him on the shoulder, he turned towards us and grinned, flashing straight white teeth. "Samyaza!" he exclaimed, slapping Sam on the back. "Where have you been, bro?"

"Here and there," Sam replied casually.

The man laughed as he stepped aside to let us enter the club and turned his attention to me. "And who's this?" he asked, intrigued.

"I'm her babysitter while her Guardian is off on an errand for me," Sam explained.

The man's smile grew as he looked me up and down. "I approve," he declared. I scoffed at his behavior. "Like I need your approval."

"Feisty one," the man chuckled.

"You have no idea," Sam said, pulling me along as we entered the crowded club.

"A Watcher friend of yours?" I asked once we were out of earshot.

"Not exactly."

The dimly lit club was packed with people, their bodies moving and swaying to the loud music that filled the air. Flashing blue, purple, and pink lights illuminated the crowd's faces, giving off a magical and hypnotic vibe. The bar we passed had a neon sign that read *The Arcane Mirage* in bold, glowing letters. I could feel the press of bodies against me, the room's heat causing a sheen of sweat on my skin. The vibrations from the music reverberated through my body, making my heart race. I had never been in a place like this.

Sam led us to the back of the club, through a crowded dance floor, and up a short flight of stairs. At the top stood another large man, his muscular frame imposing as he held a velvet rope to block people from entering. Like the man at the door, this one seemed happy to see Sam and waved us by with a friendly nod.

We found ourselves at a table that overlooked the dance floor. Immediately, a pretty girl with a high blonde ponytail stopped to take our order.

"Order whatever you want," Sam said, leaning across the table toward me. "It's on me."

I smiled at the girl and ordered a Coke. Sam shook his head and ordered something I couldn't make out over the booming music.

Looking around the club, I felt my foot tapping to the beat. The music wasn't typically my style, but it was undeniably catchy and had me wanting to dance along. As the girl returned with our drinks, I noticed Sam's glowing bright green and bubbling.

He pulled out a wad of cash and handed a bill to the girl, who beamed at him and gave him a playful wink. "Does everyone know you here?" I asked him incredulously.

He took a sip of his drink and passed it to me. "Take a drink," he offered. "And yes, I know quite a few beings in this establishment."

"Beings?" I echoed, remembering how the man at the door had addressed him by his full name. "Are they all Watchers?"

"Not exactly," he replied, pushing the drink closer. "Try it. I think you'll like it."

I eyed the drink suspiciously before taking a tiny sip. Fire filled my mouth, and I coughed, caught off guard by its

intensity.

Sam chuckled. "Try it again. it tastes better once you get used to the burn."

"What is this?" I asked, still recovering from the shock of the drink.

"It's called a diabolical elixir."

"Fitting name," I muttered before taking another cautious sip. Surprisingly, it did taste better.

My attention was drawn to a statuesque girl with fiery red hair as she approached our table. Her long locks fell over her shoulders, and her eyes sparkled devilishly. She stopped by our table, whispering something in Sam's ear. As she glanced at me, I could have sworn I saw her eyes flash red. Without hesitation, Sam pulled her onto his lap.

"Who's the girl? Did you bring us a little snack, Samyaza?"

"Rhi, this is Valentina." Sam's hands roamed over her back and into her hair, eliciting a pleased response from her. "She's not a snack, Val. I'm just looking after her for now."

Valentina snorted, and unease clawed in my chest.

"What are you?" I murmured, thinking she couldn't hear me over the noise of the music.

Her eyes narrowed on mine, examining me like an insect she wanted to squash. Yes, her eyes turned red again before they went back to blue.

"What am I?" She replied, her voice oozing with confidence. "The real question, honey, is what are you?"

Sam abruptly lifted her off his lap and stood her on her feet before him. "Time to go, Val," he said sternly. "I have business to attend to."

Valentina pouted but sauntered away with one last glance over her shoulder at me before disappearing into the crowd.

I scooted my chair closer to Sam and grabbed his arm tightly. "Okay, Samyaza," I spoke over the blaring music. "What was that all about?" My eyes flickered toward where Valentina disappeared. "Her eyes turned red!"

Sam took a long sip of his drink before replying, causing me to cringe at the memory of how strong it burned going down.

"Yes, they did," he confirmed, his gaze fixed on something across the dance floor. Now, kindly remove your hand from my arm."

I obeyed but glared at him with determination. "Where did you bring me?"

"This club is called *The Arcane Mirage*," he said, swirling his drink around in its glass. "And these are some of my acquaintances."

"Acquaintances who know your real name?" I pressed. "Are they Watchers?"

"Some are, yes." He lifted his gaze to look over the dance floor once again. "Some others have known me for a long time," he admitted, finally meeting my eyes. "But enough talk. This is a great song, let's dance."

With an angry slam, I brought my hand down on the table. "I don't want to dance. I want to know why Valentina called me a snack!"

Sam chuckled, his dark eyes sparkling with amusement. "You are quite stubborn, aren't you? Poor Kiran has his hands full with you." He tilted his head, and a sly grin appeared on his lips. "Or so he wishes anyway."

I narrowed my eyes at him. "What is that supposed to mean?"

With an exasperated sigh, he demanded, "If I answer your questions, will you finally dance? Because honestly, this conversation is boring me."

Crossing my arms over my chest and leaning back in my chair, I gave him my death stare.

Sam leaned forward, a wicked twinkle in his eye. "Alright, alright. This is not just any club, Rhiannon. It caters to those who are different." His grin grew wider. "Watchers, demons..."

Trepidation curled around me at the mention of demons. "Demons?" I hissed.

"Yes," Sam confirmed nonchalantly as if it were the most normal thing in the world. "And some fallen angels."

"Why did you decide to bring me here?"

"Why not?" Sam answered, tilting his head and scrutinizing me with a gaze so intense it almost felt like being under a microscope. "Rhiannon," he began slowly, seemingly measuring each word before allowing them to escape his lips. "You'll blend in just fine."

Sam's eyes twinkled mischievously as he held out a hand to me, "I answered your questions; now you must hold up your end of the bargain and dance with me."

"You're insane."

He cocked his head at me, studying me for a moment before nodding in agreement. "Wandering the earth for billions of years will do that to you."

With a firm grip on my hand, he lifted me off my seat and led us down to the dance floor. Around us, people moved to the beat of the music, their bodies swaying and twisting in sync with the pulsing lights that danced above.

As we reached the center of the crowd, I caught sight of Valentina, her lengthy hair swinging around her face as she danced. Sam pushed through the sea of bodies until we were in the heart of the dance floor. Laser lights flashed, and disco balls cast tiny sparkles across the room.

Sam's hands found my waist, causing me to tense up. He pulled me closer to him and whispered in my ear, "You need to loosen up and feel the music."

"Kind of hard when I'm surrounded by demons."

"Not just demons." He whispered, and I felt his hands reach for my hips. "Move your body." His hands grasped me hard, and he moved with me.

My face felt hot with embarrassment. I felt like everyone was watching me, but as I looked around us, no one seemed to be paying any attention to us. I spotted Valentina again. I couldn't believe how well she danced with stiletto heels on.

"Is Valentina a demon?" I asked Sam as the music picked up the pace.

He spun me around so my back was against his chest. "Indeed, she is," he breathed into my ear.

"Why do you hang around with Mia when it's obvious you enjoy hanging out at places that cater to the supernatural?"

Sam let out a soft tsk and pulled me closer, his hand firm on my waist. "Are we dancing, or are we playing an infinite round of twenty questions?"

"Can't it be both?"

Sam rolled his eyes and drew me back. As the music shifted, he effortlessly caught the new rhythm, as if the beat was synced with his heartbeat. "For one, she's incredibly loyal," he said, his voice filled with admiration. "I have taught her ancestors for hundreds of years the ways of magic, and it's her turn." He grinned, showing the sharp white of his teeth.

His arm wrapped around my waist, and he turned me again so we faced each other. His playful smile was disarming as he said, "So what would dear Kiran think if you were in a club surrounded by monsters?"

"He wouldn't be happy, that's for sure," I scowled.

His hand slid down to the small of my back, and suddenly, he dipped me, sending my heart into my throat. But his hold was secure, and he pulled me back up effortlessly. "I won't let them touch you, sweet cheeks. I am the oldest one here and the most powerful." With a swift turn, he positioned me with my back against his chest once again, his chin resting on my shoulder.

As we danced, his closeness became increasingly unsettling. I had never danced with anyone like this before, and it made me feel uneasy. His breath was hot against my cheek, and little pinpricks broke out across my skin.

"Power isn't everything, you know," I retorted, turning within his arms to face him fully, my brown eyes meeting his smoldering gaze.

"And what is?" Sam countered, his smile nearly neon in the electric wash of strobe lights overhead.

I thought about his question for a moment, the world whirling around us in a blur of multi-colored light and shadow, "I think love is," I finally said.

"Love, huh?" he laughed above the pounding rhythm as he twirled me again. "Love can also be dangerously deceptive. It can sweetly charm you while silently weaving chains around your heart." A new song whirred into existence around us. "Kiran knows what I'm talking about."

The mention of Kiran's name caught me off guard. What did he mean by that? Before I managed to ask, Valentina and another girl appeared in front of us. Sam didn't stop moving, though, ignoring them both. Both of the girls were dressed in dark, revealing clothes. The girl I didn't know had wild hair like raven's feathers. Valentina's eyes glittered with mischief while the raven-haired girls held a dangerous edge.

"Samyaza," Valentina purred. "Why are you being so greedy with this little flower?" Her eyes roamed over me suggestively, her tongue darting out to wet her lips.

"Go away, Val," Sam snapped, a hint of anger flashing in his eyes.

"As you wish," she said, turning to leave with her friend. Before they could go, however, Valentina ran a slim finger along my cheek. "I'll see you later."

"Not likely," I blurted out.

"Oh, really?" she lifted a brow in a challenge. Shaking her head, she extended her arm out, palm up. "Take my hand."

Before I could even react, Sam suddenly stood before me, blocking the girl's reach. His expression hardened as he sneered at her. "I told you to leave Val," he spat.

They stood just inches away from each other, their eyes locked in a tense standoff. Suddenly, the raven-haired girl let out a rich, throaty laugh. "Samyaza," she purred, her voice dripping with honey and malice. "Why so protective of this one? You're no Guardian."

My hands began to tremble as I watched the exchange between them. My heart longed for Kiran, and I silently called out to him amidst the chaos around me. Suddenly, all three of them turned to look at me.

"Rhiannon, don't call him," Sam mouthed the words to me urgently.

Confusion flooded my mind, and my body felt like it was vibrating with tension.

"You're bound to her," Valentina stated matter-of-factly. Sam didn't respond, but his dark eyes creased at the edges, and I could feel the ground rumble beneath my feet. A pungent smell of smoke filled the air, and I let out a scream as I felt myself being pulled away from the club.

We were immediately transported to a dark cavern with flickering torches lining the rough stone walls. My eyes darted wildly, searching for Sam, who suddenly appeared before me. "What...what just happened?" I stammered, my voice echoing off the cavern walls.

"We're beneath the city," Sam replied calmly. "I teleported us here. There are many tunnels and caves hidden beneath New Jersey and New York. Some were used by the Lenape tribe for shelter and storing food. Others were created during Prohibition for smuggling," he explained, brushing off his jacket as if this was a normal occurrence for him.

"Why are we here?" I asked breathlessly.

Sam casually crossed one leg over the other and leaned against the wall, the flickering light from a torch casting eerie shadows across his dark features. "Because you had to go and call your Guardian," Sam replied.

"I-I only did so in my head," I stammered.

"Yes, but we can hear you. You don't know how to cloak your thoughts," Sam explained sternly.

My heart began to race as I processed his words. Demons, angels, Guardians... it was all too overwhelming.

"And because you did that, they realized a part of my soul is in you, and that is something they would love to get their demon hands on," he continued. "An angel's soul is mighty."

"I don't understand how they would know that," I interjected, struggling to keep up.

"You just don't get it," Sam said, frustration evident in his voice as he pushed himself off the wall and came closer to me. "When you talk to Kiran that way, it's through your soul. You exposed your soul along with mine since our souls are entwined."

His intense gaze held mine, and I couldn't help but squirm under his dark stare. "Ugh!" Sam huffed, "Kiran should have taught you to shield your thoughts when you soul speak." Sam suddenly slammed his hand into the wall beside my head, causing me to jump in surprise, "I'm beginning to think you're more trouble than you're worth."

"How was this happening?" I thought to myself, feeling completely overwhelmed. My mouth went dry, and I licked my parched lips before speaking. "I'm sorry. I didn't know," I managed to say, feeling utterly powerless.

Sam's hand remained against the wall, but his head lowered until our eyes were level. He spoke in a low tone. "You're ridiculously naive. You should learn to defend yourself," he stated firmly. "My brothers and I taught humans how to make weapons and use magic for this exact reason. It's unfair that you were created and left with no means to protect yourself from the supernatural.... and your own kind." He let out a long breath, "I'm sorry. I shouldn't take my frustration out on you." One side of his mouth ticked up. "Please forgive me, and I will teach you how to mind shield so this won't happen again."

"Thank you, Sam," I said quietly. "I appreciate you looking out for me."

He nodded and reached for one of the torches that lined the walls. as he did so, I took in my surroundings - the rough, rocky walls covered in moss and lichen, the stalactites hanging ominously from the ceiling, and the musty scent of the cave filling my nostrils.

"Here." Sam took off his jacket and draped it around my shoulders.

"Thanks," I muttered, pulling it tighter around me. "Come," he urged, stepping forward and gesturing for me to follow. "The faerie hole is just up this way."

"The faerie hole?" I repeated, intrigued.

"It doesn't really have faeries in it," he chuckled. "It's just a name the locals came up with, but it is blessed by the Lenape."

We turned a corner and suddenly came upon a large opening. Sam guided me towards one side and lifted his torch to reveal strange symbols carved into the rock wall. My eyes widened in wonder as he explained their significance.

"These are symbols blessed by the Lenape," he said, his voice hushed with reverence. "They considered this cave sacred." Sam turned to face me, his dark eyes glowing in the torchlight. He moved the torch over the symbols and up the wall until I could see petroglyphs resembling people.

"This is the story of their creator and their demon of death."

"Like God and the Devil?" I asked, tracing my fingers over the carvings.

"Yes," Sam nodded. "Similar to monotheistic religions. Look here." He pointed to a large circle with animals carved around it. "Before creation, there was nothing. An empty, dark space. But a spirit existed, and this was their Creator.

Pretty boring to sit in nothingness, wouldn't you say?" He gave a soft laugh before continuing. "While sleeping, he dreamt of a world with mountains, forests, animals...and man. He was so enthralled with his dream that he created Earth just as he dreamed it. In his dream, he saw opposites, which created balance. So he created light and darkness, male and female, hot and cold, and good and evil."

I studied the old images as I pulled his jacket tighter around me.

"Sound familiar?" Sam asked me, turning to meet my gaze with his dark, intense eyes.

I rubbed my arms. "It sounds like what we believe," I said.

"Indeed." He moved with a silent grace, his footsteps barely making a sound against the earthen ground. "So, then a spirit of darkness was created called Matantu, and darkness came into being.

"Like Lucifer," I said, my voice echoing softly in the ancient chamber.

"Much like Lucifer."

I turned to him in awe of what I was hearing. "Are they the same being?" I asked, my mind reeling with this new knowledge. "And what about angels? Do the Lenape believe in angels?"

"Yes, they are called the manëtuwàk. But Matantu is not one of them. He is not Lucifer because Lucifer was, or rather is, an angel," he replied solemnly.

"How can that be? What is Matantu then?"

"Just like there is a hierarchy of angels, so it is with demons," Sam explained, his gaze scanning the walls adorned with symbols and carvings. "Matantu would be considered one of the highest demons."

I was drawn to the ceiling, where more intricate symbols were etched into the stone.

"A demon trap," Sam stated grimly. This is an ancient one made by the Mëteìnu of the tribe."

"What's a Mëteìnu?" I asked, my curiosity piqued once again.

"Basically, a medicine man or woman. Mia's grandmother is one. That's why we came here," Sam continued, turning to me. "Valentina and Sorcha can't come in here."

"Are you afraid of them?" I asked.

A laugh escaped his lips. "God, no!" He found a perfectly shaped hole in the wall and placed his torch inside. "They can't harm me, not really anyway," he shrugged. "You were about to be abducted by a lesser entity, which is a fate I find terribly dull for you, Rhiannon. So I intervened."

He touches the tip of my nose with a long finger. "But you'll forgive me for the tactical extraction. I am bound to keep you safe after all."

"So why take me somewhere that demons hang out?"

"Because you are, contrary to your own opinion, perfectly safe with me." He nudges me lightly with his shoulder. "If you hadn't thrown a wrench in our plans by soulspeaking to your Guardian, we'd still be making up new dance moves."

He shook his head as his gaze swept to the ceiling, "See that?"

I looked and spotted vines covering a hole and, beyond them, the starry sky.

"If you are ever on the reservation and need to get away from a demon, look for vines lining the ground. Push them aside and you'll find a rope. Climb down into a tunnel, and you will be in a demon trap, so they won't follow you."

My phone chirped in my pocket, causing me to jump anxiously. I fumbled for it in the back pocket of my skirt, my heart racing as I saw several texts from Justin waiting for me. *"Hey, Rhi. I'm almost done with work. Should I come by?"* and then another about twenty minutes later: *"Rhi? Where are you?"* But the one that caught my attention was the most recent: *"Rhi, I'm getting worried! Why aren't you answering me? I went by your house and climbed up the roof to your window. You're not in your room. Call me!"*

Sam looked at me curiously. "Lover boy?" he asked, amusement evident in his tone.

I scowled at him and began typing a response, but I found myself at a loss for words. How could I explain where I was and what I was doing? Finally, I managed to type out a brief message: *"I'm okay. I went out with Sam. Remember him? Mia's friend."* My fingers hovered over the screen, unsure of what else to say. *"Be home soon. I will text when you can come by."*

Almost immediately, Justin replied: *"Sam? Really? Thought you barely knew him. Where are you? I'll come get you."*

I looked up at Sam, who was still watching me intently. "He wants to come get me," I informed him.

"That's not going to work," he said bluntly. "We must stay here until Valentina is dealt with."

"Dealt with?" I repeated, "What does that mean?"

"Exactly as it sounds," Sam replied grimly. "My brothers will handle her and then come to retrieve us. I'm not going to lose that piece of my soul."

"Oh, don't worry about me," I said sarcastically.

"Like I said before, sweet cheeks. You're more trouble than you're worth."

Just then, my phone rang. It was Justin. "Damn it," I cursed under my breath. "What do I tell him?" I looked to Sam for guidance, but he just shrugged his shoulders.

Feeling panicked, I answered the call and immediately regretted it as Justin's loud voice blared through the phone. "Where the hell are you?!"

Grimacing, I held the phone away from my ear as Justin continued his frantic rant.

"Quite a catch, that one," Sam said as he studied me.

Finally, I raised my voice to be heard over Justin's angry ranting. "Justin, I'm fine. What is wrong with you? Sam is just a friend. I was hanging out with him and Mia. She had something to do, so Sam...." I paused, thinking of how to explain. "Sam suggested we take a ride on his motorcycle."

A new stream of expletives left Justin's mouth, and I hung up on him, feeling frustrated and annoyed. He immediately called back, but I let it go to voicemail. I quickly typed in a text, barely containing my anger. "I can't believe you! Leave me alone." The phone rang again, and I shut it off, shoving it back into my pocket.

"Well, that went well," Sam said dryly.

I glared at him. "He's never been that way before."

"He has a jealous streak," Sam stated flatly.

"I guess so," I said, defeated. I had never been in a relationship before, let alone one in which a boy told me he loved me and acted possessive.

I yanked the phone back out of my pocket. Maybe I should try calling him back.

"Don't," Sam said, placing a hand on my arm.

"Ugh, when are your friends going to be done? I want to go home." I heaved, feeling exhausted from the whole situation.

"It shouldn't be much longer. They would have had to be discreet. We don't want to start wars or cause disturbances here on Earth."

"A war?" I asked incredulously.

"Those of us bound to the earth have an unspoken understanding. We all enjoy living here and don't want to disrupt the balance of good and evil by causing any..." He paused. "Disturbances."

"And you taking care of them would be considered a disturbance?"

"It would."

"Don't you think the others on the dance floor noticed your disappearing act?" I pointed out. "That isn't a disturbance?"

"Oh, that?" Sam chuckled. "They wouldn't have noticed, really. You did because you haven't experienced it before."

"I can't say I have," I replied dryly, still overwhelmed by everything.

Sam's lips widened. "For us, it's just another night. They would have assumed I wanted some alone time with you." He smirked, and I felt my cheeks flush.

"See! That's why I call you sweet cheeks. It's so easy to make you blush."

I took a deep breath before asking, "So, do Watchers just pop in and out of places?"

"Not just us. Demons do it, too. But I like to add a little pizazz," he replied with a wink.

His arrogance made my eyes roll involuntarily. "Yes, you're quite the pizazzler." I mocked.

I stopped twirling the phone in my hand and turned it back on. Seven missed calls from Justin and a text from Taylor that read: *"Hey, is everything okay? Justin called Scott, all upset about not knowing where you are."*

I quickly typed a reply to Taylor, saying that everything was fine and that I would be home soon. I stuffed the phone in my pocket and turned to where Sam stood. "How long do you think Kiran will be gone?" I asked, feeling anxiety bubble up.

Sam seemed to ponder my question, rubbing his chin with his hand. "If he doesn't get sidetracked, I think he should be back sometime tomorrow at this time. That's if he's quick."

"Why would he get sidetracked?" I asked.

"Let's just say that interesting things can appear in the veil."

"Why are you so cryptic?"

"Am I? I hadn't noticed."

"You are, and you know it," I spat. "Why don't you just answer with straight answers?"

"I didn't think you appreciated my bluntness," he said with a raised eyebrow.

I scowled at him.

"Now, now, you don't want to get those little wrinkles between your eyes from glaring at me so much," he teased.

"Ugh, you're impossible!" I exclaimed, throwing my hands up in exasperation.

Suddenly, electricity crackled in the air, and a man with short auburn hair appeared before us, "That he is," the auburn-haired man said.

Sam walked towards the man and clapped him on the back. "Thank you, my friend," he said, smiling at the man. The man extended his hand towards me, and I hesitantly reached out to shake it. His eyes were the lightest blue I'd ever seen, almost translucent.

"I expect our impossible friend Sam has been taking good care of you?" He grasped my hand firmly. "My name is Armaros."

"My name is Rh.."

"Rhiannon. I know."

"You do?" I asked, surprised.

"Yes. We all do."

As my eyes flicked to Sam, I could see his expression tinged with annoyance and impatience as he leaned casually against the wall. "Who is 'we'?" I asked curiously, turning back to Armaros.

Before I could register his movement, Sam suddenly stood before me, blocking my view of Armaros. "I think it's time for me to take you home," he declared firmly.

As Armaros' eyes narrowed in suspicion, Sam seemed to tense up. "What's going on with you, Samyaza?" Armaros demanded.

"Nothing, nothing at all," Sam replied smoothly. "Rhiannon just mentioned wanting to go home, and with everything that's happened, I think it's best to get her there."

Armaros seemed to consider this for a moment before speaking again. "Don't you want to know where I put the demons?" he asked slyly.

At this, Sam's head snapped up in surprise. "Put them?" he questioned.

"I could have easily destroyed Valentina," Armaros began, "but Sorcha is another story."

"Why?" I interjected, remembering the dark-haired girl from earlier.

"Because she is the daughter of..." Armaros began before being interrupted by Sam.

"She is the daughter of someone powerful against whom we don't wish to declare war," Sam finished tersely.

Armaros shook his head in disbelief. Turning to me, "She's the daughter of Vincent Moretti."

Chapter Twenty-Eight

My heart beat frantically in my chest, making it hard to catch my breath. "Wait, what?" I managed to choke out, my voice trembling. "You mean Justin's biological father, Vince?"

Sam's shoulders slumped, and he let out a deep sigh. "I didn't want you to find out like this."

"Find out? Find out what?" I demanded, my mind reeling with the implications of Armaros' words. "That Vince has little demon children! How is that even possible?" I exclaimed to Sam.

"We can mate just as humans do," Armaros interjected calmly.

Sam shot a scolding look at Armaros. "You already have your hands full with Kiran. I didn't want to bring Vince or Justin into this mess."

"Wait a minute," I tried to take a deep breath, but it kept getting caught in my throat. "Is Vince a demon?"

They both shook their heads.

"See what you did, Armaros!" Sam hissed and then turned towards me. "Vincent Moretti is a Fallen. A fallen angel."

I gasped, having a hard time catching my breath. "Is Mrs. Rizzo a demon?"

"No, she is human."

"Then that makes Justin...."

"A Nephilim," Sam stated tersely.

A gnawing fear coiled within me like a tight spring ready to explode.

"Rhiannon," Sam says, "I need you to listen." His stare is intense. "Justin doesn't know what he is."

My mind spun, refusing to process the whirlwind of information being tossed in my direction. The world as I knew it was unspooling into chaos, and I felt like a leaf tossed in a storm. Sam looked at me reassuringly with a tight grip still on my arm. "I'll explain everything when we get back to your house."

I had so many questions tangled inside me like a ball of yarn, but I nodded.

Grabbing my arm and pulling me closer, Sam turned to Armaros, "Thank you, brother."

Armaros studied Sam's face and then nodded.

With a wave of Sam's hand, the ground beneath us began to shake and swirl once again. Coils of smoke surrounded us, and I squeezed my eyes shut tightly, trying not to scream as we were transported back to the street in front of the club.

My words hissed out through gritted teeth as I glared at Sam, my heart still racing from our sudden escape. "A little warning would be nice," I scolded him.

"Now, what is the fun in that?" he laughed nervously, shifting his weight from foot to foot. Throwing his leg over the bike, he motioned for me to do the same. All around us, the night seemed alive as shadows seemed to dance menacingly at the corners of my vision.

When we got back to my house and into my room, I collapsed onto my bed, groaning in frustration. My gaze drifted up to meet Sam's intense stare. "What?" I demanded.

"Nothing, sweet cheeks," he teased, but his voice had a hint of concern.

I studied him for a moment. He seemed desperate to get us back here and away from Armaros. He knew something, not just what he had promised to tell Kiran about the danger I was in. He knew more, a lot more.

"Out with it, Sam," I said, rolling onto my side to face him. "You promised to explain things when I got home. Well, here we are. So start talking."

Ignoring me, Sam began sorting through my music collection. "They don't make music like they used to," he mused. "Oh, wait!" He pulled out a CD with a triumphant grin. "You like The Doors?" Without waiting for an answer, he popped it into the player. "Jim Morrison was quite the frontman," Sam reminisced. "I saw them once in L.A."

"Stop," I said sharply as The Doors music began to play, the lively keyboards filling my room. "You're avoiding the conversation."

"No, I'm not." He feigned innocence.

Frustrated by his evasiveness, I pushed myself up and swung my legs over the edge of the bed, glaring at him. "How long have you known about Vince?" I demanded.

"I've known Vincent since..."

"Don't say 'since the beginning,' or I'll throw something at you," I snapped.

Sam chuckled, his eyes dancing with amusement. "You're so violent. I think I like it."

"Shut up," I hissed, feeling a blush rise to my cheeks. "You're like a perverted old man, you know that?"

He seemed to ponder that momentarily, his sharp eyes scanning the space around us as he considered my question. Then, with a wave of his hand, a bean bag chair appeared out of thin air, and he plopped down onto it. "Well, I haven't known him since the beginning, but pretty close," he said casually.

"But...how is that possible? My grandmother knew his father."

A slight grin appeared on his lips as he tapped his leg with his fingers to the melody of the music. "Actually, Vince and his grandfather are the same person."

I could feel my jaw drop in disbelief. "Wait, what?! My grandmother dated...." I shook my head in confusion. "That can't be right."

"Did she ever mention how much they looked alike?" he asked casually.

She had. I remembered she said Vince looked so much like his father, and Justin looked like him as well. "Yes," I whispered faintly.

"You see," he began in a low voice. "We angels have the ability to choose our physical appearance. Some prefer to stay on the younger side, like myself, while

Vincent likes to experience life as a human and ages accordingly. He typically started as a teenager and matured until about the age of sixty before restarting again. However, when he fell from grace, he was closer to looking around forty-five in human years and has remained in that form ever since. He can no longer change himself now that he is a Fallen."

I furrowed my brows in confusion. "But won't people notice him not aging?"

"He makes up stories and just returns as a son or cousin. He was the one your grandmother knew before he fell."

We sat in hushed silence. The gentle hum of the stereo filled the room as I mulled over Vince's fall from grace. "What did Vince do to cause him to fall?" I finally asked.

"Well, there were two reasons," Sam continued. "Firstly, Vincent had a weakness for human women."

"Like my grandmother," I whispered.

"Yes. Like her and others. We, the Watchers, are not the only ones who, once they were here and involved with humanity, started to be lured by the feelings you all convey. Love, well, it can get the better of us."

"So he fell because he fell in love?"

"Not just that. He did not just fall in love with humans but also many things humans engage in."

With a flick of his wrist, the volume increased on the stereo.

"My grandmother." I began to protest.

"Relax. I put a glamour on her. She is completely unaware of our presence and cannot perceive any sounds coming from this room," Sam assured me with a confident smile. "Like I was saying, Vincent began to lust after money, women, and worldly things. But what sealed his fate was when he fell in love with a demon."

"Is that Sorcha's mother?"

"God no, Vincent is not a one-woman or one-demon individual. He likes to play the field, as you humans say."

I couldn't hide my surprise and confusion. "Is Sorcha older or younger than Justin?" I asked.

Suddenly, Sam's eyes darted to the window behind me. "Speak of the devil," he grumbled.

Confused, I turned towards the window and heard a tapping sound against the glass. I immediately knew it was Justin.

I quickly slid off the bed and approached the window, where I saw his green eyes peering back at me. Panicked, I whispered to Sam, "You should hide or whatever you do."

"Too late, he's seen me, and I'm not about to let him know what I am by pulling a disappearing act."

"Great," I uttered and slid the window open.

"What are you doing here, Justin?" I whispered urgently.

He pushed past me, one of his long legs crossing the window, then the other, until he stood before me, his emerald green eyes blazing with anger.

"The real question is, what are you doing with him?" he spat, gesturing disgustingly towards Sam.

"Nice to see you too, Justin." Sam drawled lazily, not budging from his spot on the bean bag chair.

"Shut up," Justin growled at him.

"Justin!" I snapped my voice sharply. "My grandmother is sleeping. Lower your voice."

He turned his gaze to me, his eyes blazing. "Why Rhi? Why are you cheating on me?"

"Cheating on you? What are you talking about?" I struggled to come up with an explanation. "I was hanging out with Mia. She was gathering lightning bugs. She loves bugs."

"What the hell does that have to do with anything?"

"Will you let me speak or keep interrupting me?" I snapped back at him.

He fell silent, but his eyes continued to smolder with anger.

"Mia had some family business to take care of, so Sam and I were left alone," I continued. "He asked if I wanted to see his motorcycle, and I said yes."

"So that's all it takes for you to go out with another guy?"

"I'm not your property, Justin. If you can't trust me, you don't need to be with me."

Justin turns, pinning Sam with a dark stare. "And you? What the hell are you doing, creeping around with someone else's girlfriend?"

Sam lifts one elegant eyebrow. "I offered to show her my Ducati. But if you want to take it as seduction…"

I can almost hear the snap in Justin's head, because before I can blink, he launches himself at Sam.

Sam sidesteps neatly and appears behind Justin. He gently touches the back of Justin's head. A small beam of white light emitted from his fingertips, and Justin collapsed to the floor.

"What did you do?!" I cried out, rushing to kneel next to Justin's limp body.

"His temper was like a raging fire, consuming him. I could see it in how his eyes blazed and the muscles in his jaw clenched. So, I just put him to sleep."

I held Justin's head in my lap, and my hand pressed against his chest. I could feel the steady rhythm of his heartbeat. He seemed peaceful in his slumber, like a child resting after throwing a tantrum.

"I can wipe his memory of tonight if you desire," Sam offered.

I snapped my head to look up at Sam. "No. He needs to remember how he treated me." I frowned, "Who does he think he is anyway?"

Sam laughed a deep, husky laugh. "He's the son of a Fallen. He's a Nephilim."

Chapter Twenty-Nine

I decided to let Justin sleep it off, and maybe he would be calmer in the morning. With Sam's help, we moved his large frame to my bed, where he took up most of the space. I carefully removed Justin's oversized shoes and placed them on the floor beside my bed. "I have no idea how I'm going to explain this to Nan in the morning," I said.

"You don't have to worry about that. I can keep the glamour on until he leaves in the morning," Sam assured me.

I wasn't entirely comfortable with Nan being under some kind of angelic spell, but I reluctantly agreed. I didn't want her to worry.

"I still don't understand." I mused aloud.

Sam rolled his eyes at me. "More questions, I'm guessing." I frowned.

"Yes, wouldn't you have a million questions if you were in my position?"

"I suppose so. On with it then."

"How did Vince and Mrs. Rizzo end up together? I mean, they're so very different."

"I can't say for certain, but my guess is that Vince used some kind of glamour on her as well."

"He what?" I said in disbelief.

"There's no way that kind-hearted, godly woman would cheat on her husband willingly. Vince must have used some sort of magical persuasion to convince her to be with him. And before you ask, no, I don't know why," Sam explained patiently.

"One more question."

"Of course there is," Sam groaned.

"Why are you so afraid of Vince?"

"Oh, my dear Rhiannon. I'm not afraid of him." Sam chuckled.

"Then why wouldn't Armaros take care of Sorcha? Why did we go to that ominous cave she couldn't enter?"

"It is not fear," Sam stated solemnly. His dark eyes held a calm determination as he spoke. "Vince is not only a Fallen, but he also has a small army of other fallen angels and demons, along with unscrupulous humans, in his employ."

"And you're scared of him," I concluded.

Anger flashed across his face momentarily before he composed himself again. "I am not afraid. I simply do not wish to start any kind of war. I prefer to keep the peace," he explained, "It would be a bloody mess, and I quite enjoy my existence here, as well as some of the beings in his crowd." A smile spread across his face. "If you know what I mean."

"Eww" I crinkled my nose, "You mean you hooked up with both of them?"

Justin mumbled something in his sleep, and we both turned to look at him. He turned on his side, his hair falling across his face.

"And to answer your question, yes, both of them. I'm actually quite fond of Sorcha."

"But you asked if she had been dealt with."

He shrugged. "I did. I would hate to end things with her, but my soul is more important."

His eyes flitted to mine. "I'm going to go."

I opened my mouth to protest when he suddenly placed a finger against my lips, silencing me. "I will know of any danger before you do. No harm will come to you," he reassured me with a slight pat on my arm. "My vow and my soul, remember?"

"Yes, it's all about your soul. I don't matter at all," I grumbled.

"Nothing personal," he said with a small smile. "And you are starting to grow on me." With that, he vanished into thin air.

The room was dark, the only light coming from the soft glow of my stereo and the moon filtering in through the curtains. I sat on my bed, watching as Justin lay beside me. I quickly shed my clothes, slipping into sleep shorts and a baggy T-shirt before tiptoeing downstairs to wash my face and brush my teeth. I peeked in on Nan. Sure enough, she was sleeping soundly, her radio playing lightly by her bedside.

When I returned to my room, I turned down the volume on my stereo and left The Doors playing on the CD player. Gently pulling back the sheets, I slid into bed next to Justin. It felt strange and unfamiliar, but also oddly comforting. This was uncharted territory for me—aside from Kiran, I had never had a boy in my bed before. But Kiran wasn't really a boy; he was an angel—my angel.

I turned to face Justin's sleeping form. He looked so peaceful. His features relaxed and free of the anger that had been present earlier. But even as sweet as he looked at that moment, I couldn't let go of the anger and hurt.

Feeling angry all over again, I turned onto my side, away from him. That's when I noticed my phone on the nightstand. It was 2 AM, and two new messages were waiting for me. One from Taylor asked if I had made it home safely, to which I quickly replied, hoping it wouldn't wake her. The other was from Justin: *"I'm coming over. You'd better be home."*

"Better be?" I muttered angrily to myself. How dare he speak to me like that! I wanted to kick him, but instead, I turned back over and punched him in the shoulder.

"Ow!" he exclaimed, suddenly jolting awake. He blinked rapidly, disoriented and seeming unsure of where he was. "Rhi?" he asked in a thick, sleepy voice, his hair falling across his eyes like a curtain of midnight silk.

I continued to scowl at him until I saw the striking resemblance between him and Sorcha. Oh my God! It was uncanny, and they both looked like Vince.

"What happened?" Justin asked, pushing his hair away from his face.

"Better be?" I repeated the words from the text message, still seething with anger.

"What?" he questioned, clearly not understanding what I was talking about. But then it seemed to click for him as he looked down at his rumpled clothes and took in our surroundings.

"Who do you think you are, Justin? Bursting into my room?" I ranted, my emotions still running high. "For one, we aren't in an exclusive relationship. Two, nothing happened with Sam. Three, it's none of your business anyway. And four, don't you ever speak to me that way again!"

He sat up slowly, looking even more confused. Sam had told me he wouldn't erase Justin's memories of what had happened earlier, but maybe he had changed his mind.

Justin furrowed his brow in concentration before a scowl formed on his face. "You went out with that Sam guy," he said, shooting a quick glance my way.

"I did," I admitted, "but that doesn't give you the right to..."

He bowed his head. "I acted like an ass." He conceded, sounding remorseful. "But you could have just sent me a text or something so I knew where you were."

He had a point. But that still didn't excuse his behavior earlier.

"I could have," I said, my voice cold and flat. "But I didn't realize I needed your permission, nor had to report my whereabouts every second of every day."

He nodded. "You're right. And you can't be that mad at me if I ended up in your bed." His smile turned mischievous, but his brows furrowed in confusion. "Although, I don't remember how I got here." He rubbed his face roughly with his hands, clearly trying to jog his memory. "The last thing I recall is us arguing and Sam acting all high and mighty and-"

I cut him off. "Regardless, it still doesn't give you the right to behave like you did."

"You're right," he admitted, his tone contrite. "I don't know what came over me. I've never acted so jealous or irrational before in my entire life."

But his words were forgotten as he reached for me, pulling me closer to him. Despite my anger, I gave in to his touch, not able to help myself. His strong arms encircled me, and he gently kissed my forehead. It was hard to reconcile this tender side of him with the boy who had been consumed by rage earlier.

"I'm at least glad we're here; we haven't had any alone time like this since we fell asleep together on the beach," he spoke in a hushed tone, and I felt him smile against my temple. He began to kiss me, his lips leaving soft sweeps along my face.

Suddenly, he shifted beneath me and fell back onto the bed, bringing me along with him. Our bodies pressed against each other in ways they never had before, igniting new sensations that sent sparks through my body. His breath was ragged as our lips met again, this time more fiercely.

I pulled away and gasped for air, my lips tingling. "Justin," I breathed.

"Shh," he whispered, placing a finger on my lips. "Remember, I said nothing would happen unless you wanted it to."

Conflicting emotions were warring inside me. Did I really want this? My body screamed yes, yes, yes! But my mind was sending out warning signals, telling me to stop. I was angry with him, and if I were honest, I would say he had scared me earlier.

I rolled off of him and flopped onto my back on the bed. Justin turned onto his side and propped himself up on his elbow. "I take it that means you're not ready?" he asked gently.

I shook my head, feeling dizzy. "No."

"I get it," he said, running his finger up and down my bare arm, causing tiny goose bumps to rise.

I turned to face him, searching his eyes. "Do you really?"

His gaze dropped to the sheets, and his long lashes fanned his cheeks. "Well, kind of," he whispered. "You give off mixed signals sometimes, Rhi."

"What do you mean?"

He looked back at me, his eyes blazing green fire. "Sometimes, when you kiss me, it feels like I'm the only one in the world for you. It feels like you want me...*really* want me."

A blush crept up my neck and spread across my cheeks. "Justin..."

"Let me finish," he said, cutting me off. "But other times, you're so standoffish. Like when I told you I loved you and you just shut down."

I couldn't deny what he was saying. Love was a scary word for me. My mother had always said she loved me, but she stayed with that monster. And my father...All I had from him was a note saying he loved me. But where was he now?

I had no idea. No boy had ever said they loved me before. My grandparents always did, but if I was being honest, I had locked away my heart and thrown away the key. I didn't want to feel the pain of love anymore.

But nestled within my fear and hesitation, there was love—love for Kiran, Nan, and my cousins, who had always been there for me. I could feel their warmth and acceptance radiating from within. As much as I craved their love, I was afraid to open up the guarded chest where I kept my deepest emotions.

"Are you still with me, Rhi?" Justin's voice cut through the haze of my thoughts as his hand brushed along the curve of my cheek. His touch lingered on my skin in a comforting caress, and I leaned into his warm palm.

"I'm sorry if I act distant or strange, Justin. I know I can be odd at times. Sometimes, I wonder if I know how to truly love someone."

"That's nonsense." He said with a small smile that tugged at the corners of his lips. God, how badly I wanted those soft lips on mine again. My hormones really needed to get under control.

He pulled me closer and rested my head against his chest. "Even though I know what love is, my life hasn't exactly been filled with hearts and flowers." One of his hands came to rest upon my hair, stroking it gently.

A heavy feeling crushed my chest. Justin was right. He had experienced hardships that most people couldn't imagine, yet he still made himself vulnerable when he professed his love for me. "Have you ever said those words to another girl before?" I asked timidly.

"And meant it?" His laughter reverberated through his chest and sent gentle vibrations through my body.

I playfully slapped his arm. "Yes!" I scolded. "And you should only say it if you mean it. It's hurtful to find out someone lied to you about something so precious."

"You're right, it's not funny," he said sincerely, "I have never said it and meant it until you."

Until me, the thought made my heart begin to flutter like a million tiny butterflies trying to get free. "How do I know I'm not just another girl you're lying to?" I asked quietly, my insecurities slipping through.

There was a long pause before he answered. "I guess you don't. I guess you need to trust me."

Trust him. There it was. Trust.

It was even more of a scary word than love. To trust someone was to give over all of your power, release all the memories of past betrayals, and take that leap of faith. The weight in my chest increased, a heaviness born from the scars of past wounds. It reminded me all too well of the pain that comes with misplaced trust.

Did I truly trust anyone? I wasn't sure. I didn't know if I would ever be liberated from the chains of fear and doubt.

"I guess that means you don't." Justin's sigh broke through my thoughts.

I lifted my head to meet his gaze. "I'm so sorry, Justin. The last thing I want is to hurt you." His other hand joined the first, gently stroking my hair as if to soothe away my worries. "Trust is fragile, and when you came here tonight so angry and full of jealousy, it felt like you broke a piece of it."

His hands paused in their movements. "I know I did, Rhi. And I wish I could understand what came over me." He pulled me closer, wrapping his arms around me tightly. "I'm grateful that you didn't immediately break things off with me, and maybe I can have a chance to redeem myself."

He embraced me tighter, kissing the tip of my nose, seeking comfort in our closeness. "Just let me hold you for a while, and then I'll go before your grandmother wakes up."

I nodded sleepily, feeling drained from the night's events. So many unexpected twists and turns had taken place. Letting my eyes close, I hoped I wouldn't dream of strange clubs, fallen angels, and demons.

Chapter Thirty

The world around me was a winter wonderland, the snow falling softly and coating everything in a blanket of white. I could feel the cold flakes hitting my skin as I began to tremble.

"Rhi! Rhi!" Kiran's voice echoed through the forest, but I could only see the endless expanse of snow-covered trees.

"Kiran, where are you?" I called out, spinning around in search of him. Suddenly, a figure appeared before me, barely visible through the swirling snow. It was Kiran, his form flickering like a ghost until he became solid. I ran into his arms, seeking warmth and comfort.

"I've missed you," I whispered, burying my face in his chest.

"I know."

"But this isn't real, is it? It's snowing, so I must be dreaming."

"You are dreaming, and I am dream walking in your mind. I have entered your subconscious mind to be with you in your dream."

"Why?" I questioned. "Are you still in the veil?"

"Yes," he breathed out. "But listen carefully, Rhi. My time here is limited. I will return to you as soon as I can, but for now, there is something important I must do."

"I know," I moaned. "Deliver that note for Sam."

"It has been delivered. But there is more...I learned something from Samyaza's daughter."

"So she really is his daughter? He wasn't lying?"

"He surprisingly was telling the truth," Kiran confirmed. "The longer I stay here, the more I realize how little I truly know about our kind."

He held me tighter against him. "You must be cautious, Rhi. While Samyaza has promised to protect you, other forces are at play here."

"What do you mean?" I pulled back slightly to meet his stormy gaze.

"His daughter knew that you could hear our soul song. She said you're special. When I pressed her for more information, she revealed that Samyaza knows more than he lets on but will only share enough to fulfill his end of the bargain."

"I knew it!" I exclaimed.

Kiran's eyes narrowed in confusion. "Knew what?"

"It's a long story, but I met another watcher, actually several. I also had a run-in with a demon and a...."

"A what?!" Kiran hissed, stepping back as he locked his gaze onto mine.

"I told you it was a long story, but the most important thing I learned was about Vince," I said, lowering my voice as I leaned closer to Kiran.

"What about him?"

"He is definitely a Fallen, and I learned why he fell," I whispered, the words heavy with the weight of truth. "And Kiran, he has a daughter about the same age as Justin, but she is half demon."

Kiran's eyebrows shot up in surprise, and he suddenly turned as if he heard something. My heart raced as I realized our conversation may have been overheard. But Kiran spoke again, his tone urgent. "Someone is coming. Listen to me, Rhi. I dream-walked into your dream to keep our conversation private. I heard you call out to me last night, and I'm sure Samyaza told you not to. It will attract all sorts of celestial beings to you because you house a part of his soul. That's probably how you had a run-in with that demon."

I nodded, anxiety whirling through me as I thought about the danger I had put myself in. But before I could say anything else, Kiran's form began to dissipate, turning translucent like a ghost. He turned and looked over his shoulder again before speaking urgently, his hand sweeping over my cheek once more and tilting my head up to look into his worried eyes.

"Stay by Samyaza's side," he instructed firmly. "Do you understand?"

I nodded again, feeling a sense of urgency. I opened my mouth to try to tell Kiran that Sam had left me alone last night.

"I will be home by tonight. It will not take me much longer. I need to find the Archangel Raziel."

His image faded more until I could barely make out his form. "But, Kiran! Who is Raziel?"

"The keeper of secrets." He said, and then was gone.

I awoke abruptly, my eyes darting around the dimly lit room until they landed on Justin, sound asleep beside me. The soft glow of early morning light filtered through the curtains, casting a warm golden hue across the walls. My hand reached for my cell phone on the nightstand, squinting to make out the time. It was only five-thirty in the morning. Nan would already be up and bustling around the house - she was always an early riser.

Turning back to Justin, I watched him sleep for a moment. How was it possible that he was a half-angel and had no idea? My mind wandered to his half-sister Sorcha, who obviously knew her true identity, or else she wouldn't have been at that club. Why did she know, and Justin didn't? But then a realization hit me.

Maybe he did.

No, that couldn't be right. I gazed at him again, taking in his long lashes resting against his cheeks as he breathed peacefully and the cross that lay across his chest. Sam told me that Justin had no knowledge of his angelic heritage, but could I really trust Sam? Kiran certainly didn't seem to think so.

As the sun rose higher in the sky, beams of light filtered through the windows and danced across the room. Tiny particles floated within the rays, appearing like magical fairies.

"Good morning," Justin's sleep-filled voice broke through my thoughts.

I looked down at him, and a sweet smile crossed his lips. "Good morning," I replied.

Suddenly, he rolled over and pinned me beneath him with a roguish grin on his face. "I've wanted to wake up next to you for a long time," he whispered in my ear, causing me to shudder involuntarily.

My body responded instinctively, yearning for him and craving his touch. I squirmed beneath him, and he let out a low groan. "Keep doing that, Rhi, and I may never let you leave this bed," he whispered huskily in my ear.

I turned my head towards him, resting my hand on his chest. "My grandmother's still here."

"I'm sorry, Rhi. I was so content cuddled up next to you that I couldn't bring myself to leave earlier."

"It's okay," I said softly, snuggling closer to him. "She usually leaves around six-thirty. We can stay in bed quietly until she goes to work."

His lips pressed against my neck, trailing down to my collarbone as his hand slipped beneath my shirt and rested on my stomach. Gasping at the sensation, I tangled my fingers in his hair and brought his lips to mine.

A moan escaped me, and he pulled away, his eyes sparkling with mischief. "Justin," I panted. "We can't. My grandmother will hear us."

"Is that the only thing stopping you?" He teased, nuzzling my neck.

"Not the only thing," I breathed into his ear, feeling him shiver against me.

He lifted his head, and our eyes met; his jade eyes filled with desire. As much as I wanted to give in to him right then and there, this was not the right time. Nan was awake downstairs, and Kiran could probably sense what was happening between us, which made me flush with embarrassment. Plus, there was Sam. He was supposed to guard me and might even be invisibly watching us now. The thought cooled me off quickly.

"World to Rhi," Justin said, and my eyes snapped back to his.

"Sorry, I was just thinking," I replied sheepishly.

"About how undeniably sexy I am," he said with a devastating smile.

I burst out laughing before quickly covering my mouth, hoping Nan hadn't heard me.

"You know it's true," he said confidently.

Suddenly, I felt a vibration against my thigh.

"Ugh, seriously?" Justin groaned, pulling out his cell as he lifted himself off of me, rolling onto his side.

"Seriously, Vince?" he groaned.

"What now?" "What's going on?" I asked, sitting up.

"He has a lead on a car he's been trying to get his hands on," Justin explained as he quickly typed a reply. "I have to go to the shop and grab a truck." He groaned. "He has the worst timing."

He swung his legs off the bed and began putting on his shoes.

"My grandmother is still here," I reminded him.

"I'll be careful. I'll go out the window," he reassured me with a playful smile. "Lots of practice."

"Well, that makes me feel special."

"It should. You're the only one I've ever woken up with. I usually leave before the sun rises."

I couldn't help but frown at his words, but before I could say anything, he kissed me quickly on the forehead. "We can hang out later if you want. Just don't plan on taking a ride on Sam's motorcycle," he added with a grin.

I scowled at his words, and he threw up his hands in surrender. "Kidding!" he laughed.

I knew I needed to find Sam, and Kiran insisted that I did. "Mia wanted me to stop by, but probably later, we can hang out," I said.

"Cool, I'll call you," Justin replied as he stood and headed toward the back window. Before climbing out, he turned back to face me. "And Rhi?"

"Yeah?"

"I really am sorry about how I acted last night," he apologized sincerely.

"I know, Justin."

"Good, because I love you," and he disappeared out the window without waiting for my response.

My heart did a little skip at his words. I scanned my room and whispered for Sam. There was no response. That was weird. I touched the place in my arm that contained his soul. It just looked like my skin, but I remembered where it was. Gently rubbing my fingers over the area, it suddenly came alive with a soft glowing light, pulsing in time with my heartbeat.

"Strange," I mumbled to myself. It was still early, but I knew Nan would be leaving soon. Hurriedly, I selected a pair of shorts and a cute tank top from my closet. I padded down the stairs towards the shower and heard the door close and Nan's car engine start up.

The house was eerily quiet, almost too silent. "Sam?" I whispered again, still receiving no answer. I felt uneasy, but I pushed aside the growing anxiety and quickly showered. Wrapping a towel around myself, I hastily brushed my teeth before hurrying back upstairs to my room. Somehow, I felt safer in my room without really understanding why; being in my room made me feel protected. I turned on the CD player and let Jim Morrison's voice fill the space, creating a rhythmic background noise.

Sitting cross-legged on my bed, I attempted to untangle my wild waves. My phone buzzed beside me. I picked it up to find a text from Taylor. *"I'm glad you made it back safely. Where did you go last night?"*

My hands hovered over the keyboard, thinking of how to respond. This was Taylor; I could tell her the truth. I typed a reply saying I went out with Sam, Mia's friend, to some club.

The response was instant. *"You went to a club? Who are you, and what have you done with my cousin?"* Taylor's teasing tone was evident, accompanied by a laughing emoji.

"Haha," I typed back, a soft chuckle escaping my lips. *"You're right, though. It wasn't really my scene."* I readjusted the phone in my hand and continued typing. *"Is the baby up?"*

Taylor quickly replied that the little one was screaming to be fed. I felt a pang of guilt for potentially waking them up last night.

"I hope I didn't wake you last night," I replied. *"But I thought you'd want to know I made it home."*

A few seconds passed before another message appeared on the screen. *"You didn't wake me,"* Taylor texted back. *"It was Justin calling and texting Scott and wondering if we had heard from you. Seriously, that boy is obsessed with you."*

I let out a small sigh, unsure how to respond to her comment. Instead, I settled for sending a shrugging emoji.

Another text came through. *"Did he finally get a hold of you last night?"*

I hesitated, contemplating whether or not to confide in Taylor about what had happened with Justin. But then again, she had never been a big fan of our relationship in the first place. So, I replied with a quick *"Yes."*

Running my hands through my tangled hair, I stepped away from my bed and looked around my room. Still no sign of Sam. Anxiety clawed inside of me. It was still early, but Mia may be awake by now. Without much thought, I texted her to see if she would reply.

I stared intently at my phone, willing for a response. But nothing came. Frustration and worry began to bubble up inside me, and I got up from my bed to pace around the room. Walking over to the window, I threw open the curtains and squinted toward Mia's house. Her bedroom curtains were open, but I didn't see her. Maybe she was in the shower.

I waited by the window, feeling like a stalker. Finally, I saw movement, and relief swept over me. She noticed me standing by my window, and I waved awkwardly.

She approached her bedroom window and motioned for me to open mine. I struggled with the stubborn lock, finally pushing it open and feeling the warm, humid air hit my face.

"Lady Bug! What are you doing, girl?" She called out across the yards.

"I couldn't sleep. Been up since five this morning."

She laughed. "Must be something in the air. I couldn't sleep either."

"Any chance you've seen Sam?" I asked, trying not to sound awkward.

"Sam? He's never up this early. He's a night owl," Mia said, and I realized she was probably right. But then again, he was an angel and didn't need to sleep like humans. Or maybe, as a Watcher, he had to rest at some point. I didn't really know.

"Why don't you come over? My Gram is making her world-famous banana almond smoothies," Mia offered.

My stomach grumbled at the mention of food. "I'll be right over." I shut my window and quickly slipped on my sneakers before grabbing my keys and locking the door behind me.

As I descended the stairs, I got a strange feeling. The hairs on my neck stood up, and I scanned the street for any signs of danger. Seeing only a man tending his flowers across the street, I picked up my pace and practically ran up Mia's stairs to her front door.

She swung the door open with a warm smile. We passed through the living room and into the kitchen, where her grandmother stood holding two glasses of smoothies.

"Thank you," I said gratefully as she handed one to me. Her dark eyes seemed to see right through me.

"It appears you're without your usual shadow," she stated matter-of-factly. Alarm bells started going off in my head. How did she know Kiran wasn't here with me?

"Shadow?" Mia asked, confused.

Her grandmother's head turned towards Mia. "Spirits, child. You know I can sense them." Then she focused back on me. "The one who is usually with this girl is not with her now." Her eyes squinted as she grabbed my arm, right where the shard of Sam's soul had been placed. She muttered something under her breath, and her grip tightened as she said. "Our Watcher has marked you."

My throat constricted as a sudden realization hit me. She knew exactly what Sam was and wasn't afraid to use the term "Watcher." Mia's eyes darted between us, confusion evident on her face.

"Gram, what are you talking about?"

Mia's grandmother seemed to snap back to reality, her hand slumping from my arm as she picked up her glass and hobbled out of the kitchen.

"That was weird even for my family," Mia said with a shaky laugh. "Let's sit in the backyard before it gets too hot."

We went through the screen door and onto the back patio, where a small table awaited us. The yard was an oasis of green, with a sprawling garden filled with abundant vegetables and herbs. I admired the neatly placed signs labeling each plant- some familiar, like chamomile, sage, and lavender, while others were foreign to me, like wolfsbane and rue.

We sat for a while chatting about the herbs and their uses, witchcraft, and her relationship with Sophie.

Her grandmother waved at us from the back door to come inside. Mia and I exchanged glances and headed back into the house.

"Give me your right palm, Rhiannon," she instructed me as we entered the kitchen.

I reluctantly held my hand out, and she wrapped her leathery fingers around mine. "Someone will be in contact with you soon," she said as my hand began to warm between hers.

I thought she must be talking about either Kiran or Sam. She began to mumble words I couldn't comprehend. The scar on my palm tingled, and I felt the urge to pull away.

"It is done," she announced before letting go. She picked up her half-drunk smoothie and took a sip. "It will help," she stated cryptically. "But it is up to you to have the strength to fight evil."

"Okay.....?" Mia drawled out, looking between her grandmother and me in bewilderment. "Come on, Lady Bug, let's go up to my room."

Mia and I lounged on her bed, surrounded by piles of notebooks, papers, and the book that she had inherited from her grandmother. I touched the place on my arm that housed part of Sam's soul, wondering where he could be.

I glanced at the book in Mia's lap and wondered if there was anything about angels mentioned in the old book besides Samyaza. "Hey Mi, are there other names in there besides that Samyaza?"

Mia's nimble fingers flipped through the pages, "There's one called Sariel."

"What about Raziel? Have you seen that name before?" I asked, thinking about the name Kiran had told me.

She furrowed her slim brows in concentration, "I think so." She continued flipping through the pages until she stopped and flipped the book towards me, pointing to the name. Unfortunately, that was the only word I could make out.

"Can you read what it says?" I asked, hoping Mia could decipher it for me.

"Sure thing, Lady Bug." She pulled the large book back onto her lap and skimmed over the page. "It says he possesses a book containing divine secrets of both celestial and earthly knowledge."

My phone vibrated in my pocket, causing me to jump in surprise. I quickly fished it out and saw Kacey's name on the caller ID.

"Hey, Kace," I answered, expecting her usual bubbly voice. But instead, her words were hushed and strained. "Rhi..."

"What's going on?" I asked as unease washed over me.

"Rhi...don't do what..." Her voice was cut off abruptly, replaced by a smooth, sinister voice that made my blood run cold.

"I nicely asked you to come to my house for dinner. Because you didn't, I have some other guests here," Vince said.

I could hear Kacey's muffled screams in the background, and a wave of fear washed over me like a tidal wave.

"As I was saying," Vince continued smoothly, "I have my son here and your cousin."

"What?" I breathed.

"You come to me, and I will let the girl go. If you don't, I will take more of your family until you do," he threatened darkly.

My hands shook around the phone as Mia scooted closer, wrapping an arm around my shoulder, "What is it?" she whispered.

"Do we have a deal?" Vince purred.

"Yes."

"Wonderful! I will send a car to pick you up."

The line went dead as I turned to face Mia, "Vince has Kacey and Justin," I choked out, struggling to hold back tears and panic.

Chapter Thirty-One

Mia pulled me into her arms, "I'll go with you," she offered, her eyes filled with concern. "It'll only take me a minute to grab..." she began, but her grandmother's shuffling footsteps approached until she stood in the doorway, interrupting her.

"Mia, let her go," the older woman said. Mia opened her mouth to protest, but her grandmother's stern look stopped her. "Listen to me, child," she continued. "Let her go."

Reluctantly, Mia released my arm. Where was Sam? I thought to myself as I stood to go.

Mia's fingers grabbed my arm, her nails digging in slightly. She pulled me towards her dresser and reached behind her neck to unclasp a necklace with a pretty green stone on it. "Take this with you," she said, carefully placing the necklace around my neck. "It's malachite, a stone for protection."

I thanked her, and then she searched my face with her deep brown eyes. "Give me something of yours," she pleaded. I quickly rummaged through my pockets and found nothing but my hair tie. "Will this work?" I asked, holding it out to her.

In a swift motion, Mia snatched it from my hand and clutched it tightly, "Yes."

A car horn sounded outside, and I hugged Mia tightly, trying to hold back tears. "I'll be okay," I whispered, hoping to convince us both.

The blacked-out town car was waiting for me outside. The window opened, and Sorcha slid down her dark glasses and stared at me.

"Good morning, Rhiannon."

Wherever Amaros had put her, she obviously had gotten free. I glanced back at Mia, who stared back at me with concern etched into her delicate brow. Gritting my teeth, I approached the car and got in, feeling the cold leather against my bare legs.

Sorcha appraised me lazily from behind her glasses. "I'm not afraid of you," I told her, surprising myself with the vibrato of certainty woven through my words.

"It's not me you should be scared of."

A strange silence fell between us after that. When the door opened again, Vince's face appeared in front of me.

"Hello, ladies," Vince purred with a charming smile. "Come now, Rhiannon. Justin and Kacey are waiting for you," Vince continued smoothly as he led us toward a massive house with a sprawling lawn. I glanced over my shoulder at Sorcha, who stood behind me. The driveway curved behind her and ended at a towering metal gate. Even if I could outrun them, I doubted I could scale that gate.

Vince climbed the grand staircase leading to the enormous black front doors of the house. Sorcha pushed me forward, and I reluctantly followed him to the top, where he held the door open for us.

A cool rush of air caressed my skin as we entered the house. "Where are they?" I demanded, scowling at Vince.

"Right where I left them," Vince replied smugly, extending his arm for me to hold onto.

I sneered at him, wanting to punch him in his arrogant face.

"That is no way to treat your host," he scolded me before wrapping his firm grip around my arm. Despite my attempts to pull away, his hold only tightened.

We passed a grand staircase leading up to a landing above us, then through a long corridor lined with multiple doors on either side. Finally, we reached the end, where Vince pulled out a key and unlocked the door. "Can't be too careful," he chuckled as he swung open the heavy door.

The inside was dark and musty, but with a flick of his wrist, multiple torches blazed to life along another narrow and steep staircase leading down into a dark abyss.

It felt like an eternity before we finally reached the bottom of the stairs. The air was colder and damper down here, and as Vince pulled me further into the room, more torches ignited to reveal a large, cave-like chamber.

The walls were made of smooth stone, adorned with intricate carvings and vaguely familiar symbols. I realized they were almost identical to the ones I had seen in the cave with Sam. At the center of the room stood a grandiose throne, its design so ornate and detailed that it almost seemed alive. It looked like it had been carved from the very rock surrounding it, emanating power and authority.

A low, ominous noise echoed through the darkness, sending shivers down my spine. I strained my eyes to see in the dimly lit cavern, but all I could make out was a faint sense of movement and the unmistakable scent of danger. Suddenly, Vince snapped his fingers, and the remaining torches blazed to life, casting an eerie glow around the room.

As I scanned the room, my breath caught at the sight before me. Chains dangled from the ceiling, their metal links glinting in the light. The air was thick with the smell of ancient earth and the metallic tang of blood. And there, in the corner, was Justin - bloodied and battered. His voice, weak and hoarse called out my name. I rushed to him, ignoring Vince's taunting laughter.

Justin's face was bruised and bloody, his nose twisted painfully to one side. He was bound by chains hanging from the ceiling, barely able to keep himself upright. I cupped his face in my hands, trying to ignore the pain in my heart seeing him like this.

My gaze flicked to where his hands were bound, and I saw that the metal was cutting into his skin, blood flowing freely down his arms. My anger flared as I whirled around to face Vince.

"How could you do this to your own son?" I seethed through gritted teeth.

Vince prowled closer, a cruel smile on his lips. "He is just one of many of children I've fathered," he said coolly. "And certainly not one of my favorites."

Sorcha stood near the throne, her eyes flashing with a hint of anger before quickly returning to a blank expression. Beyond her, I saw Kacey tied to a chair, her eyes wide with fear.

"Kacey," I whispered.

"Come, sit with me," Vince gestured towards the throne, and another chair slid across the room to rest next to his.

I balled my hands into fists, summoning all my courage as I stepped forward and punched Vince in the nose. Blood spurted from his nostrils as he clamped a hand over his face. "So violent," he cackled. Slowly lowering his hand, the blood had disappeared without a trace. "Did you really think you could hurt me?" His narrowed gaze bore into mine. "Now sit." He growled.

Some unseen force compelled me to move forward. I fought against it, but it was no use. I was being controlled somehow, and when I reached the chair, I refused to sit. But it felt like a heavy weight was pressing down on my legs, forcing them to bend until I was seated in the chair.

Vince prowled towards me, his steps deliberate and calculated. "I'm sure you're wondering why you're here," he said smoothly.

I scoffed. "Maybe because you're some psychopathic fallen angel who enjoys torturing people for fun?"

With dramatic flair, Vince covered his heart with one hand, feigning offense. "I'm hurt that you would think so lowly of me." A smirk danced across his features as he continued. "No, my dear, I never torture for fun. There is always a reason." He strolled casually back to the throne and sat, throwing one booted foot atop his knee as he tapped his fingers against the large armrest. "What I can't figure out is where your Guardian is." He cast a quick glance in my direction before turning to look at Justin in his shackles, with his head hanging low.

My heart was a frantic drumbeat in my chest, the sound deafening in my ears. Vince's eyes bore into me with an intensity that made my skin crawl. He knew. He knew about Kiran, and I could see the anger and frustration boiling beneath his calm facade.

"So, where is the lovely blonde angel?" Vince's voice was deceptively mild, but his eyes burned with rage. "Don't play dumb with me. I know you know what I'm talking about." His words were laced with a dangerous edge.

"Why take Justin and Kacey?" I managed to ask, my voice trembling slightly.

Vince's expression turned bored as he glanced towards where Justin hung. His head hung limply, but his eyes were sharp. "He doesn't listen to his father," he replied casually. "And they were my means to get you to cooperate."

Vince turned his bored stare towards me. "You have nothing else you would rather ask, such as why you are here?"

I shook my head, unsure of why Vince had brought me here. Had it been to use me as leverage against Justin or Kiran?" I struggled again against the invisible force holding me in the chair, but it was useless.

"Nothing?" Vince drawled, leaning back in his seat.

"Because you're a psychopath?"

A small smile tugged at his lips. "Perhaps I am," he admitted. "But I am a brilliant one."

I let out an indignant snort.

Someone behind me giggled softly and approached with light steps. Sorcha appeared before me, her eyes sparkling as she leaned down to grab my chin and tilt my face to meet her gaze. "I like this one, Daddy," she purred, turning my head from side to side as if inspecting a prized possession. "Can I have her when you're done with her?"

I jerked away from her grasp, giving her a defiant glare, but she winked and slinked away like the snake I believed she was.

Vince waved his hand, conjuring a beautiful wine glass that glinted in the cavernous room's dim light. He raised it to me with a smile, the crystal catching the light and casting prisms on the wall. "Would you care for some?" he asked, his voice dripping with smugness.

I could feel hot, intense hatred building within me, burning through every fiber of my being. I narrowed my eyes into fiery slits, refusing to let him see any weakness.

His smile faltered for a moment before he shrugged it off. "I guess that's a no," he said casually, sipping the wine. "Your loss. It's exquisite."

I glanced at Kacey, her eyes wide with fear. My heart broke for her. It wasn't fair that she had to suffer because Vince wanted me here.

"Now, where were we?" Vince interrupted my thoughts, his confident tone returning. "Ah, yes, the stories you must have heard. How many religions across the world share similar themes and beliefs? One of them is that humans are viewed as God's greatest creation...his children." He waved a dismissive hand in the air. "But let me tell you something. We were created before you and considered His most prized creation for centuries. My brothers and sisters worshiping the ground He walked on...quite literally."

I couldn't help but glance at Justin, still hanging limply within his chains. Through the strands of hair that hung in front of his face, I could see his green eyes boring into Vince.

"Do you know how difficult it is to watch you greedy, ungrateful, and down-right despicable creatures, get praised and loved while we were tasked with protecting you?" Vince scanned my face, but I remained impassively calm despite his words. "No?" he sneered. "Of course not. A spoiled little brat like you wouldn't understand."

I narrowed my eyes as I glared at him. "I am far from spoiled," I retorted, my words laced with bitterness.

In an instant, Vince shot to his feet and stood directly before me, his nose almost touching mine. The intensity of his angry gaze made me shudder involuntarily. "Don't interrupt me while I'm speaking," he spat, his voice dripping with venom. Slowly, he began to circle around the cavernous room, his wine glass still in hand. He moved with a controlled grace, like a predator stalking its prey. "Your friend Samyaza knows exactly what I mean." Vince let out a cruel laugh that echoed off the stone walls. "Tell me, did you enjoy your little outing to the club with him last night?"

Justin growled, pulling at his chains.

He turned and continued to strut around the room, sipping his wine. Each step he took seemed to reverberate off the cold floor, adding to the tense atmosphere. "Some of us couldn't resist what the Watchers were doing," he said darkly, walking over to where Justin hung helplessly from his restraints. "You mortals do have something about you that draws us in." He stopped, eyeing me curiously, and then continued. "But, you see, the Watchers taught humanity how to make weapons, and so when the wars began as they inevitably would, more of us were dispatched to protect you, fragile humans."

He turned his back to Justin and stared directly at me. "I was once one of the greatest at fulfilling my duty," he began, his voice becoming ghostly. "But as time passed, it became clear that humanity would never learn. Wars continued to escalate, and weapons grew more destructive."

He set down his wine glass with a harsh clink on the floor before suddenly grabbing Justin by the hair, yanking his head back in a vicious display of control.

"Stop!" I cried out, fighting against the invisible bonds.

Vince slowly turned towards me. "This one here is a perfect example. He never learns." With a cruel twist of his hand, he let go of Justin's head and let it fall forward. With a burst of defiance, Justin spat at Vince.

Vince wiped away the spittle from his face with slow deliberation. "You just proved my point, boy. No matter what I give you, no matter how much your mother and family love you, you still continue down a path of self- destruction."

He picked up his wine glass before facing me once again. "I was dispatched during both great wars," he reminisced with a hint of bitterness in his voice. "But it was during the second that I was put in charge of protecting the United States' seaports." He swirled the wine in his glass absentmindedly as if lost in thought. "I wasn't exactly thrilled about it. I mean, humanity had barely survived one World War, and now they were sending their sons off to fight another?"

His piercing gaze locked onto me, searching for any sign of response or reaction. "It was then that I met your grandmother," he said wistfully. "She was breathtaking, not just in physical beauty but in the depth of her love and laughter. For the first time, I saw what the Watchers saw in humans - their capacity for love, joy, and all the things we angels could only observe but never truly feel." A heavy sigh escaped him as he continued, "I grew tired of being nothing more than a soldier for Heaven. I longed for a simple life with someone who loved and accepted me for who I am, not just as a blind, obedient soldier."

The restraints holding me in place felt suffocating as blind fury enveloped me. "You bastard," I spat out, my voice dripping with venom.

Vince chuckled darkly at my outburst. "Well, I can't argue with you there." His gaze wandered around the room like he was searching for something...or someone. Probably Kiran. "But it was not meant to be," he continued, sighing heavily.

His expression seemed to be tinged with genuine sadness. "Your grandmother left me. You can't imagine how deeply that hurt me. Even when I told her about my efforts to help in the war, she still refused me." He paused, lost in thought.

"You're sick," Justin sneered, disgust evident in his voice.

"Am I, son?"

"Don't call me that," Justin hissed through clenched teeth. "You, my dear boy, are just like me," Vince snarled cruelly.

"Tell me, what would you do if you knew your Rhiannon loved another?"

"I'm not-" I began to protest.

"Shut up!" Vince snapped at me, throwing his glass across the room, where it shattered against the wall.

"You know what he is, don't you?" he snarled, his eyes burning with anger. "Well? Don't you?"

My heart jackhammered against my chest as I struggled to meet his intense gaze. "Yes," I admitted quietly.

Justin's head snapped towards me, confusion evident in his emerald green eyes.

"Tell him," Vince said, his voice dripping with malice.

I searched Justin's eyes for any signs of understanding but found only confusion and frustration. How could he not know? Especially now, when the truth was staring us all in the face. I took a deep breath, trying to soften my expression as I spoke softly. "I only found out recently," I said, my words barely above a whisper. "Vince is....is a Fallen. A fallen angel. That makes you a Nephilim."

I saw a muscle in Justin's jaw tick as he clamped his teeth together. "You have her believing this garbage, too?" he said, turning towards Vince with fire in his eyes.

Vince waved his hand dismissively in Justin's direction. "He doesn't believe me," he paused, rubbing his jaw contemplatively before continuing. "You see, son, when someone requests protection for another person, that person receives a Guardian - a supernatural being tasked with keeping them safe. Your beloved Rhiannon has one, which wouldn't be out of the ordinary except that her Guardian has revealed himself to her in his angelic form. Something strictly forbidden."

Vince sauntered over to me, his eyes gleaming with maliciousness. "Now the question is, where is he now?"

"Why do you care?" I snapped.

"That's the real question, isn't it?" Vince paced back and forth in front of me. "All this exposition leads up to one thing - my desire to get back into Heaven. As a Fallen, I can't enter."

"You're insane," I said in disbelief.

Vince chuckled darkly. "As a Fallen or a Watcher, we've lost our grace and therefore can't enter the pearly gates, as you all like to say," he explained with a vindictive look in his eye, "But just like that little piece of Samyaza you have placed next to your own soul," he leaned in closer, his breath hot against my face, "I can take a piece of his grace and return."

"He'll never do that!" I exploded, feeling tears pricking at my eyes.

"Oh? Not even for you?" Vince taunted, relishing in my pain.

"I won't let him."

"You see, that won't matter, you stupid girl." Vince shook his head in mock disappointment, "Your Guardian will do anything for you, not just because it is his duty. You just heard me say I gave up my duty for your grandmother's love. Samyaza gave up his for a woman, too."

Sam, where are you? I said in my mind.

I shook my head incredulously. "It doesn't matter what either of you did. Kiran would never do something like that. He is too good."

"Hmm," Vince hummed, "Yes, he is quite remarkable considering who his father is."

My eyes narrowed on him. "You know nothing about him."

He laughed so hard that tears came to his eyes. He wiped them away absently before saying, "This is truly like a bad soap opera." In a blur of motion, he stood in front of me again and grabbed my chin roughly, forcing me to meet his gaze. "He will do it, and you know it, because he will do anything for you."

Chapter Thirty-Two

A heavy weight pressed down on my chest as I whispered a single word, more to myself than anyone else. "No." The sound was just a breath, barely audible, but it echoed in the room's stillness.

I ripped my face from Vince's hand and spat at his feet. "You're nothing but a manipulator, and you always will be. Why would I believe for one second he'd help you?"

He chuckled wolfishly. "You want to see him so desperately as a saint, little girl. It's almost touching."

I braced myself, straightening my shoulders like armor. "You're wasting your time. He'd never do it."

There was a shift in the air. Vince's eyes glinted, gone dead-flat and cold. "You don't understand how easily saints fall, Rhiannon," he said. "All it takes is a little push. Or a little pull. Or a little...*need.*"

"You have no idea what you're talking about," I spat.

In amusement, he raised one dark eyebrow, locking his gaze with mine. "No?" His lips curved into a wicked grin. "I guess we shall see when he finds you." His words sent icy shivers down my spine as I realized the gravity of the situation. "I've laid the trap; now I just have to wait for him to walk into it."

My thoughts scattered as I tried to devise a way to stop Kiran from falling into this trap.

Vince chuckled darkly, circling around me like a snake. "Just so you know, I have my people watching your other two cousins and your grandmother," he boasted. "If your Guardian doesn't appear soon, I will be grabbing another of them."

I glanced at Kacey, her eyes large with fright. I sat up tall and met his dark gaze head-on. "You don't know anything about me or my family," I declared, my voice trembling but determined, and Kiran will never fall for your trap."

Vince strode towards Justin, "You know, son. Your darling mother was so easy to manipulate."

Justin sneered at him.

"I wanted your mother to see what I was," Vince said smoothly, his words dripping with deceit. "You know what a devout believer she is." He chuckled darkly. "And they are often the easiest to seduce, especially when you come in angel form."

"Who would believe an angel would come asking for...for...that?" I scoffed incredulously.

"Oh, it's easier than you think," Vince replied, "Gabriel came to Mary and told her she had found favor with God. All believers would love to hear something similar from an angel."

My mind spun like a whirlwind, and the topic of conversation turned my stomach. Vince's nonchalance about his twisted manipulation tactics made my skin crawl.

"You look confused," Vince said with an obnoxious smirk. "You see, I just tell them they are chosen and that our baby is destined for the work of God."

"You're sick."

Vince shrugged his shoulders in indifference. "Whatever, it gets me what I want." He chuckled darkly. "I had such high hopes for you," He sneered at Justin. "But, you just turned out to be a disappointment."

"Don't talk about him like that!" I screamed, my anger bubbling over at Vince's callousness towards Justin.

I struggled against my invisible restraints, desperate to escape and protect Kiran from Vince's grasp and get Justin, Kacey, and me out of here. I locked eyes with Justin and saw the pain and sorrow in them. This was all because of me - if I wasn't part of his life, Vince wouldn't know about Kiran, and Justin wouldn't be caught up in this nightmare.

I closed my eyes and squeezed them tightly. My head began to throb, and I wished I would wake up from this nightmare. I took a deep breath and tried to calm myself. Vince had come to sit beside me again, his fingers tapping the arm of the chair in annoyance.

"I'm getting impatient." He grumbled and snapped his fingers. "Sorcha."

"Yes, father." Sorcha's velvety voice came from behind me.

"Hurt her."

My head snapped toward Vince, his face twisting into a cruel expression. "Her Guardian must need some motivation to show himself." He sneered.

Sorcha glided around my chair with an air of grace, her eyes meeting mine with a flicker of empathy before hardening into coldness. As she crouched before me, I braced myself for the inevitable. Suddenly, a searing pain ripped through my thigh, unlike anything I had ever felt before. An animalistic scream filled the room, but it wasn't mine – it was Justin's.

I glanced down at my leg, seeing the silver glint of a dagger protruding from my thigh, causing a wave of white-hot agony to course down my leg. I swallowed hard, fearing I would throw up at the sight of the wound. Tears burned behind my eyes, but I clenched my jaw and refused to give Vince the satisfaction.

"Good girl," Vince cooed at his daughter, praising her for inflicting pain on me. My fingers dug into the chair with such force that I feared they would snap. I couldn't feel Kiran's presence or protection, and panic rose within me as I remembered that time passed differently in the veil - he may not have felt my pain or fear right away.

Vince gazed around the room, looking for Kiran to suddenly appear. "Hmm."
He mused. "Still nothing. Where is that Guardian of yours?"

Panic surged through me, and my heart spasmed wildly in my chest.

"We'll give him five minutes," he declared. "Then my associates will be taking
the next cousin, and we'll hurt you again."

"No!" Justin's voice echoed through the room as he strained against his chains.
There was a loud cracking noise, and tiny rock fragments rained down from the
ceiling brackets where Justin hung. My jaw dropped in shock as he broke free
from one of the chains, and it crashed to the stone floor.

Vince let out a maniacal laugh and clapped his hands together. "Oh, son,
finally," he exclaimed as he stood up from his chair. He walked over to where
Justin struggled against the other restraint. "Should we stab her again and see if
you can break the other one?" he taunted, staying just out of Justin's reach.

"I'm going to kill you," Justin growled, his voice full of rage as he pulled at the
remaining chain.

"You are powerful," Vince said blithely. "But let's not forget, you're only
half-angel. You're no match for me."

"Don't bet on it," Justin sneered, his eyes flashing with determination.

Vince's eyes bore into him intensely, his gaze unrelenting. "Sorcha, again." He
growled.

Sorcha tightly gripped the knife and twisted it in my leg, causing me to turn
away and bite down hard on my lip to muffle the agonizing scream. But it escaped
regardless, echoing through the room. Just when I thought I couldn't bear the
pain any longer, a familiar sensation flooded over me.

Kiran was here.

Chapter Thirty-Three

I frantically scanned the room, desperately searching for any sign of him. *"Kiran, no! It's a trap, it's a trap!"* I screamed inside my head.

His response came as a soft whisper in my mind. *"My Ahavah, do not worry for me. I must protect you, and I will not fail."*

Suddenly, a burst of blinding light erupted in the room, burning my eyes. I forced myself to look, and I caught Kiran standing at the center of it all. No... that wasn't quite right. Kiran was the source of the light; it seemed to emanate from within him and crackle around his body. Our gazes met as he looked directly at me, but his usual silvery eyes were replaced with glowing orbs of light.

"Kiran," I whispered, overwhelmed with emotion.

"Well, it's about time," Vince's voice cut in callously.

"You will pay for what you've done to her, Fallen," Kiran's voice reverberated off the walls.

Vince responded with a deranged laugh. "You're kidding me, right?" He raised his hand and sent a blast of blinding white light towards Kiran. But Kiran vanished before it could reach him and reappeared behind Vince.

"I think you've lost your touch, old man," Kiran sneered as he effortlessly lifted Vince up and threw him across the room. With a sickening thud, Vince collided against the wall, and blood began to pour from his lips. He looked up with a gruesome smile, his teeth and lips coated in crimson that slowly began to fade away.

"You may be faster than me, but you're not stronger," Vince taunted as he used his powers to send a chair flying towards Kiran, knocking him to the ground.

"Noooo!" A guttural scream tore through my throat as I instinctively jolted upright. Intense pain shot down my leg and forced me back into the chair. But to my surprise, I realized that Vince's invisible restraints were no longer holding me in place.

In the center of the room, Kiran and Vince stood facing each other, their eyes locked in a fierce stare-down. I could feel tension prickling at my skin. Suddenly, a hand rested on my arm, and I whipped around to see Sorcha standing beside me. My instinct was to flinch away from her touch, but she placed a finger to her lips in a silent command for me to be quiet.

With trembling hands, she pulled out the knife that had been embedded in my leg moments before. Immediately, blood poured from the wound, but something strange happened - the bleeding stopped, and the skin began healing. Confused, I looked up at Sorcha for an explanation.

"The blade is coated in angelica," she explained with a sense of urgency in her voice. "If someone has been enchanted or cursed with any kind of magic, including angelic magic, angelica can break it. It also acts as a form of revenge magic. I coated the knife in it. Whatever spell Vince used on you last, you can now use it on him with the angelica-covered knife."

None of this made any sense to me. But before I could question her further, a blinding light erupted from the center of the room, causing rocks and debris to rain down on us.

Sorcha quickly rose to her feet, fear etched across her features.

"Hurry," she urged me. "Your Guardian won't withstand much longer." She turned towards the opposite wall where Kacey sat looking pale and frightened. "I will be back with help," she called out over the chaos.

"Wait!" I grabbed her wrist, "Take my cousin with you." She nodded and headed towards Kacey.

I scrambled to my feet, the knife firmly in my grip as I approached the two battling angels. The room was filled with dust and debris from the crumbling walls, making it difficult to see. Vince had his back to me, unaware of my presence as I crept closer. Kiran caught sight of me, and his eyes widened in surprise. He shook his head slightly as if trying to warn me, but I had distracted him. Vince struck Kiran square in the chest with an intense burst of light, sending him crashing to the floor.

The sound of my own heart pounding in my chest was deafening as I watched Kiran slump to the floor. My feet carried me towards him, drawn by a primal need to help him. But before I could reach him, Vince whirled around with an outstretched hand and pinned me against the wall right next to Justin.

"Rhi!" Justin cried out, his voice filled with desperation as he tugged at the last chain binding him.

Vince slowly advanced towards us, a bloodthirsty gleam in his eyes. "Now that we've had our little play time, let's get down to business," he said, his voice dripping with malice.

I was pinned against the wall, but I knew his chaining spell wouldn't work on me. With angelica coursing through my veins, I was immune to that spell. Slowly, I pushed the knife behind my back in the hope he hadn't seen it. If he got close enough, maybe I could get the knife in him, putting the chaining spell back onto him. He stopped before me, and I glanced over his shoulder at Kiran, still motionless on the ground. Large gashes marred his body, and a deep wound ran across his cheek.

"This all could have been so much easier," Vince snarled, wiping blood from his mouth with a shaking hand. "Too bad none of my children are obedient." He swore and grabbed Justin by the neck.

I started to pull the knife out from behind me when he snapped his attention back to me. "Such a pretty girl." He said in a slimy voice that made my stomach turn over. Then he turned to look over his shoulder. "She is so very pretty, don't you think, Guardian?"

Kiran began to stir and rise to his feet.

"It's a pity, really, that I have to hurt such a pretty girl. But it will all be worth it when I finally have my hands on your Guardian's grace," he taunted, squeezing his fingers tighter around Justin's neck. "And if he doesn't give it over, then I have no use for any of you. I will kill you first so he can feel the pain I'm inflicting on you."

Kiran's voice echoed in my head, a desperate plea. *"I can beat him, Rhi. Don't do as he asks, and don't try to take him on with that knife!"*

My gaze flicked to Justin, who was struggling against the shackles binding him to the ceiling. His face turned a sickening shade of blue, and panic gripped its claws in me.

But then, an idea sparked in my mind. "Please stop," I pleaded, pretending to sound scared – a role that wasn't too far from the truth.

"Tell him to relinquish his grace!" Vince demanded, his eyes shooting angry daggers at me.

"I...I..." I stuttered before pretending to faint, letting my head loll to the side and my body go limp.

"Oh, for heaven's sake," Vince fumed, but I could hear the gasps of air coming from Justin. The plan had worked.

Sort of.

I heard Justin choke out a coughing fit beside me. Then Vince grabbed my face roughly, squeezing so hard I wanted to scream. But I didn't. I kept quiet, digging my fingers into the knife in preparation to stab Vince when he least expected it. Then chaos ensued. A loud noise like thunder sounded through the room, and Vince let go of me with a growl of frustration. "Damnit!"

"You will never hurt her," Kiran's deep, staunch voice rang out through the room.

My eyes flew open, and Kiran once again emanated a bright light that surrounded him. Making up my mind, I stepped forward, intending to stab Vince in the back with the knife clutched tightly in my hand. But then Justin's voice called out to me.

"Rhi, unchain me! I can take him down," he urged desperately.

Turning to look at him, I saw his ordinarily vibrant green eyes were now bloodshot and full of rage.

"Rhi!" Justin screamed, but before I could act, a sharp blow landed against my temple. My vision blurred as stars danced at the edges of my sight, and I swayed on my feet.

Dust and debris rained around us as I reached out to steady myself, but I fell to my knees instead. Through the haze, I saw Justin finally break free from the other chain with a grunt of effort. He knelt down beside me, cupping my face in his hands.

"I'm going to kill him for this," he growled fiercely, his eyes searching mine.

With immense effort, I pushed myself up from the ground, and Justin quickly wrapped an arm around me for support.

Through the chaotic flashes of light between Kiran and Vince, I struggled to get closer to them. My pulse raced as I prayed that Sorcha had not misled me about the power of this blade. Just a few more steps and...

Justin suddenly let go of me and hurled himself at Vince, knocking him aside with a fierce blow. A bolt of pure energy crackled through the air, slamming into the ceiling and opening a hole. Coughing and rubbing my eyes, I could barely make out Justin wrapping one of the chains still attached to his wrist around Vince's neck.

But Vince just laughed maniacally. "Stupid boy, you think this will kill me? I'm immortal!" he sneered.

I summoned all my strength and made it to their side, the knife Sorcha had given me clutched tightly in my hand. With one swift movement, I plunged the blade into Vince's chest. He looked down at it, still laughing like a deranged madman. "That won't kill me either, little girl," he spat.

"But I can," came Kiran's voice from behind me.

"My Ahavah," he whispered, pressing his warm hand against my cheek. Suddenly, warmth flooded through me, like the gentle caress of a tropical breeze. And then...I felt fine.

Kiran had healed me.

Vince let out a howling laugh as he struggled to break free from Justin's grip. "Now, isn't that sweet?" he taunted, glancing up at Justin.

In a fit of rage, Justin slammed his fist into Vince's face, and I heard a sickening crunch of bone. Vince's expression twisted into pure fury, and he struggled against Justin's grip; I could see the realization dawn on his face that he was now trapped in the same spell he had used on me. With wild eyes darting between Kiran and me, he sneered through bloodied lips, "Well, son, looks like you've got me," he snarled, spitting blood from his mouth. "Treacherous children."

Justin's grip on the chain around Vince's neck was tight and unrelenting. The metal links dug into Vince's skin, causing it to turn red and raw. With each pull, Justin's voice grew more angry. "I'm treacherous?" Justin snarled. Vince gagged, struggling against the force of Justin's hand. But it was no use.

Vince coughed. His eyes narrowed as they landed on Kiran, who had a vise-like hold against his chest.

Kiran's expression darkened as he pushed down even harder on Vince's chest, causing him to cough and sputter. His wounds were healing, though. Slowly, but still healing. Vince gagged but managed to raise a single finger in my direction. "He...he has lied to you."

"Shut up!" Justin snapped, tightening his grip even further. But as I turned to Kiran, I saw anguish wash over his face.

"Stop choking him," I yelled at Justin, my eyes pleading with him to listen.

His head snapped up in surprise. "What?!" He exclaimed.

Vince's face broke out into an evil grin. "He can't move," I said, grasping the knife. "There's a spell on the knife."

Justin looked at me with confusion in his eyes, but he loosened his grip on the chain slightly. Turning back to Vince, I spoke through clenched teeth. "Kiran doesn't lie."

Vince's menacing grin only widened at my words. "Well, that is true," he wheezed, "but he can certainly leave out certain facts."

My gaze shifted to Kiran, and our eyes met briefly before he looked away, a muscle ticking in his jaw.

"Should I tell her, or shall you?" Vince taunted, his voice dripping with amusement.

"Shut up!" Justin and I said in unison.

Kiran's expression fell, and his long lashes hid his silver eyes from view as he spoke heavily. "I didn't tell you who my mother is," he began. His brows furrowed with a pained look. "She is Mary Rizzo."

My hand flew to my mouth in shock, but it was Justin who spoke first, his voice barely audible. "What the hell are you talking about?"

Kiran turned to Justin, his expression strained. "I am your twin," he confessed.

Vince cackled loudly, obviously reveling in the chaos that had erupted between the three of us. Kiran's words echoed through the grimy, dust-filled room, floating in the air like an invisible wreath of betrayal. Justin pulled back instinctively, his green eyes wide with shock and disbelief.

Vince's laughter was a harsh caw that pierced the heavy silence following Kiran's confession. "There you have it," he wheezed, coughing up blood as he spoke. "Now, isn't this a lovely family reunion?" With a grotesque grin splitting his bloodied face, Vince craned his head to look at me. "I always liked you, Rhi. You remind me of your grandmother— stubborn, a little wild. No wonder you've got both my boys twisted up." He snickered.

"Kiran," Vince sneered, "All that angelic training and he's still got the same idiot vice as everyone else. He wants a girl he's not supposed to have." Vince winked at me, lashes sticky with blood. "Or did you think nobody would notice how he looks at you?"

Justin gathered himself, fists balled. "You don't know what you're talking about." He snapped the words out at his father.

Vince raised both hands, as if surrendering. "Oh, I know you love her, too. I was counting on it." He rolled his bloodied knuckles over his chest as he coughed again.

Kiran kept his face blank, but his hands trembled. Justin watched him, suspicion and something like betrayal lingering in his eyes.

"Justin," Kiran's voice was soft yet firm.

"Shut up!" Justin's voice cut through the room like a blade of steel. His grip tightened back around Vince's neck. "You shut the hell up!" He snarled at Kiran, but his gaze was locked on mine.

The once vibrant green of his eyes now looked murky as a swamp, clouded with anger and uncertainty. I wished I could reach out to him, speak words that made sense, and soothe his confusion, but I was too stunned myself.

I turned to Kiran, who was watching Justin intently and ignoring Vince's derisive laughter. "You've known all this time?" My voice came out as a whisper, but it must have reached Kiran because he immediately turned towards me.

"Yes," Kiran replied in a grief-stricken tone, regret clear in his silver eyes. "I have always known my mother's name; Archangel Michael told me. I knew I had a twin and could sense his presence, but it wasn't until you moved back here that I realized my twin was Justin." He reached for my hand and took it in his own. "I did not know that I was a child of this...Fallen." His teeth gritted with anger. "And I have never felt any otherworldly connection with Justin. I don't understand why."

A voice broke through our conversation, coming from behind us. We all turned to see Sam standing next to Sorcha.

Sam pointed a long finger at Justin. "That necklace you wear," he demanded, his eyes narrowed and intense. "Where did you get it?"

Justin's eyebrows furrowed in confusion as he stared at Sam. "From my mother," he replied slowly, unsure where this was going. "Why?"

Sam leaned forward slightly, voice low and knowing. "It's a cross, correct? With a shining, pearlescent stone nestled in its center."

"How did you know?" Justin asked, seeming to grow more wary by the second.

"It's a moonstone. It creates a sort of shield around you so other supernatural beings can't see what you truly are, and you can't see them. It's very powerful magic."

Sam took a step toward us as he continued, "I'm curious as to whom or what gave that necklace to your mother to give to you. Do you know?"

Vince looked perplexed, "There's no way anyone could have known," he muttered. "Who would have given such a powerful object to Mary to give to him?"

A dark look came over Sam's face as he spoke again. "It pays to know a witch," he said cryptically. "When a Nephilim is born, angels on Earth and Heaven can sense it. And the closer you are to the Nephilim, the stronger that sense becomes."

He circled around us and came to stand next to Vince; his gaze focused on the blood-splattered fallen angel lying on the ground. "I felt it when Justin was born - I've lived in this same place for centuries and never sensed another Nephilim as strongly as him. So I paid a visit to my witchy friend, who cast a finding spell." His smirk grew wider. "And then I visited Mary in the hospital, disguised as a priest. I knew that there had been some manipulation to get this good, God-loving woman to have a child with another besides her husband."

He knelt down next to Vince, his tone turning somber. "I saw the sorrow in that poor woman's eyes. She asked to speak to me privately to confess her sins. She told me the lies you had told her, she so gullibly believed. His eyes flicked towards Kiran. "The Archangel Michael took you when you were conceived, Guardian, to become what you are," Sam said softly before turning back to Vince. "I knew that nothing good could come from this situation. The angelic father must have been up to something, so I gave Mary a gift. I told her it was blessed by...."

Justin cut him off, finishing his sentence. "...the Pope," he said as realization dawned on him.

Sam nodded. "I instructed her never to let anyone take it off her son. It seems to have worked," his gaze flicked to Justin. "And I have stayed here watching you as I was asked to do."

"What a fool you are, Vincent. Justin is indeed truly powerful; it is only the necklace that blinded him to himself and others."

Vince's face turned a deep shade of red as anger radiated from him in waves. "How dare you, Watcher!" he seethed, his voice trembling with rage. "Interfering in the affairs..."

"Affairs of a Fallen?" Sam interrupted coolly, crossing his arms over his chest. "Although, with all you've done, you're more like the Morningstar himself." He shook his head disapprovingly.

Vince's voice grew stronger as he spoke, a fierce determination shining in his eyes. "We'll see about that, won't we? After all, the Morningstar may have fallen from grace, but he is still one of the most powerful angels ever created." He struggled to sit up, his hand clamped around the handle of the knife embedded in his chest.

With a guttural sound, Vince ripped the knife from his body and swiftly swung his arm, throwing Justin across the room with surprising strength. Kiran jumped to his feet, his wings unfurling behind him, rustling like leaves on a quiet wind. The soft glow of ethereal light reflected off their snowy white feathers, casting an otherworldly aura in the dimly lit space. And then, to my astonishment, Sam's tattered wings also erupted into brilliant light.

Kiran's gaze met mine, determination burning bright in those silver depths. But there was something else there, too.

Love.

He nodded at me before returning to the chaotic scene unfolding before us. "Take Justin and get out of here," he commanded, his voice radiating authority.

But I refused to leave without him. "I'm not going anywhere without you!" I screamed over the sounds of battle.

Suddenly, Sorcha appeared at my side, her hand gripping my shoulder urgently. "How did he break free?" I demanded, searching her scared face for answers.

"He's just too strong," she replied, pulling me to my feet. "There's a handle on the floor next to where Kacey was bound." Her eyes darted around the room, taking in the chaos surrounding us. "Go down the tunnel there and follow it until it forks. Take the right path, and you'll find a ladder; climb up and get out."

She pushed me in the direction she wanted me to go, and I stumbled forward, scanning the room frantically for Justin. He was already on his feet, heading straight for Vince once again. But Sorcha threw out her arm, casting him towards the exit she told me to go. He slammed into the wall with a resounding thud. "Get out, brother!" She screamed.

I hurried over to where he lay. "Justin, you have to get out of here," I urged him, trying to pull him to his feet. "You can't take on Vince, he's too strong."

"I will finish this and then deal with that....that half-brother of mine," he growled.

My heart sank at his words, but before I could respond, Justin was sprinting towards Vince. He stopped abruptly and picked up something from the ground - it was the knife that had impaled Vince's chest moments ago. With a fierce cry, Justin lunged at him and drove the blade deep into Vince's arm. But in an instant, Vince retaliated and wrapped a muscular arm around Justin's neck.

"No," I screamed, the sound echoing around the room. Panic gripped me as I watched helplessly.

Kiran, stepping forward, blasted a beam of pure light directly into Vince's body. He stumbled back, releasing Justin from his grasp. And just as suddenly, Sorcha appeared at Sam's side, and they both began chanting feverishly. With a wave of her hand, a ring of fire erupted around Vince, trapping him inside.

As Kiran struck Vince with another powerful blast of energy, there was an explosion of smoke and rock as the ceiling above us gave way completely. I braced myself for impact, sure that this was the end.

But then, a warm wash of light enveloped me, and the gentle softness of feathers surrounded me. I opened my eyes to see Kiran shielding me with his own body as rubble fell upon us.

Chapter Thirty-Four

K iran's eyes filled with intense emotion. I reached out and touched his face, feeling the warmth of his skin against my fingertips. "Rhi," he breathed, relief and emotion evident in his voice. "You are safe."

The noise surrounding us dissipated as Kiran pulled his wings back, and the fire circle died down. Amid the rubble, Sam and Sorcha stood atop a pile of debris.

Kiran stood up and offered me his hand to help me to my feet. My heart raced as I scanned the room for Justin. "Is Vince gone?" I asked in a shaky voice.

"He was wounded badly, but he managed to escape," Kiran said in a somber tone. "I stopped the ritual to come to you."

My focus immediately shifted to Justin. "Where is Justin?" I pleaded, my voice taking on a desperate tone. "Please tell me he's alright."

"Guardian," Sam called out from where he stood beside Sorcha. "Your brother-"

My head snapped in their direction, and then I was running. I saw Justin lying amid the wreckage, blood seeping from a wound on his head, while a large wooden beam and rocks covered his lower body. With tears streaming down my face, I cradled his head in my arms, feeling the warmth of his blood soak through my clothes.

"Oh God, he's going to die!" I cried out in anguish as my tears mingled with rock, blood, and dirt. The air was thick with the metallic scent of blood and the acrid smell of burning wood. Kiran appeared at my side, crouching silently next to us.

"Kiran, do something, please," I pleaded desperately.

"Rhiannon, I can't." His voice was like a whisper in the wind.

A surge of rage filled me at his words. "You can't?" I seethed, my voice rising in volume. Sobs wracked my body as I pulled Justin closer to me. His skin felt cold and clammy against mine, and he coughed weakly, blood dripping from his mouth. Gazing up at Kiran through tear-blurred eyes, I cried out in anguish. "I came out of this fight without a scratch, while Justin lies broken in my arms. You could have helped him, too. Kiran. He's dying!"

"He is," Kiran replied simply.

"Damn you, Kiran!" I sobbed, my anger and desperation growing with each passing moment. "He's only eighteen, and I know his soul is worth saving."

"He is your Guardian," Sam said from behind us. "He cannot heal anyone but you."

"Then you do it!" I screamed at Sam, unable to accept that there was nothing anyone could do to save Justin.

"I am hurt, child," Sam sighed as he knelt beside us. "I used all I had to fight Vincent. Only his own Guardian or the Creator can save him now."

Desperate for some glimmer of hope, I leaned forward and pressed my forehead against Justin's, willing my life force into him. "Where is his Guardian?" I pleaded. "His mother must have prayed for one."

Sam's reply was solemn. "I'm guessing his mother thought he was holy because of Vince's lies, and she didn't think he would need a Guardian."

A chill suddenly swept into the room, causing my skin to prickle. I could see my breath in the air as I cried out, "Please, please don't let him die."

"Azrael," Sam whispered beside me, and I heard the others gasp.

I could sense the tension in the room grow. Suddenly, a gust of wind swept through the space, causing me to turn my head towards its source. My eyes widened in awe as I beheld a being of immense size, at least ten times larger than Kiran or Sam. His wings were massive and the darkest black I had ever seen. He carried a sword nearly the size of his own body, and his raven hair swirled around his face wildly. The glow of his piercing white eyes reminded me of Kiran's earlier transformation. He glided across the floor and pointed his sword toward Justin.

"It is time," came his deep rumbling voice that shook me to my core.

I caught movement out of the corner of my eye. Kiran was reaching out and touching Justin's cheek, and when I glanced up, I could see the terror in his eyes. Was this really it? Justin coughed, and I heard Kiran let out a startled cry.

"Kiran, is he...?" I trailed off, afraid to even speak the words. All the time I had known him, I had never seen Kiran terrified; what could possibly make an angel tremble? As if sensing my thoughts, Kiran turned to look at me, his silver eyes somehow seeming different.

"Kiran?" I breathed, lifting my face to meet his intense gaze.

Azrael's head snapped towards us at our interaction, and in an instant, he stood right in front of us.

"What have you done?" His voice boomed as his fiery gaze fixed on Kiran. "Answer me, Guardian."

Kiran hung his head low, just like Sam had done earlier. "He is my brother," Kiran answered quietly.

In a swift motion, Azrael lifted Kiran off the ground by his collar, bringing him face to face with his towering figure. "We are your brothers and sisters," Azrael bellowed.

Meeting Azrael's intense stare, Kiran bravely raised his head. "I did not do it for myself," he said firmly. "I did it for my ward."

"You cannot cheat me of a soul," sneered Azrael.

My arms tightened around Justin's body as he stirred in my embrace. His voice was weak and trembling as he spoke. "Rhi?" he whispered. I gazed down at him, relieved to see that the blood and bruising were gone from his once-battered features. I ran my fingers along his jawline, feeling the warmth of life returning to his skin. Kiran had healed him, but now he was paying the price.

I tore my gaze away from Justin and focused on the scene before me. The Angel of Death stood before us, his presence looming over the room. A mix of fear and determination surged through my veins as I gathered my courage and stood up. Justin sat up beside me, his gaze darting around the room.

"It wasn't his fault," I said, directing my words towards Azrael. My heart ached for Kiran, knowing that he was suffering because of me.

Azrael's sly grin only made him look more intimidating. "Maybe I should take you instead," he mused, his hand reaching out towards me.

"No!" Kiran yelled out as Azrael dropped him to the ground.

Azrael stood before me, his cold touch burning against my skin as he grabbed my chin to tilt my face towards him. "You," he whispered. "Your soul...it is part of The Warrior's."

Confusion and disbelief swirled inside me as I tried to understand his words. "What?" I mouthed in disbelief.

"If I may, Azrael," Sam spoke up reverently. He had been kneeling on the ground this whole time, unnoticed by Azrael until now.

Azrael's gaze shifted, eyes narrowing as he sighted Sam on the ground. "Speak," he commanded coolly.

Drawing a deep breath, Sam rose slowly, focusing his attention on Azrael. He cleared his throat before speaking. "I am bound by a seraphence oath," he began, "I cannot speak about the oath except that it is bound by the prophecy foretelling the return of The Warrior's spirit."

A pause hung in the air, heavy and suspenseful; Azrael's gaze never faltered from Sam's face. "That spirit would be reborn in another body, born of The Warrior's bloodline."

Azrael inclines his head, and the gold flecks in his irises catch the candlelight. "I am aware of the prophecy," he says in a low voice. "And I know precisely what was asked of you, Samyaza."

Sam's fingers twitch, and he looks ready to vanish, but he stands his ground. "Then you know I cannot say more."

Azreal's ethereal gaze shifts between me and Kiran. "You are connected to my most revered brother. I will not punish you, but your Guardian..." He trailed off, turning his attention towards Kiran.

Fear clutched my chest, desperate to protect my angel. "Please don't hurt him," I pleaded with Azrael. "If what you say is true about me, then I beg for his safety."

After a moment, Azrael turned back to me and spoke in a tone that sent cold waves over my body. "I will spare him this time, but by breaking one of our laws, he has become a Fallen."

With those final words, a blinding burst of light filled the room, and Azrael was gone.

A familiar voice called out from above us, calling my name. "Rhi? Lady Bug! Are you here?" Mia's head appeared through the caved-in ceiling, her eyes widening in shock when she saw us.

"Mia?"

"Rhi!" She squealed. "Are you okay? Wait, I need to get you all out of there!"

"Mia," Sam called up to her. "Meet us at the Witches Well. The tunnels here will take us there."

"Sam? What are you doing here?" She squinted down the hole. "And Justin?"

"I'll explain later," Sam interjected before I could answer. "Just meet us there and bring your mom's van. There isn't enough room for all of us in your car."

"Got it," Mia replied before disappearing from our view.

Together, we made our way through the narrow hatch on the floor, following Sorcha's directions. The tunnel was dimly lit by flickering torches, casting eerie shadows on the walls. As we reached a fork in the tunnel, two familiar figures emerged from the shadows. Sorcha and Kacey's eyes widened at the sight of all of us.

"I'm sorry," Sorcha said with a shaky voice. "I had to leave when I saw Azrael." She frantically rubbed her hands through her dust-covered hair.

Kacey rushed towards me, throwing her arms around me in a tight hug. Her body was trembling, and tears streamed down her cheeks. "Rhi, thank goodness you're safe," she whispered. "What happened up there?"

I squeezed her back, feeling grateful she was safe. "I'll explain everything later, Kace."

Sorcha went back to Vince's through the tunnel. Before she left, Justin grabbed her hand. "Thank you," he whispered gruffly.

Mia was waiting for us with her mom's van when we emerged from the well at the end of the tunnel. "How on Earth is there a tunnel from Vince's house to the Witches Well?" Mia asked incredulously as we piled into the van.

"It's a long story," Sam replied wearily. "There are lots of tunnels that run all around here."

Mia seemed to notice Kiran. "And who is this handsome guy?"

Kiran glanced at her under his disheveled hair.

"You can see him?" I said.

She looked him up and down. "Girl, I can, and I like what I see."

Kiran gave a surprised look at her. "I figured I should allow myself to be seen by your friend and your cousin." He shrugged his shoulders. "Everyone else here can."

She ushered us all into the van. "Well, you can thank a witch for finding you all," Mia said as she pulled off Thirteen Witches Road and onto the reservation's main road. "My Gram did a location spell." She turned and looked over her shoulder at me. "She made me wait until finally she said it was safe to go to Vince's house."

Justin and Kiran were both quiet. Justin stared out the window while Kiran buried his head in his hands. I could see the weight of everything that had happened settling heavily on their shoulders.

We decided to go to Mia's to wash up. I couldn't let Nan see me covered in blood and dirt. Sam cleaned our clothes with a wave of his hand and healed Justin. Steve had come to get Kacey after Sam had wiped her memory of what had happened. The less she knew, the safer she would be, he told me.

It was late when Justin, Kiran, and I finally left Mia's. Sam had explained everything to her, including who he really was. She was enthralled by the story and even did a little dance when he finished. "I can't believe my best friend is a Watcher!" she exclaimed gleefully.

Standing together by the curb on the street, both boys had their hands jammed in their pockets, looking eerily similar. As I studied them closely, I finally noticed their striking similarities. How had I never seen it before? Kiran was slightly taller, but Justin was more muscular. Their hair and eye colors differed, but so did Justin's and Scott's. Despite their differences, they shared certain features - the slope of their cheekbones and the shape of their eyes. I blinked to clear my vision. I stood between Kiran and Justin, my gaze flickering between the two boys- my two boys.

The silence stretched between us until Justin finally broke it with a question. "So... he's always there, with you? in your room, even when you sleep?"

I nodded, my voice quiet as I confirmed, "That's what Guardians do."

"But you see him," Justin pressed, his expression troubled. "You know he's there."

A sudden realization seemed to dawn on Justin before he could finish his thought. "Wait, have you been there when we..." He trailed off, unable to bring himself to say the words.

Kiran's head snapped up, his own expression horrified. "No, no," he insisted. "I don't want to see that."

Justin's eyes narrowed as he processed this information. The tension between them was palpable. "Humph." He grunted out.

"I know there are still many unanswered questions," I said, wanting to diffuse the tension between them.

Justin turned to me, his eyes flashing a mix of love and desperation, "You know I love you, and I would do anything, anything, Rhi, to keep you by my side."

I felt Kiran stiffen beside me.

"You need to choose," Justin said, glancing at Kiran. "I can't share you with ....with him." His eyes darkened with frustration.

My gaze fell on Kiran as he stood next to me like a sentry. His expression unreadable. He was my Guardian and so much more.

"I will not make you choose," Kiran said quietly.

"Of course you won't," Justin sneered.

I sagged with the heaviness within my heart. The truth was, I wanted both of them, and that meant I was a coward and maybe a bit selfish. Justin was completely unpredictable, full of fire and passion. And Kiran, my sweet devoted angel, who had done the impossible and saved Justin because I asked for it.

I looked between them again, but Kiran couldn't meet my gaze, and Justin would periodically shoot him accusatory glances. "Justin...I.."

He threw up a hand to stop me, "Scott will be here soon to pick me up and take me to the shop to get my car." There was a flicker of hurt in his eyes. "Call me when you make a decision."

A car pulled around the bend in the road and stopped before us. "Hey, guys," Scott called from the car window.

Justin turned on his heel to leave without even saying goodbye.

"Justin?" I called out after him.

He stared at me for a long moment before finally letting his head fall. He looked defeated and hurt. With that, he climbed into the car beside Scott, and they drove off. I turned to Kiran, feeling overwhelmingly sad.

"There has always been pain in Justin's heart," Kiran explained softly. "And now, with the added torture and revelations about his true parentage, he is trying to protect himself from more painful truths."

My gaze drifted up towards the house, where I could see the lights on in the living room. Nan must still be awake, probably watching one of her old black-and-white movies. I had called her earlier when we arrived at Mia's house and told her where I was and that I would be home later.

Kiran gently tugged on my hand, bringing my attention back to him. "Come, you need to rest," he urged, leading me up the stairs.

"And what about Nan? She can't see you," I trailed off as we reached the door.

He lifted my hand to his lips and kissed it gently. That was new. "Only if I choose to let her."

"So Vince allowed everyone to see him?" I asked.

"He did," Kiran confirmed, a hint of sadness in his voice. "But now, there are some things I need to explain to you."

With trembling hands, I fumbled with my keys and unlocked the door. As I entered, I was met with the comforting sight of Nan sitting on the couch, her favorite movie playing in the background as she sipped on a cup of tea.

"Hello, dear," she greeted me with a warm smile, setting down her cup.

I made my way over to her and gave her a tight hug, feeling the weight of the day's events on my shoulders. "I love you, Nan," I whispered into her ear.

She gently patted my back with her small hands. "I love you too, Rhi," she replied softly, pulling away to look at my face. Thanks to Kiran and Sam's magic, you couldn't tell I had been through so much earlier in the day.

Forcing a smile, I said, "I'm exhausted. Mia has more energy than I can keep up with."

Nan chuckled knowingly. "She always has," she teased. Then her expression turned serious as she searched my face. "Is everything alright?"

"Yes, yes, of course it is," I reassured her, trying to sound convincing. "I'm just tired." Saying goodnight, I headed upstairs, where Kiran was waiting for me.

As I entered my room, I noticed the lights were off, and the only light source came from the small lavender-scented candle on my nightstand. Kiran was sitting on the floor next to my bed.

"The candle?" I questioned curiously.

A slight smile tugged at his lips, but a deep concern was etched across his features. "It's relaxing. I thought you could use it."

Locking the door behind me, I made my way over to my bed and sank onto it with a long sigh. "I have so many questions," I said, looking at Kiran expectantly.

He was quiet for a moment, studying my face intently. I stared back at him, silently urging him to speak. After what felt like an eternity, he finally seemed to come to a decision based on what he saw etched upon my features.

"Where do I start?" he sighed heavily.

"I find the beginning is usually the best place," I replied with a timid smile. "Come sit up here with me, Kiran." I patted the spot next to me on the bed.

He hesitated momentarily before uncrossing his long legs and standing in front of me. "Maybe you should get comfortable up there with your pillows." He gestured to the top of the bed. "I'll sit down here."

Confused by his request, I did as he asked and kicked off my shoes, tossing them haphazardly onto the floor.

Kiran sat down timidly on the edge of the bed. "The beginning," he began, raking his hands through his honey-colored hair before resting his elbows on his knees and burying his head in his hands. "I'm sorry; this is all so difficult for me." He shook his head in despair.

"The beginning was my awakening, as we call it. I was visited by the Archangel Michael, who revealed to me my true identity and purpose. He told me that while I was conceived and had a soul, it was not meant for this world. I was to become a guardian angel, and when the time came, I would hear the song of my soul mate." He lifted his head to look at me, and I could see the pain in his eyes as he continued, "I could never be a part of my mortal mother's life. I was only allowed a few visions of her."

I clutched my extra pillow tightly, burying my face into its softness. Justin's lingering scent still clung to the fabric, but I pushed it aside and focused on Kiran. "I'm sorry," I whispered, trying to make sense of everything he told me.

He shook his head, a pained expression crossing his features. "He also told me I had a twin, but his path was to remain on Earth." He paused, letting that statement hang between us. "But he didn't tell me anything else about him."

Desperate for him to continue, I stayed silent.

"When you returned here and met Justin, I felt a strange connection to him and didn't understand why. That was until your cousin's shower, and my mother was there. I had only glimpsed her in a few visions before. That was all that was allowed." A twinge of pain flickered across his features. "As I watched all of you together, I saw Scott and Justin and wondered which one was my twin."

"I counted the mortal years since I was awakened and realized it was Justin." his eyes became troubled. "What I did not understand was if he was my twin, then how come I couldn't sense anything celestial about him or see his aura?"

His words were heavy with grief; tears welled up in his eyes.

Tears.

They never fell as he took a deep breath and continued. "I was so confused and angry. Angry that he, Justin, could have my mother and I could not." Kiran ran a hand roughly through his hair, his gaze distant. "He didn't even appreciate her, and then....then he started to take you too."

His gaze met mine again, his eyes no longer holding unshed tears. "Angels are not human, and humans are not angels. Angels were created before humans to serve and be messengers of God's will. But we are punished without forgiveness when we make mistakes because we should know better. Hence, why those who disobey are called fallen angels."

"On the other hand," he trailed off, a small smile playing on his lips, "Humans hold a higher position than us. You are considered more holy and can even be forgiven for terrible acts because you are God's children."

"But...," I interjected.

He raised his hand, halting my words. "Please understand, it is a magnificent experience to be an angel," he said. His voice was tinged with an otherworldly quality, every word carrying deep meaning. "But something deep inside me longed for the life I could have had if I were the one to remain on Earth instead of Justin."

His silver gaze caressed me as he spoke. "When I heard our song, I realized that, besides my love for the Creator himself, I had never felt anything so powerful before. Not even for my own mother." He buried his face in his hands, rubbing his temples. "The first time I laid eyes on you...I will never forget it. And let me tell you something I haven't shared before - besides hearing your soul, we can see it, too. And yours was the most beautiful sight I have ever seen. It glows with a lavender hue." His hands twisted in his lap. "I hope to see it again someday." His words were barely above a whisper.

"So...you can't see it anymore?" I asked, feeling a pang of sadness in my chest.

He shook his head slowly, and then I saw them again - tears glistening in his eyes. They fell freely down his cheeks, and my heart broke seeing him like this.

Without hesitation, I threw aside the sheet and went to him, cupping his face in my hands and wiping away the tears.

"Oh no...no, Kiran! This is entirely my fault!" I cried tidal waves of guilt. How could I have done this to him? It was because I couldn't let go of Justin.

His expression turned solemn, and he spoke with a quiet intensity. "Rhiannon, my sweet girl, the suffering I would have endured if I had lost you would have been far greater than this."

"You would never have lost me, Kiran," I whispered fiercely.

He arched an eyebrow at me, his lips clamping down. "Wouldn't I? If I had let Justin go, if he had died today, wouldn't you blame me?"

The memories flooded back, engulfing my mind in a whirlwind of emotion. It seemed like a dream that Kiran had saved me from certain death. I could still vividly feel the pressure of his strong, angelic arms wrapped tightly around me as the ceiling collapsed around us. I begged him to save Justin's life, placing the blame on him for not saving both of us at the time. And though he granted my request, it came with a heavy price.

His voice trembled as he spoke again. "I couldn't take the chance of losing you. In your eyes, I saw desperation, love for Justin, and, worst of all, accusation towards me. I couldn't bear the thought of being blamed for his death and losing you forever." There was a flicker of hurt in his eyes. "I also couldn't bear to let my twin go."

A burning tear slipped from my eye.

"So I did what I had to do, not knowing exactly what consequences it would bring." Kiran's voice trailed off as he was transported back to that room in Vince's mansion.

"I told you I could see souls. I saw Justin's fading away, leaving this Earth. Then Azrael appeared and affirmed my fears. I tried to establish a connection with him, sending him visions of you and his family, anything to make him want to fight and stay here with us." Kiran's eyes were distant as he relived those moments. "But despite my efforts, I could still see him slipping away. And he was terrified."

His voice was barely audible, a quiet murmur. "His fear was otherworldly, and that scared me. So, I grabbed his soul. I was there with him, in that plane between this here and the veil. Others were there, watching me, screaming at me from both sides. I had never been in a more frightening place. I have never seen so many of the dark ones. They scratched at both of us. They wanted me to let him go, and I thought if I didn't do that, I might go down with him. The pain was horrific, but I could also see the angels, whether they were real or in my mind's eye; I couldn't tell you. I took strength from their presence, though." He seemed to return to the present and stroked my face gently with his fingertips. "I also took strength in you and wanted to get back to you. I felt that is what Justin was clinging to also...your presence." And then, just like that..." He snapped his fingers, "We were back in that room, with an intense electric charge around us, and just as quickly, it disappeared."

As he continued, Kiran's gaze again took on a distant, ethereal quality. "As I lifted my hand away from Justin's face, I felt something change within me. I was cold, and my vision was blurred. I couldn't see Justin's soul anymore, and when I looked at you...I couldn't see yours either. It was as if a part of me had died."

Anguish filled my heart, knowing that my selfishness had put him in this predicament. But what else could I have done? Not ask for his help to save Justin's life? The guilt weighed heavily on me as I realized how much he had sacrificed for us both.

I pulled Kiran's head to my shoulder, stroking his tousled hair. The scent of vanilla enveloped me as he leaned into my embrace, seeking comfort and solace. "I will take care of you, Kiran," I whispered softly, "like you have always taken care of me." As my tears fell onto his hair. I could feel his body trembling with emotion.

Kiran heaved a sigh, his voice quivering as he spoke again. "You may change your mind once I tell you everything."

"What could you possibly say that would make me not want to help you?" I asked, genuinely confused. "You saved Justin's life. You have saved mine. You are a part of me that I cannot live without." There was a vice grip on my heart as I held my Guardian close, his breath warm against my collarbone and his hair soft against my chin. My angel meant so much to me. My heart constricted more. My mind reeled. I felt so overwhelmed by the weight of everything that had happened in such a short amount of time. Closing my eyes, I lay my cheek against the soft top of Kiran's head. "I will help you, Kiran. Always."

"You are making this harder on me with your kindness," Kiran murmured against my skin. "I don't know that I deserve it."

But I wouldn't hear any of it. "You are a part of my family, Kiran," I insisted, my voice breaking with emotion. "I would do anything for you."

He pulled his head away from me, and as I looked into his eyes, I saw heaven and hell collide, his expression full of sadness and regret. "My Ahavah,"

I couldn't tear my gaze away from his intense stare. Damn, his beautiful, ethereal voice. The deep timbre of his voice when he called me Ahavah snaked into my soul and set it ablaze. He reached up to stroke his fingers along my cheek, and I felt that same wave of electricity along my skin.

"I must tell you this, though," he said solemnly. "I knew so much about Justin's heart because...I could sense things about him. Things that I had never been able to sense in another person except you." His words hung in the air, heavy with sorrow and pain.

But all I could see was Mrs. Rizzo's sorrow. Justin's rage. Kiran's grief. My own confusion. "Brothers," I whispered.

"Yes, Rhiannon," Kiran confirmed with a pained expression. I'm so sorry I couldn't tell you sooner, and you had to find out the way you did." His voice cracked with emotion, cracking my heart wide open. "He is my brother, but...I am your Guardian."

There was something in his gaze that made my heart hurt for him even more, "I understand why you didn't tell me, Kiran."

His voice was guarded, "You forgive me then?"

I nodded, and my thoughts turned to Sam and his wings. "Will your wings deteriorate like Sam's?" I asked quietly. I hoped not, knowing it would only bring him more pain.

"I haven't encountered many fallen angels before," he mused. "And when I did, they didn't have their wings out. Come to think of it, Vince never exposed his either." His gaze grew distant as he thought back. "I honestly don't know."

He returned his attention to me, his silver eyes locking with mine, swirling with icy fire. "I found who I was looking for in the veil for Sam," he said softly. "She opened the note he sent, and a sad smile crossed her lips. She misses Sam." He paused, lost in thought for a moment. "It was Sam and she who helped me."

Confusion swept over me. "What do you mean?"

"I don't know everything in that note, but she told me Samyaza wanted her to introduce me to someone."

"Introduce you?" I questioned, struggling to understand.

He nodded. "That's part of why it took me so long. She brought me to Raziel - the angel of secrets and keeper of all magic."

"Why did Sam want you to meet this angel?"

"His knowledge is vast," he explained. "It was his writings that were passed down to the Watchers themselves. They learned their magic from him."

"I still don't understand."

"Samyaza was told by Sorcha that Vince was after me and planned to use you as bait. Sorcha doesn't like her father at all, and she and Sam....well, they're intimate with each other."

"He told me."

"Sam knew that the magic Raziel possessed could help defeat Vince. His expression darkened. "The angel Raziel," he said, his tone grave. "Knows magic beyond anything I have ever known."

I was taken aback by this revelation.

Kiran's voice was soft and apologetic as he spoke, "I know Sam left you, and I'm deeply sorry for that. But when I learned the reason why he had to go, I found it in my heart to forgive him." He paused a moment before continuing, "Sam's note explained that he was bound by a vow, but he wanted his daughter to guide me toward answers."

"So she led me to Raziel," Kiran's tone held a hint of awe. "He is unable to pass through the veil between worlds and speaks only in riddles, leaving me to piece together the truth on my own. After our conversation, he promised to make an appearance to Sam and instruct him to retrieve a powerful rune."

"A rune?" I asked, curious.

Kiran's hand slipped under his shirt and emerged, holding a smooth, polished blue stone. It seemed to glow slightly, with a slanted Z etched on it." This is the eihwaz rune," Kiran said, his voice low and reverent. "It was gifted to humanity long ago by a Watcher named Armaros." He lifted an eyebrow. "I believe you met him?"

I nodded quietly, remembering my encounter with the ancient Watcher.

"Armaros taught humanity how to fight against evil spells, create wards, and use runes," Kiran explained, "And to keep the original most powerful talismans safe, he hid them all away."

Kiran stared at me with watchful eyes, "Sam and Armaros went to retrieve this rune specifically to help fight against Vince."

"So Sam was trying to help us both," I murmured.

"Yes," Kiran rubbed the stone that hung from his neck, turning the smooth, light blue stone over in his hand, "This stone is angelite, it's believed to have healing properties for emotional wounds and grief." His eyes twinkled as he continued, "I wonder if that's why Armaros chose this stone for me to use. Not just to give me an advantage over Vince, but also to help both of us heal from everything that's happened."

"When I returned, Vince had already taken Kacey and Justin," he said coldly. "And Sorcha was on her way to him with you."

"He had Kacey," I replied, trying to keep my own emotions in check.

"I know," his expression hardened. "Sam had also included Sorcha in his plan," he continued. "I don't like working with demons, even half-demons, but it was necessary."

A bitter taste filled my mouth, thinking of how manipulative Vince was.

"I need to ask you something," I cut in, "When Sorcha picked me up, she didn't say a damn word about... any of this. Not the plan, not Kacey, not you, not even Justin. Why keep me in the dark like that?"

He shakes his head, hair brushing his collar. "Sorcha's afraid of making mistakes. She's been playing Vince's games all her life, and she was terrified of the plan unraveling—especially if you tried to intervene. It's not logic, Rhi. It's survival instinct." His voice got quiet. "She didn't want her father to realize what she was doing, either. The less you knew, the less you could give away."

I chew that over. "So, she was protecting the plan. Or... protecting herself?"

"Both."

He looked me dead in the eye. "Sorcha despises Vince. He wasn't kind to any of his children."

"So you all planned to attack him together?"

He nodded grimly. "But then Sorcha called Sam in a panic. She told him that Vince had taken Justin and Kacey. He was going to use them to lure you to him. Vince trusted Sorcha, thinking she was on his side, and revealed his plans to her."

I felt a chill like my body had been plunged into ice water as he continued, "Raziel told me with the combination of this rune, Sorcha's, or any demon blood, and one of my feathers, we could banish Vince, if not kill him. I knew Vince figured out who I was after he saw me with you at his garage. I have no idea how he knew I was his son. Because we are related, the grace I have would bind to him more easily. Justin has grace, too, and I'm sure it infuriated him not to understand why he could never feel it. I didn't know about Justin's necklace, hiding that part of him from me and everyone else, including Vince." He chuckled ruefully. "All that time, the grace he sought was right there under his nose."

"I will forever be grateful to Sam for what he did to protect Justin," I said.

"I know," he said softly.

"Okay, so you, Sam, and Sorcha concoct this plan to take down Vince. continue."

"Sam is a powerful angel, but waited in the tunnels for Sorcha to open the hatch in the floor to Vince's dungeon." And it indeed was a dungeon - a hellish place of torture and nightmares that sent a chill through me as I recalled the feeling of being there. "He didn't want to be the one to take on Vince first. He stayed until he was needed. He said he didn't want to start a war with Vince." He shrugged his shoulders. "Watchers, demons, and Fallen all coexist here in the mortal realm. Sam said turning on each other disrupts the power dynamic."

"I didn't know about Samyaza's plans when he asked me to deliver his message to his daughter. But now, I will forever be grateful to him." His voice was weak as he gave me a faint smile. "There is more." His voice dropped. "Raziel told me that because my of my father." His lips twisted in disgust. "Vince is one of the most ancient of angels, and because his blood flows through mine, I am no ordinary Guardian."

Ominous feelings pressed down on me as his eyes met mine. "Both Justin and I are Nephilim, but because the Archangel Michael took my soul and I became a Guardian, I have more power than normal Nephilim. I am an Alpha Nephilim."

"Kiran?" I said with uncertainty in my voice.

He turned towards me, his face looking worn and exhausted. "Yes, sweetheart?"

"What about what Vince said? How did he know that you have....have feelings for me?"

He froze, his body going completely still.

"I don't know how he could have known that, but Kiran..."

He hesitates, searching my face. "Vince knows how to put pieces together. Most of the Fallen, have a nose for weakness. Especially the kind you try to keep hidden."

He shifts forward, his knees almost touching mine. "He saw me when we went to his garage after your beach trip. I think he started to put things together then."

I try to remember every second I spent in that garage. The way Vince smirked when he saw me. "So I was leverage."

He laughs, hollow, shaking his head. "I always thought I was hiding my feelings for you so well." His eyes flicked away swiftly, "But I guess...maybe I wasn't hiding it as well as I thought." He nervously rubbed his palms against the front of his jeans. "I know what love is. It encompasses us all. I understand that love means unwavering support and acceptance, a deep emotional connection with another person. And I know that when two people have that connection, it brings intense feelings of joy, happiness, and contentment whenever they are together." His silver gaze turned to me. "It's why I call you Ahavah- *my love*."

My throat constricted, and tears pressed against the back of my eyes. I pressed my palms against my face and tried to take deep breaths, but I couldn't catch my breath. Despite my efforts to push them down, my emotions broke loose.

Hot, salty tears flooded my palms, and I collapsed back onto my mattress, curling into a tight ball. A loud, guttural sob tore out of me, releasing all the pain and anger that I had been holding in and burying deep within myself. It was like a dam breaking, and the flood of emotions washed over me with an intense force that cracked my battered heart apart.

I cried for my father, who had abandoned my mother and me when I was just a baby, leaving a void in my life that could never be filled. I cried for the loss of the mother I once knew before she changed into someone unrecognizable. And then I cried for Justin, who had been through so much already but now had to face the harsh truth that he had been used and lied to about his own identity.

But mostly, I cried for Kiran.

At that moment, it felt like all the pain and suffering in the world rested on my shoulders. Like it was my fault, somehow, for coming into Justin's life and bringing him nothing but turmoil, and my fault that Kiran lost his grace.

I gave in to the grief.

I didn't hear the song at first as it spread throughout me. I was so caught up in my emotions, but I felt Kiran's strong arms wrap around me and pull me into his lap. His wings brushed against my skin in a comforting caress. Our song, the one that made us soul mates, filled us both.

I felt his pain as well, and it crushed me. Kiran held me tightly, his cheek pressed against my own, and I didn't know if the wetness that covered my face came from just me or both of us.

We clung to each other, our bodies trembling with emotion. He whispered words in a language I didn't understand, but the tone conveyed his love and comfort. We stayed like that for what felt like hours, lost in the melody of our song and the protective embrace of his wings.

As my tears finally abated, I eased my grip on him and pulled back slightly. "I'm sorry," I croaked out in a hoarse voice.

"You never have to apologize to me for your feelings," he replied softly, brushing away the stray strands of hair clinging to my face. "Do you feel any better now?"

"I feel like I'm drowning," I admitted. "It's all just too much."

"It will be okay," he reassured me.

Taking a deep breath, I rested my hands against his chest and felt the steady beat of his heart beneath my palms. "I do feel like I can breathe a little better now."

"Good." He shifted slightly, creating some space between us before snapping his fingers. A steaming cup of tea appeared in front of me.

"What?" I said in surprise.

"Chamomile tea. It helps relax you," he explained with a small smile as he handed me the cup.

"Not that, since when do you make things spontaneously appear?"

His lips twitched into a smirk. "I don't like to show off."

Taking a sip of the tea, I found it was perfectly sweet - just how I liked it. "You're way too modest," I commented. "The power you displayed today was...just incredible.

Kiran's head dipped as if he were embarrassed, but I could see the pride shining in his eyes. We both fell into a comfortable silence, knowing that there was so much more that could be said between us but not needing to say it out loud.

I could feel our bond even stronger now, a connection that went beyond that of Guardian and ward. But there was also something else – a yearning, an unspoken desire that we were both trying to ignore.

"Kiran?"

"Rhiannon." My name was a prayer on his lips. "You can shed tears now."

He sighed heavily. "I can. I still feel the burn in my chest, but somehow releasing tears subdues it a little." His lips kicked up slightly on one side. "I don't mind it."

"Is it because you....you fell?" I asked softly.

"I believe so." His head dipped slightly, and his hair fell around him like a halo. Kiran's expression was calm, but there was a storm whirling in his eyes. "Rhi, love is something you cannot control. Nor is it simple."

My heart clenched. I knew, knew deep in my bones what was coming. Justin had insisted I make a choice. Even if I chose him, Kiran would not leave me. So, how would our relationship ever work?

This decision hung over me like a guillotine.

I took a deep, calming breath and said, "I'm in love with both of you." Saying the words out loud made me feel raw and exposed. "I don't know how to make this right. I can't tear my heart in two."

I shuddered, a sob catching in my throat as I stared at my angel. My beautiful, tortured angel whose heart I held in the palm of my hand.

He scooted closer to me as his silver eyes locked onto mine, holding an ocean's depth of patience. "Rhiannon," he said, his voice caressing my soul like a lover's kiss. "Do not tear yourself apart over this."

I could see the truth in his eyes, and my heart ached at the realization of how deeply he loved me, regardless of my feelings for Justin. I knew there would never be an easy way around this situation, no magical solution that would make everything right. I needed them both just as they wanted me. For all its beauty and purity, love was turning out to be cruel.

I nestled into his chest, allowing myself to take comfort from his warmth - from his existence itself. Kiran remained silent for a while. When he finally spoke, his voice was soft and heartbreakingly gentle. "For you, Ahavah, I would brave heaven and hell. But I cannot force your heart."

I churned over my thoughts, knowing that no amount of self-flagellation would birth the right answer. My mind was weary from the constant battle, stuck between the stoic angel with silver eyes who'd sworn to protect me and the boy from New Jersey who'd effortlessly stolen my heart.

Every time Justin's hardened exterior would crack, revealing a soft underbelly filled with pain and trauma he desperately tried to hide, my insides would clench in fierce protectiveness. And yet...my feelings for him were so different compared to my feelings towards Kiran. With Kiran, there was tenderness and unyielding devotion. Whether I want them or not, I have strong feelings for him, which scare me so much that I can hardly breathe.

Kiran seemed to want to say more, and he reached into his pocket, retrieving Justin's cross. The tiny stone that sat in it seemed to glow. "Justin gave this to Sam to give to you. Justin told him he didn't want to hide what he was anymore."

He placed it in my palm, and energy pulsed through it, igniting my insides. I closed my fingers around the cross, feeling its cool surface against my skin. I was not the girl tossed around by life anymore, since meeting Kiran and Justin.

I had slowly turned into a girl who wouldn't allow herself to be broken again. But as I sat there, cross in hand, I felt it. A tingling sensation rippled beneath my skin, something ancient, stirring to life.

Waking.

Kiran looked at me sharply, as if he felt it too. "What was that?" he whispered.

I didn't answer. I didn't know how to.

All I knew was something inside me had shifted, and whatever it was....it was only just beginning.

www.ingramcontent.com/pod-product-compliance
Lightning Source LLC
Chambersburg PA
CBHW060413030726
47495CB00003B/555